The Runes of Sorcery

Jane Welch was born in De... ... ... years she and her husband  resort in Andorra. This is ...

By the same author

THE RUNES OF WAR
TE LOST RUNES

Voyager

JANE WELCH

The Runes of Sorcery

Book Three of
The Runespell Trilogy

HarperCollins*Publishers*

Voyager
An imprint of HarperCollins*Publishers*
77–85 Fulham Palace Road,
Hammersmith, London w6 8jb

The *Voyager* World Wide Web site address is
http://www.harpercollins.co.uk/voyager

A Paperback Original 1997
1 3 5 7 9 8 6 4 2

A catalogue record for this book
is available from the British Library

ISBN 0 00 647023 8

Set in Goudy by Rowland Phototypesetting Ltd,
Bury St Edmunds, Suffolk

Printed and bound in Great Britain by
Caledonian International Book Manufacturing Ltd, Glasgow

For my parents,
Tom and Peggy Davies, with love,
gratitude and admiration.
And of course for my husband Richard,
whom I can never thank enough for
his endeavour, guidance and craft, helping to
write this trilogy.

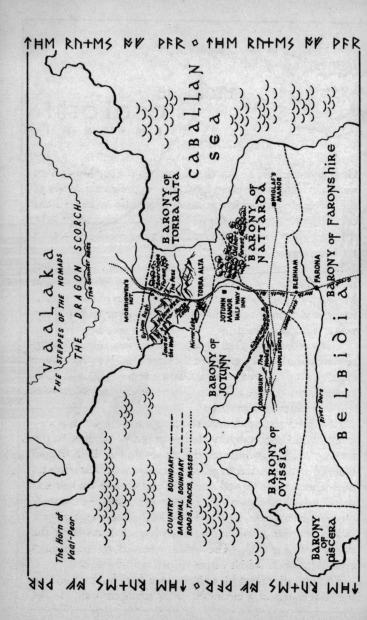

Prologue

Gasping for breath, he struck out through the tumbling white water rapids for the eastern bank, the scything cold waters of the Silversalmon sucking at his strength. He welcomed the cold after the scorching flames of the fire. Pinpoints of light sparkled where minute ice crystals were beginning to form in the fast running river.

Blue with cold, he scrambled breathlessly to the bank and slunk into the snow-muffled, eastern ranges of the Yellow Mountains. The water trickled from the tufts of his cropped fringe and crisped to points of ice. He sucked in the sharp winter air and grinned.

'Great Vaal-Peor, God of Ice, your breath already claims the land,' the warlock muttered to himself, his breath a steamy cloud curling into the frosty air. Behind him a pillar of angry flames lit the sky like a beacon, as a towering inferno engulfed the west tower of Torra Alta.

He moved quickly through the trees lining the lower slopes, intent on finding fresh, dry clothes before he perished in the freezing northern winter of the mountains. A lone trapper hiding from the Vaalakan enemy offered him his first opportunity. The warlock slipped a toothed dagger from his belt and soundlessly slit the man's throat from ear to ear. As the wolf-trapper bled to death, he stripped his leather leggings, wolf-pelt jacket, bearskin cloak and cracked leather boots from the slowly writhing body. The blood glistened on the frosted crystals as a rich scarlet carpet spread around the body.

The warlock ripped his sodden cloak from his back and, in the cool waters of a mountain brook scrubbed away the last smuts from his blackened face. Finally satisfied, he sank down amongst the frosted ferns and spat towards the besieged castle, a dry cackle rasping through his throat. He coughed to clear the last remnants of smoke from his scorched lungs, then a thin laugh escaped from his cracked lips. Bitterly, he wiped his hand across his mouth, wincing as the singed flesh on the back of his hand brushed against his chin.

He ripped off his wet black garments, now shredded and charred in his escape, and redressed in the tough leather hides of the trapper. He wrapped his easily distinguished black clothes and fine shoes into a tight bundle and, kneeling, scraped at the frozen ground with his dagger. He dug beneath the roots of a blackthorn, whose battered branches leant with the prevailing wind. It was only a small hole but large enough to bury his clothes. Satisfied with his work, he stood and sucked in the keen, raw air of the crisp month of Hunting.

A self-satisfied smile twisted his narrow face as he stared at the distant turrets of the besieged castle and then down at a small object whose brilliance glistened in his hand. He closed his fist possessively around it and headed straight for the steeper scree slopes where the wind had blasted away the snow. He would leave no tracks on bare rock. Dragging the wolf-pelt tightly around his shivering body, his snarling face mimicking the toothed grin of the wolf's head dangling over his back, he enveloped himself in the heavy brown bearskin cloak.

Zealous energy spurred him across the boulder-strewn terrain until at last a lonely hunting lodge, cowering beneath the snagged peaks of the mountains, beckoned him from the treacherous cold. Content that no one could track him across the scree, he risked descending into the snowbound valley. Wading through the deep snow, he stumbled in drifts up to his thighs, the icy snow biting through his breeches and stinging against his skin. The numbing pain of cold hardened his heart as he shouldered open the weather-beaten door that had set fast in its rusted hinges.

Damp logs were stacked up against the hearth and it took many minutes for his shaking hands to entice life from a flint.

The miserable flame teased at a wisp of kindling. Eventually, he crouched down beside the thin fire as it wheezed in the grate, cradling in his numb hands the sparkling object that he had taken from his forsaken home of Torra Alta. He gazed into the heart of the brilliant blood-red crystal as his lips peeled back into a bestial scowl.

The ruby was an unusually circular jewel and embedded deep within its crystalline structure were fracture lines like white threads that flawed its perfection. The threads formed a circle subdivided by three radiating lines into three segments. He stared deep into its heart though the sight of the circular sigil burnt painfully into his watery blue eyes.

'The sacred rune of the Mother,' he sneered. 'But I have it now.' The blood-red ruby scorched into his palm and he gasped, painfully drawing breath into his smoke-damaged lungs. A sinister smile drew out his thin lips as he relished the sweet torment of his victory. He had the ruby now and Torra Alta would suffer.

He thought back on how he had been forced to flee Torra Alta. The fire in the castle had all but consumed him but he had needed the flames to be fierce so that he could slip furtively away in the distraction. All the others had failed him: Kullak the Vaalakan shaman, the weak curate Dunnock, the monstrous Cailleach. Now he would do his own work. He wondered how many tears dear Baron Branwolf had shed over his death, and how long it would take him to discover the damage to the runes of war rimming Torra Alta's heartstone. He laughed fitfully at the thought, then abruptly flicked his gaze back to the jewel in his long-fingered fist. He clutched it with feverish possessiveness, certain that the rune of the Mother held the key to the secret location of the Druid's Egg. Instinct urged him that the sacred pattern held some further meaning and would lead him to the talisman. But he didn't yet possess all the pieces of the puzzle.

He knew he must go south to Caldea and pick up the trail at the point where Kullak had failed. There he could start to trace the threads of the pattern and begin to piece together the puzzle. He had to get to the Druid's Egg first. He and his servants had failed to slay the witch who had conspired with the world against him. Now his only chance of destroying her and avenging the death of his mother was to claim the Egg and gain its ancient, awesome power first.

Warmed by the fire, he slept fitfully through much of the night, but before dawn he was slapped awake by a trembling energy flooding through his veins. The air within the cabin crackled with power. His inner senses tingled with foreboding. He stepped outside the hut and kicked away the snow to press his palm onto the bare soil, feeling for the pulse of the loathsome Great Mother. Something was trembling through the bones of the earth. The Great Goddess was stirring. He felt a magic awaken and radiate through Her lines of power. He sensed the energies stir, felt the rousing magic blending with the elements.

The runes from the ancient cauldron had been found, he was certain, but there was more . . . another magic . . . something unexpected. The power tingled like a new life sizzling through the earth. He had spent his childhood amongst those who taught the lore of the old ways and it had heightened his innate sensitivity to the power of runespells. He instinctively knew that the force radiating through the earth's mantle would rekindle life into the ancient creatures – creatures that possessed the natural power to sense the moods of the Great Mother from whom they sprang. These were runes of great sorcery rushing through the energy lines of the Mother.

He dismissed the thought of this unexpected magic and turned back to contemplate the lost runes of the cauldron. If they had found the lost cauldron then they must also know the runes that would lead them to the Egg. But he had the rune of the Mother.

He looked down at his clenched palm and slowly uncurled his slender fingers to sneer wickedly at the ruby. The rune, the pattern of the rune . . . if only he could fit the pieces together . . . He had to get to the Egg first.

Torra Alta must fall to the Vaalakans and the witch must

be destroyed. His mother would be avenged. He thirsted for the satisfaction that would come from the suffering of all those at Torra Alta. All those years they had despised him and now he would be avenged. All he needed was the Druid's Egg.

Chapter 1

'It's not safe to leave it here.' The priestess glanced warily at the mist surrounding the clearing.

'Well, we can't very well take it with us, can we, Brid? We'd need a wagon and a team of six to shift that great thing,' Hal reasoned, his words sharp, resentful.

'I'm not stupid, Hal. We'll have to destroy it,' the young maiden replied decisively.

'Destroy it? That's even more stupid! It's half a ton of solid metal.'

'Absolutely. But the runesword will shatter it.'

The dark youth looked uncertainly at the weapon, rotated it in his hand and eased his grip further into the quillons that spanned the hilt. He flexed the fingers of his left hand. His eyes fixed on the knotted red scar that had once been his little finger before Gatto's mercenaries had severed it. 'It may have shattered mail and badly forged blades, but that . . .' He fixed on the solid mass of the rune-engraved cauldron. The black sooty metal looked as old and as solid as granite, contrasting dramatically with the sword's bright steel.

'You can't destroy it. You haven't told us what the runes say,' Caspar objected. 'I've got to know!'

Brid ignored him, her dazzling green eyes still warring with Hal's.

Caspar bit his tongue and eyed the mist. Something was out there, lurking, he could feel it.

'Destroy it!' Brid ordered again.

The noble youth made no move to obey her. Instead he plucked up her clenched fist and soothed the back of her hand with surprising tenderness. 'After last night you could be a little sweeter with me.'

'Hal!' Brid looked exasperated but there was a faint flicker of pleasure in her eyes before she suddenly stiffened. 'That didn't mean anything. I needed the magic, that was all. I wanted to enhance the elemental powers released by sacrificing myself to you.'

'Sacrificing?' Hal's voice was teasing. 'Are you sure?'

'Yes!' Brid glared at the handsome raven-haired youth for a long hard moment and then laughed lightly. 'But fortunately I didn't have to in the end, did I? Really, Hal, we haven't got time for this. Please do as I ask.'

He bowed gallantly, grinned and turned his attention to the sword. The taut contoured muscles of his face flexed along his jawbone as he approached the cauldron, both hands firmly gripping the hilt of the broadsword. The pearly light of dawn danced on the runes engraved along its length as the youth swung it around his lithe body. His graceful movements, enhanced by the hazy light, made him look like a warrior stepping out from a book of legends. Seven paces from the cauldron, he leapt forward, the rage of determination screeching from his lungs, swirling the sword back in readiness to smite the soot-black iron of the great cauldron.

Caspar clapped his hands to his ears as the pain of the noise slammed into his head. A splinter of bright metal ricocheted out into the glade. The cauldron appeared unmarked but a chip had broken off the edge of the runesword. Hal was on his knees, staring with horrified shock at his damaged sword. Brid's hands clapped to her mouth and her brilliant eyes were momentarily startled but she quickly wiped away the alarmed expression.

'You weren't clear in your mind, Hal. Give me the sword. We have to destroy the cauldron.'

'No!'

'Give it to me!'

'No! Haven't you done enough harm already? You've already ruined the runes of war!' He ran his fingers lightly over the nick in the sword's edge. A dark ball of liquid appeared on one of his fingers and smeared across the bright metal.

A rare look of self-doubt clouded Brid's face. 'It's my fault. I shouldn't have stirred the potion with the runesword. But I'm sure I didn't spoil the runes of war,' she flashed hotly at Hal, defending herself.

Again Hal's anger flared in his eyes as he remembered how Brid had inadvertently altered the runes on his sword by using it to stir the contents of the cauldron. The runes emblazoned on the fuller were now blood-red and extra symbols had appeared. Brid had called them the runes of sorcery. At the precise moment they had been drawn from the cauldron's spell-womb Caspar had first sensed the malevolence prowling in the mist.

'Look at it! Look what you've done!' Hal was shouting now. 'You've broken it!'

'It's not broken; it's chipped and it's only a tiny chip on the edge. Now, give it to me!' The dark youth stood up but, rather than handing the sword to Brid, he let it fall ungraciously to the ground. Stooping she grasped the hilt of the weapon. The length of the blade seemed almost as long as her body and the tip dragged in the earth as she pulled at the hilt.

A sardonic smile lifted one corner of Hal's mouth. 'Oh come on, Brid, what are you playing at? You can't even lift it.' He placed his hand on the sword, arresting her efforts. 'Why don't you tell me how to focus my mind and let me have another go?'

The stubbornness was sliding away from his voice and reason filled its place. He raised a questioning eyebrow at her and finally her resolve softened. Her arms sank down to let the earth bear more of the sword's weight.

Hal eased her fingers from the ornate hilt and drew the sword up. 'Right that's better. Now, tell me what to do.'

Brid brushed herself down and smiled. 'When you're not being stubborn, there's a lot of hope for you,' she said. 'Now look. Read the runes on the blade and it'll help.' She pointed them out one by one. 'Ignore the runes of sorcery and concentrate on the others. Most of them are vicious hateful runes. Runes of revenge, runes of hatred, runes of victory, runes of maiming and this one is ↑: Tiw's rune, dedicated only to war.'

Hal fixed his eyes on the sigil and nodded. Caspar looked at the rune over Hal's shoulder. 'It looks like an arrow,' he observed.

'Until now you have used the sword without understanding,' Brid continued to lecture the raven-dark youth. 'But this rune here is the rune ᛉ: Nyd, the rune of necessity or need. You cannot use hatred against another artefact of the Great Mother so you must concentrate through the rune of need. You wish to destroy the cauldron because you must and not because it is your enemy. Focus through that rune and when you strike the cauldron, strike with the part of the blade that's level with it.'

Hal fingered the plain geometric pattern near the hilt of the blade. 'Do you really think a rune will make any difference? If I strike so near the hilt, I can't drive as much power through the sword.'

'It'll make all the difference. Think through the rune. Try and free yourself from all the other aggressive, cold feelings of hatred that the sword induces. Think only that you must do this for the greater good.'

The youth nodded and grinned. 'If the sword breaks in two, I'll never forgive you.'

'Trust me,' she smiled back.

'Yeah!' He let the tip of the sword rest on the ground and took slow deep breaths, concentrating his energies before drawing his arms back and pacing towards the cauldron. With nothing more than a grunt of effort, he twisted the blade and brought it down heavily on the cauldron's rim. Dust and smuts filled the air and somewhere at the back of his mind Caspar heard an intensely sorrowful song. The song of the sword at last, he thought; it was the saddest sound he had ever heard.

As the dust settled, Caspar looked for the cauldron but it

4

had gone. All that was left was a heap of slag and soot. Hal was coughing on his knees. One hand gripped the sword and the other clutched his side. Blood oozed between his fingers. Brid rushed to him, reaching him only a moment before Caspar.

'Are you all right, Hal?' Caspar asked anxiously.

'You do ask stupid questions,' Hal spluttered and the younger boy could see the tense lines of pain in his uncle's grimace. 'The wound in my side has reopened so what do you think?'

Brid eased up his shirt to examine the bloody gash. 'It's not too bad; it's just where the scab's torn apart a little. Try not to stretch your side too much,' she advised as she bound the wound with a strip of cloth from her shirt.

'Try not to move too much, she says, when she's just got me to charge around, smashing up a mammoth-sized cauldron.'

Brid stirred the dust of the cauldron with her toe and looked at it ruefully. 'I'm sorry, Great Mother. I had to do it. The Keepers have abandoned their duty. There was no one left to guard the cauldron; no one left to protect the knowledge of the Druid's Egg; I couldn't leave it.'

Hal took a moment to admire the sword as if savouring his mighty feat of destruction. 'We should go,' he boomed, his muscles still twitching with the after-shimmer of power bestowed on him by the runesword. He spoke like a warrior-chief, every word an order.

'I'm not ready,' Brid defied him.

A look of exasperation crossed Hal's dark face.

Caspar was getting impatient. Brid had ignored him ever since she had deciphered the cauldron's runes and still refused to tell him what they said. He had been unable to read the esoteric writing on the bottom of the cauldron and knew only that it told of the Egg, a great talisman that the Goddess said would save his mother. It had dark powers, a sorcery that Caspar did not understand, but it was the only means to rescue Keridwen and restore the Trinity of high priestesses. And once the Trinity was reunited, the Great Mother had vowed to repel the Vaalakans from the borders of Belbidia and so save Caspar's home, and birthright, the frontier castle of Torra Alta, from destruction.

Caspar's heart caught in his throat as he thought of his mother incarcerated in the cold heart of the Vaalakan glacier, at the mercy of the evil Ice-God, Vaal-Peor. The magical eye of the moonstone had unveiled more than the reality of her torturous, deathlike state. It had revealed a radiant vibrant woman with red hair swirling about her shoulders and piercing violet eyes welling with love from her soul.

His father had been stricken with grief at her loss. Though Baron Branwolf had filled the bleak wilderness of his loneliness with a stream of smiling feminine faces, he had never again found a love to match the one he shared with Caspar's flame-haired mother. At about that time, King Rewik outlawed the Old Faith from Belbidia thus forcing Branwolf to suppress all mention of Keridwen's pagan status. If she had been found alive, preaching the word of the Great Mother, she would have been branded a witch and burnt at the stake. Caspar had been brought up in the New Faith, oblivious to his mother's heresy, and had learnt only recently that she had been a high priestess of the Old Faith.

'I will have no more delays. We must get back to Ceowulf and Cybillia,' Hal demanded loudly at Brid's back.

The Maiden was hurriedly searching for her herb scrip that she had mislaid in the spell-casting frenzy of the previous evening. She completely ignored Hal, who was now impatiently preparing the horses and cursing at Trog, the white terrier that had joined their retinue. 'We haven't got forever, Brid. The Great Mother only bestowed the runes of war on Torra Alta for three seasons. That was at the end of Shedding. It's already taken us two months to find the cauldron and we've only got until the last day of Fallow, or had you forgotten? At this rate it'll be another month before we even get out of this wretched yew forest.'

'I can't go until I've got my herb scrip. I can't leave this clearing and pass through the mist while I'm awake. I need

Faronan henbane and Salisian wolfsbane to cloak my mind in sleep before I put one toe in the mist.'

Hal looked at her as if she were mad. 'What's so fearsome about the mist and why do – ? '

'Can't you feel them?' Caspar interrupted his uncle, his voice catching in his throat.

The pagan priestess flicked her eyes warily towards the eerie dun cloud that surrounded the glade. 'The runes of sorcery on the sword have stirred bestial ghosts from the Otherworld. The parallel world of spirit is close. Something knows we are searching for the talisman and they desire that power for themselves.'

Hal sheathed his sword and the blazing anger in his eyes subsided though he still refused to join the search for the herb scrip. The terrier, however, was greatly enjoying snuffling through the crisp bracken alongside Brid, who was on her hands and knees now, combing the undergrowth. The dog evidently found it a great game.

'I still don't see why you have to be asleep,' Hal said more reasonably.

'I can't pass through the mist awake, because I know what's written on the cauldron. Don't you remember what it was like when we first entered the mist? The way it seeped into our minds, forcing us to share each other's thoughts? I can't allow my knowledge of the cauldron's runes to be shared with those creatures out there.'

'So that's why you've spent all night copying down the details from the cauldron and refused to tell us what they mean!' Caspar exclaimed, suddenly enlightened. He recalled how she had used the back of his map and a stick of charcoal to trace out a complicated design of squares, crescents, circles and runic letters.

Brid looked at him as if he had been a little slow to understand. 'Of course! Now help me find my scrip.'

Hal was pacified for a little while but when the search was still fruitless his patience failed. 'It's late Fogmoon now which means the castle only has a little over seven months before the runes on the heartstone fail. Are we to spend every day of those seven months here? Can't you use anything else to put your mind to sleep?'

'You could hit me over the head I suppose, Hal, but really I'd rather you didn't.' Brid smiled sarcastically.

'I'm hungry,' Hal continued to complain. 'And we haven't got time to waste. If the Great Goddess really wanted to protect us, She would have given us the runes unconditionally.'

Caspar sighed. 'Who are we to judge the deeds of Gods?'

Hal spat disgustedly. 'Spar, you sound worse than Father Gwion with his incessant sermonizing about the New Faith.' He kicked through the dusty remains of the cauldron and glared at the young auburn-haired youth. 'It must be in your blood, all this sanctimonious preaching; I can't bear it.'

Caspar sulked. Gwion might be his mother's brother but he was nothing like the self-righteous priest. The youth withdrew into the vivid landscape of his own thoughts. Hal's temper and irreverent words had unnerved him. He couldn't listen to any more of it.

'Trog, no!' Brid shouted, suddenly chasing after the white dog. 'No! Drop it! Give it to me!'

Caspar was relieved that at last they had found Brid's herb scrip but despaired when none of them could catch Trog. The Ophidian snake-catcher was running in delighted circles around them, tossing the scrip into the air and snapping at it with his long white fangs. Gleefully he scattered herbs and various articles of divination, including a bat's wing and what Caspar imagined to be tails of mice and the claw of an owl.

Hal's nose wrinkled at the sight of the withered fragments and Brid wailed. 'Trog, you stupid dog, look what you're doing.' She fell to her knees and scrambled about in the short tufts of grass that managed to grow in the shade of the trees, gathering up the strewn objects and muttering as she went. 'Bladderwort, saxifrage, loosestrife, melilot ... good, more loosestrife, wolfsbane.' She twirled a purple veined stem in her hand and then stopped short as she sifted through the remaining herbs. 'Oh Mother!' She looked up in horror at the dog who was dancing triumphantly away from Caspar. The youth was chasing after him as the terrier chomped on something in his mouth. 'Oh Mother! He's eating it! Hal, get that dog; he's eating the Faronan henbane!'

She raced after the terrier who skipped from left to right, pausing briefly on his short tautly sprung legs before bounding away just as Caspar's fingers brushed against his tail.

'Trog, stop. Come here; it's not a game. Drop it! Drop it!'

The dog's dark slit eyes gleamed wickedly back at them. He turned to leap out of reach but stumbled, shovelling his blunt nose into the dirt. Lifting his head, he swayed and staggered a few ungainly paces before collapsing, his breath coming short and sharp. Pitifully he wagged his tail as Brid approached. 'Oh Trog! What have you done?' she sighed sorrowfully.

The three companions stood over the dog and stared down forlornly as the animal began to snore.

'Will he be all right?' Caspar asked anxiously.

'He'll sleep for a week I should think, but most of what he's eaten won't do him any harm. At least he didn't touch the ergot wheat, or the dragonfire or the wolfsbane, but he's eaten the woundwort, the hyssop and, worst of all, the henbane.'

'Won't that just make him sleep?' Caspar was fascinated by Brid's skilful magic.

'Yes, it'll make him sleep but –'

'But you were going to take it to empty your mind,' Hal finished for her. 'Faronan henbane and a tiny bit of Salisian wolfsbane, you said. Can't you just use the wolfsbane?'

Brid looked pale beneath the smooth bronze of her skin. 'I suppose I'll have to. Wolfsbane's poisonous but without Faronan henbane there's no alternative and I'll have to take a lot more of it to have the desired effect. Well,' she sighed as if steeling her resolve, 'let's get ready.'

Caspar pulled her round to face him. Red blotches appeared on Brid's arms where his anxious fingers dug into her flesh. 'Are you sure you know what you're doing?' he demanded, tightening his knuckles.

She prised him off and snapped tartly, 'Oh Caspar, it'll make me sick, that's all. And I'd rather be a little nauseous than have my mind devoured by whatever's out there.' She pushed him further before instructing them what to do once she became unconscious.

'Yes, Brid, of course we understand,' Hal snapped impatiently as she finished. 'Is this self-inflicted illness of yours going to be gruesomely awful? Because if I'm going to carry you out of here I don't want . . .' His words petered out as she turned away.

Brid wasn't listening. She swallowed hard then moistened her dry lips before taking a mouthful of Salisian wolfsbane. Dipping her cupped hand into the stream, she scooped up some water and gulped it down, washing the poisonous herb into her system. She sat perfectly still for just a moment, then began to rock back and forth, her head swaying before she was gripped by spasmic coughs. She fell writhing to the ground. Her throat and face turned a deep puce and a thick foaming tongue choked her mouth. She coughed and retched and clawed at her mouth, her eyes bulging in pain.

'Brid! Brid!' Caspar cried pitifully, grabbing the Maiden's arms to prevent her from shredding her skin with her nails. But gradually the violence of her convulsions lessened and she lay still, eyes wide, pupils rolled back, the whites ridged by deep red blood vessels. Caspar leant forward and pressed his head to her chest. He could hear nothing for his rasping breath. A cold sweat broke out on his forehead. He held his breath and at last there it was; the flutter of a faint, rapid heartbeat.

'Oh Hal! She's only just with us.'

Hal's forehead grooved into lines of concern but his voice was steady. 'Time to leave. My mare will be steadier than Cracker. Lift her up to me and we'll get out of here.'

Biting back his fears, Caspar passed the Maiden's limp form up to his uncle before checking that the drugged dog was securely fastened to his own fiery steed. Now that Brid was no longer awake, he felt vastly more vulnerable, guessing that her waking presence had been shielding him from the threat in the mist.

The raven-haired youth grasped the girl firmly around the waist and nodded at Caspar, 'Lead on, nephew, future Baron of Torra Alta. Deliver us from this place of ghouls.'

Firecracker shrieked out a wild fiendish whinny and reared, hooves slashing at the insubstantial form of the mist. The freckled youth spurred his heels into the animal's side. Fearing what the runes of sorcery had awoken, he gritted his teeth and braced himself for what he might find in the irksome mist.

At first he sensed nothing. His horse's jangling curb-chains seemed shockingly loud, like the chime of a leper's bell, and he felt like an intruder in the murk-filled world. Slices of mist clung to his skin, damp and cold, creeping into his pores, invading his body. Swirling drifts massed around his head, befogging his vision and when he turned to look back at Hal, he could only just discern a dim shadow, half-eaten by the mist.

'Spar!' Hal's voice came muffled through the ground-hugging cloud. 'Keep going. I'm right with you!' Then suddenly his voice was startlingly clear. *'Keep talking to me, Spar,'* Hal spoke in his head. *'I'm right with you.'*

Caspar tried to concentrate on his uncle rather than contemplating what might be in the mist. Hal's mind leapt from one thought to the next, snatching glimpses of Torra Alta and of Baron Branwolf fighting alongside his men with a longbow in his fists. Archers fired flaming arrows down into a deep canyon; Vaalakans screamed. They were wishful thoughts where Hal yearned to be: battling alongside his older half-brother, rather than here in Caldea searching for the Egg.

'Don't think about it. Think of something else, anything else, but don't think about it,' Caspar warned.

Hal's mind turned to the Maiden in his arms. Brid's contorted face and wall-eyed look filled him with a sense of sinister evil, the remnants of ingrained fear of the pagan people clouding his reason. Fleetingly, he imagined her withering until she was like an old witch, possessed of the Devil. Then she was beautiful and vibrant, free and wild, full of the promise of blossoming youth.

Surging emotion howled and Hal's mind flooded red.

Caspar's unbridled love screamed jealously green and for a while the two colours roiled in tempestuous conflict before slowly the colours faded until it was as if they had never been.

Hal's image of Brid melted and the form of another beautiful maiden filled his thoughts. Her eyes were dusky smudges of colour, like the hazy sky in the full heat of harvest, and long rippling waves of rich golden hair framed her pale face. The image distorted and coloured red. Her glorious hair was now cropped to short spikes of grimy stubble. Her skin was soiled and bruised and the scars ... Knotted raised weals puckered her cheeks where the pagan stellate symbol had been carved into her flesh.

Cybillia, poor Cybillia! For her the stigma of the pentagram on her face was worse than death itself. The daughter of the Baron of Jotunn, she came from lowland Belbidia where all men and women, peasant or noble, were true to the New Faith. Hal jerked at her pain and self-loathing. The image of her disfigured face soured his thoughts and filled his mind with guilt-laced revulsion. He turned back to gaze at the Maiden.

'No!' Caspar railed against the thought. 'You can't have her!' And then his mind was racing, galloping across grassy plains beneath a beating sun and he realized that his thoughts had melded with the bestial emotions of his horse.

Their minds galloped wildly, weaving through scrubby bushes, chasing, desiring, warring with guiltless savagery. A shadow swept over them at twice their speed, drinking up the sun's heat, obliterating thought and drowning comfort in a fearful stampeding panic. He was in the misty yew forest now, the urge to bolt, to crash through the overhanging branches, overwhelming. He grappled to throw off his instincts and pull away from the herd. Desperately he struggled for his individual self, grasping for the fresh air of logic.

Hal's calm mind was with him now, guarding him, shielding him from the malevolence stalking them through the mist. But still something cold crystallized in the boy's mind. Appalling cold. The frost of death was creeping through his veins. Needles of ice pricked at his eyes, stabbed at his ears, pierced his mind, delving for the secrets of his soul, seeking the knowledge of the Egg.

Hal's red anger lashed out and beat at the blue terror of the cold.

Firecracker's wild shriek of fright shattered the stillness of the muffling mist, breaking through the barriers of their minds. The horse reared and slashed at the air, throwing Caspar forward against the stallion's neck. For a brief second he thought he saw a more solid whiteness in the mist. Above it, the point of a single horn was just visible through the swirling shroud. Caspar began to shake. He tried to tell himself that the white was merely the mist and the darker lancelike horn no more than a dead branch, but the deathly cold remained.

The fierce warmth of Hal's emotions charged through his mind one last time and then he could hear nothing but the roar of Hal's voice bellowing out the Torra Altan battle-cry. Pride in his noble ancestry brought heat to the boy's soul and he joined his uncle in the fearsome war-song. A streak of bright metal flashed through the cloying mist. He could see the runesword and the shape of the black markings on Hal's piebald mare became clear.

'I'm with you, Spar. Just keeping talking. We'll soon be out of the mist,' said Hal in matter-of-fact tones.

Gradually the shrouding vapours rolled away and they eased into the stillness of the drowsy yew forest. The fear of the unnatural creature was gone and the eerie sense of spell-craft that had charged the air diffused into the healthy reality of the late autumn morning. A squirrel, startled by their approach, spiralled up the dusky-brown bark of an ancient yew and vanished into the dark green canopy, its chattering cry scolding them for their rude intrusion into its territory. Caspar's memory of the malevolence in the mist drifted to the back of his mind. He sensed it dimly, only as he might remember a dream at the point of waking, recollecting little of what happened but still left with the lingering stain of dark emotion.

He urged Firecracker to a faster pace, winding and dipping between branches that dragged at his clothing and teased his hair. Morning light slid through the trees and up ahead he could clearly see the edge of the forest. Caspar drew a deep breath and filled his lungs with the fresh air. At last free from the trees, his gaze stretched out over the smooth rolling downs of Caldea, Belbidia's southernmost barony, and across a grey-green sea to where the distant twin peaks of the Hespera Islands crowned the western horizon. With the morning sun warming his back, he looked down as his long shadow stretched out across the springy grass.

For the briefest of seconds a cloud swallowed his spindly shadow, a rearing shape enveloping his long sticklike image. Then the sea-breeze stirred the air and the image was gone. Scudding clouds raced away across the sky and with relief the boy felt the warmth of the sun soak through the supple leather of his jacket.

A branch snapped behind him. He jumped round, startled, convinced that the presence still hovered at his back. But it was only Hal as his horse brushed apart the last of the dark green brooms of yew to join him in the open. They pressed their heels to their horses' flanks and with Brid bouncing awkwardly in Hal's arms, they cantered south over the downs and through the regimented strips of Caldea's famous vineyards. Finally they sped across the dirt road that linked the port of Ildros to the Baron of Caldea's castle at Tartra and on towards a thicket of blackthorns that were crowded round the convex rise of a distant chalky down. Two figures greeted them: a tall bulky man leaning heavily for support on the shoulder of a spiky-haired girl.

Caspar reined in at the very last possible moment and slid from his horse, the hot-blooded red roan dancing round at the end of his reins. With a confident air of one totally at ease with horsemanship, the boy steadied his steed and unbuckled the straps that secured Trog's heavy slumped mass to the cantle of the saddle. He dragged the white dog over the horse's back and let him thump to the ground before turning to greet Ceowulf and Cybillia.'

'We were worried,' the solidly built knight greeted them quietly. A look of pain still covered his face and he clutched at his shoulder where a throwing axe had hacked into his upper ribcage. It was obviously still painful for him to breathe and he leant heavily on the tall slender girl, who carefully kept her face turned away to prevent them from scrutinizing her scarred cheek.

Ceowulf watched silently as Hal and the two heavy-boned war-horses thundered up the rise. Brid's arms flailed helplessly in Hal's embrace.

'Brid! What's happened to her?' Ceowulf raised his arms to help ease the Maiden from the back of the piebald mare but flinched with pain and grasped at his shoulder. Caspar rushed to help and eased Brid's poisoned body to the ground. The whites of her unseeing eyes, ridged with purplish blood vessels, stared at the four noble Belbidians. All, bar Caspar, grimaced.

'May the good Lord have mercy. May He cleanse her soul of these demons,' Cybillia prayed in alarm.

Caspar gave her a harsh look. 'Don't, Cybillia. Your God will do nothing to help her.'

'What can we do to help?' the dark, sunburnt knight asked insistently.

Cybillia bundled up two bearskin cloaks and handed them to Hal, making sure she kept her distance from Brid. He eased one under the Maiden's light frame and wrapped the other skin warmly about her, all the time keeping his eyes averted from the agonized expression contorting her face.

'She's poisoned. I don't know how long it'll take to wear off. She told us specifically just to let her rest,' he explained to the knight.

'Poisoned! And the dog too! Why? Who poisoned them?' Ceowulf's face was anxious beneath his straight dark eyebrows and he scanned the western horizon as if looking for a ship that might be harbouring Vaalakan spies. Caspar shuddered at the thought of Kullak, the fiendish Vaalakan shaman, and the bear-like warrior, Scragg. It was hard to believe that it was only five days since the Vaalakans, their hired mercenaries and the traitor Ulf had attacked them.

'She poisoned herself to forget the runes, because of the

15

thing in the mist,' Caspar blurted, realizing instantly that his words made no sense at all.

'Heretical madness,' Cybillia snorted, one hand pressed firmly against her scarred cheek to conceal the damaged skin.

'Be quiet,' Ceowulf ordered with surprising fierceness and Cybillia instantly deferred to the man's authority. He turned back towards the two youths. 'Now try to tell me what happened. Is she going to recover and what thing in the mist? Tell me quietly and steadily. Let's see if you two hot-headed lads can make sense so I can decide what to do.'

Caspar liked Ceowulf even though he had been a mercenary for fifteen years, fighting foreign wars in the far south. There was something innately disloyal in offering your lance for the highest price but the man's practical skills and easy manner made him an agreeable companion. Caspar sensed his uncle's hackles rising at being ordered around, even though Ceowulf was of equal status, much older and more experienced.

'There isn't anything to do.' The dark Torra Altan youth levelled with the swarthy Caldean knight. 'Brid said we were to wait until she comes round.' He sat down next to the Maiden as if proving his point. 'And that's what we're going to do.'

'Well, it had better not be too long,' the knight said quietly. His face looked wan and dark smudges under his eyes betrayed the toll on his injured body. 'Last night the sky was alive with strange colours and this morning we heard the great knell of a bell, a monstrous sound that pealed out across the downs. The Inquisitors may well have sailed for Dorsmouth on their way back to King Rewik's court in Farona, but such strange and inexplicable commotions will alert them all too quickly.'

Hal's distrustful expression changed and he looked eagerly at the youngest son of the Baron of Caldea. 'If we come under your banner, will your father, Baron Cadros, help us?'

Ceowulf shrugged. 'I very much doubt it. I haven't seen him for fifteen years. He might welcome me but, more likely, he'll cast me out. As a penniless free-lance, I would bring only disgrace to his house.'

'But I thought . . .' Caspar began, remembering the sight of the knight glistening in polished armour beneath the red and white chequered surcoat, when he had charged to their aid. 'I thought you had already been to Tartra to claim your horse and colours.'

'No, I risked a meeting with a friend, my old tutor Morgrimm, who purloined the horse and knightly paraphernalia. No, I couldn't risk going to my father's castle and neither can you. He and my brother are as devout as Rewik in their following of the New Faith.'

'Quite right,' Cybillia muttered under her breath, but Caspar was too busy worrying about Brid to defend the Old Faith.

'We've got to get out of Belbidia before we make enemies of our own countrymen,' Ceowulf continued. 'Any ship that will take us away from Ildros will do.'

Hal shook his head. 'We can't go anywhere until Brid comes round. Unfortunately she's the only one who knows where we're supposed to be going.'

'What? You mean . . .' Ceowulf drew his hand up to his forehead and rubbed at his temples. 'You'd better explain from the beginning.'

Caspar drew a deep breath and described the enormous Mother Cauldron and the intricate pattern wrought into its metal. Briefly, he explained that the flashes Ceowulf had witnessed were caused by the magic potions and roaring fire that Brid had conjured to coax the meaning of the runes from the cauldron's mysterious design. Then in hushed tones, he described the mist and the malevolence they had sensed and how it tried to invade their thoughts.

'If Trog hadn't eaten all the Faronan henbane it would have been much easier,' Caspar concluded the explanation.

The dog was still lying on his side, his breathing much calmer than the Maiden's shallow rasped breaths. The animal's white paws were twitching as if he were dreaming.

'Ceowulf's right; we should get out of here fast,' Hal decided. 'Since he's unable to offer us safety at his father's castle, we'll have to buy passage on a merchant ship. It doesn't much matter where we go: we just need to get out of here quickly before either the Inquisitors or the Vaalakans return. If Spar and I ride into town we could purchase a cart. We could put Brid in it and slip into the docks without too much trouble.'

They wasted no time in argument, but took Ceowulf's advice to go to the nearest vineyard rather than into Ildros. They couldn't afford to draw any more attention to themselves.

With Hal leading the borrowed cart-horse, the two Torra Altan youths galloped off. Before long they turned off the Tartra Road and down a track that squeezed between walled vineyards towards a large flint house with a low terracotta roof. Chickens and geese scratched in the earthy forecourt amongst wisps of straw that stirred in the lazy breeze. Two vast barns shaded the house and, through a crack in one rickety barn door, Caspar could see huge oak vats, which he presumed were used for fermenting wine. His attention was caught by a door to his left. It banged in the breeze and, through it, he glimpsed a two-wheeled open wagon amid a collection of broken barrels. Perfect, he thought to himself and followed Hal towards the shuttered farmhouse in search of the proprietor.

He was surprised that no one had come forward to meet them. Not even Firecracker's hooves striking sparks on the cobbles in front of the flint house had brought any sign of life from the farmstead. Caspar had the uncomfortable feeling that the place was deserted.

'Hello!' Hal bellowed in a deepened voice. 'Anyone at home? Hello!'

'Helloo, helloo,' a mocking voice called back and a man with a pudgy face and blank eyes looked down at them from the top of a wall. 'Helloo, neeone a hooome.' He giggled childishly.

'Good morning,' Hal addressed the man politely, though he himself seemed somewhat taken aback.

Caspar wondered what a fully grown man could usefully be doing sitting on top of a wall during the working part of the day but, noticing the man's faraway expression and the slack drooling jaw, he surmised that he had to be simple. The man beat a stick rapidly against the wall before grinning at them and repeating, 'Helloo.'

Hal sagely avoided repeating the greeting and grinned back at the childlike man. The simpleton flicked his head around like an owl and looked back at the dark youth, nodding gravely at his horse, Magpie.

'Big horse!'

'Yes, isn't she?' Hal replied soothingly. 'Where is everyone? Is the master in?'

'Don't know. They told me to stay here.' The man beat his stick against the wall more fervently. 'I wanted to see the dead pig. The horse is killed, then the pig is killed too. Who killed it?'

'I don't know about the pig,' Hal replied, beginning to sound a little edgy.

Then an anxious female voice shouted from behind the wall. 'Lucky, just who're you chattering to?'

'Just two boys. They have horses,' Lucky replied matter-of-factly.

'Strangers! Lucky, you know you mustn't talk to strangers.' A young brunette appeared from behind the wall, dressed in a stained apron that was stretched over her swollen stomach. With a baby in her arms and heavy with child, she was obviously too preoccupied to bother with the killing of a pig.

Hal inclined his head politely. 'Good morning.'

'Morning,' Caspar hurriedly followed his uncle's example.

'Who are you and what do you want?' the woman demanded.

'We're a long way from home and one of our companions is ill. We need to buy a wagon because she can't ride,' Hal explained.

'My husband is out and I'm not bartering with no strangers,' she replied curtly. 'Now go on, get out of here; we've got enough trouble as it is.'

'First the horse and then the pig,' the simpleton muttered to his stick.

'Shut up, Lucky.'

'They wouldn't let me see the horse neither,' Lucky gravely informed them. 'He was all hacked up.' He squinted defiantly at the pregnant woman when she gestured at him to be quiet.

Slouching grumpily, he continued to disobey her. 'They said it was all chopped up with an axe.'

The woman looked thunderously at Lucky but Caspar hardly noticed; the word *axe* jarred in his thoughts.

'An axe!' He turned towards the brunette woman as she struggled with the squirming baby.

She sighed resignedly as if deciding that these two polite Belbidian youths were unlikely to be any real threat. 'Yes. It was shot through the head with a bolt and the rump was hacked out like someone had taken it for meat. Now, we don't eat horse in these parts so we're on the look out for vagrants or strangers who might do such a thing.'

'We don't eat horse either,' Caspar hurriedly assured her. A shiver ran up and down his spine. A crossbow bolt and an axe! Brid was wrong, Kullak and Scragg must still be nearby. She had thought that they had fled Caldea but this suggested otherwise.

'And we didn't kill the pig,' Hal promised her. 'We just want a cart.'

'I know you didn't kill the pig.' The woman's tense face was half-curtained by a sheet of lank brown hair. 'It weren't a man that killed the pig. My lad found him early this morning. Our prize boar. His side's been ripped open and he's shredded with claw marks. It weren't the work of a man; it were the work of a beast, a huge beast.' She hugged protectively at the huge bulge of her stomach. 'We've sent for the reeve. He'll alert the town to look out for strangers. Evil times,' she murmured fearfully. 'May the good Lord protect us.'

Caspar looked at Hal as he tried to take in the meaning of the woman's words. They couldn't go into the port to buy their passage out of Caldea now. They would have to seek sanctuary in Caldea. Moreover the Vaalakan spies and a vast beast were abroad.

Hal was already turning Magpie and clattering out of the courtyard. Caspar burst past him and streaked recklessly through the vineyards and back towards the blackthorn thicket.

His only thought: to protect Brid.

Chapter 2

The willowy Jotunn maiden bravely held a dagger in her trembling hand. Ceowulf stood over Brid, his steel broadsword unsheathed and fiercely gripped in his left hand, his injury still preventing him from baring its weight in his sword-arm. Trog, on stumbling legs, swayed groggily, his hackles stiff and his short pricked ears pressed back onto his thick skull. With a relieved wave, Ceowulf stumbled forward to greet Caspar as he galloped up the rise.

'What's happened?' the boy gasped, dropping Firecracker's reins and running straight to where Brid lay wrapped protectively in the bearskin cloak. She was still asleep but her eyes had closed and her breathing was quieter.

'It was strange. We didn't see anything but the air was suddenly cold. It was just a feeling . . . ,' Ceowulf began. 'Like the feeling you get when there's a wyvern in the next valley. You can't hear it or see it but you know it's there.'

Hal thundered up the rise towards the blackthorn thicket and hauled Magpie to a halt before dismounting. He took one look around him and, without asking any questions, told them all to gather up their belongings.

'I hope you're fit to ride, Ceowulf. We've got to get out of here right now. We can't go towards Ildros; the port authorities have been warned to stop and question all travellers. There's talk of strange things abroad and with Brid like that we won't stand a chance of getting through to the port.'

'Steady on a bit, lad,' the older knight started to object. 'I think you should tell me what's going on first.'

'There isn't time. I'll tell you as we go,' Hal told him firmly and the knight nodded his head in understanding and set about the task of gathering their belongings.

Hal threw a rug over the cart-horse and cinched it with a girth. Cybillia struggled to help Ceowulf strap his armour, bound neatly in cloth, onto the cart-horse's back while Caspar caught Trog. Once he had secured the white Ophidian snake-catcher by a leash, he carefully organized his pack, stowing his ornate ivory-inlaid hunting bow with the various blankets and pans that they carried with them. He kept the plain holly and stagbone bow, which the woodsfolk from Oldhart Forest had given to him, ready to hand. It provided impressive range and accuracy and he prized it far above his more expensively crafted weapon. Once his pack was arranged, the youth turned towards the white terrier who was looking anxiously around at the bustle of activity.

'Sorry, boy,' Caspar told the drugged dog, 'but you don't look quite fit enough to run around yet. You'll have to come with me.' With Hal's help Caspar lifted the terrier onto the back of his saddle.

'I think we should leave him behind. He's nothing but trouble,' his uncle argued.

Caspar set his jaw decisively. 'He saved Brid and me from the snakes when we crossed the sands; we can't possibly leave him now.'

Hal didn't answer but swirled round to look at Brid's limp body. 'We couldn't get a cart so I'll have to take her with me. Cybillia, you'll be all right with Ceowulf?'

The girl nodded without argument and within a minute they were all set to ride.

Hal looked towards the sun-drenched mercenary. 'We're in your hands, Ceowulf. We can't go to Tartra or Ildros and we can now presume the Vaalakan spies are still nearby. We're in your barony; where can we hide out until Brid recovers?'

'The marshes,' the knight replied decisively as he slipped his right arm into a sling to ease the pressure on his injured shoulder. 'There's an old wildfowler there I can trust. We need to get off the road and keep heading south-east. If we can get there I can send word to Morgrimm. He has influence and should be able to help us with a passage.'

Cutting through the valleys and winding between the vineyards, it was slow going, avoiding the highways and farmsteads for fear of drawing attention. The time allowed Hal to tell the knight about the farm and the savaged pig.

Ceowulf nodded and explained in turn about the ice-cold wind that had whipped through the bare branches of the blackthorns. 'I don't understand what happened to you in the yew forest last night but you stirred up something. The air had the smell of wyvern about it – a sort of bitter taste, but there was silence too, absolute chilling silence. I thought it was my imagination until Cybillia sensed it as well.'

'When Brid comes round perhaps she'll be able to explain, but what we do know is that the Vaalakan shaman and that warrior Scragg are out there waiting for us,' Hal said practically.

At the mention of the savage butchers who had mutilated her face and ravaged her body, the young Jotunn lady clung tightly to the comforting bulk of the Caldean knight. Ceowulf looped his reins round the pommel of his saddle and reached back with his one good arm to squeeze her hand reassuringly before turning to Hal. 'At least you killed that moon-faced Torra Altan peasant – though you were, perhaps, a little extravagant.'

The Torra Altan youth growled in his throat and drew his dark brows together in a scowl. 'That traitor. To think my brother gave him food and shelter and a worthwhile job. He was always so . . . gruesome, so macabre, but why would he turn against us like that? We looked after him. What could he have possibly gained by joining with the Vaalakans?'

'Perhaps he enjoyed their barbaric mentality,' Ceowulf suggested.

Hal shook his head. 'He was too simple. They would have laughed at him.'

Caspar nodded at this conversation, keeping a tight grip on Firecracker's reins as the high-stepping stallion plunged into his bit. 'Maybe someone was using him, playing on his sick delights. Ulf was an idiot but really quite harmless. Someone else must have incited him. I know a few of the younger soldiers were concerned at my father restoring the Old Faith to the castle, but I can't believe any would be so outraged as to turn against him for it. After all Father Gwion assured them that they could still worship the one true God if they pleased.'

'Perhaps they didn't trust him anymore,' Hal mused. 'He is your mother's brother after all and many of the younger men might not have known she was a pagan. I mean, Keridwen did disappear over twelve years ago. If they didn't know that, just like you and I didn't know, they wouldn't have known that Gwion had once been brought up in the ways of the Old Faith. They might not have liked him so much after finding that out. It does explain why King Rewik's bishops refused to promote him even though he was related to a baron. Think about it, Spar.' Hal's olive eyes searched the violet-blue of his nephew's. 'Branwolf returns to Torra Alta with two high priestesses and Gwion rants and raves that they should be burnt. Then quite suddenly, when he realizes that he needs them to rescue his sister, he accepts them into the castle. Many men may feel that a chaplain's loyalty should be to his God first, not his sister. Some might feel that it was their duty to rid the castle of the heretical Old Faith because their chaplain had failed to do so.'

'I agree,' Caspar gravely nodded, giving the cart-horse a quick jerk with the lead-rein to remind the animal to stop lagging. 'And Ulf could not be working alone: you said he kept mentioning someone called the Master. So whoever this Master is probably incited him to the treacherous betrayal . . . and the Master could still be after Brid.'

'The Master,' Hal echoed pensively.

Ceowulf looked at him blankly.

'First, the Vaalakan I killed in the Dragon Scorch and then Ulf; they both referred to someone called the Master,' Hal explained.

'Possibly a swordsman then. At home our chief sword master was referred to simply as the Master.'

'Hmm, but not in Torra Alta,' Caspar broke in. 'There, it's a general term of respect. Hal and I and even the poor old engineer who looked after the well, we were all called Master. Master Catrik . . . ,' he sighed regretfully, mourning the loss of the old man who had been so much a part of their childhood. He couldn't help letting the corner of his mouth curl up as he thought of how the old Wellmaster had always had some proverb to fit every occasion. But he had died after being injured, trying to rescue him in the Torra Altan caverns. They all fell silent for a while, contemplating the brutality of the past events. Caspar looked edgily around him at the sweeping downs, wary of any ambush.

Ceowulf studied him. 'You don't need to worry so much. The mercenaries have gone and there were only two Vaalakans. I might have injured my sword-arm but we'd still be a match for them. After all one of them is a shaman, you say, only some kind of tribal priest.'

Hal looked down ruefully at his sword. Sheathed in its plain scabbard, it bounced against Magpie's back and Caspar knew that his uncle was thinking about the chink in the blade's edge. He wondered whether Hal's confidence was similarly damaged and if that would affect the power of the sword.

'I wish Brid would wake up,' Caspar sighed, looking at the Maiden's lolling head, as it rubbed against Hal's shoulder. 'We need her.'

The dark solid knight looked at Brid and murmured, 'The world needs her.' He seemed taken aback by his own words.

Caspar stared at him in surprise, wondering why such a practical, war-hardened free-lance would say such a thing. 'The world needs her? What do you mean?'

The Caldean nobleman shrugged, 'I don't know. The thought just came to me. Something that one of my tutors used to say. A long time ago when I was about your age I had three teachers. The one I saw most often made me learn literally word for word the holy scriptures of the Book. It seems my father was intent on me becoming a man of God. He was a rigid inflexible man and what always seemed strange to me was he didn't seem to care what the words meant. He was merely intent on stuffing my mind full of words so that I could quote them chapter and verse.'

'Well, at least that impressed King Rewik,' the freckled youth remarked, turning Firecracker in a circle to keep the hot-headed stallion level with the rest of the company.

'It's funny how words can impress even when their meaning is lost,' the knight agreed. 'Then there was my second tutor. He was a man of many talents. He taught me courtly sophistication, the rituals of protocol, the history of our country as well as the layout of the world and the major languages of the Caballan Sea.'

'We had much the same schooling,' Caspar said, 'though archery and strategic warfare were of greater importance in Torra Alta and I fear I never mastered any of the languages.'

'My third tutor, though, he really understood the world.' There was a sparkle in Ceowulf's dark brown eyes and the corners of his mouth lifted, creasing the edges of his eyes, where the harshness of the southern skies had prematurely toughened the skin. 'Morgrimm not only taught me the meanings of the Book but also explained much about the Old Faith and its secrets. He knew a good deal about it and though he truly worshipped the one true God there was a sparkle in his eyes when he spoke of the old ways. It seemed that much of his soul still belonged in the clutches of the Great Goddess. He used to say that man depended on the one true God but that the Earth depended on the worship of the Great Mother. Though he's always appeared outwardly disapproving of anything I do, he was the one who fetched Sorcerer for me and, once we get to the wildfowler's, I shall send for his help again.'

'Are you sure we can trust them – Morgrimm and this wildfowler fellow?' Hal asked sceptically.

'Mallart and his wife Aida live deep in the marshes. It's a secluded place and I often visited them in my childhood. They're loyal and good-hearted. I'd trust them with my soul and Mallart will go into Tartra to fetch Morgrimm for me. I daren't trust any common messenger now, like I did last time.

And although Morgrimm might be stern and disapproving, he won't betray Brid and if she doesn't wake up soon he may be able to help her recover. We need her. She must understand what's happening here in Caldea. Ever since last night, it's as if we've awoken something that's too mysterious or awesome for us to comprehend. We need her to show us how to protect ourselves.'

'The runes of sorcery,' Caspar muttered. 'She said she had miscast her spell and then the new runes appeared on the great sword. She said they evoked an ancient magic.' He shuddered.

They rode on for over two leagues before Hal started to complain that his arm ached from holding Brid. They decided they should stop and rest at the next chalk stream where they could water the horses. There was little by way of sustenance left except for some cold spit-roasted rabbit and Caspar still felt hungry after they had divided out the meagre rations. Hal had laid Brid down on the ground, easing his cloak under her head as a pillow. She was breathing softly and Caspar crept over to her and pressed his head against her chest to listen to the rhythm of her heart. The pulse was still a little weak and unnaturally fast but it was stronger than before. Then he felt another life-force beating strongly, an entity full of energy, and the boy remembered the moonstone secured in a lattice leather pouch strung around the girl's neck. Guiltily he slid his hand inside the soft folds of her shirt and Hal flashed him a look of thunder.

'What do you think you are doing?' Jealous possessiveness darkened the youth's features.

'Who do you think I am?' the younger boy protested, flushing vigorously. 'I was just worried about the moonstone.'

'Yeah, I bet,' Hal growled and watched suspiciously as his kinsman slid the leather leash over the Maiden's head and teased the moonstone free from her clothing. The little red salamander clutched hold of the orb, its scaly body dangling in mid-air.

'Oh no, please don't use that thing.' Cybillia's cheeks paled to ash almost as white as the creamy surface of the moonstone itself.

The stone was about the size of an apple. At first glance it looked like nothing more than marble but as their eyes were drawn into its energy, the scudding cloudlike patterns skimming beneath its surface became more visible. The stone excited Caspar's heart and his pulse raced as he dangled the magical orb by its leash and took a firm hold of the squirming fire-drake.

Ceowulf sat bolt upright suddenly alert. 'Is it safe?'

'No it's not safe,' Hal warned, speaking more to his nephew than to the sunburnt knight. 'Spar doesn't know how to use it correctly and its magic blinds his mind like a thunderbolt each time he touches it. I don't like that thing.'

'I can reach my mother or maybe Morrigwen,' Caspar explained. 'Perhaps they can tell us what to do.'

'Don't touch it,' Ceowulf insisted. 'The energy of magic is loud to all those who understand it and the moonstone might draw that malevolent presence to us.'

'How do you know?' the boy queried, though he was already obeying his companions and stringing the orb around his own neck for safe keeping.

'I don't know, but my tutor used to say that magic sings and only those who already know the words of the song can hear it. Anyone or anything practised in the arts would sense you probing the magic of the moonstone. I think we'd better be getting across to the marshes as fast as possible.'

'I hope your friend has a brace of duck ready for supper,' Hal said eagerly.

'We won't get there by supper. It's well over to the east and about three leagues south of Tartra. It was only because it's so close to the castle that I know it so well. It's been a long time though . . .' he added wistfully, remounting Sorcerer and manoeuvring the black war-horse near to a tree stump so that Cybillia could climb more easily up behind him.

Struggling to help his uncle heave Brid onto Magpie's back, Caspar mused that the spoilt young noblewoman from Jotunn was becoming considerably more capable as she bravely withstood the harshness of life. He wondered how her father, Baron Bullback, would take the news of her mistreatment at the hands of the Vaalakans. Cybillia swore that she could never let her father look on her again, not now when she was so hideously scarred. Caspar felt deeply sorry for her.

They rode on through the afternoon, the shadows stretching out in front of them. The western horizon to their rear became a blaze of fire as the sun lingered behind the downs and they marched onwards into the dark of the eastern sky. Caspar's stomach was rumbling and he had a gnawing discomfort in his belly. He was about to complain when he thought of his father and Morrigwen at home in the besieged castle. When they had left Torra Alta, they had already been rationed to siege supplies. The limited food stores would have to last until they returned with the Egg and drove the vile Vaalakans back out of the rift valley.

Nine months, he thought in despair, and time was rolling past, sweeping rapidly through the days. It was nearly Wolfmoon already and by the end of Fallow the runes of war would fail. Before then they had to find the Egg and restore the Trinity of high priestesses. All three women had to live and yet all three were in mortal danger. Morrigwen was besieged in Torra Alta with a traitor midst the castle garrison, Brid had succumbed to an unnatural sleep and Keridwen . . . He could hardly bear to think of his mother trapped in the crushing teeth of the glacier. He wrenched his mind away from the tormenting image.

It was nearly fully dark now and the dapple grey of the cart-horse and the black silky coat of Ceowulf's destrier had been swallowed into shadow. Trog slumped over precariously behind Caspar's pack and he had stopped to tighten the straps that secured the dog. Now only the ghostly white patches of the piebald mare and the dim outline of Cybillia's spiky golden hair were visible ahead. Caspar mounted quickly, feeling uneasy at being left so far behind. A twig snapped somewhere behind him and he wheeled Firecracker round as he tried to pierce the gloom. He couldn't see or hear anything but his imagination drew out dark shapes and shifting shadows. He told himself fiercely that there was nothing there but, as the wind soughed in his ears and rustled the trees in a nearby spinney, a coldness ran through his body.

Seeker, Seeker, the hissing whisper seemed to be saying. His flesh felt clammy and his fear must have transmitted itself to his horse as Firecracker laid his ears flat and reared, lashing out with his pale hooves.

Caspar spurred the red stallion on towards the others.

Macabre curiosity begged him to look over his shoulder to face his own fears galloping behind him. He imagined a great black wraithlike horse with claws in place of hooves snatching out of the dark, tearing towards his neck. He told himself not to look round, lest his action gave credence to his imagination and caused the creature to materialize.

Hal's anxious face looked ghostly white in the dark, his eyes black sockets too dark to see. He had halted Magpie and was waiting for his nephew.

'Spar, whatever is the matter?' His voice was full of concern.

The moment Hal's calm rational tones filled the night air, the sensation of something stalking Caspar's footsteps melted away. 'Nothing, nothing,' he gasped. 'I stopped to secure up Trog, that's all,' he stammered, still not daring to look over his shoulder.

'Well, don't gallop about in the dark like that. The last thing we want is the horses spooked. Are you sure you're all right? You're breathing very hard.'

'I'm all right,' Caspar snapped back, smoothing the red hide of his stallion, more to calm his own nerves than to quiet the horse, who tossed his head and rattled his curb-chains. 'It's just the dark. I heard a twig snap and then I thought I felt that presence again.'

'I bet it was only a fox. We only sensed the *thing* before because the yew forest mist disturbed our minds.' The older youth sounded reassuring rather than scornful, which Caspar found surprising. Normally Hal would have laughed at him for thinking such things.

'Who ate the pig then? The pig wasn't in the mist,' Caspar argued.

'We never saw the pig. That tale could have been grossly exaggerated. Half-wits and pregnant women. We're not going to rely on their judgement now, are we? It's bad enough relying on Brid.'

Caspar noted jealously that his uncle had the Maiden securely wrapped in his arms. The sight at least drove away his fear of the dark as they marched ever eastwards. He ruefully mused that whereas Ceowulf shared his horse with the Lady Cybillia and Hal cradled Brid in his embrace, he only had Trog for company. Typical, he thought.

'Hal, why did the Goddess give us three seasons to find the Egg?' Caspar asked, swaying to the rhythmic strides of his colt. 'I mean why three seasons, why not four or two?'

'Morrigwen said it was because the spring rains would wash away the runes of war by the end of Fallow, but I don't know. The Goddess has a woman's mind and there's no guessing at such logic. It's just like a woman to think of nine months.' He laughed but Caspar cringed, thinking that his uncle's words must surely be blasphemous.

Hal groaned at his nephew's reaction and shouted ahead, 'Hey, Ceowulf, I'm hungry. How much further?'

'Give me a chance, lad,' Ceowulf retorted. 'It's dark and it's got to be sixteen years since I was last here, so I can't tell you exactly.'

'But, I'm hungry,' Hal repeated.

'We know,' the man replied patiently. 'You've told us a dozen times. I should think every owl and every bat in the south of Caldea knows you're hungry.'

The dry thuds of the horses' footfalls were turning to a splattered squelch as they entered the marshes. The spongy mosses sucked at the horses' hooves and the party fell into single file, carefully following Sorcerer's large rump as Ceowulf picked a way through the network of paths criss-crossing the lakes and streams of the gurgling swampland. Cybillia had been asleep against the knight's back but as the destrier waded through a shallow stream, sending muddy droplets splattering up around his flanks, the girl shook herself upright.

'Where are we?' she asked anxiously.

'The marshes,' the noble Caldean knight replied succinctly.

'The marshes? Is it safe?' she wailed anxiously. 'It's dark. We could ride straight into a bog and be up to our necks before you could say –'

'Will-o'-the-wisp,' Caspar suggested, looking southwards to where a ghostly, glowing shape shimmered over the mire before dancing out of sight.

Cybillia gasped and clutched tightly onto Ceowulf. 'Will it attack us?'

'It's only gas,' the knight reassured her. 'The marsh gives off a gas and it ignites very easily. It's like a fireball.'

'How do you know?' Caspar asked uncertainly. 'How do you know they're not the souls of men that have drowned in the marshes?'

'Spar, you're always the first one to believe in fairies,' Hal growled at his nephew. 'It's so embarrassing. If Ceowulf says it's gas, I'm sure he's right.'

Caspar was perversely comforted by his uncle's sharpness because at least it made him feel that the world was returning to normal.

Ceowulf halted abruptly and Magpie and Firecracker bumped into each other as the company came to an unexpected halt. Through the murk ahead, they could see that the path divided and a choice of three routes spread out before them.

'Well?' Hal demanded.

'I'm not sure,' the knight admitted.

'I wish Brid were awake; she would know the way,' Caspar unexpectedly declared.

'She couldn't,' Ceowulf objected. 'She's never been here before.'

'Brid always knows the way,' the boy stiffly contradicted, feeling defiantly loyal towards the high priestess.

'You've no idea at all?' Hal sighed, addressing the Caldean knight.

Ceowulf didn't reply but Caspar, though he couldn't see him clearly in the dark, guessed that the squarely built man was probably shaking his head.

'I think we should just stay put till daybreak.' Cybillia's thin voice slid into the murky silence of the marsh. A low mist was swirling around the horses' fetlocks and the splosh of a frog or a water vole flopping into the water to their left made Firecracker dance up on his toes.

'I'm not staying here in the dark,' Caspar protested, glancing anxiously at the dim light of a will-o'-the-wisp sliding behind the spikes of some bulrushes.

'I'm not waiting here either,' Hal declared in a practical, matter-of-fact tone. Decisively, he urged Magpie past the destrier in front. 'We'll take the middle path. I bet they all meet up again anyway.'

The reflection of the crescent moon in the shallow waters to either side at least gave some broken light to guide them along the narrow way. Occasionally the path dipped beneath muddy waters or was overrun with reeds and each time they had to splash through shallow mud for a few paces before the hooves beat out a firm rhythm once more.

'Hal,' Ceowulf warned, 'not so fast. Don't be so impulsive; you don't know where you're going.'

Hal muttered something disrespectful under his breath.

'Is he always so heedless of advice?' Ceowulf asked, and without waiting for Caspar's reply continued, 'I guess it took me a long time, too, before I learnt to control my impulses. Though I don't think I was ever quite as hot-headed as young Hal here.'

Caspar wanted to explain that Hal was the way he was only because he was always trying to prove himself. But out of loyalty to his kinsman, he kept his criticism to himself. Instead he kept his eyes peeled back to make sure Firecracker kept safely to the dry path and asked, 'How deep are the marshes?'

'Don't know. You can certainly take a small boat into them. We used to get a lot of duck from the boats. I was quite handy with a catapult in those days. Mallart used to say –'

A sudden heavy splash and a startled yell, followed by Hal's spluttering cries for help, sent Caspar's throat dry with fear. Without a moment's hesitation he flung himself to the ground and sprinted to the edge of the mist-shrouded mire. Hal's white face was visible above the deep black of the mud as was the surging shape of the piebald mare as she frantically kicked and heaved, the bubbling suction of mud clawing at her flanks.

'Hold onto the horse, Hal,' Caspar shouted. 'Get hold of the horse; she'll get you out of there. Where's Brid? Where the hell's Brid?'

'I can't reach her. Oh God, Spar, I can't reach her.' Hal's cry was a shriek of despair and he fought against the panic, which scattered his wits. A dark shape glugged off to his right and Hal thrashed a white arm out towards the gloomy form of Brid's cloak, as it slowly sank into the mud. His efforts were hopeless: he just couldn't move through the bog to get closer to her.

Without further hesitation, Caspar took a running leap and dived into the splattering mud, stretching out towards Brid. He closed his fists around the sodden spongy hem of her cloak just as his face hit the mud and he was swamped by treacly black liquid.

He couldn't breathe. The mud was dragging him downwards, drawing him deeper and deeper into the mire. He wrenched his head back and forth, trying to break free from the weight of mud, and finally he was able to flick his head up, haul one arm out of the mire and fling it forwards until he found the soft mass of Brid's hair. She was face down in the mud, motionless. Spluttering choking slime from his mouth, he wrenched her head up, hoping that she would breathe, but she lolled lifelessly in his grip. Dragging his other arm out through the mire, he frantically clawed at her face to clear the mud from her mouth and nostrils.

'Please, Brid, please be alive,' he begged almost in tears, as they both gradually sank inch by inch into the dark liquid.

Strange half-strangulated gurgling sounds were bubbling from Hal's mud-strewn face. Tongues of thick treacly slime dripped from his hair and nose, and a curtain of black mud stretched across his mouth. Caspar found himself shrieking helplessly at his uncle to grab hold of Magpie, whose great body heaved and swayed in the mire. The mud spat and sucked around her sides as her legs stirred in the depths of the marsh. Caspar's wild panic ceased, as Hal's hand finally grasped hold of the mare's black tail and he slowly hauled himself forward along the surface of the mud. Inching along the mare's body, he was very gradually nearing firm land. The quicker Hal was out of the bog, the quicker he could do something to help Brid.

Caspar concentrated on holding Brid's head up. He knew that kicking frantically would only make him sink faster so he steadied himself and looked towards Ceowulf for help. The knight had wasted no time. He had thrown the reins over Sorcerer's head and stood Cybillia at the edge of the marsh to steady the animal. He was now wading out towards him, stretching one arm across the bottomless mud whilst still gripping firmly to the reins. The broad-shouldered man moved painfully slowly, forcing his way through the life-sucking mud, and Caspar stretched his arm forward, elongating his fingers. Ceowulf reached the end of the reins and, almost invisible in the dark, his black destrier sank onto his haunches to counterbalance the knight's weight dragging on the bridle.

'Come on, Spar, reach,' Ceowulf pleaded. 'I can't quite get to you. Come on, you've got to get nearer to me.'

'I can't; I'm sinking.' Caspar knew his voice was thin and quaking. 'I can't reach you, not without letting go of Brid. Do something, Ceowulf, we're sinking.'

'Hold on, lad, just hold on.' Ceowulf's voice was calm and the man's level tones helped the boy find his courage.

'It's all right, Brid,' Caspar whispered to the soundless Maiden. 'It'll be all right.'

'Spar, hold on, just hold on,' his uncle's desperate voice filled the air. 'As soon as I get to the bank I can help you.' There was a bursting snap of air as the piebald mare broke the suction and heaved herself another foot towards the bank, dragging Hal behind her as he clung to her girth. He was still several yards from firm ground.

'It's all right, Spar,' Ceowulf repeated. 'We've got everything under control.'

Even though Caspar knew this wasn't true, the words were comforting as he felt the bog's embrace draw him closer to its depths. He felt encased in lead. The half-moon overhead shone down onto Brid's blue-white face. Only her head and neck were visible above the grasp of the mire. The bog was like some vast mouthless monster, which absorbed its prey through its skin. He sensed it had a life of its own, hungrily, greedily drawing them towards its stomach. Desperately, he tried to pull her further out of the mud but as the mire released an inch of her fine-boned body, he found himself in turn being pressed further down into its depths. The embracing mud crushed his chest, restricting his breathing.

'Mother,' he prayed, 'Mother, release us from this terror.'

'Cybillia, get hold of Sorcerer's reins and come in here towards me,' Ceowulf commanded. 'We'll form a chain.'

'No,' Cybillia replied quietly and firmly.

'Do it! Now!'

'But the mud . . . I can't.'

'They're sinking, girl. Now do what I say,' Ceowulf's voice whipped the air.

Nervous whimpers came from the girl as she worked her way along the reins and slid down into the sludge alongside him.

'Wrap the reins round your wrist. Good, now in the name of mercy, don't let me go.'

'I won't be strong enough,' she sobbed.

'You have to be. You've just got to hold on until Hal can get to you.' The knight raised his voice across the marsh. 'Are you going to make it, Hal?'

'Nearly there,' the youth grunted. 'Go on, Magpie, get up.' There was another sucking slurp of mud and a gurgling pop as the gruel-thick slime released bubbles of air onto its sludgy surface.

'Right, Cybillia, have you got me?' Ceowulf demanded.

There was no reply but just as Caspar felt the cloying mud creep up around the back of his skull, the firm grip of the knight's hand grappled for his outstretched fingers. Ceowulf grunted with the pain as he stressed his wounded shoulder but the sinew in his arms knotted as he hooked his fingers into Caspar's flesh. For a second Caspar stared gratefully into the man's moonlit face, but suddenly Brid's body was snatched under, wrenching his joints.

Urgently he dug his fingernails into her flesh and dragged at her with all his strength. But she was being jerked away from him, just as if a great king salmon had snatched at the hook of a fishing line.

'Brid, no,' he screamed as bubbles plopped up onto the surface where her head had been a second earlier.

A giant fin violently split the surface to his left, splattering mud into the air. He felt Brid being pulled away again. Tightening his grip, he was abruptly dragged another six inches deeper into the mud. He wrenched his neck back, stretching his face up towards the moonlight, gulping in precious air. Then, with another jerk, his world went black. Mud engulfed his mouth, nose and eyes. His body was stretched between Ceowulf and Brid, who was being fiercely tugged away from him. His lungs burst with the agony of suffocation and he lashed and kicked with his feet, fighting for air, fighting for his life. He knew the strength of his frantic kicks was weakening but he could no longer tell if he was being dragged deeper or not.

He must not breathe. He must not open his mouth to let the death-dark bog seep into his lungs and drag away his life. His mind was heavy, dizzily fading away from a sense of reality, and he fought to retain his will. All he need do to save himself was to let Brid go, but he must not. He must hold on. He must hold on to Brid; he must hold on to Ceowulf. His strength was fading fast. He could still just feel the bittersweet pain of the knight's fingernails digging into his flesh, holding him tightly, but Brid was slipping slowly from his grasp.

His mind was slithering down into the empty depths of the bog. Reality, hope, life were sliding away . . . His will to fight was ebbing; his desperate need to live, to save Brid, to breathe life, was being seduced by the apathy of suffocation.

It would be so much easier just to let go. It hurt so much. If he could just let go and slide softly down to sleep . . .

Great Mother, help us, he prayed, and his blurred mind filled with the gentle, loving image of his mother's face as she rocked him in her arms.

Chapter 3

Hal lunged for the reed bed and dragged himself hand over hand towards the bank. He was vaguely aware of the great piebald war-horse floundering in the shadows but his main thought was for his nephew. Spitting mud from his mouth, he struggled onto the bank and crossed to where Cybillia, waist deep in the mud, screamed incoherently. She was fearfully clinging to Sorcerer's bridle with one hand and Ceowulf's outstretched arm with the other. The knight was submerged up to his chest in mud and there was no sign of Caspar or Brid. A large black coiling shape slashed back and forth in the marsh where his nephew should have been.

'Spar,' yelled Hal in helpless panic. Though his brain was strangled with paralysing grief and despair, his body continued to move purposefully forward.

'I can't hold on,' Cybillia shrieked.

The black destrier was snorting, crouched low on its haunches with its great thick neck bowed over under the weight that dragged on its bridle.

'Hal, I can't hold on. Help me,' Cybillia sobbed.

'You've got to,' Ceowulf cried desperately. 'Spar's dragged under and his grip's failing.'

Hal threw himself back into the mud, snatching Sorcerer's reins with one arm and clawing at Ceowulf's stretched forearm with the other. Cybillia's grip slithered loose and for a second the knight slid further away before his grip retightened on Hal's wrist. Hal pulled on the reins and tried to drag the knight towards him but the weight was too great. There wasn't enough time . . .

'Spar . . . Spar!'

He knew his face was wet with tears of desperation. Spar was down there drowning in the mud and he couldn't do anything to save him. He was overwhelmed by the desperate fear of losing his nephew, his lifelong companion whom he loved as a brother.

'Get to the horse, Cybillia! Pull yourself out and get him to back up!' Hal knew he was shouting angrily. Cybillia's frightened face turned away determinedly to do as he ordered.

The black coiling shape arched above the surface of the mire and plunged down again, leaving a razor-sharp fin proud of the surface. Hal thought the muscles on his chest would burst as he desperately attempted to pull Ceowulf towards him. He prayed that the man still had hold of his nephew.

'Don't let go of him,' Hal pleaded. 'Don't let go of him. Oh God,' he screamed out into the night. 'Help us! Please, God, help us!' he screamed louder and louder.

Cybillia was beating against Sorcerer's chest with her fists and the animal was snorting in panic and wrenching its head from side to side. Despite his huge bulging muscles, the destrier was unable to drag them out.

'Get Magpie, Cybillia. Get a rope round her neck.'

'What rope?! What rope?!' she yelled back at him.

'Stand aside, lady.'

Suddenly another voice was in their midst, steady and calm, heavy with the burred accent of southern Belbidia. The whistle of an arrow whipped past Hal's ear followed by a distinct soggy thud as its barbed head embedded in flesh. The stranger loosed a flurry of arrows at the triangular fin. A few sloshed harmlessly into the mud though a couple had a satisfying crunch to them and suddenly the destrier lurched backwards, dragging Hal a yard out of the water.

'Steady does it now. That's it. Go on, horse, up with you,' the stranger urged.

There was a second sudden slurping rush as Caspar and then the limp body of Brid were hauled to the surface. Hal's face scraped over the hollow-stemmed reeds as he was dragged through the shallows, still holding Ceowulf. Within a few more seconds the chain of Belbidians was dragged free from the bog. With relief Hal saw that Caspar was breathing, though in short rasping gulps, between spluttering coughs. His fiercely white hands were still hooked into the Maiden's shirt and his nails had torn great rents in the fabric. One finger was hooked through the strap of the leather scrip that hung across her body. It was only that leather strap that had saved her from being dragged from his grasp.

Caspar refused to let go. Someone was trying to prise his fingers open and someone else was turning him over and wiping the mud from his face. He still couldn't see.

'Spar, Spar,' Hal's familiar voice was shouting in his ear but it sounded somehow distant and remote.

Caspar's mind focused on Brid. I mustn't let go. Whatever I do, I mustn't let go, he told himself. His body still felt leaden and his lungs were raw with pain as if a giant had taken him in his fist and wrung his chest out like a wet cloth. Brid, he thought helplessly. All other thoughts were distant and vague and he tensed his fingers against someone's prising efforts to sever his grip on her. He felt cold, horribly cold and the blood-chilling sensation that something was watching him returned to his half-conscious mind.

'Spar, it's me. Wake up!' Hal's voice was insistent. An unexpectedly sharp slap across his cheeks brought Caspar's eyes blinking into the light of a firebrand held close to his face.

'He's lucky. He's been very lucky,' a strange voice was murmuring and Caspar tried to focus on the dark outline of an unfamiliar figure that was peering down at him.

'Brid,' the boy found himself moaning. 'How is she?'

'Now just stay calm, lad; the others are looking after her. Just try to breathe steady now.'

'Brid!' Caspar yelled, pushing himself up on his elbows. A sickening heaviness swam through his head. The light of the firebrand swirled around him and he felt himself falling –

falling endlessly back into blackness through time and space, not knowing whether he would ever reach the bottom. Someone was coughing wretchedly in the blackness and disjointed echoing voices were yelling and shouting, clashing and jarring against his head and yet he couldn't understand them. Someone was calling his name. He could hear them repeating it over and over again. He wanted to answer. He wanted to say sorry for being so much trouble and for upsetting everyone but somehow the effort was too much. His eyelids were too heavy to open and his jaw felt set in stone. He felt giddily sick and his world lurched and swayed.

'Have you got him now?' a strange voice shouted in the distance.

'Yes, don't worry. Just make sure you bring the girl. Cybillia, hold that firebrand high. We don't want to miss our footing again.'

Caspar vaguely knew that voice. He was sure it was familiar. It wasn't Hal's, he knew that. Maybe it was his father's, he wasn't sure ... No, it couldn't be. Somehow he knew his father wasn't with them.

'Brid,' he tried to shout, suddenly realizing that his hand no longer gripped hers. 'I've let go of her . . .' He thrashed his arms, trying to reach her, but they wouldn't move properly. 'Brid!' he yelled again though he heard his voice only as a murmur.

That familiar voice was soothing in his ears but did nothing to reassure him. 'Hush, Spar. We've got her.'

A warm touch gripped his hand and with great relief Caspar knew that Hal was beside him. He let his mind drift. Hal was there so everything would be all right. Hal would look after him; Hal would look after Brid. He relaxed to the rocking motion and gradually, as his mind began to clear, he realized he was being carried.

'Not far,' a deep rich voice reassured him. Caspar remembered now that the voice belonged to Ceowulf.

'Is he with us yet?' Hal's anxious voice drifted into the boy's head.

'Hal,' he groaned. 'Hal, is Brid all right? Is she alive?'

There was no answer at first but, after what seemed to be an eternity, Hal's voice broke very close to his head.

'Spar! You're awake. We're nearly at the place Ceowulf was taking us to. Mallart found us and dragged us out of the bog. As soon as we arrive, he's going to Tartra for help.'

'What's happened to Brid?' Caspar asked feebly.

Hal's hand tightened on his nephew's arm and Caspar sensed the fearful tension. 'I don't know, Spar. We got her out of the bog. You never let go of her but we don't know yet . . .'

'Is she breathing?' Caspar was suddenly wriggling, trying to escape from Ceowulf's arms, but he didn't have the strength.

'Yes,' Hal whispered uncertainly. 'I think so. Her hair smothered her face, forming a seal over her nose and mouth so she doesn't seem to have inhaled any of the mire – well, not much anyway. Her breathing is shallow and intermittent . . . but she is breathing.'

But she is breathing. The words went round and round in Caspar's mind and he comforted himself with the thought. He drifted off only to awaken to the soft reflection of warm firelight flickering on a low ceiling. He was smothered in thick rugs and he had to twist his head to take in the view of the room. A rocking chair was creaking to the rhythmic movements of an old woman who pushed herself back and forth with her big toe. His movement had evidently caught her eye because she pushed herself up and shuffled over to him.

'Well now, look who's awake,' she said with a kindly smile that revealed only two front teeth and a gummy lower jaw. Her grey hair was tucked up under a shawl and her face was like scrunched parchment. The folds of sagging skin beneath her jaw flapped as she mashed her mouth up and down. Uncurling her knobbly hands, she soothed his forehead. 'Thank the good Lord for sending Mallart out into the night. He heard the birds shrieking and thought there might be poachers about. I think he must have found you only just in time,' she mumbled, tucking the blankets tightly round him again.

Brid! The single thought of the Maiden swamped the boy's mind. Despite the old woman's efforts to restrain him, he kicked his legs free and struggled out of the blankets only to find himself completely naked. He grabbed at a rug and wrapped it round himself. Then with a strenuous effort to control his swimming head, he looked vaguely around the dimly lit room. He instantly recognized Hal's glossy black hair poking out from under a heap of rugs in the corner. But right by the fire, near where the old lady had been sitting, was a bundle wrapped in fur-lined cloths.

Caspar stumbled towards the bundle, muttering Brid's name and falling to his knees to tease back her cloak from her face. He recoiled at the sight of her ash-grey face and purple lips. 'Brid!' he cried in horror. 'Brid, wake up.' He was overwhelmed with the desire to pick her up and shake her, to somehow make her respond, but his arms were fiercely pinned by two strong hands. Hal, dressed only in leggings, was at his side.

'Leave her be, Spar. Mallart's gone to Tartra to get help. We can't do anything now except keep her warm.'

Wrapping the rug around his body, Caspar sat down next to the girl. He fixed his eyes on her face, not daring to remove his gaze for one second in case, in that moment, she slipped away from him.

'Come back to us,' he softly pleaded.

'Back to bed and rest yourself, right now,' the old woman ordered. 'Both of you. There's no good to be done crooning over her like that. It's not so far to the castle and Mallart will be back with help soon enough.'

'Where is Ceowulf?' Caspar asked, trying to fit the pieces together.

'Settling the horses,' Hal quickly explained. 'I offered but he thought it better if I was close by for when you woke up.'

Just as the youth spoke there was a creak at the door and a white snub nose rapped heavily against the wood, flinging the door open. Trog burst into the room. Hal caught the terrier by the collar before he could trample all over Brid in his enthusiastic efforts to wake her. Ceowulf and Cybillia, both still smothered in mud, anxiously followed. The broad-shouldered man beamed warmly at Caspar.

'At least you're with us,' he sighed, though his anxious brows and tense eyes betrayed his worry over the Maiden.

'Here, let's get you two cleaned up,' the old woman fussed. 'I've a tub in the other room. Now, young lady, I'll put the kettle on for some hot water and we can get the mud off you first. Oh my, oh dear Lord, you've scratched your face something terrible in the struggle. I'll have a look at it for you.'

Cybillia slapped her hand to her cheek and turned her face away, hiding the pentagram-shaped scar in the shadows.

'No. No need. I'll look after it,' she stammered and fled into the other room.

A thick layer of dried mud encased the lower half of Ceowulf's body and the rest of him was bespattered with dark blobs of slime. Cradled in his left arm, his right shoulder was held at an awkward angle. Obviously in pain from his traumatized injury, he slumped down next to the fire, but not a murmur of complaint crossed his lips.

'Oh, dear boy.' The old woman fled to him. 'I mean Lord Ceowulf, you're hurt. What can we do?'

The knight fended her off with his good arm. 'Don't fuss, Aida, don't fuss. It's an old wound and tonight's efforts in the mud have only torn the tissue slightly. The bone's not yet properly knit, but I'll be fine, really. It's Brid we need to worry about.'

'Well, I can't do anything for her right now but I can do something for you. I remember when you were knee high to a water-hound and you used to toddle down here on your scruffy little pony. Mallart would teach you to use a catapult and you would get into such trouble at the castle. You were such a blithe and bonny lad and you think I'm just going to sit here now with you in that state. Come on, I'll have no more of your fussing. Now, let's get your shirt off.'

Ceowulf reluctantly resigned himself to the woman's well-meant ministrations, trying to disguise his grimaces of pain as she dabbed at his wound with a clean wet cloth.

'Oh, it grieves me, my dear Lord Ceowulf. How ever did you get this?'

The wound where Tasso's throwing axe had hacked into the flesh of Ceowulf's chest, crushing his collarbone, had knitted into a purple scar. The scar had split and, where the scabs had burst apart, greenish liquid seeped between slits in the half-healed skin.

With thankful admiration, Caspar looked at the man's dark eyes frowning beneath his straight black brows. Despite the agony it must have put him through, Ceowulf had held on to him unfailingly when he had been dragged into the bog. He was indeed a brave and noble man.

'Now what were you doing out there at such a time of night anyway? You of all people should know how dangerous the marsh is,' Aida scolded him, as she poured a dark red liquid from a stoppered gourd over his wound. The man's neck muscles sprang up into bars with pain. Caspar recognized the pungent aroma of a particularly strong fortified Caldean wine.

'We're in trouble,' Ceowulf muttered between gritted teeth. 'We need your help, but please don't ask me to explain because I can't.' He looked into Aida's deep-set green-brown eyes. 'Please don't ask me any more, will you?'

She shook her head fondly at him. 'The good Lord saw fit to make me the wife of the wildfowler; now is it my place to question the Baron's son?'

Trog had wriggled free from Hal's grasp and was slinking forward on his belly to nuzzle up against Brid's bloodless face. He whimpered pathetically.

'Whatever you do, keep that dog away from her legs,' the old woman warned.

'What's wrong with her legs?' Caspar leapt at the concern in Aida's voice. It came back to him, the black fin, the coiling humps of reptilian flesh and the vehement force with which Brid had suddenly been snatched under the surface of the mire.

'Whatever that bog monster was it has left teeth marks in her flesh,' Hal informed him.

'It was a marsh lindworm, I'm sure,' Ceowulf muttered ominously. 'Mallart used to tell tales of such a beast, a sort of shrunken slimy dragon without wings that slunk away many hundreds of years ago to hide in the bogs.' He turned to look sorrowfully at Brid. 'Her legs are a mess.'

'Oh Mother,' the boy exclaimed in horror, which twisted Aida's face into a shocked frown. She turned back anxiously towards Brid.

'Such a little mite. I've never known one so cut up. May God bless her, she'll have to have the strength of a lion to pull through.'

'But . . . we've got to do something for her. We can't just sit here,' Caspar protested.

'Aida's dressed the wounds. There's nothing more we can do but wait till Mallart gets back with Morgrimm,' Ceowulf said calmly. 'The best thing you can do is keep quiet and calm.'

'Where's the moonstone?' Caspar demanded frantically, suddenly realizing it was no longer hanging round his neck. 'I've got to do something for Brid. We can't wait for Mallart.' He grabbed hold of Hal's collar and found himself vigorously shaking him. 'Give it to me. I know you've got it.'

A heavy hand on the boy's shoulder pulled him away from his uncle.

'You've got to control yourself, lad,' Ceowulf growled. 'Now, Aida, please will you leave us,' he asked in a polite tone that still carried all the threat of command. 'Why not give Cybillia a hand?'

Aida looked at him suspiciously. 'There's something afoot here which I don't like but I'm merely a peasant woman and I won't be meddling in the ways of noblemen.' Her haughty, hurt look softened, 'May the good Lord protect your soul, Ceowulf.'

The moment she had shuffled from the room and pulled the ill-fitting door shut on its latch, Caspar held out his hand for the moonstone. 'Give it to me. I must try to reach Morrigwen.' Whenever he had touched the moonstone previously,

47

it had always taken his mind straight to his mother, but he feared that Vaal-Peor had almost claimed her in the crushing jaws of the Vaalakan glacier and that if he drew on her powers again, he might fatally weaken her tenuous grip on life. From now on he could call only on Morrigwen for help.

Reluctantly Hal returned to his bundle of bedding and, using just a thumb and forefinger, teased out the leather leash that held the moonstone. He studiously kept it at arm's length and held it out distastefully to his nephew. The red salamander groggily swung from the orb, still determined never to let go. The little fire-drake looked paler after its immersion in the bog but Caspar was relieved to see that it was still alive. Brid had said that the animal, whose thoughts were only ever of fire, fed its heat to Keridwen through the channels of magic opened up by the moonstone. The warmth from the salamander, like the heat from the mutant dragon that had treasured the orb over the last twelve years, had kept her alive.

Caspar felt his heart racing with vigorous energy. The magical orb threw its white pearly light into the shadows of the dimly lit room, chasing spiders back to their cobwebs and creeping into the darker crevices. It had the effect of bringing the walls and ceiling closer to them. He drew in a deep breath, preparing himself for the jolt produced by the mind-wrenching power of the moonstone. He studied the orb's smooth creamy white surface as it swirled and stirred before his eyes. Carefully he slid it from its lattice pouch onto the palm of his hand.

The shock jolted his forearm, throwing his muscles into spasm, jerking tight his grip. The white-hot pain sliced into his brain and stunned his mind. Flashes of lightning zigzagged through his thoughts and he gritted his teeth against the blinding agony.

'Morrigwen,' he whispered, staring into the racing patterns of white cloud. 'Morrigwen,' he demanded again, forming the image of the old Crone in his mind, picturing her long white hair and her strange blue eyes flecked with slivers of silver.

The opaque white patterns whisked aside and a clear vision of Torra Alta beneath a half-moon filled the orb. The moon was stained red by fires that lapped up the sides of the walls. Torrents of flame, like great tongues of dragonfire, spilt out of the crenellations where the garrison poured burning oil onto the Vaalakans below.

Standing above the other solid square towers of the castle, a circular turret stretched towards the moon. Caspar felt the orb yearn towards it and then swoop down towards the lower keep. Suddenly the air was rushing past his face as he swept across the distance and squeezed through an arrow-slit into a small dimly lit chamber.

The ancient woman flicked her head up and stared straight into his eyes. Beside her stood a small chestnut-haired girl who clutched at her hand. Caspar found her strangely like Brid and his soul was drawn towards her before he was distracted by the old Crone. Morrigwen looked pale and terribly thin, but at least now she was sitting up. She stretched out her hand to reach him. Her mouth moved over soundless words and Caspar could hear nothing. Suddenly he felt himself being sucked away, spiralling high into the heavens, drifting on the biting cold ice-currents of the winter sky. He was flying northward. The air was thin and harsh as he swooped across the Dragon Scorch. Below him he could see the coiling trail of Vaalakan soldiers as they converged on the Pass. He soared higher and clipped over the three barren black peaks of the Black Devils. Then he glided down to the vast sleeping monster of the glacier that crouched in the mountains at the southern tip of the tundra.

His mother was calling him.

He could feel her presence crying out to him. Though he had tried to reach Morrigwen, the bond with his mother was too strong. Suddenly he was staring through frosted ice onto the black shadow of a body lying buried several feet below the surface. Then he was next to her, the dreadful cold piercing his body and slicing into his veins. He felt it creep into his brain, slowing his thoughts and bringing with it a screaming pain. A skeletal hand reached out and snatched at his arm. Very slowly he forced his head round to stare into her dead eyes. Her black mouth was stuck fast in an agonized scream that distorted her face with twisted anguish. One hand clawed at her throat as if trying to fight back the agony.

Looking up, he could see someone above the surface and he sensed a madness, a malevolent hatred. He was slipping back in time to just before the deathly cold rivers gushing off the Vaalakan tundra had turned to solid ice, as his mind joined with his mother's and he relived her memories. An arm reached down through the freezing waters, seizing Keridwen by the throat and plunging her deeper into the river. She clawed at the arm, her nails shredding flesh. His blood seeped out into the water and frostbite ate into the wounds. Caspar fought to tear away the man's grip and suddenly Keridwen's nightmarish memories faded. The lacerated arm withdrew to the surface and the waters froze around them.

'Mother, Mother,' he screamed, willing the warmth of his body to her, trying desperately to ease her torture. The clutch of her arm bit deeply into his flesh, the pain of the cold so fierce that it seemed like fire raging through him. He willed the heat from his body towards her, pumping the blood through his constricted veins to bring her life. Slowly her eyes melted then suddenly blood gushed through her veins and her ice-blue skin glowed with the vibrancy of health. He had finally reached the living soul trapped in her near dead body and now her mind was free to wander with his.

Violet-blue eyes were framed by a heart-shaped face and fiery red hair. Caspar immediately felt embraced by her overwhelming love. He could see the blood-red lips moving but her words were soundless. For a second there was a flicker of delight and relief and then her eyes narrowed suspiciously and she seemed to be looking beyond him, anxiously searching the shadows. Her eyes fixed back on him angrily. *What are you doing, child? Keep away from the channels of magic in the Druid's Eye. You don't know what you are meddling with. There are powers all about you.*

Caspar was shocked. 'Mother, Mother, it's Brid. I tried to reach Morrigwen but –'

Keridwen's eyes filled with understanding as she read his thoughts and he knew that further explanation was needless.

She whispered in his head. *While Brid's mind is asleep you are in danger. You have cast a runespell that you cannot control. The ancient beasts of power, banished to the Otherworld by the first druid, are stirring. Their shadows slip between the two worlds, trying to reach you. The fearful beasts that still haunt the world, like the krakens and the marsh lindworm, are aware of your presence. You seek the Egg and they hope for you to lead them to it. If they claim it for themselves they will have dominion of the Earth. You are in danger from shadow and monster alike. While Brid sleeps, she cannot protect you.*

'But Mother, she's hurt. The monster in the bog lacerated her legs.'

The flesh will heal. It's her mind we must reach, Spar. Trust me. Reach out to her. Hold her palm against the Druid's Eye.

Caspar felt inside the blankets for Brid's limp hand. It felt horribly cold. Still holding the moonstone, he pressed her hand to the crystalline orb. Her body stiffened and jolted as if a great shot of raw energy had slammed into her slender frame. Gradually her muscles relaxed and Caspar let his mind be drawn back into the stone. He felt his mother's touch and her lively mind right there beside him. Her closeness felt real, though he knew she was hundreds of miles away in Vaalaka. He sensed her hand close protectively round his and he felt safe and blissfully secure. Then they were walking through what he thought was a murky forest only he couldn't see any trees. There was a stillness to the atmosphere, a ghostly quietness, and Caspar couldn't see the way ahead. He held tightly to his mother's hand.

'Brid! Brid!' Keridwen called into the gloom. 'We're here. Wait for us, Brid. We will find you.'

There was something very strange about this place. Caspar knew they weren't alone and could sense mysterious powers stalking him. They seemed very close, watching him, waiting for the moment he released his mother's hand, to snatch him away.

'Don't let go of me, Spar. Whatever happens don't let go. Brid!' she cried again into the insubstantial murk. Caspar wasn't sure what he was treading on, whether it was soft grass or crisp leaves. He wasn't even sure whether there was any ground there at all.

'Brid,' he called, adding his own forlorn voice to his mother's call. 'Brid, where are you?'

Something lurched out from the right as if it had leapt from an overhead branch. Caspar caught the image of talons and the great curving fangs of a cat but only for a second. Keridwen wrapped her cloak around him and shielded him from the assault, driving back the creature with a vehement attack of her mind. A flash of white hooves came next, thundering across the earth. Caspar felt the jab of an ice-cold sword in his side, but Keridwen enfolded him in her arms and breathed her warm breath over his face. 'It's not real, child. They're not real. They are only the shadow of unicorns long since banished to the Otherworld. They can't harm you.'

Ahead a cold blue light drew closer. Caspar thought he could see branches about him but gradually he realized that they were moving, coiling and slithering. A flickering forked tongue darted out of what he thought was the broken bough of a smooth-barked beech and a silvery-grey snake reared its head ready to strike. Keridwen focused her mind on the reptile and it withered away while her son cowered behind her. Not snakes, he murmured tremulously to himself. Anything but snakes. He was mortally afraid of them. The very thought of their writhing legless coils and sibilant tongues froze his blood.

His heart stopped. Surrounded by ice-blue light, a pack of hunched animals crowded together, fighting over something in their midst. The air was full of snarling, fetid breath as they grizzled and growled and tore at their prey. He knew at once that they were trolls: large cumbersome beasts, with short whippy tails, hunched backs and coarse hide with hoglike bristles sprouting along their jutting spines. One of them turned its flat face and small round human eyes towards him. It opened its mouth as if to smile but instead of the yellow upturned fangs of a troll, its mouth was filled with icicles.

The Seeker, it roared in his mind as its eyes fell on him with recognition.

'Stay close,' Keridwen warned. Then she yelled out into the murky drifting world, 'I am the Mother. I am the mortal embodiment of the Goddess herself. I fear no one. I fear nothing. I am life.'

A warm glow of energy throbbed through her body and drove back the ice-death chill that lingered around the trolls. Suddenly Caspar realized what their salivary tongues hungered for. He knew what scrap of meat was in their midst. A slender frame, with long, soft coppery brown hair, flailed limply as she was tugged between the grunting troll-pack that raked at her with bear-like claws.

'Brid! They're killing her, they're killing her,' Caspar shrieked, trying to run forward to her rescue.

'No, Spar,' his mother caught him in a terrible grip, her strength made more potent by the summoning of her powers. 'It isn't real. We are walking through Brid's mind and it's filled by the ghosts of creatures. They are digging for her thoughts; they wish to possess her knowledge. With the runes of sorcery, you have woken an ancient power, which the Druid's Egg controls. We must have the Egg before these shadowy creatures from the Otherworld discover it and wield its power. Strengthen your mind. Their claws are not real. We must walk through them and steal Brid away lest she wakes in their midst.'

Keridwen strode determinedly forward, seeming to grow with each stride until she was huge like a great ogress and the boy felt he was clinging to her calf. With an angry slash of her hand she threw one of the monstrous trolls aside. It curled up into a whimpering ball and slunk away until it was absorbed by the shadows. One by one the cowering creatures trembled before the blinding fury of the Goddess as Her power was channelled through Keridwen.

At last Keridwen cupped the Maiden in her giant hand and the girl looked peaceful and serene. The lacerations that had ripped apart the flesh on her cheeks, chest and legs smoothed over and healed to a delicate bronze. Her dragon-green eyes opened and, like an infant looking lovingly into the eyes of her mother, she blinked.

Caspar's mother was shrinking rapidly until at last she hugged Brid in her arms. The murk around them was beginning to brighten but as it did so Keridwen seemed to waver like a rippling reflection in a millpond. Her outline became hazy as if Caspar were looking at her through a web of dew-dropped gossamer sparkling in the first rays of morning.

'Find the Egg, find it soon, my children.' Her voice became a distant echo. 'We haven't much time.' Suddenly her mind leapt forward. The colour had sapped from her cheeks and her ruby lips had dulled to sickly purple. Her eyes were glazed. *Keep the doors and windows closed and the fire burning high. Tonight the cold breath of Vaal-Peor is riding in the wind. He is the God of cold places and there His strength grows quickly. Stay out of the channels of magic. You must not look into the Druid's Eye; the loud song of its magic alerts Vaal-Peor's servants to your presence. Beware, those who seek you.*

Caspar could barely hear her now. Suddenly he was blinded by a burning brilliance and the shadowy murk around him vanished into bright light. It wasn't the raw white light of the moonstone but the light of life, like looking directly into the heart of the sun.

His mind reeled away and just for a moment he heard Brid's voice, gentle and loving.

'Spar, don't go. Don't go.' But he shrank back from the dreadful power of her waking mind, fleeing Brid, fleeing the small beautiful girl for the awe of the Goddess within her soul. 'Don't go, Spar,' she pleaded. 'Don't go. I'm afraid of the trolls. I'm afraid of the cold.'

Suddenly Caspar was looking at the bare earth floor and realized he was lying on the ground in the small dimly lit room. He shook himself fully awake and turned to look at Brid. She was breathing softly and a warm blush of colour plumped out her previously grey-white cheeks. Gently he lifted an eyelid and saw that the dead white walls of her rolled back eyes had returned to their healthy dazzling green. She was sleeping peacefully.

'Vaal-Peor!' Caspar tried to explain incomprehensibly. 'The trolls of Vaal-Peor. We must stay close to her and keep her warm. Check the windows. Keep them shut; there are spirits out there. They found Brid's mind and now they are looking for us.'

'I don't believe in spirits,' Ceowulf sniffed, looking anxiously over his shoulders.

Caspar crept towards the windows and peered out into the night. In the moonlight he could see the reeds and bushes whipping to and fro in the breeze. 'The wind is picking up,' he murmured. 'And over there, look, there's one of those ghostly marsh lights. And it's coming towards us. We should close the shutters.'

Hal was by his side, looking over his shoulder. 'That's only a lantern. You'll get us all spooked if you go on like that. If it makes you feel better we'll get the shutters closed.'

Not even Hal's steady words eased Caspar's fears. He didn't want to go out into the night but he knew he must to seal out the rising storm. As he put his hand on the front door, he felt the latch being ripped away as a blast of cold air pulled the door open and buffeted him in the face. Quickly, they ran round the small hut, slotting the creaking shutters into place and latching them firmly closed with wooden crossbars. The outside world suddenly seemed much darker as the last of the light from the dwelling was shuttered in. Caspar tried not to look over his shoulder as the wind howled in his ears and he hurried back to the entrance.

The lantern was closer now and the silhouettes of two figures striding towards them were clearly visible in its halo of light. One was short with bowed legs and hobbled on a stick. He took quick paces to keep level with his tall companion who was wearing a sweeping cloak and a broad-brimmed, peaked hat.

Ceowulf, who had come to the doorway, strode eagerly forward to greet the man. 'Morgrimm! Morgrimm!'

'Into the house,' Morgrimm ordered without returning the welcome. 'The marsh is alive with spirits tonight.'

They huddled round the fire, closely guarding Brid who still slept soundly. Her skin was flushed with a healthy glow and she softly mumbled meaningless words in her sleep. The dog lapped insistently at her face.

Morgrimm looked around him. He was thin and very tall with stern cold features. Only his eyes and long white hair and beard gave away his age. The beard was braided into three long plaits and his hair fell from beneath his broad-brimmed hat like a frozen waterfall. He didn't wait for explanations or introductions but fixed them all one by one with a discerning stare. 'Someone's been meddling with things they don't understand,' he said accusingly in a deep mellow voice.

'Get everyone into the room. Mallart, find your wife. We'll have everyone in the same room and then we'll seal up all the cracks. Build up the fire, Ceowulf.'

Once Aida and Cybillia were seated by the fire, Caspar laid rugs along the cracks at the bottom of the door and then crept back close to the hearth to be near Brid. Cybillia was wrapped in a shawl, which she clasped tightly to her face, hiding her cheek, and Ceowulf slumped next to her, gripping his wounded shoulder. The freckle-faced boy looked around the company and decided they looked a sorry sight, completely unfit to protect themselves. But he was relieved by the presence of the tall stranger from Tartra.

'Ceowulf, you should have gone to your father for help,' Morgrimm said reproachfully. 'He is old and longs to see you before the barony passes into the hands of your brother. A few days back he heard rumours of a magnificent knight baring the Caldean colours and he murmured from his bed, "If only that were my son Ceowulf."'

'How could I? You must understand, Morgrimm, the girl . . .'

'Yes, I understand. She is of the old ways. She has brought evil spirits down on this place. Mallart has told me about the marsh lindworm. The monster had passed into folklore, unheard of even in my lifetime, but the presence of the girl has lured it back from Hell.'

The wind rattled at the shutters and hummed in the eaves and for a second the fire dulled in the hearth. Morgrimm stirred it with a poker until sparks spat out and the flames regenerated with a roar.

Aida clung to her husband. 'Ceowulf, how could you do this? You have brought the Devil into our home. You should put her out into the dark and let the spirits have her.'

'Hear our tale before you judge her,' the nobleman replied. 'There are worse evils on the northern border of Belbidia. The Vaalakans are marching south and they threaten our whole country. Torra Alta is the only thing that holds them north of the Yellow Mountains and this small girl is the only one that can save Torra Alta. If she dies Torra Alta falls and all Belbidia will be lost to the Vaalakan hordes.'

Gradually he unravelled their mysterious tale and explained how the fearful talisman they sought would drive back the hated Northmen. 'Aida, they sacrifice their own offspring to the Devil-God Vaal-Peor. Surely you can shelter this girl if it means that we save Belbidia?'

A scratching noise at the shutters and a low groaning wail outside silenced Morgrimm's words and Caspar felt the hairs on the back of his neck stand on end. They huddled closer together and the tall tutor ordered them to hold hands in a tight circle. 'Don't listen to it. Don't look over your shoulders. Stay focused on the warmth of the group.'

Caspar tried not to listen to the noise outside but he couldn't ignore the sound of something dragging across the ground and the steady pacing of a large animal. A fiendish shriek cut through the wailing moan of the wind and Caspar prayed for morning. They all prayed.

Morgrimm insisted that they talk through the night. 'I know many things about the old ways but I do not know their Gods,' he sighed. 'This girl may be a priestess of the Great Mother but Ceowulf tells me there is goodness in her heart so I will pray for her. I will pray for the mercy of the good Lord to protect her immortal soul from the demons.'

Silently Caspar prayed to the Mother, while nearby the old couple from the marshes, Cybillia, Hal and the tutor from Tartra murmured words from the scriptures – words he knew by rote and could recite in his sleep but words he no longer believed in. At first he wanted to scream out against them and protest that the prayers to the one true God would harm the priestess: she had, after all, struggled all her life against the New Faith.

Morgrimm placed a wise hand on the boy's shoulder as if sensing his chagrin. 'We must each pray to the God in our own hearts.' The old tutor fixed Ceowulf with a stern look. 'And you, who ran away and fled your duties as the son of a baron to slaughter men in the name of shame as a free-lance, you must pray too.'

'I know no gods,' Ceowulf retorted. 'I know many words, many psalms, many scriptures – all of them the written word of *men*. But I know no gods.'

'You were always stubborn,' Morgrimm acknowledged and returned to chanting the rhythmical psalms.

Caspar looked longingly and protectively at Brid and tried to shut out the prayers around him. He needed to form a picture of the Great Goddess in his mind and reach out for the warmth of Her love but no image materialized. Instead he saw Brid, his mother Keridwen and the old Crone Morrigwen standing all together, but it was enough. The mere thought of the Trinity drove away his fears of the rattling taps and snorts that circled the hut.

When morning broke, the wind whispered away and the disturbing sounds of the night were replaced by the sharp clear tones of a reed warbler claiming its territory. Caspar looked around him at the drooping eyes of the sleep-deprived company and breathed a sigh of relief.

Yet one image from the night still haunted him. He couldn't rid his mind of the vision of the lacerated arm, the arm that his mother had clawed and shredded with her nails in her attempt to save herself. He remembered the man's presence leaning over the freezing waters and the sickening sense of hatred he brought with him. Caspar's mind held the image of the forearm scarred with furrowed black frost-bitten gashes.

Chapter 4

Brid was still asleep when a cry from outside brought her blurrily to her senses.

Aida ran into the room, gasping and gesticulating incomprehensibly at the window. 'Outside! Look outside!'

Caspar ran to see what had caused the commotion and stared with horror at the devastated landscape. Trees were uprooted and the reed beds were combed flat. But far, far worse were the deep raking imprints of large clawed beasts that circled the house.

The youth returned to the fireside to see Brid blinking and looking bewildered as she clutched hold of Trog, who had remained faithfully by her side throughout the night. Aida immediately fled into the kitchen to hide from the piercing dragon-green eyes of the pagan priestess.

'Spar,' the girl murmured faintly, 'what's happened? Where are we? Why are we here?'

'You ate some Salisian wolfsbane,' the boy started to explain.

'Rubbish! I wouldn't have done anything so stupid. The last thing I remember was searching through a curious mist looking for the cauldron and its runes.'

'We found the cauldron but we had to destroy it to prevent anyone else from reading its secrets.'

'Destroy the Mother Cauldron! Spar, you've been having terrible dreams. I would remember finding the cauldron and I would certainly never have destroyed it. You've either been dreaming or you're playing a cruel joke on me.'

'I'm not,' Caspar pleaded. 'You copied all the runes down. You put the parchment in your scrip. You had to take the

Salisian wolfsbane because Trog ate the Faronan henbane, which would have been less poisonous. You couldn't risk any of the creatures entering your mind and finding out the location of the Egg.'

Brid looked back at Caspar blankly.

'Then Hal dropped you in the bog,' the Belbidian youth continued, 'and a monstrous marsh lindworm tried to drag you under. Then last night after I used the moonstone, strange creatures flooded to the house and prowled all around. Keridwen saved you from the ice-trolls who were fighting for your mind.'

'You *were* there in my dream,' Brid said uncertainly. 'You were there but you ran away from me and Keridwen was there in the distance, fading away. Is the rest of what you say really true?' she asked suspiciously. 'Give me my clothes and my herb scrip. Maybe I'll believe it when I see the parchment.'

Caspar retrieved the leather pouch and flaked off the caking of dried mud. The leather itself was stiff and cracked from its soaking. She unlaced the leather thongs that knotted it shut and tipped the bag upside down. A sodden sludge of muddy herbs and bits of small dead animals fell out onto the floor and there, lying in the middle of the sorry mess, was a folded piece of parchment. Brid pinched a corner between her thumb and forefinger, gingerly lifting it out of the pile. Trog immediately plunged his nose into the debris, snorting and splattering mud and tiny pieces of withered carcasses over their clothes. Ignoring the dog, Brid delicately peeled apart the folded wad of parchment and looked at the blurry mud-ruined scrawl that had once been her own clear writing.

Hal stepped into the room and grinned warmly at the priestess. 'So you're back in the land of the living.'

Brid didn't reciprocate his greeting. 'This is all your fault. You dropped me in a bog and now look at it!' she exploded, causing the raven-haired youth to take a backward step at her unexpected attack before looking suspiciously at his nephew.

'What have you been saying to her? She makes it sound

like I did it deliberately. Magpie stumbled, that was all,' he defended himself.

Brid snorted stiffly. 'I bet. Now, both of you leave me alone; I want to get dressed.'

Hal was goaded to anger. 'What are you being so coy about? We've seen it all before, haven't we? You were all over me in the yew forest. To think I carried you all the way across Caldea while you were unconscious and all the thanks I get is you yelling at me like this! Crazy witch!' He spat out the last two words and stood glowering down at her.

Caspar was mortified. How could his uncle speak to the high priestess like that? She had removed her clothes and flung herself at him only to increase the potency of the spell that she had hoped would break the cauldron's silence. But, thankfully, his own interventions had made her sacrifice unnecessary.

Brid stiffened with indignation. Her brow hooding her face like storm clouds, she scowled back at Hal. 'You mean you tried to take advantage of me when I was casting a spell?! You, a Belbidian of noble blood!'

'As I recall it was very much the other way around,' Hal retorted with a dignified sneer. 'You tried to take advantage of me.'

'Never! In fact I wouldn't touch you with . . . with . . .' Her fists clenched in anger but suddenly the cold fury in her green eyes swept away and was replaced by a look of complete indifference. Serenely she closed her mouth and dismissively turned her head away as if she simply couldn't be bothered with him.

Caspar didn't believe it. She was clearly hurt by Hal's reaction otherwise she would never have been so angry. 'She doesn't remember,' he whispered and tugged at his uncle's arm. 'Leave her alone.'

But Brid hadn't quite finished, her angry green eyes warning of the intensity of her emotions. 'Don't ever forget who I am, Hal. I'll never be at your beck and call like some smitten damsel. You can't claim or take advantage of me like you might one of the Torra Altan girls who can't stop you because of your position.'

'Take advantage!' Hal's nails dug into his clenched fists in an effort to curb his boiling anger.

Caspar dragged anxiously at his arm. 'She doesn't mean it, Hal.'

'I do,' Brid spat back.

'She doesn't,' the younger boy insisted, trying desperately to defuse the charged atmosphere. 'She's just hurt and confused. She doesn't remember and you upset her by being coarse about seeing her naked.'

'I upset her! I like that.' Reluctantly the dark-haired youth let himself be led away to the window where he pretended to studiously examine the ravages of the night. 'She shouldn't treat me like that. Not after what nearly happened in the yew forest,' Hal snarled.

'But nothing did happen.' said Caspar without sympathy. His uncle was clearly confused and hurt by the Maiden's outburst but he didn't care. Hal didn't deserve Brid; he was too insensitive. She needed someone more like himself.

They stared mutely at the flattened vegetation, grim black mires and rippling ponds interspersed with the huge root mounds of fallen trees whose broken limbs dipped their branches in the debris-strewn water. A hoarfrost coated the reeds and the window-pane was opaque with crystals of ice.

Caspar frowned. Frost usually came on still clear nights: how could it have formed when there had been so much wind? A flight of geese, in an arrowhead formation heading south, broke the picture-like scene and a dribble of melting frost ran in broken bursts down the glass. Caspar began to feel the warmth of morning though the sun was only a pale yellow and its heat barely penetrated the grey gloom of the marshes. He was still gazing out of the window when Hal nudged him insistently in the ribs.

'We'll get some more logs in for the fire,' the older youth told him and Caspar nodded obediently before following his kinsman over to the log pile at the back of the dwelling.

Shortly after, the others returned, stamping their feet and

clapping their hands together, wide-eyed from studying the ravages of last night's storm. They all turned to look at Brid.

She had wasted no time in getting fully dressed and was now halfway through plaiting her long coppery brown hair. She had propped the parchment up at the edge of the hearth to let it dry out a little, keeping her eyes fixed, hawk-like, on the sodden wad. When she had finished her hair, she sat in the rocking-chair by the fire, gently moving to and fro, deep in thought, and massaging her temples as if she were rubbing at a nagging pain. She totally ignored the company of Belbidians who starred expectantly at her.

Aida looked uncomfortable and mashed her jaw and sucked at her lip. 'In my house! Here in my house! What's the world coming to? What are we to do?'

'Put the kettle on?' Mallart suggested pragmatically. 'If we all have some nice nettle tea, I'm sure we'll think better.'

Above the fire dangled a black iron hook from which swung an old battered kettle. Aida stepped carefully around the girl, pulling her shirts close to her so that they didn't brush against the girl's pagan body. For a moment Brid grimaced at the woman's back but then sighed and her features relaxed.

'I'm not some kind of demon, you know.' Brid sighed, rose from the rocker and picked up the parchment. She took it to a rude table by the window and very carefully teased apart the parchment where it was stuck together with mud. Caspar crowded over her shoulder and no one spoke as she gingerly worked at the fragile paper.

'Be careful; it's tearing,' Caspar warned her.

'Look, give it to me,' Hal demanded. 'I'll be much better at doing that than you.'

'I'm not giving anything to you,' she snarled. 'And as I said earlier it was your fault in the first place.' Brid cut him a razor-sharp look. 'Now, stop breathing on me. I want some space.'

Caspar edged away, but still craned his neck to see over her shoulder as gradually she peeled apart the sheets of parchment. On one side, the contours of a map showing the Caballan Sea and its surrounding countries was still clearly visible though a little washed out. Brid tenderly turned the fragile parchment over only to reveal a smudged and blotted pattern. Her charcoal writing had not survived the immersion in treacly mud as well as the cartographer's ink. At the parchment's centre Caspar could make out an oval shape with squiggly lines radiating out from it. Embracing the pattern was a circular formation of squares each with a rune at its centre. The top right-hand corner and the centre of the pattern were nothing but smudges. Brid lifted the parchment to the light and tilted the page back and forth, trying to make out the lettering that was drawn over the central oval figure.

Hal was beside himself with frustrated curiosity. 'What does it mean? Tell us, Brid. You wouldn't tell us before.'

The priestess looked perplexed. 'I'm not sure. The central circle must be the Egg but I don't know what the squiggles are.'

'They're snakes. On the bottom of the cauldron they were definitely snakes,' Caspar said eagerly.

'Snakes then,' Brid conceded. 'I don't know why. I wish I could remember. But this pattern of squares, it's oddly familiar. Did I say what they were?'

Hal shook his head. 'You didn't tell us anything. You were too afraid of the *thing* in the mist.'

'I don't believe I was afraid of anything,' she retorted calmly. 'Wary perhaps . . .'

'And the runes. Can you read the runes?' the younger boy persisted, feeling that Brid might be taunting them by holding back the information.

'Well, of course, I can read the runes.'

Caspar looked over her shoulder and studied the curious patterns.

ᚠᛖᛚᛚᛟᚹ ᚦᛖ ᚹᚪᛁᚷ ᚢᚠ ᛏᛖ ᛋᚾᛏ ᚪᛏ ᚦᛖ ᚹᚪᛁᚷ
ᚢᚠ ᚦᛖ ᛗᚢᛦᚱ ᛏᛟ ᚠᛁᛏᚻ ᚦᛖ ᚻᚢᛗᛖ ᚢᚠ ᚦᛖ ᛞᛏᚤᛟ

ᚴᚱᛁᛗᛒ   ᚠᛒᚢᚪᛗ ᚦᛖ ᛈᚱᛖᛁᚷ ᚱᚢᛚᛚᚷ, ᚱᛁᚷᛗ ᚾᛖ
ᚠᛒᚢᚪᛗ ᚦᛖ ᛋᚴᚱᚱᚢᛈ

Brid read them aloud. ' "Follow the dying of the sun at the dying of the year to find the home of the dead." And then this bit I can't read at all; it's all smudged.' She looked coldly at Hal. 'No doubt it was important otherwise I wouldn't have written it down. The last bit says, "Climb above the weeping rocks, rise up above the sorrow." '

'That's it?' Hal was aghast. 'That's all we've got to go on?'

'Well, that's not my fault, is it?' Brid defended herself. 'We can stay here and rest only until we're strong again and then we must leave. We haven't got much time.'

'It's only just Wolfmoon. We've still got six clear months to find the Egg,' Hal reasoned, 'but even that's not long, especially since you don't seem to know the first thing –'

'No, I didn't mean that,' the priestess interrupted, 'I meant until the dying of the year, which means the winter solstice and that's at the end of Wolfmoon. We have less than the span of one moon, to find this place.'

'Which place?'

She drew her finger round the squares rimming the outside of the circular pattern. 'I reckon these squares must represent a standing circle – a stone henge. We've got to find it before the winter solstice.'

'Where is it and how can you be so sure?' Hal frowned sceptically.

'Because I'm sure.' She carefully turned the parchment over to reveal the ancient map, which Caspar had secreted from the library in Farona. 'Now even if this map is old – and we know the world is far bigger than this says – it's still not as old as the cauldron. So the known world of this map must include the known world at the time of the cauldron. The circle must be here.'

'But it's vast and there are lots of circles. Look!' Hal exclaimed in exasperation, poking the parchment in half a dozen places. 'Here, here, here, here, lots of them. How do we know which is the right one?'

'Well, one of them will look right,' Brid vaguely explained as she counted the square shapes on her smudged diagram.

'Twenty-one stones. That's a big henge.' She turned the parchment over again. 'There are certainly none in Belbidia with twenty-one stones so we can discount all of this area. Vaalaka and Camaalia have two each. Glain has one, the Farthest Isles of Ophidia have one and of course there's one on Gorta. I don't know anything about any of them,' Brid sighed. 'But the Druid, he put such structure into his enigmatic messages; there must be a significant reason for choosing precisely this particular henge.' She pouted, drumming her fingers as she stared intensely at the map.

'Spar, it's the sort of thing you should know,' Hal said mockingly to his nephew. 'You usually know some silly nursery rhyme about how many miles to market. Couldn't you for once know something useful like how many stones there are in each circle?'

Caspar looked stiffly at his uncle but couldn't think of a suitable retort, deciding instead to keep as much dignity as possible by ignoring the gibe.

'I know,' the deep voice of Morgrimm suddenly cut into their conversation.

Brid jerked round and glared suspiciously at the cloaked man who had to stoop to avoid grazing his head on the beams of the ceiling. 'Ah, yes, the tutor,' she managed to say in such a way that she conveyed both suspicion and derision all at once. 'The tutor who told our Ceowulf so much about the Egg. You are not of the old ways; how can you understand the things of the Primal Gods?'

'You misunderstand me, young lady. I don't claim to understand your world of magic and spirits, but I know much of your lore. My great-grandfather, you see, came from Gorta and was a druid.' The man unfurled his long fingers to reveal a fistful of knuckle bones. Each was engraved with a rune. 'He gave me these on his death-bed and in his dotage he whispered many secrets, which I, with hungry ears, listened to and remembered.'

'Can you read the runes, then?' Brid challenged abruptly, as if she found his knowledge threatening in some way.

'No, I don't understand them. Their knowledge is hidden from me. But I know of the Egg because it's a druid's tale. I know it is a terrible thing of awesome sorcery and he who possesses it controls ancient powers.'

'Maybe,' Brid said frostily, obviously wary of this gaunt old man. 'But we do not seek the power. We seek only to return the Egg to the bosom of the Goddess. She is the one, the only one with the total love and understanding to wield such power. The power is too formidable for mortals. You should not preach of things you do not understand.'

The old man pulled at his plaited beard. 'You are very young and very small to speak to me, a man of many years and much learning, in such a way. How can you, a mere child, know anything of these matters? But then I suppose it is in the nature of female minds to think they understand everything when they merely grasp the fringes of a subject.' He pulled off his hat, revealing his bald pate, and studied the pheasant feather that decorated it. 'I think you are an ungrateful little girl. I, after all, know how many stones are in each ring.'

'I might be small and young but my knowledge has been faithfully handed down from generation to generation. I have the accumulated understanding of a thousand priestesses before me.' Brid's wide eyes sparkled with anger as she stared defiantly up at the tall man.

'Knowledge does not always imply understanding. Understanding comes with the years and perhaps when you are older you will have better judgement and treat those more worthy than yourself with greater respect.'

'You are wrong,' Brid retorted smugly. 'Judgement comes with experience not age.' Her sweet smile threw Morgrimm totally off balance. 'I bow to your greater experience of henges. Humbly I beg you, tell me about them.'

'Right, well, yes, the standing stones.' said Morgrimm, a little bemused by Brid's sudden change. 'They are ancient temples of worship designed for sacrifices as well as to mark the tombs of kings.'

'Well, that's not true,' Brid started to interrupt but Hal elbowed her in the ribs and she clamped her mouth tight. The old man, like the best of teachers, hardly noticed the momentary distraction and continued with his lecture.

'There are thirteen henges of the known world. Twelve for the twelve moons in the year, plus one. Five of them have twenty-one standing stones: the circle on Gorta, the one on Ophidia's Farthest Isles, the two in Camaalia, and the one in Glain near the Smokies. The henges are laid out across the surface of the earth in the shape of a rune. Though I don't know what it means I know its shape.' He sorted through the chips of bone held in his palm and placed one on the rough surface of the table.

'ᛒ: Beorc, the rune of birth or rebirth,' Brid agreed. 'That makes sense.'

Caspar didn't understand but didn't dare distract her as she traced the pattern of the rune over the map. The henges did indeed all fall along the lines of the rune, except one. 'The one henge that falls beyond the pattern of the universe, the one henge that reaches beyond life's circle of death and rebirth. It has to be that one.' Brid drummed the largest island in the centre of an archipelago lying off the western coast of Ophidia and beyond the narrow straits that led out of the Caballan Sea. The straits were clearly labelled as 'the Teeth'.

'The Farthest Isles,' Caspar read the name of the islands aloud.

Brid stood up but then clutched at the table as she suddenly swayed on her feet. She slumped back down onto the stool cradling her head.

'I think you're still under an ague from the infection in your wounds,' the old tutor suggested. 'You need to lie down and rest.'

'I'll have time to rest while you procure a ship for us. A ship big enough to take us through the winter storms of the Caballan,' Brid added.

Caspar smiled; Brid was her usual commanding self again. Now that she was awake and in charge, he was sure that the evil around them, the hungry presence that sought him, would be repelled.

'A ship for all of you?' Morgrimm asked. He looked doubtfully at the assembled company. 'As you are, you'll have difficulty getting through the marsh without being stopped and questioned, let alone a port.'

'You'll get us through, though, won't you?' Brid smiled confidently, looking up at him with big pleading eyes.

'With Ceowulf's wounds, Lady Cybillia's scars and the look of you and the young boy? Everyone knows there's witch trouble in Caldea. The whole barony's on the alert for strangers.'

'So?' Brid retorted calmly. 'That just means it'll cost a lot more. You'll buy the favour of some old sea-dog and get him to moor up at a quiet bay where we won't attract attention. Someone willing to take the money is bound to know of a good harbour for smuggling.'

Morgrimm looked at Ceowulf. 'Do you always let this girl tell you what to do?'

Ceowulf shrugged and grinned fondly at Brid.

'I've never heard of such nonsense,' the old tutor said incredulously. 'Is this really what you want me to do, sir?'

The knight nodded. 'The lady's right. It will cost more. Only a disreputable man will take you on board and disreputable men charge high prices.'

'Hal will give you the money,' Brid decided flatly.

The youth pouted at her. 'It's not a bottomless pit, you know. Branwolf didn't give me Torra Alta's entire treasury.'

Morgrimm took Ceowulf's sleek black destrier and rode out into the crisp morning, heading for the Hook of Caldea, the nearest sizeable port. His pouch jangled with the gold Hal had reluctantly handed to him.

'Can we trust that man?' he asked Ceowulf. 'He's got half my money.'

'Our money,' Caspar corrected him. 'Torra Alta's money.'

'Torra Alta's money, then,' Hal grumbled. 'Excuse me, I

suppose that means *your* money, nephew.' He turned back to the Caldean knight. 'Ceowulf, can we trust Morgrimm with *Lord Caspar's* money.'

The young boy wished he hadn't said anything.

'Of course we can trust him.'

'He could of course go straight to Baron Cadros,' Cybillia said and everyone looked round, surprised to hear her voice. In Jotunn the young ladies were normally excluded from any conversation that went beyond the colour of their gowns. She blushed, as they all turned towards her, and said defensively, 'It was only an opinion.'

'He won't. He did after all get Sorcerer and the armour for me. How he explained away the loss of one of my father's great destriers from the baronial mews, I can't imagine, but he's a wily old thing beneath that grumpy exterior.'

Brid laughed. 'Well, if he managed that, he'll manage to find us a ship. Now we've got work to do. Cybillia, I need some herbs. You'll have to go out and search for them, because I need to rest.'

'She can't go alone,' Caspar protested.

'I didn't say she would. You can go with her.'

'You deserved that,' Hal grinned at his nephew but Caspar wasn't listening, instead he was struck by the look of hope that suddenly flooded into Cybillia's eyes. She had worn a permanent sadness on her mutilated face and Caspar hoped they would find the herbs that might cure her injuries. No one could bare such sadness and humiliation forever.

'We don't know anything about herbs so how do we know that we'll get the right ones?' Cybillia asked, though she was already standing eagerly by the door, wrapping a thick cloak about her shoulders.

Brid smiled as if trying not to laugh at a child's simplistic view of the world. 'Just search in lots of different places and find as many different plants as you can. That'll be good enough. I'll sort them out later.'

Caspar reluctantly left Brid carefully studying the parchment while Ceowulf and Hal stood by the fire, listening to Mallart telling tales of poachers. He picked up his bow and trotted after the tall daughter of Baron Bullback of Jotunn.

After a long hour in the marshes, where they kept diligently to the well-trodden paths, Caspar had accumulated a good bundle of herbs. He thought one of them might be woad of which he was very proud since he knew it would please Brid, fond as she was of daubing woad patterns on her body. A spinney of weeping willows, their long whip-like tendrils drooping into the dark marsh, swayed with the wind and he thought of the pain-killing bark that the priestess prized so much. With his knife he sliced off the smooth grey-brown bark and added it to his bundle.

They decided that between them they had enough to satisfy Brid and trudged homeward. Cybillia had barely said a word over the last hour and now she pulled at her hacked hair and stared ruefully into the still waters of a pool, mournfully studying her rippling reflection.

'I'm sorry, Cybillia,' said Caspar, trying to comfort her. 'Your hair will grow again, Brid will heal your face and then you'll look as beautiful as the dawn again.'

She smiled back at him. 'You've got a soft heart, Spar. You don't look at me any differently. You're the only one who sees me as the same person. Ceowulf looks at me with pained sympathy, Brid looks at me now as if she owns me and Hal . . . well, he won't look at me at all.'

Caspar smiled back, not knowing what to say. 'Come on, the others will be worried about us.' A flight of ducks skimmed the water and skidded to a halt forty yards away near the far bank. Quickly he raised his bow and chose two short-quilled arrows to compensate for the long flight. He released one and then a second an instant later. A startled beat of panicked birds scattered into the sky, leaving two fowls dead in the water.

They ran round the perimeter of the shallow waters and Caspar found a broken branch long enough to reach the ducks and scoop them towards him. He flopped the first out of the water at Cybillia's feet.

'Well, pick it up then,' he said as she stepped back and looked at it distastefully.

'But it's dead. I can't touch a dead thing,' she complained.

'Why ever not? It's only a duck. It means we won't have to eat rabbit again. I never want to eat another rabbit as long as I live.'

'I just can't,' she said squeamishly, taking another step back.

Caspar couldn't fully understand the girl's reluctance and returned to the task of retrieving the other bird. Just as he managed to hook it with the tip of the twig, he saw a large dark shape sliding through the water. Hurriedly he flicked the duck onto the bank.

'What's the matter?' the yellow-haired girl asked, her wide eyes mirroring the boy's startled expression.

'I thought I saw that thing again in the water – the thing that got Brid –' Then, realizing that he was frightening the girl, he added, 'but I'm sure it was only a pike. Come on, let's get back.' He worked the arrows out of the ducks and returned them to his quiver before hurrying after Cybillia.

Hal greeted the sight of the two ducks with as much pleasure as Brid welcomed the herbs, though she dismissed more than half of them merely as different types of grass. 'They'll do more good to the horses than anything else,' she told them but nevertheless seemed pleased with their efforts.

'Is there anything that can heal my face?' Cybillia asked anxiously.

Brid shook her head. 'No, dragonfire is rare; we won't find it in such wet conditions. On the way to the Hook perhaps . . .'

Cybillia kept the shawl wrapped round her face, which made her look as if she had toothache.

They waited two days for Morgrimm to return, by which time Ceowulf was a great deal stronger, though he still kept his right arm in a sling, and Brid was back to her usual, sprightly self. Armed with her herbs, she was able to suppress the fever and so allow her body to heal faster.

Hal and Caspar were becoming increasingly impatient.

Caspar busied himself practising with his new bow, using the knots of trees as targets while at first Hal was intent only on his hand as he mourned the loss of his finger. Thanks to Brid's herb lore, the knuckle joint had healed cleanly but all the same he scowled at his damaged hand. Then, as time passed, his concentrations turned to the sword. The small nick halfway down its edge was barely visible but he fussed over the damage.

'Do you think it's done any harm?' he asked Ceowulf. 'Has it diminished its power?'

The solidly built knight reached an arm out to examine the sword and, momentarily, Hal's grasp tightened on the weapon. Then he relaxed and, graciously turning the weighty blade, he offered the ornate hilt to the Caldean knight.

The lines on Ceowulf's weather-worn face instantly tightened as he felt the power in the sword. He scrutinized the great white-steel runesword with its elaborate quillons and the hilt crafted in the image of two dragons with their claws locked in mortal combat. Where their claws interlocked, there was a circular gap, which had once held a ruby.

While Hal and Ceowulf inspected the blade, Caspar fell to thinking on the ruby. When they had tried to free Keridwen from the glacier, he remembered how the ruby had developed a strange pattern within its structure. A pattern representing the rune of the Mother. He recollected how his father had removed the ruby from the sword and set it in the centre of Torra Alta's heartstone to show the Great Mother that the castle was once more dedicated to her worship.

The circular sigil had filled him with a sense of joy and well-being.

Ceowulf's eyes ran down the length of the burnished metal, following the pattern of blood-red runes engraved into the central fuller. The shadow of greed, resentment and jealousy flickered over his face.

'There's so much hatred in it,' he shuddered. 'It's full of the horrors of death.'

'I know,' Hal said flatly. 'But it also makes you feel like a king.' He eagerly held out his hand to retrieve the sword and laid it across his lap, possessively stroking the flat of the blade. 'But the nick in its side – will it weaken the blade?'

'I don't know much about the artistry of the swordsmith, but I'd say a weapon like that would take a year to forge. And it would cost the best part of a herd of Jotunn's finest oxen, possibly the price of the golden gates of Farona itself. The sword isn't a laminate but a single pattern forged from one single sheet. No, I don't think the nick will weaken it.'

Brid was frowning. 'Here, let me look. How did that happen?'

Hal explained about the cauldron.

'A piece of white steel from the sword chipped off?' she echoed in disbelief. 'I must have been beside myself. I can't believe I let so many terrible things happen. And what about these runes? They mention the creatures of power and the spell for awakening them.' Her mouth dropped as she studied them in horror. 'These are the runes of sorcery! What have you done? How did they get there? Now the ancient creatures of the Earth will be struggling out of the shadows to follow us in the hope that we will lead them to the Egg.'

'You stirred the cauldron with the sword,' Hal said stiffly. 'You did it yourself. It had nothing to do with me.'

'But – but,' Brid was momentarily speechless before blinking away her dismay. 'Describe it to me. Describe everything on the cauldron.'

Caspar told her how she interpreted the design inscribed around the girth of the vast metal pot, how it told of the elements of the earth and the beasts of power trapped and crushed in exile. 'It showed fire-breathing dragons and vast wolves with fangs like daggers,' he expounded.

'The magic in the sword reached into the design and touched the beasts,' she deliberated. 'How could I?' She retreated back to her task of studying the ragged parchment as if she wanted to shut out all other thoughts until Morgrimm returned.

Caspar watched her as she studied the map. 'When Morgrimm said that the henges were arranged in the pattern of the rune of rebirth why did you say that made sense?' he asked curiously.

'What?' Brid asked distractedly. 'Oh that. Henges are stone or wooden circles where the Old Tribes took the bodies of their dead. The bodies were left out in the open to be picked clean by carrion and only when the skeletons were completely dry were the dead taken to the burial mounds or barrows. It is during the time in the henges that the soul is thought to be reborn. First it has to pass through the Otherworld, the parallel universe of shadow, then on to the bliss of Annwyn where all souls merge with the power of the Primal Gods. And from there they are reborn to this world. It is all part of the cycle.'

Caspar mulled over the details of the pattern. He thought it extraordinary that the ancient people had managed to recreate the rune with such accuracy across so many thousands of miles. 'It's an incredible achievement,' he observed.

'The Goddess has her design in all things,' Brid replied and turned the map over to study her blurred notes.

At last the tall, bearded tutor returned and, after a last brief meal with Mallart and Aida of pan-fried snipe and watercress broth, they were eager to move.

'I'll feel much safer out of Belbidia. None of the other countries of the Caballan Sea are so fanatical in their witch hunts. In fact some like Camaalia don't believe in witchcraft at all,' Ceowulf explained, sharing his knowledge garnered over many years roving abroad with different companions. After saying gracious farewells to the couple from the marshes, he followed the others towards the barn where the horses were stabled.

Caspar noted how he adjusted his sling, rotated his shoulder in his socket and grunted in satisfaction. Evidently it was beginning to pain the ex-mercenary a great deal less. The auburn-haired youth turned back to preparing their mounts. They only had four horses between them. All six Belbidians looked competitively at the three fine horses and turned their backs on Herren's cart-horse.

Caspar patted the animal affectionately, 'Poor old cart-horse, we never even learnt your name, . . . now let's see, if I take Brid with me and Hal takes Cybillia –'

'That leaves Morgrimm to ride the cart-horse,' Hal cut him short.

'I'm not so stuffed with pride that I'll feel the slightest shame,' the tutor replied, eyeing Firecracker cautiously. 'Besides I'd rather take this old thing any day than that demon.'

The red stallion raked at the ground and danced round on the end of his reins as if to prove his reputation was not unfounded.

When they were fully tacked up and the packs loaded, Caspar was suddenly aggrieved to see that Hal had already lifted Brid up behind him, leaving Cybillia hanging her head disappointedly. Caspar was determined that the noble girl shouldn't feel rejected, and rode forward to take her, but Ceowulf was already there.

'Fair maiden,' the knight said, looking straight into her dusty blue eyes and ignoring her wretched scars, 'may I have the honour of your company?'

She smiled gratefully but there was no joy in her eyes. She gave Hal a guarded look. Caspar recognized and understood all too well the jealous emotion behind it.

As they wound their way out of the marshes Caspar was glad of the morning sun warming through his clothing, though the air was becoming sharp with the chill of late autumn. He gave vent to his frustrations by encouraging his hot-blooded colt to leap over the trunk of every fallen tree he could find along the way. They had delayed too long and time was slipping through their fingers.

As the twisting marsh paths gradually gained more definition and the ground became firmer, the countryside opened up into rocky moorland and then rough grazing just as the first village came into sight. Morgrimm thumped his heels into the side of the cart-horse to get the animal to lumber reluctantly forward alongside Ceowulf.

'We'll cut round Nettleymarsh and head straight towards

Campionlea. It's a secluded run-down port and I'm sure we won't pass too many people.'

At last the smooth silvery waters of the Caballan Sea stretched out across the horizon and the dank smell of stagnant marsh water, which seemed to have been following them all day, was finally swept away by a refreshing briny breeze. Caspar yearned to get clear of Caldea's turgid atmosphere, stifled with superstitious fears of witchcraft and paganism. Over to their left a curving spit of land known as the Hook of Caldea arced out into the rippling sea. He could just make out the port, its crammed buildings jostling for position along the harbour wall. Schooners with deep draughts and broad beams for carrying valuable cargoes across the calm waters of the inland sea swung at anchor.

Morgrimm urged his horse off the road and turned away from the Hook towards a cove some three miles to the south. Even from here Caspar could make out the single mast and poorly furled red sail of a ship moored at the end of a narrow jetty, gently rocking on the swell.

'There she is,' Morgrimm announced. 'The *Queen of Tutivillus*. A small vessel, I'm afraid, built for the sheltered waters of the Caballan, but she's headed for Langost on the Crest of Ophidia,'

'Near Cocklebay,' Ceowulf interrupted, his eyes momentarily brightening.

Morgrimm nodded. 'Yes, which takes you in the right direction, and the ship's master took your gold without so much as a raised eyebrow. He told me she's a traditional Belbidian schooner from the Barony of Piscera so I dare say she's seaworthy.' He paused and then hastily added, 'She'll get you out of Belbidia and south-west towards Ophidia anyway.'

Caspar was none too comforted by the last remark.

The path dropped steeply down towards the waters and Caspar watched as Cybillia shut her eyes and clutched tightly onto Ceowulf's back as Sorcerer slipped and slithered on the loose flint. Even the knight looked perturbed by the descent, but the three Torra Altans never blinked an eyelid as they approached the edge of the cliff and headed their horses down the steep incline. Leaning back in their saddles, they allowed the animals to ease the weight off their forelegs. Ceowulf looked decidedly relieved as his horse reached the sandy half-moon of the beach and Cybillia tentatively opened her eyes and looked up at the cliff. 'Did we really ride down that?' she asked incredulously.

Caspar laughed. 'You've never been to Torra Alta, have you? Now that really is steep.'

'No,' she agreed. 'I haven't and I don't suppose I ever will now.' There was a heavy resignation in her voice as she put her hand to her lumpy cheek.

'Don't worry. We'll find some dragonfire,' Brid murmured encouragingly without releasing her possessive grip on Hal's waist.

Cybillia's dusty-blue eyes widened and she cast the Maiden a look full of hope and for the first time Caspar realized that the young Jotunn noblewoman no longer feared Brid or what she represented. 'Can you really heal my scars?' she asked softly and, as the pagan priestess nodded warmly, the willowy girl returned the smile.

Morgrimm signalled to the vessel that was moored up alongside an old rotting jetty. Campionlea had once been a busy herring port but the fish had moved on and the town had dwindled. Now only a few bewhiskered lobstermen scraped a living from the shallow banks off the coast. The quay was quiet and dilapidated as they approached but the two girls pulled their cloaks up round their ears and lowered their heads to avoid catching anyone's eye. Caspar studied the *Queen of Tutivillus* doubtfully. Buckets and ropes, anchor chain and unstowed cargo barrels littered the deck. Three unsavoury-looking characters sauntered bad-temperedly along the boards. They were dressed in wide baggy trousers of an indeterminate grimy colour and their torsos were covered by garish short-sleeved shirts. The eldest man was further distinguished by the size of his belly. This man, evidently the ship's master by the way the others deferred to him, spat out the weed he was chewing and, brushing his hands down his trousers, swaggered across the gangplank to meet them.

Without muttering a word, he scanned the party, sized them up and spat again. He wiped the back of his hand across his stubbly mouth before offering to shake hands with Morgrimm.

'So you brought them then.'

The tutor nodded. Caspar took a strong dislike to this sailor. He stank of drink and had a surly down-turned mouth dragging at his coarse, weathered cheeks. He looked like he hadn't smiled in years.

'Well, let's get you on board then. I want to get underway before the tide turns.'

Caspar dismounted and began to lead his horse forward when the ship's master turned on him

'I didn't say nought about horses.'

'Well, we can't leave them behind,' Hal objected. 'They're valuable animals and we need them.'

'If they're that valuable you won't mind paying a fair price then,' the master argued and Hal looked reluctantly at his depleted purse. 'I'll have thirty pieces of gold, and gold with good King Rewik's head on it if you don't mind, for them four horses.'

'That's daylight robbery,' Hal grunted. 'Twenty would be fairer.'

'I don't have so much space on my ship and live cargo's troublesome. We'll have to pen them on the well-deck and fix up a corral. It's all mighty troublesome.'

'Twenty,' Hal argued without the slightest sympathy.

'Twenty then, though it's you that's robbing me.'

Hal diligently counted out the coins and stopped at fifteen, carefully replacing his purse inside his leather jerkin.

'You can't count, sir.' The sailor held out his callused hand for the remaining coins.

'Twenty for four horses but we're only taking three. The passage costs more than that cart-horse is worth, so fifteen seems fair to me.'

Caspar let his mouth turn up at one corner, admiring his uncle's bargaining skills.

Ceowulf bade farewell to his old tutor, instructing him to have the cart-horse returned to the innkeeper at the Causeway Inn in Northdown, and Morgrimm nodded dutifully. The rest of the Belbidians politely bade him farewell and turned to inspect their ship.

Chapter 5

May gaped at the heartstone. The ruby was gone.

A cold hand seemed to clutch at her heart as if the cruel
frost had finally found a purchase in the castle. For several
moments she just stared at the circular slab of rock, grieving
at the scarred marks where the ruby had been prised from its
central gold setting. The bright metal was torn open like the
mouth of a miniature volcano.

'Mother,' she whispered. 'Oh Mother, Great Mother, your
ruby . . .'

Every day since she had arrived at the castle, she had passed
the heartstone and sensed the warm comfort emanating from
its central ruby. At first she had thought it was the gem itself
that filled her with such comfort but, when she studied it more
closely, she soon realized that the warmth came from the
sigil engraved within its structure. The rune of the Mother,
Morrigwen had called it. Just looking at the silvery circular
pattern divided into three segments had given her a sense of
safety and solace. And now it was gone.

Stupefied, she stared at the empty gold setting at the hub
of the heartstone, too upset by the loss of the ruby to notice
that anything else had changed, but then she saw it. Yesterday
the runes of war around the edge of the heartstone had been
angry, angular marks scythed into the stone itself. They had
been plainly visible though a little more worn than they had
been during Hunting when Morrigwen and Brid had first cast
them. But now they were scoured and scratched where someone had taken a rock or a masonry axe and chipped at the
letters, defiling their image and blurring their shape.

May stood pointing speechlessly at the heartstone. She didn't notice the creeping cold of the snow as it seeped through the worn stitching of her boots or the blast of ice-cold air that smacked her face, giving her high-boned cheeks a ruddy glow. Her lips were blue with cold and her fingers numb. She had been standing too long in the cold harsh winter of the northern mountains but still she stared and pointed at the heartstone.

'Someone help,' at last she managed to cry.

A huddle of soldiers gathered around her. Stammering and shivering, she pointed at the runes, acutely aware that the vandalism foreboded terrible suffering for the besieged castle. She couldn't begin to imagine who could commit such a heinous crime; she only knew that their protection had gone. The runes of war were defiled. Now they had lost their protection against the vast hordes of starving Vaalakans that swarmed at the foot of the Tor.

Strong hands put a cloak around her shoulders. She sensed the deep angry breathing and looked up at the Baron's stubbly face. The heavy bearskin cloak, clasped around his shoulders, covered his thick hauberk and hung down to the top of his black leather boots.

'To your posts, men,' he ordered without looking up from Torra Alta's heartstone. 'Keep a keen eye about you. The fog is rising out of the valley.'

His words were steady and calm and May could only guess at the turmoil that boiled within his head. The troops looked at him uncertainly until eventually he raised his head and stared at them levelly. He turned to the two nearest soldiers, his expression calm and authoritative, any hint of emotion concealed by the steady command of his voice.

'Down to the well-room, both of you, and double the quantities of brimstone being extracted from the water. Tell the Wellmaster to make as much as he can. We may need it before the day is out.'

The men scattered purposefully to their posts.

Not daring to speak, May found her hand still clasped in the man's giant, bear-like grip. Almost as if he didn't know she was there, he marched determinedly across the inner court-yard, pulling her along in his wake. Tripping through the snow, she tottered after him.

'Captain,' he bellowed across the courtyard to the tall gaunt soldier who walked the north wall, continually encouraging the men.

The Captain looked tired, she thought, so very tired – but then so did they all. He strode over to them, his black eyebrows meeting over the bridge of his hooked nose. A sinister-looking man at the best of times, May had always been afraid of him though clearly he was greatly respected by the men.

'Sir?' The Captain saluted and Branwolf impatiently waved the formalities aside.

'Meet me in the upper keep,' the Baron growled. 'And get the old woman.'

'Morrigwen?'

'Yes, Morrigwen.' The Baron sounded angry at being questioned. 'There's no one else I can trust now.'

The Captain looked taken aback but marched determinedly towards the kitchens were the old Crone was usually to be found, mixing her potions.

May hoped that at any moment her overlord would release his crushing grip on her hand but he seemed intent on holding her. She could see her fingers turning white at the ends. Running to keep up with his long strides, she raced at his side. As they reached the stone staircase that spiralled towards the great hall she tripped. Without pause he scooped her light body up in his arms and carried her up. Once in the old hall, the Baron released her and without a word strode towards the small fire that flickered in the grate at the far end of the hall. Four deer-hounds leapt to their feet and snaked around him, nudging his hands in greeting before lying contentedly at his feet.

The Baron didn't dismiss her so May stood nervously by his chair, fidgeting with her hands. Fearful of disturbing him, she tried to keep her breathing as silent as possible and gritted her teeth against the pain as the blood swelled back into her hands. It seemed like an eternity before the Captain returned, slowly helping the old Crone up the long winding staircase. She was bent double and her crooked fingers were hooked through the Captain's for support.

'Let me carry you,' the Captain implored several times.

'The day I can no longer walk is the day I'll die,' the old woman croaked angrily at him.

She reminded May of a white wolf that she had once seen in the forest near her home. The little girl had been with her father. Oh, how she missed her pa. The sweetness of the memory brought a stab of grief to her heart. They had crept to the edge of the forest and had seen the wolf in the distance.

'The old matriarch,' Wystan had told her with awe as they spied her warming herself on a distant rock. The white wolf was so very thin, her eyes sunken into her skull with age, and yet May was sure they gleamed with wisdom. Morrigwen was like that too. Her body, decayed and withered with age, was now crippled by the effects of the poison that had nearly killed her. Yet still her eyes held the same look of knowledge and wisdom that earned her respect and authority. She might be bitterly caustic and crotchety but she understood so many things.

May loved her. Though she had not known her before arriving at Torra Alta, the days of nursing the old woman through her illness had created a bond between them. To May, Morrigwen seemed to have come from a forgotten age of peace and fulfilment. She was a fountain of fantastical tales and the young girl rejoiced at the joy of life that never ceased to bubble beneath the Crone's weathered skin.

Breathing heavily, Morrigwen looked into the room, both hands clasping the Captain. 'I will sit,' she said as if giving a command, her words bearing not the slightest deference to the Baron's rank. Her painfully thin arms seemed to barely support her body as she leant forward onto the table. 'Speak,' she demanded of the Baron.

'Morrigwen,' he began, drawing up a carved straight-backed chair and nodding to the Captain to sit. May found herself ushered forward by the soldier and, at his bidding, she climbed onto one of the chairs. She could barely see over the table's high surface. 'Morrigwen,' the Baron started again but again stopped short. He nodded at May. 'Tell her.'

With the Baron glowering down at her, the small chestnut-haired girl found her words stuck in her throat but, as she turned her eyes towards the high priestess, she felt her fear subside. In her mind she was talking only to Morrigwen. She had spent many hours in the old Crone's company, and was no longer afraid of the woman's harsh temper.

'The heartstone,' she whispered. 'I was going to the kitchens to help Ma and I passed the heartstone and –'

'The ruby is gone,' the old Crone interrupted, sudden realization darkening her eyes. 'The ruby is gone and the runes of war?'

'All chipped and scarred,' May told her. 'How did you know?'

'This morning I felt a desolation blowing in the wind,' the old woman sighed. 'It was like the day Keridwen vanished. Today, I felt again the candle of hope and joy snuff out but I had hoped it was just the whims of old age deceiving me.' She looked down at her gnarled and twisted fingers. 'Today I felt naked as if someone had stripped away the mantle of our shield.'

'Who would do this?' Branwolf asked her in a broken voice as if the words were painful to say.

Morrigwen raised a wispy eyebrow. Her long silvery hair was thin where the effects of the poisonous Vaalakan fang-nettle had weakened the roots and the light from the fire played on her scalp.

'You can answer that question as well as I. Someone who wishes Torra Alta harm.'

'My thoughts at first,' the Baron agreed, 'but now I'm not so sure. It could be someone whose heart is still true to the New Faith and thinks that Torra Alta should face the Vaalakans without the aid of the Old Faith.'

May found her eyes rising to the Captain's face. She knew

that he was still loyal to the new God from the south, the God she herself had been raised to worship, but since she had met Brid and Morrigwen and witnessed her mother's joy at the rekindling of the Old Faith, she knew that her heart belonged to the Great Mother. She understood about the trees, the water, the herbs, the animals and the balance all around her. As a woodcutter's daughter she had grown up understanding the changing nature of the seasons and how they rolled round one to the next. She had understood the concerns when they said that too many trees were being felled and the forest would not be able to replenish itself. All these things, along with the simple joy of feeling the breeze in her hair or letting the trickle of cool water tickle her toes as she dipped them into the Sylvanrush river, all these things she understood.

The new God, however, talked of sin and the threat of Hell, of the base nature of women and their evil designs upon men. This last part she didn't understand at all. When she had asked the curate about such things, he had blushed purple, muttering that she was still far too young to learn and all she should concern herself with was chastity.

She did not even know what chastity meant. She presumed it was something to do with staying at home and learning needlepoint because that, the curate had preached, was the only seemly occupation for a woman.

And the Captain . . . he was still one of the few remaining in the castle who still worshipped the New Faith. Every week the numbers attending the chapel had dwindled. More and more of the men now joined Morrigwen at the rise and the setting of the sun as she thanked the Primal Gods for each new day – and for every day they had been safely kept from the Vaalakans' barbarous axes.

The Captain nodded. 'Since the chaplain's sad departure . . .' he began, euphemistically alluding to the fire that had burnt the west tower – all they had found of Father Gwion's remains were his ring and a boot. 'Since that time a few of the more fanatical young men feel that their worship of the New Faith is threatened. They feel their religion is being slowly stripped from them. I have tried to reassure them that you, my lord, believe that all may worship as they choose but, without a priest, there are still a few who are deeply concerned for their souls. They fear the Devil.'

Morrigwen's voice cracked, 'I don't worship the Devil.'

'Forgive me, Morrigwen. I meant no personal offence but in the teachings of the New Faith any worship of a god who is not the one true God is the worship of the Devil. I myself am a soldier and I live and fight solely to serve my liege-lord and, in truth, am little worried by your superstitious ways. But still there are one or two who fear for their souls.'

'Enough to bring harm to Torra Alta?' The Baron sounded sceptical. 'Surely they fear the Vaalakans and their devilish God, Vaal-Peor, more.'

'I know of no man here that would bring harm to Torra Alta; I would swear to it. Yet someone has done this thing,' the Captain replied practically.

There was a quiet knock at the door though their senses were so tightly strung that they all started and turned as one to stare at the arched and studded panel.

'Enter,' Branwolf thundered.

A young archer, his hair crusted with snow and sticking up on end from where the wind had swept it back off his face, stamped into the room. 'My lord, Captain, I am sent by my sergeant.'

'Yes?'

'We found a grappling hook on the east side, my lord.'

'The east side?'

May didn't fully understand the reason for the incredulity in the Captain's voice.

'Aye, sir, where the Tor overhangs the river.'

'You mean to say, that a Vaalakan has somehow thrown a grappling hook up a hundred feet of sheer cliff face onto the east wall?'

'My sergeant thinks not.'

At this Branwolf rose impatiently, knocking his chair over with a crash to the floor. 'And why not?'

'It's not a Vaalakan rope, sir; it's one of our own. It matches the others from the stores, sir.'

Branwolf looked at the Captain, their eyes reading each other's minds.

May still did not understand the significance of it all. She scurried round the table and clutched hold of Morrigwen's skirts. The old woman patted her head and ran her fingers through the girl's long chestnut curls. Through the cold of winter devoid of the bright summer sun, her hair was beginning to darken and enrich into deep russets and browns.

'It means, my little Merrymoon, that it was not a Vaalakan who climbed into the castle but a Torra Altan who has fled from it.'

'But why would they do that?'

Morrigwen shrugged. 'Until today the runes of war protected our walls. Whoever has destroyed the runes and taken the ruby knows that now we only have these bare walls and a thousand archers to protect us from the mass of Morbak's army. There are a hundred and twenty thousand Vaalakans out there. Now we have only our lives with which to defend the castle. And we must defend it. We must hold until Brid returns.' The old woman looked southwards through a thin arrow-slit, her eyes narrowing as she stared into the far distance. 'Hurry, Brid, hurry.'

The archer had gone and Branwolf paced up and down by the fire. The hounds sat alert, their ears pricked, watching him intently.

'Whoever has done this terrible thing has already left. I will not waste time or men on searching out a culprit who is no longer in our midst – though I *will* know who has done this to us. We must do the best we can. We've reached Wolfmoon now and Spar and Hal may yet return long before the full allotted nine months have passed. We may yet stand fast on our own merits for a while. How difficult can it be to find this talisman?' His voice dipped and for a while all was silent. He stared into the fire without moving. At last he turned to the Captain, his olive-green eyes intent with thought. 'How much more food do we have?'

'Not enough,' the Captain said simply. 'On full rations enough for five months perhaps.'

'We have to cut the rations then,' Branwolf concluded grimly.

At the very mention of the word *food*, May felt her gnawing hunger deepen.

The Baron moved his hands across the table as if turning a page over in his mind. 'With the runes of war defiled, their power will be diminished. We must gird ourselves for the oncoming assaults. I will know who has fled my castle and vandalized the runes.' He turned his eyes on May and all thoughts were scattered from her head. 'May, you will help me. I can spare no men for this task.'

The young girl nodded dutifully.

'You will account for every man, woman and child in the castle. To set my mind at peace, I will know who is missing by the end of the day. The Captain will tell you how to do it.' He turned to the gaunt, beaky-nosed soldier. 'We can do nothing but man our posts. The Vaalakans have left us standing idly for three days. I'm certain they will attack during this fog.'

With the parchment clutched tightly in her clenched fist, May went first to the well-room where she knew her brother would be scraping out the sulphur barrels. One look at his powdered yellow face told her that Pip was jealous. He scowled at his elder sister as she came nervously down into the well-room. She sought out the young Wellmaster, who had replaced poor Catrik, and offered him the parchment already inscribed with several names.

'The Captain wrote down the name of each sergeant and those in charge of the well-room, the stores, the kitchen and the stables,' she explained. 'I'm to ask each one to account for all the men, women and children in their charge.'

'But why you, May? Why did he choose you and not me?' Pip demanded as the Wellmaster examined the parchment.

'Because I was there. Because he didn't want to waste any

more men on the task when the fighting might be fierce today. Besides you're needed here in the well-room. At least it's warm down here.'

'Sweltering, you mean.' Pip's voice echoed from within a vast vat that he was scraping for sulphur. His once brown hair was now stained yellow where it had become caked in the powder. He looked quite ridiculous since their mother, Elaine, had also cut his hair terribly short because of the filth from the well-room. It now stuck up straight like a pixie's.

'I still don't think they should have given a task like that to a girl,' Pip continued but May wasn't listening. She was patiently waiting for the young Wellmaster to finish counting heads.

May couldn't read figures so all she had to do was give the Wellmaster the parchment, which the Captain had subdivided into three columns. In the first column the Wellmaster was to write the number of people in his charge actually present and in the second, the numbers accounted for elsewhere, which in these sad times generally meant dead. The last column was for the name of anyone he could not account for. The Wellmaster wrote no name in that column.

Still wrapped in the bearskin that Branwolf had clasped about her shoulders, May made her tour, going next to the kitchens where Cook awkwardly applied her own attempt at writing.

'It's them runes, isn't it, child?' she said, stepping back from her vast cauldron of thin simmering broth.

May nodded. Her mother was there in the kitchens as usual, preparing herbs to help heal the wounded as Morrigwen had shown her. She nodded anxiously at her daughter and May scurried over. Unexpectedly Elaine gave her young daughter a big fierce hug.

'Keep yourself safe, May,' she warned. 'Believe in the Mother, love Her and She will protect you without the need for runes. Now hurry along with your duties.'

May left the kitchens to worm her way through the bustling archers and race along the parapets to find each of the sergeants. The atmosphere was tense and many yelled at her to get back to the keep where she belonged but she ignored them and thrust the parchment, dignified by the Baron's seal, determinedly under the nose of each sergeant.

When the fighting started she still had several sergeants to find. She couldn't read the names on the list and had to work from memory but in her two months in the castle she had come to know almost every person of rank, certainly nearly all the unmarried sergeants who had politely tried to make the acquaintance of her newly widowed mother. Elaine was a most attractive woman and many were interested though they seemed to treat her with great respect and kept a deferential though reluctant distance.

May was sure it was because her mother looked so like Lady Keridwen, the Baron's missing wife. If it had been said once, it had been said a hundred times and it clearly even disconcerted Branwolf for he would often watch Elaine with a strange expression on his face. May didn't like the way he stared. It was wrong. Those long lingering looks, they made her angry. She was angry, with the Baron and all his family. It was their fault her father was dead. It was because of the arrogance of the Torra Altan nobles that her father was dead, holding their own lives above those of the common people. Why should her father, Wystan, have died to save Lord Caspar?

The angry thoughts relented, though, as she thought of the time when her mind had met the Lord Caspar's in the magical universe captured within the moonstone. He hadn't been at all what she imagined. She had expected cold arrogance or at least some sense of the surly superiority which oozed from the Baron's younger brother. No, Master Spar had been different. He thought very little about himself; his mind was too busy with the concerns of others.

The short sergeant with an angry gash across his face handed back the now smudged and torn parchment. May was about to stretch out her hand for it when he was suddenly flung on top of her. For a moment the wind was knocked from her lungs and she saw only blackness. Someone was moaning weakly and hands were all around, dragging the bulky sergeant off her.

May scrambled to her feet and stared speechlessly across at a yawning rent in the battlement walls. Pebbles and hunks of masonry lay in shatters around them. The ragged parapet looked as ugly as the scars on the sergeant's face. He was still breathing, though only weakly. A few of the archers were carrying him towards the keep. May stepped back as everyone ignored her, too intent on their own business as they sent arrows flying out over the canyon in a whistling storm.

'How did those devils get the range?' an archer shouted angrily. 'Until now not one of their shots has come within a hundred yards of the Slide let alone reached up here.'

'Probably with one of those new siege-engines that appeared today. They've dragged them right across Vaalaka and they've been building more in the canyon these past days,' another replied, taking careful aim with his long war bow.

They were suspended in a moment of stunned silence as the wall before May's eyes bulged and shuddered but this time it held. Her lips were trembling, terrible fear tearing into her heart. The runes of war were failing long, long before their allotted time. It was Wolfmoon now and they should have held until the end of Fallow, six clear months away. Their only hope was that Brid would return earlier, much earlier, with the Egg.

She still couldn't see out into the canyon but she could hear the triumphant roar from the Vaalakans and smelt the stench rising from their campfires. She was being knocked and jostled from all sides as men poured from the east wall to reinforce the damaged section. White with shock, she backed off and began to retreat towards the keep.

She still had three more sergeants to find but she would wait. The Vaalakans would cease their attack at sundown and she would finish the task then. However fierce, however brutal the enemy might be, they were predictable. At night they would, with unfailing regularity, retreat to replenish their energies and fill their stomachs on sheep and Belbidian boar.

As she crossed the inner courtyard, she wanted to cover her

ears and hide as the terrible pounding of the walls continued. Urgent shouts thickened the air as, in the midst of battle, men rushed out with planking and hammers to shore the damaged battlements. Just before reaching the keep, May paused by the heartstone and looked down in despair at the gouged-out gold setting.

'Mother, Great Mother, don't forsake us,' she begged. 'We are your people.' Then with new resolve she turned towards the vast studded doors of the keep. She could at least help her mother with the wounded. A solar off the rear of the lower keep was decked with scrubbed pallets, benches and fresh linen, ready to receive the injured. After the attack she knew Morrigwen and her mother would have immediately hurried there.

The castle physician had handed over much of the administration of poultices and herbs to the old Crone while he bandaged and stitched wounds. At first they had been suspicious of each other's practices but, having seen the differing skills successfully applied to the ill and wounded, they now toiled respectfully alongside each other.

Nine men were brought in that day including the sergeant with the gashed cheek. His ribcage had been smashed by the impact of the rubble and his breathing was laboured. While the castle physician dressed and bandaged the other men's wounds, Morrigwen prepared a draught to ease the sergeant's pain.

Her eyes were filled with sorrow. 'He won't last,' she sighed. 'A splinter of bone has punctured his lungs; he's slowly drowning in his own blood. There is little I can do except ease his pain.'

Two hours later he was dead. May stared at his face. It was his body that had shielded her from the impact. The thought was too terrible to bear. In mimicry of the old Crone, she pushed the emotions from her mind and steeled herself against the pain. Only her mother wept.

'Don't, Ma.' She put her hand on Elaine's shoulder and her mother hugged her tightly.

'Oh May, how you've changed. You came here a young child, innocent and frightened, and now it's you who's comforting me. I just can't bear the hopelessness of it all. There was nothing I could do for the poor man.'

'Ah, but you did so much,' a deep voice contradicted her. May started; the Baron had crept silently into the hall and put a hand on Elaine's shoulder. 'You made a very big difference. To die with someone beside you caring, hoping, is a great ease. To die alone would be far worse.'

Elaine dipped her head and stepped a small pace away from the Baron. Branwolf also withdrew as if sensing that he transgressed. He stared at her hard for just a second and then turned towards May. 'Now, young girl. How have you done with your task? I came to get one of the young lads to relieve you of it. I should never have given the job to a young lady in the first place. Forgive me – the heat of battle.'

May wasn't sure whether she was being teased or not. But the Baron's jovial morale-boosting countenance didn't last, for he suddenly looked subdued and sombre – and terribly weary.

'I would know whose hands have caused the death of these fine young men. I will know who fled this castle having caused such treachery.'

May curtsied. 'I have all but completed the task, my lord. Please let me finish it: the men are tired.'

Pip, grubby and spluttering up clouds of yellow dust, had returned from the well-room. Hearing the last part of the Baron's conversation, he thumped his sister playfully on the back, nearly knocking her flat. 'I'll come with you – you know, to look after you.'

'Spare me,' May groaned, 'from the day I need protection from my little brother!' She frowned at him. He was growing, catching her up fast, and she wondered how much longer she would be able to call him 'little' brother.

A large number of the men were taking their turn at the refectory board in the lower keep. They looked mournfully into the watery stock and at the meagre sliver of crisp dried venison that were offered that day. One or two rubbed at cracked lips and sores at the edges of their mouths. Winter was never a good time in the mountains for fresh herbs and vegetables but now they had to be eked out and the lack of nutrition was beginning to show.

It took them no time at all to find the last few sergeants and even less time for Pip to extract the important-looking parchment from his sister's hands.

'You did all the others. It's not fair; I get to slave away in the well-room all day long while you get to play at being the Baron's personal messenger. It's not right for a girl. Give it to me.'

May gave in quickly for fear that Pip would cause a scene. Many of the soldiers were already turning to look at them. Triumphantly Pip marched around the various tables, offering the parchment and a stick of charcoal to the three remaining sergeants. Each of them counted heads around them and scratched onto the paper before handing it back to Pip.

'You don't have to strut around like a stuffed peacock, you know,' May told her brother. 'And are you sure they put the figures in the right place?'

Pip looked at the parchment doubtfully and then turned it a half-twist. 'How would I know? I can't read any more than you can.'

May finally arrested the parchment back from her brother before nervously climbing the spiral stone staircase to the upper hall where the Baron was conversing with the young Wellmaster. The door was ajar but she knocked very timidly.

Pip frowned at her. 'Can't you get anything right, sister? They'll never hear you.' He hammered a good deal harder on the studded door and one of the dogs barked in warning. Branwolf spun round and May muttered at her younger brother's sheepish grin as he looked at her guiltily. 'Perhaps that was just a little too loud,' he admitted unrepentantly.

The Baron held his hand out for the parchment and unravelled it. Staring at the figures, his dark brows knotted together and he combed back the greying hair at his temples pensively. One of the dogs circled round his legs. He pushed it absent-mindedly away.

'Some trouble?' the Wellmaster asked nervously.

'Huh?' The Baron sounded distracted. 'No, not trouble. More of a puzzle.'

He looked at May. 'You did tell the cook and the stablemaster to account for even the youngest children?'

May nodded, worried that she might have made a mistake.

At that moment the Captain entered, taking long sweeping strides across the bare oak floor. 'We've nearly got the breach shored up. I've got masons working on the largest gaps now,' he said hurriedly and then stopped short, looking down at the Baron. 'What is it?'

Branwolf flicked the parchment irritably aside. 'Oh nothing. It's just that the ruby is gone, the runes of war defaced and a man disappears over the wall . . .'

'But . . .' the Captain prompted.

'There's not a soul missing. Everyone is accounted for – one way or another.'

'Well, it couldn't have been a ghost that got up and chipped the runes away with an axe,' the Captain argued with a sour laugh.

The Baron raised an enigmatic eyebrow. 'No. I don't believe in ghosts either.'

Chapter 6

A plume of seagulls escorted the *Queen of Tutivillus*, like so many petitioning courtiers. They swooped and dived into the rolling wake, which paid out into a white pathway from the sloping stern of the creaking vessel. Aloft, the sails billowed and flapped, the luff lifting restlessly, not yet catching the full breeze as the mate took the helm and brought her closer to the wind.

The *Queen of Tutivillus* slipped slowly out of the cove's still waters and into the deep green depths of the swell that rose and fell offshore from the Hook of Caldea. Here, the wind shifted astern and Caspar felt the breeze on his neck.

'The wind's backing,' the first mate shouted forward. 'Ease the sheets; let's catch some of this breeze so that we can get cracking.'

As ropes were eased round their pins and paid out to ease the sail, Caspar sensed the wind tugging at the old vessel. As the sheets absorbed the strain from the billowing sails, they cracked, snapped taut, and with a surge of power the *Queen of Tutivillus* cut more swiftly through the waves.

Taking advantage of the last warmth of the day, Caspar hung over the bows, fascinated by the way the water raced past. He counted the amorphous brown jellyfish with their graceful tentacles as they rolled in the ship's wash. He shuddered; the tentacles writhing beneath the bigger ones looked like nests of infant adders.

The dying sun bathed the western ocean in dazzling blood-red. The colour instantly reminded Caspar of the ruby his father had set in the centre of Torra Alta's heartstone. He smiled, glad that the rune of the Mother blessed his home, offering solace to his father and the Torra Altan garrison.

The glowing colours warmed him as they slipped away from the shores of Belbidia and, for the first time in many days, he felt a rising conviction that they would succeed in their quest. The sea was flecked with foam but it was peaceful and unthreatening. They were free from the Inquisitors, and those horrible ghostly creatures lurking in the mist and the bog were far behind. Nothing and no one would follow them now.

He staggered to his bunk, amused by the rolling platform beneath his feet. The smooth lull of the sea quickly soothed his mind and blurrily he wondered why people complained so much about sea-sickness.

As they turned south-west away from Caldea, he could hear Firecracker giving out the odd wilful shriek followed by the thud, thud as his hooves connected with the planking of his stall. He fell asleep to the sound of the sailor on watch swearing at the animal. Caspar reflected that at least some things never changed.

The next thing he knew, he was being startled awake by a violent crash as the ship lurched, throwing him from his bunk to thump hard to the floor. Hal was beside him, pulling him to his dazed feet.

'What the hell's happening?' Caspar shrieked above the sound of splintering timbers. His world sheered over. The deck slewed at an impossibly steep angle. A chair was sliding over the boards towards him.

'Get up on deck,' a voice yelled from above.

Hal was pushing him up a ladder and out through the rear hatch. Sails flapped loosely and billowed like ghosts. A girl, undoubtedly Cybillia, was shrieking frantically and the ship's lanterns tossed and darted in the last of the night's darkness. Caspar was confused; the sea was glassy smooth and hardly a breath of wind ruffled the air or disturbed the smooth curve of the ocean swell, yet they were listed hard over to larboard.

Ceowulf, with one arm in a sling, was pulling Cybillia towards the centre of the deck where Brid was already steadying herself by the mast. The priestess reached out a hand to grab Cybillia, who clung tightly to her. Even in his panic, it struck Caspar how much the attitude of the two girls had changed towards each other.

The master, his experienced sea-legs keeping him happily upright on the listing deck, boomed orders to his crew as they went over the starboard gunwale on ropes. The entire cargo had shifted to larboard.

'What's going on?' Hal demanded.

The ship's master didn't reply. 'Get these landlubbers out of my way,' he yelled distractedly, calling for hammers, planking and sacking to be taken down below. 'Take a lantern and look at the hull. See if you can't shore it up,' he bellowed to one of his crew.

Ceowulf nodded to the two Torra Altan youths to come and stand by him. 'I guess we've hit a rock or something. It can't be much else in these calm waters. I don't seem to be having much luck with sea voyages lately,' he remarked wryly. 'At least this time there's no money to lose, assuming we can all swim well enough.' The lightness in his tone belied the anxious looks he threw towards the two young women.

They didn't seem to be sinking – not yet at any rate – and the busy hammering and shouts for more canvas and wood strips from over the ship's starboard side reassured Caspar that the crew had the situation well in hand.

'We're lucky it's a quiet night,' the master rumbled in his ale-thickened throat. 'We're holed above the waterline. But I don't know how it could happen; there are no rocks charted in these parts, not until we get nearer the Teeth, any road. Right, we'll have one of you overpaid sailors over the side on a rope and you can hammer some boards over the gap.' He turned to look southwards where a dun bank of brown rested on the grey sea. In the semi-darkness Caspar couldn't determine whether it was land or cloud. 'We can limp to Ophidia by midday so long as we patch the old *Queen* up for the time being.'

Though the ship's master ordered them to stay out of harm's

way on the foredeck, Caspar could not contain his curiosity and climbed the sloping deck to look over the starboard side. A ten-foot gash, bordered by splintered planking, yawned in the ship's hull. The impact had sent the ship's cargo reeling over to larboard, and kept the ship listed and most of the hole above the waterline. The fathomless depth of the water below unnerved him.

Two men, and in Caspar's opinion, two extremely brave men, were lowered on ropes, hammer in hand, to fix some spare hatchboards over the gash.

'Damn funny place for a rock to hit us, so high on the waterline,' one of the two sailors mumbled, a bearded man with a mouthful of nails gripped between his teeth.

'Well, I ain't complaining.' The second man was slight of build with quick moving fingers and already had several nails in place before the first sailor had found a suitable grip with his hammer. 'Any lower and we'd be having a hard swim for the far shore there.'

'Here, what's this?' The clumsy, bearded man suddenly stopped working and looked thoughtfully at the splintered wood in front of him. He worked the claw of his hammer back and forth until something white, about the size of a knife blade, came away in his hand.

His face went equally white to match it.

'What is it?' The nimble man turned with sudden apprehension at the look on his companion's face.

'I ain't never seen one of these in the Caballan Sea before. Now in the western oceans maybe, but not here. Here, someone!' he started to yell excitedly. 'Ahoy! Someone pull us up from here sharpish!'

'Get us up, get us up now!' the slighter man began shrieking as the sailors on deck groaned under the strain of their weight.

A prickling feeling tingled up Caspar's spine and he found himself staring into the murky depths, knowing that down there somewhere ... He automatically reached for his bow. The innocent swell of glassy green rose and fell before him, a veil across the dark secrets of the depths. He knew something was there. The water stirred and a black shape flitted away fathoms below him, but it could just have been the darker shadow of the boat on a sand bank below or maybe the shadow of a cloud. But then the black form was racing up towards the hull.

'Look out! Broad on the starboard bow!' the first mate yelled.

At first he thought they were moving over a barnacled rock as the jagged pointed head rose up from the depths but it kept on rising. A great bulbous head, a broad gaping mouth and streaming tentacles that powered the creature upwards took form in the dark depths. The mouth opened, revealing long white sickle teeth, each like a saw-edged sabre for shredding rather than crushing flesh.

Caspar felt his own mouth open in horror. As the jaws broke the surface of the waves he let loose an arrow and then a second before he had even time to think. The barbs struck deep in to the greeny-black scales but the monster continued to rise, clamping its teeth around the dangling legs of the bearded sailor. The ropes securing the man to the ship parted like thin strands of cotton as the monster thrashed its head from side to side. Blood swirled into the maelstrom of foaming water, stirred by the coiling tentacles trailing twenty or maybe thirty feet into the depths below. The stricken sailor shrieked like a panicked animal caught in an iron trap, the sound of his terror screaming out over the sea.

The man grappled and clawed at the sides of the boat and the monster flung him up above the waves. Caspar saw how his leg folded back awkwardly, held on by no more than a thread of sinew. The sea was bright scarlet now and the foaming waters boiled around the monster's mouth as it gnashed and sliced at the man's torso. Aiming at the slit eyes set directly above its cavernous mouth, Caspar fired again and again, embedding three barbs in the creature's bulbous head, but it was impossible to judge what damage was done. A black inky jet squirted out from the body of the beast and it plummeted away, its flailing tentacles thrusting straight as spears as it dived down into the depths. As it plunged away, one central barbed tail, jutting beyond the skirt of tentacles, broke the foaming white bubbles on the surface, spraying water in a shower over the deck. Then it was gone. And the sailor's body was gone too.

The surviving sailor was on the deck, gasping fitfully and pointing. It was several minutes before he could speak and by that time the excited frenzy had quelled to the uneasy stillness of fear.

'There but for the grace of God . . . ,' he spluttered fitfully before turning ominously on Brid and Cybillia. 'These women, these witches have brought us bad luck.'

'What was it?' Caspar demanded, ignoring the man's outburst. 'I got three or four arrows deep into its skull but it didn't flinch.'

The master looked heavily at his crew who were muttering distrustfully and glowering at Brid and Cybillia. 'A kraken,' he mumbled as if not daring to say the word too loud in case it summoned the monster again. 'They've been rumoured of far out in the deep western oceans but never within the confines of the Caballan Sea. Come on, lads, sheet in them sails. We'll be close hauled but it's not far to the Crest of Ophidia now.'

There were ugly growls from many of the sailors as they darted black looks at Brid's elfin beauty and verdant eyes then at Cybillia's scarred cheek. Finally there was an outburst from the back of the throng. 'Put them overboard. The good Lord is punishing us for our sins.'

Caspar's heart pounded out a thick swollen beat in his throat and within seconds he was standing in front of the priestess with his bow drawn. Hal was shouldering him with the runesword. The white metal of its blade caught the first rays of the morning sun as dawn warmed the eastern horizon. A pathway of gold spread towards them across the rippling waves to anoint the blade.

The band of sailors looked on uneasily and several drew short cutlasses from their broad-buckled belts. The master looked warily at Caspar's bow and Hal's gleaming sword, with its blood-red lettering angrily declaring its powers. He tugged at the thick looped earring that dragged at his ear and stepped calmly forward. 'Steady now; we're not in a hurry to cause any more trouble.'

Ceowulf, his sword still in its sheath, stepped calmly in front of his young, headstrong companions. 'Just put us ashore at the first port,' he muttered. 'We're all trained men and you would find it costly to attack us.'

'Men!' one of the younger sailors sniffed. He swung dextrously down from the shrouds, spiralling down a rope and landing neatly on the deck. 'I can only see one and he's got his arm in a sling. This is witchcraft. The one true God has sent that monster to slay those witches and I for one believe He will spare us if we throw them overboard.'

An older man stepped forward and laid a callused hand on his crewman's shoulder. 'Steady it down, friend. I say the good Lord is punishing us for our greed. I say we give these here women their gold back. It's taking the witches gold what's doing the harm. It makes us as sinful as them.' The eyes of the rest of the crew were still flitting between the point of Hal's runesword, Ceowulf's muscly bulk and Caspar's bow. They eyed the latter with healthy respect, having just witnessed the accuracy and speed of his skill with the weapon.

'Aye, sir, give 'em their gold back,' the general consensus filtered through the crew.

The ship's master thumped at his chest and hit the bulge over his breast, which chinked with the reassuring sound of a full purse of money. Scowling, he reached inside his breasted jacket and drew out a kid leather purse. He tossed it awkwardly at Ceowulf and, though the knight was handicapped by his injury, he caught it neatly in his left hand.

The master turned his back on them to harangue the crew, yelling at them to set the ship back on an even keel. He obviously wanted to get out of these waters fast, clearly prepared to take in a little water through the repaired gash rather than sit at sea any longer with the kraken lurking in the depths. He nodded to the Torra Altans to stow themselves on the foredeck, as far away from the helm as possible, where they wouldn't bother him or the crew.

As they looked longingly towards the grey-brown humps of land on the southern horizon, Caspar reflected that the Crest of Ophidia still seemed a very long way off.

'They're suffering from a guilty conscience, if you ask me,' Ceowulf mused as he handed Hal his purse. 'They must have done some black deeds in their time to think that God could be punishing them for harbouring witches.'

'I'm not a witch,' Cybillia sobbed.

'Oh shut up,' Brid growled, but at the same time patted the girl's hand reassuringly. 'I've told you I'll heal your face.' The priestess looked anxiously down at where the water divided around the bow, sweeping up and curling over into two diverging crests. She looked up towards the distant shore. 'Mother, it's a long way off.' Her fists clutched the rail and Hal's dark hands covered hers and squeezed reassuringly.

'We'll make it,' he murmured without conviction.

Brid looked at his hand covering hers and glanced at him quizzically. Hal caught her look and the corners of his mouth twitched in the beginnings of a smile but then he suddenly flicked his hand away and grunted incoherently. Caspar recognized the lingering look the Maiden gave his uncle and felt the jealousy rise in his throat. He swallowed hard and determinedly turned his attention towards the knight.

Ceowulf was looking southward. 'We'll make it all right. These men are as anxious as we are to get ashore. There's nothing like the combined willpower of men to make things happen.'

Rising up out of the sea, the Crest of Ophidia was now a discernible green and brown rather than the indistinct grey that had merged into the early morning clouds. Clusters of white sprang out of the background and as Caspar was just beginning to relax the first houses became visible to the naked eye. Now that he could clearly see land, he yearned to feel firm rock pushing up through the soles of his feet again.

An ominous crash from the bows startled him from his

reverie. But it didn't take him any time to realize the cause of the disturbance as the sound of splintering wood cracked through the deck and a fiendish equine shriek cut through the noise of shouting sailors. At least it wasn't the kraken.

'Get that animal under control,' the ship's master bellowed, 'or he'll feel the edge of my knife on his throat.' The cold bite to his tongue left the youth in no doubt that the threat was in earnest. Firecracker was bucking and thrashing and had already snapped a strap on his head collar. The fiery horse was now smashing through the planks that divided him from Sorcerer's stall.

'That horse of yours needs gelding,' Hal growled above the noise of splintering planks as a hunk of boarding flew off the back of the roan's heels and hacked into the bulwark that ran around the perimeter of the deck. He ran for a rope. It took Caspar a moment longer to think but he went straight for the animal's bridle. The horse needed a bit between his teeth before anyone was going to control him.

Hal was about to leap into the stall when Caspar caught his arm and pulled him back. 'Stay out; he's too excited.'

With the horse throwing his head about and lashing out with his hooves, Caspar knew it was going to be tricky. However, he managed to get the loop of reins over the animal's head and quickly had a hand to one of his soft ears, which he pulled quite hard. 'I'll put a twitch on your lip if you don't settle,' he threatened, though in a soft calming voice. As he struggled to get the bit between the horse's teeth, Firecracker threw his head up and Caspar was lifted clean off the ground. Within seconds, he had the bridle over the animal's ears and the bit between his teeth. Finally he had the beast under control.

'I need to walk him round.'

'Not on your life,' the master's bearded face peered over the top of the stall. 'I'm not having that animal loose on my deck. And if he stoves anything in I'll slit his throat, do you hear?'

Brid's small frame appeared next to the man. Her mellow tones soothed the stormy atmosphere just as Hal grabbed the other side of Firecracker's bridle in an attempt to stop the horse crushing Caspar against the side of the stall. She took the cloak off her back and very carefully eased it up over the horse's head, plunging the animal into darkness. Firecracker snorted and stamped but became instantly calmer. Caspar found himself able to breathe again. His shoulder socket hurt where Firecracker had wrenched his arm upwards and somehow he had managed to bang his nose but at least the horse was quieter now. He smiled gratefully at Brid.

'It just needs a bit of common sense,' she replied with a touch of condescension to her voice. 'I'll make up a soporific brew of Ovissian camomile and Gortan wild lettuce just to keep him calm.'

'She's infuriating,' Hal muttered. 'She always talks to us as if we're complete incompetents.'

It was half an hour before Caspar was content that Firecracker was dozing peacefully. Only then did he feel relaxed enough to take his eyes off the horse and look around him again. The sailors were reefing in the sail and the Crest of Ophidia suddenly towered over them. A black cormorant plunged into the sea over to his right and all around shearwaters skimmed across the rippling waves, their twisting flight reminding Caspar of summer swallows. The sea was immediately a more reassuring pale blue rather than the unfathomable dark green of the deeper waters. It wouldn't be long now before they reached dry land.

Cocklebay was a small but busy port and the quayside bustled with fishermen auctioning their catch and spice merchants bartering with the townsfolk. The port was full of travellers from all corners of the Caballan Sea and most of their business was conducted in Belbidian, though the native fisherman yelled their wares in a sing-songy tongue that Caspar could just identify as Ophidian. He felt reassured by their mundane day to day activities. At least they were far from King Rewik's fanatical Inquisitors. As Firecracker tripped and stumbled groggily across the gangplank leading to the pier a band of fisherman broke into hoots of laughter. The auburn-haired youth grinned sheepishly at them though Hal marched over and thrust his darkened face up against theirs, placing his hand threateningly on the hilt of his sword.

'He's far too headstrong for his own good,' Ceowulf muttered as the fishermen hurriedly retreated.

'Just because we're no longer in Belbidia, it doesn't mean that people can treat us with disrespect,' Hal grumbled.

'I'd be thankful we're not.' Ceowulf nodded towards the two girls. 'In my experience it's only in Belbidia that people are so fanatical about routing out witchcraft. At least now we're abroad, we shouldn't have the same problems as we had in Belbidia on that account.'

'Please,' Cybillia half-whined, half-whispered at Hal. 'Please don't draw any attention to us.' The tall willowy girl pressed close to Brid and kept her hood scooped over her spiky hair to shadow her face.

As Ceowulf marched forward, he eased his arm from his sling and gently rotated his shoulder. 'Well, I can't be seen out and about like this,' he muttered and removed the bandage. Though his arm was still stiff it evidently pained him a great deal less.

Caspar dragged at Trog's collar as the dog excitedly tried to scramble off the breakwater and onto the beach.

'He can smell snakes,' Brid guessed and laughed at the dog. 'He's an Ophidian snake-catcher after all and there're more of those sand vipers here than any where else in the Caballan Sea.'

Caspar's blood ran cold and his skin turned clammy. He harshly yanked at the terrier's collar. 'Come on, Trog, we're getting away from here fast.' If there was one thing that scared him it was the thought of snakes.

Ceowulf strode purposefully forward.

'You seem to have an uncanny ability for finding inns,' Caspar remarked lightly, trying to repress his phobia of the sand vipers.

'Just one of my many secret weapons,' the knight smiled enigmatically. 'You'll like this one.'

Ceowulf led them through narrow cobbled streets towards a gabled timbered building set slightly back from the main street. Caspar couldn't read the blistered sign that hung above the door because it was written in Ophidian but, through the peeling paint, he could make out the image of a crab and a lobster. He had never eaten either and wondered what they would taste like.

A neat courtyard fronted the inn and a groom hurriedly rushed out to take their horses. Caspar let him take Firecracker, feeling certain the doped horse wouldn't cause any more problems that day. Ceowulf dipped his head under the door mantle and led them into a low-ceilinged room, panelled with what looked like planking stripped from a ship's hull. A small anchor hung on one wall and the crooked beams were decorated with strings of lobster pots. Caspar was beginning to feel quite tall in this place since most of the Ophidian inhabitants seemed to be a good six inches shorter than the average Belbidian.

He was also glad that the imbibers paid more attention to Trog snuffling at Brid's heels than to any of them. The dog wagged his tail furiously at the attentions and Caspar laughed. 'Of course! Trog probably understands them. I wonder what "good dog" is in Ophidian.'

'Oh don't be ridiculous,' Hal snapped, though Caspar couldn't help noticing the way his older kinsman tried to disguise a smile as Trog rushed enthusiastically from one friendly face to the next.

One man with a broad grin leapt from his table, exclaiming loudly as he stooped towards the dog. Trog wagged his tail furiously and curtsied his head, giving out pathetic yips that were more suited to a puppy than a deep barrel-chested cur. The small man had blue tattoos, dark sunken eyes and tiny gappy teeth. He gabbled something excitedly to Ceowulf, making the knight step back and hold up his hands in mock defence.

'I'm sorry, friend,' he replied with clear enunciation, 'but my Ophidian is rather rusty.'

'Of course, of course.' The short man turned his Ophidian speech into a rapid sing-songy dialect, obviously quite adept with the Belbidian language. 'I've never met a Belbidian yet who could speak more than his own tongue.'

Ceowulf nodded apologetically at him and the tattooed man grinned with friendly welcome. 'Your dog,' he opened, stooping down to ruffle Trog's neck and thump his muscly flank appreciatively, 'can I buy him?'

'Yes,' Hal replied instantly though Brid's furious eyes stabbed at him as she clutched possessively at the dog's collar.

'He's mine,' she replied firmly. 'And he's not for sale.'

'I paid for him,' Hal protested. 'And he'll be happy in Ophidia. It's his home after all.'

Ceowulf interjected. 'Sorry, friend, the lady's too attached to him. We can't possibly sell him.'

The man looked disappointed. 'That's a shame. He's got a fine head.' Bravely the man looped his finger over Trog's upper lip and lifted the skin, showing his tapered white canines. 'Excellent teeth and very fine muscles.'

Caspar didn't like the way the man was so impressed with Trog's teeth. 'What's your interest in him anyway? You're not looking for a fighting dog, I hope.'

The man looked instantly offended. 'No, never. But it's a problem with these snake-catchers. They're very strong, brave and – how do you say in Belbidian – stoical, that's it. They have to be for clearing the wretched vipers off the sands. Trouble is we get a few stolen because they are stronger than most other hounds. Not naturally aggressive towards humans, mind. They love people but some ruffians will get almost any dog to fight once they've mistreated it enough. Oh, no, I don't fight them and I'd kill anyone that does. I breed them. That's why I fancied your dog here. He's got excellent stock in his veins.'

'Hear that, Trog? You're a prize champion dog.' Caspar thumped the terrier affectionately.

'Well, come and have a drink with us, friend,' Ceowulf offered. 'We'll talk dogs and perhaps you'd be so kind as to help us. We need a friendly ship to give us a passage west through the Teeth.'

'You don't want to be going through the Teeth this time of year. Wherever you're trying to get to, you need to go overland if at all possible.'

Fully in agreement with this line of conversation, Caspar was developing quite a liking for their new Ophidian friend. They sat on low wooden chairs, cool thick alcoholic drink soothing their nerves. It tasted somewhat between rich dark beer and cider and the boy was quite taken with it.

'We need to get round to the Farthest Isles before the mid-winter festival and there isn't time to go by land,' Ceowulf explained succinctly with an open honest expression on his tanned face.

The dog-breeder raised a questioning eyebrow. 'Well, I hope you can all swim. You've obviously no idea what it's like going through the Teeth. It's a very narrow strait and the tides of the Caballan Sea funnel through it, producing treacherous whirlpools and undercurrents. I doubt you'll find any vessel braving the straits for at least two moons.'

'We've got to.' Brid was emphatic.

'I'm sorry, miss, but I think you'll be out of luck there. He downed the last of his drink and wiped the back of his hand across his mouth. 'Well, I'm sorry I couldn't change your mind about the snake-catcher, but I hope you find what you're look-ing for.' He nodded his head politely at the two Belbidian girls and took his leave.

Caspar was crestfallen. They had to get to the Farthest Isles as quickly as possible. Even now they were wasting time drinking in this inn and he was annoyed at Ceowulf for the complacent manner with which he unhurriedly sipped at his tankard.

'Shouldn't you ask a few more people?' he demanded. 'We can't just sit here all day.'

'Oh, have patience, lad.' The knight smiled at him enigmati-cally and sat back against the wall, placing his feet up onto a stool. He kept looking towards the bar but Caspar could see nothing of interest there, except the innkeeper pouring generous portions of the amber brew into tall horn goblets. Ceowulf had an expectant look to his eye and rather a self-satisfied smile to his face. He was also keeping himself too contemplatively quiet.

At last Caspar realized what the knight had been waiting for, though Hal noticed her first. He suddenly saw Hal's olive eyes light up like a beacon over his goblet and he looked round to see a girl with rich black hair and full round curves. She was dressed in white with a blue apron draped around the curve of her hips. A black bodice squeezed tightly at her narrow waist and her eyes, outlined by long curling eyelashes, were almost black to match.

'Too young for you,' Hal challenged the older knight, male rivalry sparking between them.

'Too much for your inexperienced hands to handle,' said the knight with a wicked glint in his eye.

'Just because I'm young doesn't mean I'm inexperienced.' Hal leant forward. 'I'll wager you my best hunting knife that she'll go for me rather than you.'

Cybillia did not react well to this boisterous exchange. The colour had drained from her face and she slumped back in humiliation, pulling up the collar of her cloak. Her lower lip trembled momentarily but she bit it fiercely. Caspar realized that the Jotunn maiden was deeply offended by Ceowulf and Hal's bantering.

He flicked his eyes towards Brid, expecting to see her displeasure at this behaviour, but she looked quite unconcerned, in fact she looked rather pleased with herself. A small movement of her hand drew his attention to the bristly narrow-leafed lettuce and the small green plant with tight white flowers that she'd fed to Firecracker earlier. She was surreptitiously crumbling it between her fingers. Then whilst Hal was leering at the voluptuous figure of the serving girl, Brid slipped the crushed herbs into his brew. She sat back with a smug expression and smiling eyes. When she caught Caspar looking at her, she winked wickedly.

Caspar had to bury his chortles in his goblet as he watched his uncle greedily slurp his drink. Brid looked entirely satisfied.

Cybillia looked quizzically between the two Torra Altans. 'What are you two doing?' she demanded innocently.

The priestess gave her a meaningful look, which clearly told her to shut up, and patted her scrip.

'Oh!' the yellow-haired maiden exclaimed.

'C-y-b-i-l-l-i-a!' Caspar moaned in frustration, hoping that she wouldn't give the game away – at least not until Hal had finished his drink. Thankfully a bright blush swam up her cheeks and she gave Brid a conspiratorial grin. Hal was too absorbed in the barmaid to notice any of their exchange.

At last, Hal finally downed his drink and his expression was just beginning to look a little puzzled, when the black-haired maiden in her white skirts turned round. Ceowulf had pushed his chair back into the shadow of a central pillar, arranging his face into one of implacable meditation. Hal kicked his feet arrogantly up onto the table and snapped his fingers.

'Barmaid,' he slurred, though apparently unaware of his failing faculties. 'Another drink from your fair hand.'

Brid interceded. 'I think he's had too much already.'

'Nonsense, I've – I've only had one,' Hal complained, tripping over the words. 'Haven't I?' He was starting to look more confused.

'I'm afraid he's not used to it,' Brid apologized for him. 'He doesn't know his own limitations.'

'Do I hell,' Hal roared, leaping up and at the same time snagging his jacket in the arm of his chair and finally ending up in an undignified heap on the floor. The young barmaid looked quite confused as Caspar and Brid collapsed with laughter, but her expression soon changed as Ceowulf moved slowly forward out of the shadows.

She dropped the empty tankard she was holding in delighted surprise and flung herself at the knight, falling into his lap and smothering him with kisses. Hal was on his feet by now and looking thoroughly cheated. 'You knew her all along; that's not fair,' he slurred.

'Ceowulf! Ceowulf! I didn't think we would ever see you again.' The sound of the girl's excited voice made Caspar feel that she wasn't quite as old as he had at first thought. He decided she was probably no more than his own age, though plainly she had been quick to grow to maturity.

'How's your mother?' Ceowulf hugged her with avuncular affection and Caspar immediately decided there was some intimate connection between this girl's mother and the Caldean nobleman. Ceowulf certainly knew the girl very well.

The girl groaned. 'As fussy as ever. She spies on me all the time now.'

'Ah! So that means you have a young gentleman friend?'

'It might.' She blushed. 'Ma isn't happy about it. He's a sailor.'

'And what's wrong with a sailor?' Ceowulf asked.

'He works on the *Moonshadow*.'

'Is that meant to mean anything to me?' the knight queried.

'You wouldn't know of course. It's one of the big Ceolothian ships. She sails shortly for the far western oceans to explore the Diamond Seas. She puts in here regularly as her last port of call before passing through the Teeth. Though she has a Ceolothian master, he recruits many of his men from here. Ma said it's not right to get involved with someone who goes out to sea so far and so often. It's one of the few ships from the Caballan Sea that will put to sea in the winter and risk the Teeth.'

'Well, she's probably right. Not necessarily a wise choice for a husband,' Ceowulf said protectively.

Caspar's mind leapt at the girl's words. At least there was one vessel that might take them westwards.

'You don't understand either,' the girl protested. 'He's only doing it for a short while till he's earned enough share in the profits to buy a lobster boat like his father's. We need bigger ones now in Cocklebay because we need to put out to sea further than we used to.'

'Don't tell me,' Brid sighed. 'The lobster beds are yielding less and less each year.'

'Mmm,' the girl affirmed. 'How did you know?'

'Just a lucky guess,' she shrugged. But Caspar knew it was not. Brid was always lecturing about the way the men of the New Faith over-harvested the land and the sea.

The young girl looked round at Ceowulf's companions as if noticing them for the first time. Her skin was dark and she had big eyes beneath dramatic, arching brows. Her hair was silky black, much like Hal's.

'Let me introduce everyone.' Ceowulf smiled warmly at the girl. 'This, my friends, is Dionella, named after the brilliant rare flower that grows in the desert. She's very special to me.'

'Indeed,' Caspar tried to sound worldly. 'And her mother too, we understand.'

'This clever little chap, who thinks he knows everything, is Spar and this sleepy character is Hal.'

Hal was propped up on his elbows, looking gloomily into the dregs of his ale. 'I'm sure I only had one, I'm sure I did,' he mumbled to all but his own amusement.

Ceowulf continued, 'And these two fair and delightful maidens are Cybillia and Brid.'

'Now, Spar, you've guessed wrongly though it wasn't too bad a guess. I came across her mother, Katalin, in the deserts of Glain, well, it must be around fifteen years ago now. I was very young and had only just run away from home. Well, she'd escaped from a wicked tribe of nomads who bought and sold women into slavery, and she was lost, alone and friendless. She hadn't eaten in days and was down to her last drop of water. I took her to safety, learning on the way that her husband had been killed and that she was with child. I eventually brought her back here to her mother in Cocklebay. And I suppose I've been by a few times since.'

'But not so often as you might have done,' Dionella interrupted. 'Though Ma will be very glad to see you, I'm sure.'

'Well, my dark lady, why don't you run along and warn her that we'll be paying a visit?'

Dionella skipped from the room like a small child and

Caspar looked at the knight reproachfully. 'That was wicked. You led Hal on terribly.'

'I couldn't resist the opportunity,' the knight laughed. 'And who are you to judge? The three of you don't seem to have treated him too well either.'

'She doesn't know who you really are though, does she?' Brid interrupted. 'She thinks you're just a wandering mercenary.'

'You are uncomfortably perceptive, my dear lady,' Ceowulf conceded. 'In essence I've not led her a lie but you're right, she knows me only as Ceowulf – and I'd rather prefer to keep it that way. We'll pass through the crowds and rouse far less suspicion if we all keep our noble ancestry under our hats and pretend we're from the ordinary merchant classes. You never know when some villain is going to get some complicated ideas of kidnap and ransom into his head if he discovers any of us are of baronial lineage. They get very excited about such schemes, you know.'

Caspar nodded knowingly.

They had to help Hal to his feet, who was beginning to realize that Brid was to blame for his swimming head. He pulled roughly away from her when she offered him a helping hand.

'I don't want to go,' Cybillia muttered. 'I don't want to meet anyone.'

'We can't leave you behind,' Brid argued. 'It's not safe to get separated and if Ceowulf's got friends here they'll be better able to help us.'

'I don't want to go,' she repeated. Nobody had to ask her why as she turned her left cheek into the folds of her hood.

Brid looked at her imploringly, but Ceowulf nudged the priestess aside and caught up Cybillia's hand, squeezing it affectionately. 'Believe me, you won't mind meeting Dionella's mother. She won't pass any judgements on you.' He tugged her to her feet. 'Come on, I'll look after you.'

The spiky-haired girl didn't have the strength to resist.

Taking a rather wavy line, Hal stumbled after the others as they strode through the cobbled streets. They made their way down to the waterside and along the bright row of houses each painted a spectacular colour. Katalin's house was white, set between neighbours of garish pink and soft peach. Ceowulf didn't need to rap on the door as it was delightedly flung open by the young girl from the inn. She led them into a cosy room with bare flagstones and a broad hearth. A simple table surrounded by three benches was pressed up against one wall and, apart from several three-legged stools crouched around the fire, where a black kettle shrieked, there was only one real chair. It was occupied by an old woman wrapped in a black shawl and it creaked comfortingly on large curved rockers. She stared blankly into the fire.

An inner door, leading into the rest of the house, banged open and a woman carrying a plate of cakes and rolled herring mops worked her way sideways into the room. Her eyes lit up with delight at the sight of Ceowulf's grinning face. One half of her face lifted into a welcoming smile but the other half twisted and pulled into a grotesque sneer.

'I hope you don't mind, Katalin, but I've brought some friends.' Ceowulf welcomed her with outstretched arms.

'Friends! Of course not,' she declared, meeting them full in the face and greeting each of them warmly. She was quite short but well formed in body. She had dark olive skin like her daughter and her eyes were large and appealing. Sadly her most noticeable feature was an ugly gash across the right side of her face. It cut from the corner of her eye to her mouth, where it pulled up the right-hand side of her upper lip, twisting the skin when she smiled or spoke.

Caspar was quite struck by the way she seemed to ignore her disfigurement and didn't try to conceal it like Cybillia did hers. He watched how the golden-haired maiden let her hand fall guiltily away from her gnarled cheek in respect for the woman's own scars. Cybillia had been lucky by comparison. Her scars were no more than skin deep whereas Katalin's must have been cut through to the muscle, judging by the way the skin lifted and distorted as she spoke.

Caspar found that he was staring and quickly dragged his

gaze away from her cheek and firmly fixed it on her eyes.

She showed not a hint of embarrassment at welcoming them into her home and Caspar thought how very astute it had been of Ceowulf never to mention his noble birth. The woman would have balked at asking them to sit at her plain table if she had known they were of noble blood.

Dionella and Katalin chattered away warmly, seemingly unperturbed by Hal who was slumped forward on the table with his face buried in his arms. Every so often the young girl would trot over to the old woman in her rocking chair and patiently feed her a plain biscuit and some milk.

'Grandma forgets to eat if you don't make her,' she explained without bothering to lower her voice. Caspar guessed the old woman was either deaf or unable to understand Belbidian.

'So,' Ceowulf put his arm around Dionella, 'the young lady here has found herself a beau.'

Dionella blushed red and pouted at him.

'I told you Ma's funny about Pellam. Now you'll set her off on one of her gripes.'

'Dionella! Don't you speak about me like that.'

Ceowulf smiled at the pair of them. 'She says he's in port for a week before setting sail round the Crest and out through the Teeth. We need a passage. I'd like to meet the ship's master,' Ceowulf continued, ignoring the angry glances that flashed between mother and daughter.

'You're never wanting to sail out through there at this time of the year. And anyway haven't you heard? The port's buzzing with talk of a kraken. I should think this entire southern coast is humming with the tale. The *Queen of Tutivillus* put in and her hull's been torn apart by a huge sea monster.'

'I know. We were on her.'

Katalin blinked and looked stunned for several moments. She then swallowed hard and said determinedly, 'Well then, you should know better. Oh, dearest Ceowulf, you can't possibly go through the Teeth –'

'We have to,' Brid quietly interjected.

There was something in the priestess's tone that precluded

further argument. She spoke with such utter conviction that it stopped Katalin in mid-sentence. The woman studied the girl for a second and nodded. 'Well, I won't ask your business. Ceowulf's been on so many unmentionable exploits, I don't think I want to know anymore. Dionella, you'd best fetch young Pellam and he can take our friends to see Silus, the master of the *Moonshadow*.'

Dionella scampered from the room, catching her skirts on a chair in her haste. Her mother sighed. 'She's just too young to get her heart broken. She's crazy for this boy Pellam but I don't know that he's at all right for her.'

'I doubt there's a mother in all the countries of the Caballan Sea that doesn't say that when their daughter first falls in love,' Ceowulf remarked.

Katalin laughed, happy to laugh at herself despite the cruel expression it produced on her face.

Chapter 7

Pellam wasn't at all what Caspar had expected. In his opinion he was a little too old for Dionella and had mousy hair, thin stringy muscles and a rather irresponsible sparkle in his hazel eyes. The young Torra Altan could feel Ceowulf stiffen with displeasure as if the knight concurred with Katalin's disapproval of this young man. He had a hungry, opportunist look that contrasted starkly with Dionella's trusting vulnerable nature.

Pellam put a proprietorial arm around the small dark-haired girl and looked the Belbidians critically up and down. Caspar wondered if the look would have been any different if he had known they were of noble blood. He doubted it.

'Ceowulf, the hero! I've heard more than I can believe about you,' the Ophidian said with a dismissive laugh. He spoke Belbidian easily but with the usual sing-songy accent of the region. Caspar couldn't decide whether he was joking or not. The man's eyes never seemed to smile.

'I can't say I can return the compliment,' the knight replied with candour. 'So far I can believe everything.'

Pellam narrowed his eyes at this comment and looked at Ceowulf sideways as if trying to decide whether this was an insult. He bristled visibly and then laughed with rather too much confidence. Caspar suspected that the man's surly looks were a front behind which he hid an underlying streak of insecurity. The Torra Altan rubbed self-consciously at his freckled, crooked nose as he felt Pellam's eyes take stock of his small frame and auburn hair. He bristled protectively as the Ophidian's eyes lingered on Brid and noted with anger how he stared at Cybillia's cheek. No wonder Katalin didn't like him.

Cybillia stood up to the appraisal better than he had expected. Rather than retreating as usual into her cloak, she let her hand slip away from the ugly raised scars, allowing the foreigner to take a long cold look. The man finally averted his gaze, the flickering of an apology skimming through his eyes. Caspar smiled inwardly, thinking that Cybillia had learnt one or two things from Katalin's scars. Nobody treated Dionella's mother with any disrespect; she simply didn't let them.

Hal, who was quickly recovering from his spiked ale, clearly took an instant dislike to Pellam. His olive eyes darkened and one eyebrow rose into a look of superiority. He stared at the young man who was one or two years his senior and met him with a confident cool gaze. There was a conceited, self-satisfied look in Hal's eyes as he let them flicker a teasing challenge towards Dionella. This look was not lost on Pellam and for the first time the Ophidian became flustered and possessively pulled his girl towards him. There was something undeniably handsome in Hal's roguish good looks and Pellam appeared instantly wary.

'The five of us need a passage west through the Teeth,' Ceowulf said abruptly, obviously deciding to waive any further formalities. 'Will you take us to your ship's master? Dionella tells us that you're sailing next week and from what I hear there'll be no more ships for several months.'

Pellam shrugged. 'Well, if you think you're up to it. But it's not a journey for landsmen and if you want to take the girls they'll find it very tough.'

Brid laughed. 'We can look after ourselves; don't you worry, mariner.'

The *Moonshadow's* master was precisely what they had expected: stocky, well-built with ruddy cheeks, a full round belly from too much ale and a harsh voice that continually snapped orders. He was a plain-speaking, no nonsense sort of man who was, no doubt, looking forward to a long retirement. His crew were gathered from all countries of the Caballan Sea and, as was customary, they used Belbidian as their common language. Belbidia traded more widely than any other nation and the language was broadly understood. Silus, the Ceolothian master, didn't have a parrot nor a wooden leg but Caspar thought that neither of these would be out of place. He rasped a thick hand through his curly black beard.

'Are you folks sure you want to go through the Teeth?' he asked, his harsh monotone accent contrasting starkly with the Ophidian voices. 'Surely there must be better places to run and hide to.'

'Who says we're running?' Ceowulf replied enigmatically. He evidently enjoyed being mysterious.

'Such a curious bunch of folks: two young girls, a couple of lads, a mercenary and a lot of efficient-looking weaponry. I'd say someone's upset their overlord in some way.'

Ceowulf laughed, and let the man believe his assumptions. 'Ah, but we might be looking for treasure, mightn't we?' he joked.

'Yeah, and I might find a sea passage through to the stars. Sure I'll give you folks passage. It's just the five of you then?'

'And three horses,' the Caldean knight replied.

'And our dog,' Brid hastily added. Trog pressed himself against her knees, eyeing all the strangers suspiciously.

The two Torra Altans, Brid and Cybillia returned to the Crab and Lobster while Ceowulf went back to Katalin to chat about old times.

'Do you think there's really something between them?' Caspar asked.

'Ceowulf and Katalin?' Hal looked doubtful and raised his hand towards his cheek about to say something, but then with a quick look at Cybillia hurriedly changed his mind and tone of voice. 'Maybe. She's a fine-looking woman.'

Cybillia looked at him in surprise and the smallest smile curled up on her sad lips.

Hal continued, 'I would say Ceowulf thought her attractive anyway.'

'She's certainly a handsome woman,' Brid added firmly, 'but actually I think our friend's just very protective of her. I'd bet Hal's famous hunting knife,' she added with a grin that brought a grimace to the face of the raven-haired youth, 'that they're busy discussing Pellam and how to get rid of him. Mind you, I think they're wrong.'

'Wrong?' Hal couldn't believe it. 'He's an arrogant, self-conceited –'

'Talk about pots and kettles!' Brid laughed. 'He's no worse than you, but that doesn't mean he hasn't got a good side. We've been vainly looking a long time for your shinier side but we still believe there is one, don't we, Spar?'

Caspar enjoyed it when Brid brought Hal down to size but at the same time he had the discomfiting feeling she was flirting with his uncle in a way he couldn't fully understand.

Ceowulf didn't return until morning, which added more fuel to their suspicions and arguments. Cybillia kept quiet and looked away when the knight greeted them. Caspar wondered if she were jealous, but found the notion ridiculous: Ceowulf was much too old for her.

At last the day came when their ship was ready to sail. They led the horses through the cobbled streets and out towards the long jetty that jutted into Cocklebay's deep-water harbour. *Moonshadow* tugged arrogantly at her moorings like an impatient mare fresh and ready for a gallop. She was narrow-beamed with two tall masts and traditional Ceolothian lateen rigging, having gaffs hanging obliquely on the masts to hoist her triangular sails. With a sleek and shiny black hull and an elegant thrust to her shapely bow, she had a silver crescent embroidered in her white foresail. Firecracker immediately threw up his head and shrieked a challenge at the bright red masthead pennant, dancing sideways and thumping into Magpie who marched with serene calmness on a loose rein at Hal's side.

'Brid, I hope you've got enough of that wild lettuce and Ovissian camomile to knock that horse out again. We don't want another of his performances like last time.'

Brid patted her bosom where she kept her herb scrip and nodded reassuringly. 'I've given him plenty. It'll start to work in a few more minutes.'

'And don't forget I haven't forgiven you for slipping those herbs to me,' he added with his eyebrows raised in threat and then growled at his nephew, 'Nor your treachery.'

Pellam met them on the jetty, still looking coldly suspicious. 'Three rather fine horses, aren't they? Bit too smart for normal folks. No wonder you're wanting to slip through the Teeth. Need to throw some soul you've aggrieved off your trail, eh?'

Ceowulf growled in his throat, 'I'm going to drown this lad.'

'You're behaving like an irrational, over-possessive father,' Brid whispered in his ear. 'Give him a chance. He's Dionella's choice after all.'

'She's too young to make a choice.'

Brid snorted. 'Dionella must have been swamped with advances over the last year. Girls grow up quickly. You underrate her.'

'What is it about you, Brid, that makes me forget you're no older than Dionella?'

Brid smiled enigmatically. 'One's vision of the world comes not from how long one has stared at life but from how many angles.'

'That, I'll grant you,' Ceowulf smiled.

The horses had to be lowered into the forward hold on slings using a system of pulleys. The master refused to have them on deck, which was more usual, because of the expected weather and eddying undercurrents through the Teeth. Blocks and tackle were set up with the gaff as a fulcrum and the capstan, normally used for hoisting the anchor, was now employed to raise and lower the weight of the horses. Pawl bars were slotted into the circular head of the capstan and it took seven men to heave it round to raise Magpie's great weight. And after Firecracker had finally been coaxed into his stall, Brid stirred another generous helping of herbs into his feed while Caspar rubbed him down.

Silus showed the Belbidians to their two cabins, which were small and cramped but clean, and said that while the sea was calm they were welcome to stay on deck. Caspar liked this man very much more than the master of the *Queen of Tutivillus*. He had asked no more than a reasonable price for their passage, saying that friends of Katalin's were always welcome. He added boastfully that he'd make enough money from the pearls he was to harvest from the Diamond Seas.

Caspar found himself wide-eyed with wonder as the ship's crew related how they had ranged far across the world. The ship's galley was decorated with rows of small pointed skulls and large spiralling shells the size of Firecracker's head. The skulls, he was told, were from giant turtles from the other side of the ocean.

The only restriction Silus imposed on the group was that they stay away from the two deck-hands posted near the bow-sprit, where the ship carried a rack of harpoons. 'You don't need to worry,' he assured them. '*Moonshadow* has a fine hull and will withstand a great deal more than the rotted timbers of the *Queen of Tutivillus*. All the same, we want to be ready if that kraken stirs again.'

They spent a comfortable evening at the master's table with a select number of the crew and Ceowulf entertained them all with expansive stories of wyverns and bandits in the southern deserts. Caspar relaxed as he listened to the wonderful tales and, only because he had heard them before, did he notice how successfully the Caldean nobleman kept the conversation away from any prying questions about northern Belbidia. Ceowulf after all was a mercenary and once that sin was admitted it doused any other suspicions that there might be anything disagreeable about their voyage.

Silus in turn spoke at length about his journeys and ate a healthy plate of wheat pancakes and boiled eggs. At the end of the meal, Caspar's curiosity was roused as each sailor from the first mate down to the cabin boy took their eggshells and crushed them up. They were advised to do the same.

'Now why ever would we do that?' Hal asked.

'It's a superstition amongst sailors that a witch can cross the sea if you leave an eggshell whole for her to use as a coracle. If you crush the shell you protect yourself from spreading witchcraft.'

'Indeed,' Brid said coolly. 'The witch would have to be quite small, wouldn't you think?' She held up her half-eggshell between her fine-boned fingers.

'Most witches are small but they can make themselves any size they wish – but they still need an eggshell to cross the seas.'

'I've never heard anything so daft,' Brid laughed, 'but it's a wonderful tale.'

'We sailors are full of such yarns,' an Ophidian sailor admitted, 'though I've never seen a witch. Whenever I've gone ashore at any Belbidian port, they're always muttering on about devilry and witchcraft but we've not believed in such superstitions in Ophidia for hundreds of years. We're a great deal more civilized here in the south,' he informed them jovially.

Caspar was very relieved that these men didn't treat Brid with the same suspicions as any Belbidian would have done. Ceowulf had been right when he had said they wouldn't.

Several days into their voyage, Caspar began to relax, feeling certain that no monster had been riding in their wake. On Keridwen's advice, they had avoided any contact with the moonstone, which would have alerted any creature sensitive to its song of magic to their presence. He reasoned, therefore, that the savage spirits and dark beasts that sought him would soon lose their trail. He certainly hoped so.

They never strayed far from Ophidia's ragged northern coastline, which was comforting for Caspar – after his last voyage he never wanted to lose sight of land again. They made good time towards the narrow straits that would take them out of the sheltered waters of the Caballan Sea and into uncharted oceans. As they neared the straits, the southern shores of Belbidia were again drawing distinctly close.

'All passengers below deck!' The cry went up around the ship.

'They can't possibly think there's a problem,' Hal objected, looking at the clear skies.

'The water's changed colour,' Caspar pointed out. 'And there's a different smell in the air.'

A subtle change in the wind brought up a cool fine spray into Caspar's face. Apart from that he didn't notice anything to warrant the activity of the sailors as they scaled the ratlines and began to take a reef in the foot of the sails. But gradually the waters darkened and the clear blue sea became opaque, boiling foam skating across its surface.

Silus took the ship's wheel and set his face in hard determination.

'All passengers below deck!' the first mate ordered more irritably this time and Hal and Caspar reluctantly followed Cybillia, Brid and Ceowulf who had been immediately more obliging.

'I'm going to sit with the horses,' Caspar explained and Hal nodded, clipping his heels as he followed on his tail. Brid was already in the livestock hold.

'I thought you would be with the others,' Hal remarked.

'Well, you thought wrong. They looked as though they would be happy to be left alone for a while. Cybillia's not so upset about her cheek now and, besides, those two are good for each other.'

Hal pursed his lips doubtfully and slumped down into the hay. Taking a reed of straw, he chewed at it thoughtfully, never once taking his eyes off Brid as she fussed over the horses. They whickered appreciatively at her attentions.

The three Torra Altans resigned themselves to the idle hours below, invariably worrying over how Torra Alta fared against the onslaught of the Vaalakans. Then suddenly the boat reared and lurched violently to the larboard. Caspar was flung against the stall boarding, his face buried deep in the straw. Hal's body pinned him into the dry, sweet, breathless atmosphere and he pulled himself up with difficulty, hanging on to a post as the ship rolled upright.

Firecracker was on his side but luckily was doped enough not to do himself much damage despite the sound of the other two horses kicking and squealing as if someone were trying to murder them. The terrifying lurching eased and, at least for the moment, they sailed on more comfortably. Caspar felt unspeakably sick and dizzy, so dizzy that it seemed as if the whole ship were spinning. Hal looked grim and Brid was stumbling like a drunkard, as she worked her way towards the horses to comfort them. Firecracker remained on his side, which Caspar thought was probably the safest place for him. Trog was already retching up into a pile of straw, whimpering feebly.

The sickening motion seemed to last an eternity, by which time Caspar thought he would rather die than suffer anymore. His head was still spinning when finally he realized that the ship was sailing calmly forward again. He steadied Firecracker's head as the horse heaved himself up onto tottering legs, looking as precarious as a newborn foal. The other two animals had suffered a few minor grazes and Brid, who seemed to be keeping remarkably steady on her feet, was already checking them over.

'You two go up on deck,' she suggested. 'I'll see to the animals. A bit of fresh air will clear your heads.'

Remarkably, the deck looked much as they had left it. The sailors had done a good job of battening down the hatches and securing any loose cargo. The fresh air and the cooling salt spray that stung Caspar's cheeks cleared his head and made him feel glad to be alive. Cybillia, looking for all the world as though she had just fainted, was swaying in Ceowulf's arms.

A sailor beamed at them. 'Looking a bit green around the gills, eh, landlubbers?'

Caspar grinned back sheepishly.

'Well, not to worry. We're through the whirlpools now. By nightfall we'll hit the open seas of the mother ocean herself.'

Caspar breathed in deep lungfuls and hugged himself, suddenly becoming aware of the bruises he seemed to have developed over every inch of his body. He moved towards the bulwark at the edge of the ship and clung to the gunwale for support, happy to look down at the white rearing waves that curled away from the bow. He felt his mind drift down into the waves, exploring the rise of the bubbles and listening to the rhythmical swish of the waters being cut by the bow. His thoughts took him home. He imagined that he and his father were looking over Torra Alta's battlements down into the white waters of the Silversalmon far below. He imagined he was looking down at the white waters as they churned around fallen boulders and jagged rocks . . .

Rocks!

'Rocks!' he warned, his voice like the thin cry of a bird. 'Rocks!' he yelled again more loudly. 'Look out! Look out!'

The water had turned green and boiled around the head of an angry black shape lurking barely a fathom beneath the surface waves. Pellam's tight face was instantly behind him and after one brief sweep of his eyes over the water, he spun on his heels.

'Hard-a-larboard, hard-a-larboard,' he yelled. 'Rocks, fine on the starboard bow.' He pointed excitedly forward and slightly to starboard of the bowsprit.

Caspar found himself flung backwards as *Moonshadow* lurched away from him, turning her nose across the buffeting waves, bucking and dancing like an unbroken filly.

'There aren't any rocks here,' Silus bellowed angrily across the deck as he righted the helm. 'Pellam, what did you see?'

'It was big and black below the surface,' the young man replied. 'We barely missed it.'

There was a sudden hush over the crew as an all too perceptible change could be heard in the rhythmical groaning of the ship's timbers. *Moonshadow* was like a living being, Caspar thought, listening to her sighing, breathing and moaning with her aches and efforts. But now she creaked and strained in a drawn-out cry without pause for her usual breath between waves.

Caspar knew it and the crew knew it. They were rising, the whole ship was rising at an alarming rate on the back of a vast wave. Then suddenly Caspar's stomach was left in mid-air as they smacked back down again, all noise drowned out by a monumental crash. The ship slapped down, sending up sheets of white water from her bows and washing over the deck. Caspar clung to the gunwale with his fingernails, unable to breathe as freezing white water gushed over him. Suddenly he was released, gasping and choking, into the air.

Armed with spears and harpoons, the crew was already rimming the deck. Pellam was right forward on the bow, one hand gripping a spear while the other looped securely around a rope attached to the bowsprit. He pulled back his arm and, with a yell of effort, thrust his spear into the waves. A black hump rose out of the sea and curled away over to starboard. A tight expectancy spread through the crew as they watched and waited, their arms raised in readiness to hurl their weapons. It was the sound of sobbing that finally broke the silence.

Caspar dragged his eyes away from the threatening sea to look at Cybillia wrapped in Ceowulf's arms. She was crying softly. Caspar didn't blame her. He almost felt like crying himself.

The noise seemed to break the tension of the sailors. They eased back from the edge of the ship and looked at each other with wide stunned eyes.

'Good work. Good fast work, Pellam,' the master shouted enthusiastically across the deck. The young man arrogantly flicked his head back but Caspar caught the look of shy gratitude on the young Ophidian's face as he was slapped and thumped appreciatively by many of his shipmates. He gave them a mock bow and finally turned red with embarrassment at their cheers.

The men gathered back on the lower decks, humming with excitement and speculating on the nature of the predator that had attacked the ship. There were claims of a hundred different kinds from big whales to giant turtles to squid. Silus refused to pronounce a verdict. Just so long as the creature had gone that was all that mattered.

'Let's get this place shipshape, again,' he ordered.

Once the men had returned to their habitual bustle of activity, Caspar found Brid by his side. 'The horses are fine,' she muttered before he could ask about them. She looked surprisingly worried.

'What's the matter?' he asked.

'It sounds different.'

'What sounds different?' Hal lurched towards them, gripping ropes and halyards on his way to steady himself against the rolling sea. Caspar decided that no Torra Altan would happily make a good sailor.

'Shh! Just listen.' Brid waved them down and tilted her head slightly, pushing back her coppery hair to reveal a neat ear. Trog comically tilted his head to the same angle with one ear pricked alertly forward. The animal had an intelligent expression and an acute awareness of his mistress's emotions.

Caspar listened too. Men shouting, sheets being drawn through blocks, a sail flapping, the rush of the sea against the vessel's timbers, the beat of the spray, his own breathing, the groan of the ship as she climbed the crest of each wave and arched over its peak to crash down into the next trough. But there was also a new sound; a whining hum that came from the ship's timbers interspersed with creaks and groans and punctuated by sharp cracks. The sailors noticed it too and Master Silus took purposeful strides towards the foremast.

The Ceolothian frowned and put his hand against the broad ash timbers. 'We can't put to shore until we're round the point and reach Porta d'Oc so we'd best have a couple of men aloft here to fish-plate this mast.'

Caspar found he could not take his eyes off the mast. He watched the men strap two strips of wood to the mast about thirty feet above the deck where they had discovered a crack in the old timber. As they worked, the ominous creaking gradually eased until only the occasional large wave caused the wood to snap or jar. Everyone breathed more easily and

Caspar prayed it wasn't too far until they rounded the point.

The coastlines to either side were receding and had dimmed to soft grey, merging with the clouds on the horizon as the straits widened. And at last they sailed out into the great dark depths of the ocean. Though there was no increase in the chop of the waves that scuffed the surface of the sea, there was a sizeable difference in the mountainous roll of the swell. Fearing to lose sight of the land, Caspar strained to keep his eyes on Ophidia's west coast.

Brid and Cybillia sat on the foredeck, absent-mindedly scanning the waters, lost in quiet conversation. Caspar smiled at Brid. In her presence he could think of little else except her wondrous beauty and vibrant energy, though he did manage to muse on how well Cybillia was coping with the voyage. She had been so overbearing, petulant and squeamish when they had first escorted her from her father's manor to Belbidia's capital. She was changing and for the better.

His muscles stiffened as he heard two sailors grumbling about the girls. 'Women on board and there's always trouble. One's too pretty and the other . . . ! God, what a face! She ought to be ashamed to step out into the daylight.'

Hal had also heard the conversation and the two youths hurled themselves towards the grouching men but they were beaten to the attack by Pellam. Without a moment's hesitation, Dionella's chosen man plunged his fist into the teeth of the pot-bellied sailor who had insulted Cybillia. The flaxen-haired girl was on her feet and for a moment her cheeks puffed up with rage, but then shame overcame her. Her hand slapped to her cheek, fearful of further degradation. Brid pulled at the girl's arm and fixed her straight in the eye.

'You have nothing to be ashamed of.'

Ceowulf looked like a goaded bull, his face blotched with thunderous anger. He reached for his sword but hesitated and watched as Pellam snagged his arm round the throat of the cantankerous sailor. Taking a fistful of hair in his furious hands, Pellam jerked the man's head round to face Cybillia. 'Apologize to the lady,' the Ophidian barked.

For a young man not yet thickened out with the muscles of manhood, Pellam's determined spirit and cool words impressed Caspar.

Silus strode into their midst and broke up the furore before the offending sailor managed to spit a single word of apology in Cybillia's direction. 'Let him go, Pellam.' He turned and thrust his ruddy, bearded face up against the sailor's. 'You'll apologize without any threat, isn't that right, mariner?'

The surly man wiped the back of his mouth across his sleeve and raised his eyes to the ship's master. 'We shouldn't have women on board ship. They always bring trouble.'

'That was not an apology.'

Surprisingly Cybillia broke the thunderous silence. 'I don't need an apology from him. The man was frightened by the creaking mast. He's looking for a scapegoat, someone to blame his fears on, and just because I'm scarred and don't look like I can hit back, he's chosen me. He doesn't need to worry; the marks aren't contagious. They were done to me by Vaalakan barbarians who also chose to pick on someone defenceless.' She turned her face so that the man stared right at the ugly keloid knots that stitched the sign of the pentagram into her cheek. 'A few scratches do not change who I am though.'

Caspar thought on her words and decided that in one way she was wrong. She was definitely a stronger, more self-reliant person now than before she had suffered so brutally at the hands of the Vaalakans.

'Please, Master Silus, think nothing more of it. And send these men back to their work,' she said generously.

Ceowulf smiled proudly at the Jotunn noblewoman and Brid winked at the girl. 'Well done, Cybillia,' she praised as the sailors went back to their duties.

'Well, I wasn't going to invite further interest in my cheek by making a fuss,' she said plainly.

'We'll heal it,' Brid whispered, 'just as soon as I have the right herbs, I promise.'

Pellam's anger was not so easily quelled and he flexed his

knuckles in the palms of his hands. Grinding his jaw, he directed black looks towards his pot-bellied companion. His hair drifted across his eyes in the stiff breeze and freezing spray blew up to wet his cheeks but he didn't seem to notice.

'I would have made him apologize. He should have apologized loud and clear,' he muttered and turned towards Cybillia. 'I'm sorry he said those things. And a few scars doesn't alter the fact you're a beautiful young woman, if you'll forgive me for saying so.'

Cybillia was lost for words, the effort of overcoming her shame and keeping her dignity in front of the sailors had taken its toll on her emotions.

Ceowulf stepped forward to give her support. 'That was well said and well done, Pellam. We thank you for your honourable conduct.'

Pellam lifted one side of his mouth into half a smile. 'Yeah, well, he had no right to speak to any girl like that, no right at all.'

Later that evening as the sea pitched and the hull thumped down on the back of the waves, they gathered in a secluded corner of the galley. Silus strode over to them and drew up a bench.

The bearded seafarer coughed into his tankard as if about to speak and then sucked at his drink again. He didn't bother to wipe the froth from his moustache as he finally stumbled over his words. 'You see, we travel the broad oceans and it takes tough men to venture so far through pirate waters and high seas. And when you're short on truly tough men you need rough men who are the next best thing in these conditions. But rough men have few manners and I'm truly sorry for what that sailor said to the lady today.'

'Think nothing of it,' Cybillia muttered, catching hold of her cup as it slid across the table to the rhythm of the rocking sea.

'I'm sorry I stopped Pellam from laying him flat. Pellam might only be a light, wiry chap but he's very determined and that sort of thing gets him upset. You see, his father lost his hand many years back and it's made him sensitive. Because he lost his hand, he lost his job and it took him a long time to earn enough money to buy his own lobster boat. Pellam took a lot of stick about his father's injury and it's probably why he's got such an understanding with Katalin's daughter.'

When the master left, Brid looked thoughtfully at Ceowulf. 'Your Dionella's not completely blinded by Pellam's roguish charm then?'

The knight levelled his steady dark eyes at her and shrugged. 'It doesn't hurt to be cautious and I was worried because she's so young, but perhaps I should have listened to you. As a young maiden yourself, you probably had more understanding of what Dionella sees in him.'

'Not necessarily,' Brid said, raising her voice so she could be heard above the roar from the sea. 'Morrigwen always told me never to advise people on matters of the heart but she also said never judge a young relationship through the eyes of an old head. She says it's impossible to tell for sure who is right for whom. Everyone sees different things in different people and the age of the lovers has nothing to do with the suitability of their choice. Someone is old enough to fall in love when they fall in love.'

The galley had emptied of sailors and their thin urgent cries above deck were intermittently swept away in the raging wind. Ceowulf kept on talking, occasionally casting anxious looks at Cybillia's tight face. He didn't tell them not to worry but instead tried to distract them by telling the story of a prince, who claimed he owned the fastest horse in the desert – but no one was listening. All ears craned for the noise above deck.

A thunderous crack, like the sound of a giant's backbone being snapped in two, cut through the roar of the sea and shuddered through the ship. The rocking platform of boards beneath their feet suddenly dived away to starboard and the table swung on its rope hangings. Hal caught hold of Brid, and Ceowulf wrapped Cybillia tightly in his grasp to stop her body from being flung to the far side of the galley. Caspar grabbed at an upright beam as Hal shouted in Brid's ear, 'Go and see to the horses while Spar and I take a look outside.'

Caspar didn't argue with his uncle. He knew Brid would settle the animals better than anyone and he had a cold feeling rising up through his bones. Like Hal, he needed to see what was happening above deck.

The two Torra Altan youths struggled towards the narrow companionway that led directly on to the deck and flung back the hatch. Caspar's breath was swept away in the wind and his face was slapped by a rush of biting water. A wash of white water arched over the bow and he grappled for a hold on the sloping deck. Storm lanterns flickered on deck and the moon cast just enough light to see by. The ship was no longer cutting forward through the storm but lay floundering on her side at the weather's mercy. The mast had snapped and the top now hung folded back, dropping the gaff and sail into the sea. The sail dragged heavily in the water, and the waves pounded the gaff against the hull's timbers. It was only moments before the first of the timbers gave. The drag of the sail swung the ship broadside to the weather and water rushed over the tilted deck. Hal shoved Caspar from behind.

'Get forward. There must be something we can do.'

Caspar shouldered determinedly into the spray-soaked storm as Hal yelled at him to hurry.

Three men were already hacking at the base of the mast and Pellam was chopping at the ropes on the tack of the sail where it was secured to the bowsprit. The front tack was quickly freed and it looked as if the foresail would soon be loose but the wind had knotted the flailing ends of the ropes high up on the mast. All watched and waited with bated breath for the ropes to pull free, but they were stuck fast. The men hacking at the great trunk of mast redoubled their efforts but it was clear it would take too long to chop through. Caspar looked again at the entangled rigging thirty foot above his head. The ropes would have to be cut free. He took an uncertain look at the ocean's angry black waters. How long would they survive in that? Minutes? He doubted it.

'Get up aloft,' Master Silus yelled at two of his crew, nodding at two hatchets lying amongst the ship's tools. 'Get aloft and cut the sail free.'

They hesitated.

Before anyone could protest, Hal lunged straight for a hatchet, shoved it in his belt and hauled himself against the force of the wind towards the mast. Caspar struggled after him with the second hatchet. He wasn't afraid of climbing the mast. It was only thirty feet, nothing to a Torra Altan. He grabbed for a halyard that spiralled the thick beam of the mast.

The ship yawed over at a precarious angle. Caspar told himself that, if it weren't for the wind and the spray, the climb would only be like slithering out along the smooth branch of a beech tree. He wrapped his legs around the beam and dragged himself forward with his arms, hooking into the halyards that threaded around the mast. The ship rolled and pitched and he felt as if he were clinging to the arm of a giant who was trying to shake him off. Breathing was hard as the wind sucked away his breath and the sea polished his face with abrasive salt. He did his best to tuck his head down to shelter behind the mast. There was little space for a foothold and he had to rely on the strength in his arms to pull himself up from one knot of rope to the next.

Hal missed his grip once and slithered a foot down the mast until his feet connected with Caspar's tensed hands. The younger boy shoved him forward. 'Get up there, Hal. We've got to make it.' But he doubted that his shout carried above the screaming wind. He daren't look down – not because of the height but because of the lashing waves beneath his feet. Caspar had no trust in the sea. The ship bucked and lurched hard over as a wave smashed sideways against the hull. He felt his legs flick away from the mast and his body snapped taut, torn between the pull of the wind and his own desperate grip as he clung on fervently. He kicked back and hooked an ankle round the post, breathing hard.

'Spar,' Hal's worried cries battled through the wind. 'Are you all right?'

'Keep going,' Caspar yelled back by way of reply.

Another minute saw them nearly there. Where the wood was broken away, jagged splinters knifed out into the dark. At least the luminescence of the moon reflecting off the storming white waves that bucked around the black shape of the hull gave them enough light to see by. Caspar wriggled round beneath Hal and braced himself. To use the hatchet he would have to let go of the mast with one arm.

The mast dipped towards the sea, again soaking them in a curtain of white, bitingly cold spray. Another acre of sail was swamped beneath the waters, lurking like some huge ghostly ray, its bat-like wings rippling beneath the surface of the waves.

Caspar curled his ankle around a length of rope, did the same with his left wrist and finally freed his right hand from its grip. The handle of the hatchet stuffed into his belt was wet and slippery and he had difficulty fumbling for it but at last he had it in his hand. Hal was sawing away with his knife at the taut ropes that still secured the top, trailing section of the foresail to the ship. As Caspar hacked furiously amongst the broken timbers, one by one the shrouds catapulted away.

The sail released its grip on the ship in a sudden rush. Like a mighty tree felled in a gale, the remaining broken timbers smashed onto the deck below and then, pulled by their sail-bound tethers, slipped overboard into the sea. The white sheet of the sail swirled downwards. Everything happened so quickly that Caspar didn't have time to think. The ship snapped upright and his hands lost their grip on the slippery timber. Upside down, he saw the hatchet slip from his fingers and felt himself falling fast only to be jarred to a halt as something bit into his ankle.

The wind whipped him like a rag doll and he tumbled and smashed into the mast and then the rope jerked out another length and he found himself hurtling downwards. A buffeting wave smacked into the beam of the ship and, as *Moonshadow* yawed over, Caspar found himself flung out sideways. The ship pitched again and he was jerked beyond the gunwale and over the side, dangling helplessly above the waves.

Frantically he fought to pull himself upright as he was

slapped back and forth, cruelly aware of the tongues of water greedily lapping towards him and the black bottomless belly of the sea calling for his sacrifice. He bounced once against the hull's planking before he felt the cold touch of the water sweep over his head. White bubbles churned around his face. He couldn't breathe. For a split second he was aware of two huge eyes, striking out from a vast black face, then a sudden gash of teeth appeared in the murky depths. A solid grip crushed his ankle and he was spluttering for air as he was hauled upside down towards the deck.

The first thing he saw was Pellam's face as the young man dragged him onto the deck and fell on his chest to pump any water from his lungs. Hal tumbled down the last dozen feet of the mast and scrabbled towards his nephew, flinging crewmen aside in a frantic effort to reach his kinsman.

'Spar, you idiot! Are you all right?'

Smarting from grazes where he had been scuffed against the hull, Caspar looked up with startled eyes into his kinsman's face. Too tired to speak, he merely raised his hand, and Hal gripped it firmly. He was carried below decks where the men pressed round him, jostling and shouting and offering their thanks and praise.

Silus ushered them out. 'Man the pumps. We might be upright now but we've taken on tons of water. We're just going to have to ride this storm as it takes us.'

Caspar grinned at Pellam. 'Thanks.'

'You were like trying to catch a slippery fish for a moment but, for a landlubber, you were damn brave and I couldn't let you go.'

There was nothing to do but wait for dawn and take turns manning the pumps that spat water from the bilge back over the side. Without its foresail, the ship drifted and crabbed with the current though Silus fought with the helm to keep a rough course that would take them round the point.

Chapter 8

Dawn brought a happier view of the world. Caspar ignored the gashed deck and the ravaged remains of the foremast and fixed his gaze on the white cliffs no more than a few hundred yards to the east. He beamed at a sloping blue-green swathe of marram grass that dipped towards the brightly coloured houses of Porta d'Oc.

Silus, looking several years older, still staggered at the helm. Some of the crew worked now with heavy buckets to supplement the pumps and the remaining sail strained to drive the weight of the black-hulled ship through the swell.

With the help of several rowing boats, which put to sea at the sight of the stricken vessel, they were towed into the port and made fast alongside the jetty. The weary passengers scrambled ashore and watched as the horses were unloaded. They led the sweated beasts inland, their heads hanging low between their knees. Only Trog looked none the worse for the ordeal.

'I would like to have been able to take you to the Farthest Isles as you requested,' the old Ceolothian sea-dog muttered. 'Especially after the bravery of these two lads here. I feel right bad that it was you what went aloft and not my men. Those two won't be on board when we put to sea again, I can tell you. But I can't get you to the Farthest Isles since *Moonshadow*'s not going nowhere until I've found her a new mast. But what I can do is ask about for a reliable skipper who'll take you the last few miles.'

Caspar's heart sank. He really didn't want to put to sea again. But as Silus waved his arm westward to where the sharp lines of a mountainous isle reared out of the sea he was a little more comforted.

'So it's not that far?' he asked hopefully.

'No, not more than ten miles. Pellam!' *Moonshadow*'s master spun on his heel to address the young Ophidian. 'I'm going to keep you out of trouble while we're in port. You can go and find a ship that'll take our friends over to the Farthest Isles.'

Pellam nodded. 'That won't be hard.'

He was back within the hour. 'I've found a local who says he'll take you in three days' time. The weather's not going to settle for a while but after that, he assures me that, by the smell of the wind, it'll clear. He's only got a small boat and he doesn't want to risk the winter storms.'

The moment they were alone Brid turned to her companions, a look of concern on her face, 'If we wait three days here in Porta d'Oc, we'll only have three days on the Farthest Isles before the winter solstice.'

When he wasn't working on the repairs to *Moonshadow*, Pellam offered to guide them around Porta d'Oc. The five Belbidians anxiously took up his offer as it was far more convenient to have a native with them rather than struggle to make their Belbidian tongue understood. They repaid him with riding lessons on Magpie.

The youth was strong and determined and what he lacked in balance and feel he made up for in determination.

'I'm really quite good now,' he declared on their last day in the port.

Ceowulf laughed at him. 'You'll only be good when you can stay on the back of Cracker.'

'It can't be so hard if Spar can manage him,' Pellam cockily retorted. 'He's only little.'

Refusing to hear the insult, Caspar grinned knowingly and was tempted to let the man try before deciding it was too cruel. Pellam didn't know the first thing about horses; he had no idea how difficult a feisty stallion could be. Magpie was a sweet-natured animal and never protested if she were kicked or jabbed with awkward movements. She had given the man a false belief in his new-found skills.

'I think you'd need a few more days' practice,' Ceowulf calmly assured the man.

'When I get back from our voyage I'll buy me an animal like Cracker,' he boasted, 'then I'll show you I can ride.'

'He'd cost more than a lobster boat,' Caspar informed him and instantly regretted his words.

Pellam's eyes narrowed. 'Where did you get him from then? You make strange friends for Katalin, turning up with princely animals and curious weapons. I guess the old free-lance gave them to you. Battle trophies? Or taken from your liege-lord's manor perhaps?' he taunted.

Hal was reaching for the hilt of his sword at the insult but Ceowulf stepped in front of him and smiled coolly at the Ophidian. 'Let's just say they're battle trophies, and leave it at that,' he replied firmly and deftly changed the subject. 'Well, is that boat ready for us tomorrow?'

Pellam nodded. 'Sure and I'm coming with you. I've been given a few days' leave and you landlubbers can be a nuisance on board ship so I thought I'd give the skipper a fighting chance.'

Ceowulf didn't think it was a good idea but he couldn't see how they could turn down the offer without arousing suspicion.

Brid and Cybillia had kept themselves quietly to themselves over the last three days, staying in their room within the tavern. On the first day after a short search inland, Brid had found the required Ophidian pennywort and the rarer red-stemmed dragonfire to heal Cybillia's scars. She had been preparing and applying the salves at regular intervals ever since. Sometimes Caspar could hear the Jotunn noblewoman sobbing at night from the pain of the burning herbs. She wasn't allowed to expose the raw swelling to sunlight but she wouldn't even come out to eat with them so Brid kept her company in the room.

The priestess was displeased when she heard that Pellam

was joining their party but agreed that they couldn't really turn him down. 'He's only looking for adventure and probably wants to learn more about Ceowulf and his curious connection with Katalin.' She shrugged. 'Besides, he'll not betray us because of Ceowulf's connection with Dionella's mother. He won't want her dragged into anything.'

'I just wish he weren't so damn arrogant,' Hal complained.

Brid laughed and Ceowulf gave the raven-haired youth an indulgent smile.

'Have you ever looked in a mirror?' he asked, cocking one eyebrow at the youth.

Hal scowled.

Early the next morning they followed Pellam down towards the quay where a small red ketch sulked at its moorings. It was a cold day with a light breeze blowing down from the north but at least the sea was a peaceful grey-blue. Gone were the threatening, choppy white horses whose foaming crests had broken with the stormy waves during the three days of their sojourn.

The voyage to the Farthest Isles was an uneventful one. To the west as they approached, lazing on the ocean swell, lay a cluster of small flat-topped islands with one large central island dominating their midst. A volcanic core thrust up at its centre to give the island its imposing height and the shores were henged with pillars of basalt standing shoulder to shoulder like an army of petrified giants. Above the cliffs, green hills merged back into heathered moors and sparsely vegetated crags. There was no beach nor any sign of a harbour and Caspar wondered where they could land.

'You really must be looking for treasure,' Pellam muttered.

'Well, that's what we said,' Caspar retorted. 'How do we get onto this island anyway?'

His question was soon answered as they sailed close up against the bold cliffs and around to the west shore. Here, the land sloped more gently into the water and a channel, cut into the island, formed a sheltered bay. The ketch glided gracefully up alongside a rickety old jetty, its timbers rotted and blackened. Pellam leapt nimbly ashore, grasping a length of rope that he looped over a mooring post while the skipper organized a plank for the Belbidians to disembark.

He had agreed to sit at anchor for a few days so long as he was paid for his time, explaining that he would do some fishing just out of the harbour. He suggested that they signal him from the high ground when they wanted to return.

Brid said they would be a few days, and the schooner owner looked pleased. It was going to be a few days of easy work for him.

'How do you know we'll only be three days?' Hal queried as they gingerly negotiated the slippery jetty, crackling over seaweed and worrying over the strength of the structure. Ceowulf kept a tight grip on Cybillia and Caspar looked warily around for any sign of sand vipers though he knew they must be safe on the shingle.

'We can't be any longer than that, because it's the shortest day of the year in three days' time.'

They looked around at the bleak landscape. There was scarcely a tree with only coarse grasses and crisp red heathers lying between fallen boulders that had crashed down from the sides of the central scarp. Apart from the constant shrieks of gulls and the soundless splashes of elegant cormorants plunging into the water, there wasn't a single sign of life. The Belbidians all looked to Brid.

She raised her hands defensively. 'Well, I don't know this place any better than you do. We'll just have to look.'

They spent the morning skirting the perimeter of the island and found nothing of note except for a track that led up from another bay towards the central volcanic mount. 'That has to be the way,' Brid decided.

They climbed with renewed vigour up the steep incline. Caspar felt a strange sense of freedom at moving upwards; he liked the heights. The further they climbed the more they had to wait for Cybillia, who was beginning to tire. Caspar curiously studied Pellam's face as they waited. He had been uncharacteristically silent for some time and his eyes were brightly alert, eagerly searching the slopes ahead. He really does think we're looking for treasure, Caspar thought and smiled inwardly when Pellam, much to Hal's scowling annoyance, turned to Ceowulf, who he evidently thought was in charge.

'Are there any clues about where to look?'

'Not very complete ones,' the knight freely admitted.

Brid made a face at his candour but Caspar felt quite unperturbed. There seemed to be no harm in pretending that they were looking for treasure.

Brid studied Pellam's face carefully for a few minutes and then shrugged as if dismissing her fears. 'No, not very complete ones,' she echoed and flung a black look at Hal as if blaming him for this defect in their plan. 'We're looking for a henge.'

'A henge?' Pellam had evidently never heard the word.

'A circle of standing stones.'

The Ophidian made a face. 'That's a bit sinister, isn't it?'

'Who cares if it means treasure?' Ceowulf retorted, affecting the callous tone of a mercenary.

Pellam nodded. 'Yeah, who cares?'

Hal saw it first. He had marched impatiently ahead and had come to a sudden halt fifty paces in front of them where the track curled away behind a fold in the rock's strata. Seeing his kinsman reaching for his sword, Caspar sprinted forward to shoulder him.

As he approached the bend of the road, he too stopped. The path led directly into the steep face of the mountain and an enormous effigy of a bull's head, carved from the solid rock, stared out at them. The giant horns must have been twenty foot across. The track led straight to its open mouth and disappeared into its black shadow.

The others drew level and gasped at the size of the statue. 'Father would like that,' Cybillia murmured mostly to herself, reminding Caspar of Baron Bullback's pride in his vast oxen herds. Pagan idol or not, the bull's head would have greatly pleased the Baron of Jotunn. Ceowulf winced a little as he drew his sword. His right shoulder evidently still pained him and he eased it several times through its full range of move-ment. Caspar bent and strung his bow and tentatively they crept forward.

'I feel a bit naked without a weapon,' Pellam complained, obviously rather shocked by the sudden aptitude of his new-found friends to defend themselves.

'You've got eyes and ears,' Brid whispered pragmatically. 'That'll do.'

They warily approached the huge statue and peered through its open mouth into the dark.

'There's a light at the end,' Caspar whispered, though his voice carried into the cave and echoed raucously back at them. 'It looks like some sort of short cut through the rock.'

There was an unnatural quiet as they tiptoed through the tunnel and Cybillia clung tightly to the Caldean knight. Plunged into darkness, Caspar felt his senses sharpen and his ears prick as a stone tinkled from the roof. He felt very uneasy.

'The place might be deserted.' Brid's soft voice cut through the silence, as they emerged into the cool light beyond. A fertile valley opened up before them, held in the bowl of rock formed by the crater of an extinct volcano. Its grassy slopes were sheltered from the wind by the surrounding wall of basalt.

'No, these paths are used frequently,' Hal corrected her, nodding towards the beaten path at their feet.

'I suppose you're right.'

A red-crested eagle launched into the sky above their heads, spiralling upwards on a rising thermal and skimming the cliff face. Caspar felt certain it was watching them. They crept forward a short distance to where the track began to tilt down-wards, giving them a sweeping view of the sheltered valley. Positioned proudly in the centre of the valley floor, twenty-one standing stones marked out the perimeter of a ritualistic circle.

Brid smiled in deep satisfaction. 'We needn't have worried. This is going to be easy after all.'

'Ever the optimist!' Ceowulf looked at her with the wary eyes of a long-lived mercenary. Keeping his oiled sword comfortably balanced in his right hand, he signalled to the others to stay behind him, though Hal ignored the gesture and pointedly paced level with the knight.

'There's no one about. Why do you suppose there's anyone dangerous here?' Pellam asked.

'Because of that great big bull's head. It's been well-cared for, no lichen or moss clinging to the stone, so clearly someone is still worshipping it. No idol worshipper will welcome strangers for fear of persecution, so we'd best be wary,' Ceowulf counselled as they crept forward. He was worried about their approach route. Surrounding the central circle of stones countless armies of boulders were scattered across the entire valley. Any number of people could be hidden behind the rocks.

Cybillia tugged at Ceowulf's sleeve. 'Won't we be safe with . . . ?' she dropped her voice and looked warily at Pellam who was walking a little apart from the rest of the group. His eyes were raised, watching the swoop of the eagle with fascination. When she was certain that Pellam couldn't hear her, she continued in a hushed whisper, 'We can't come to any harm if we're with Brid, surely.'

Hal looked at her. 'Of course you don't remember the Priory in Ovissia. Just because they are pagans doesn't mean they are under the benevolent guidance of the Great Mother.'

Brid looked pleased. 'Benevolent, Hal? Don't say you're softening.'

Pellam turned round. Seeing them all whispering, he gave them a curious look but said nothing.

A shriek that could have come from a banshee stopped them in their tracks.

'What the hell was that?' Pellam exclaimed.

Caspar instantly recognized the distorted sound. 'It's a horse. A very frightened horse.'

The deep wail of a haunting clarion echoed within the crater walls, bouncing from one outcrop of rock to the next. It was impossible to judge whether there was one horn or several. Caspar felt his flesh creep. Trog marched on elongated legs close to Brid, his hackles like stiff hog-hairs ridging his spine.

Ceowulf pushed Cybillia behind him as a long shadow betrayed someone's presence lurking behind a lichen-covered boulder. 'We do not intrude as enemies,' he declared in forceful tones.

'They might not understand you,' Brid reminded him. 'Pellam, can you repeat that in Ophidian?'

'What have I let myself in for?' he muttered, nodding and repeating Ceowulf's words in his own musical tongue.

Five figures stepped out onto the track. Cybillia gave a startled scream.

Four of them were masked in horse skulls and were draped in what looked like horse-hide cloaks. Beneath, they wore very little else despite the chill of the day. The fifth figure was very much taller. A bull's head with giant horns sat on his shoulders, imprisoning his head, and gold amulets clasped his arms, bright against his dark muscly skin. A black bull-hide hung over his back and a strip of leather covered his loins. His ribs and muscles were contoured with blue dye and looped chains of animal teeth necklaces adorned his body. But to Caspar's eyes it was the four figures beneath the horse skulls that were the most curious; they were women and he was shocked to see women so grotesquely dressed. Tall and slender with smooth skin, their taut naked muscles were defined with the same blue dye.

The man beneath the bull's head leapt forward, spreading his legs wide and crouching in an aggressive pose. He rattled his tooth necklaces at them and shook an ornate spear. For the first time Caspar realized that the spear rattled with miniature skulls. Sick to his stomach, he realized that they were the skulls of infants.

'The saints preserve us,' Pellam prayed.

'Hush,' Brid warned him. 'We'll be fine so long as we keep our heads.'

'I presume you mean that literally,' he replied with surprisingly wry humour for the circumstances.

'Tell him we have come to worship at the stones because it is the dying of the year,' she told the Ophidian calmly.

Pellam looked at her askance. 'Are you sure?'

She nodded reassuringly.

The man coughed and mumbled a few uncertain-sounding words in Ophidian. The central bull figure thumped out a solemn dance with his bare feet and at least two score men and women stepped out into view from behind several of the larger boulders. They moved onto the track and surrounded them.

'Ever had the feeling you're trapped?' Hal muttered in spirited defiance of their predicament. 'But tell me, Brid, why is it that it's always on one of your sacred days of the year that we seem to end up in trouble?'

She scowled at him and approached the bull shaman with fearless determination in her eyes. She touched her hand to her heart and raised her arms above her head, touching her fingers together to make the circular sign of the Mother. The bull shaman furiously rattled his bone spear and arched both his arms forwards to mimic the horns of a bull. He pawed the ground with a hooked leg to emphasize the threat. Suddenly he leapt aside and pointed them towards the henge. The unmasked followers closed in around them, jostling them forwards. It seemed pointless to resist so Caspar lowered his weapon and followed Brid's example as she walked towards the stone circle.

The islanders jeered and gabbled at them incomprehensibly, their voices harsh and the Ophidian they spoke far less tuneful than Pellam's. They were very much taller than their mainland countryman and had fair hair and pale skins, which was also unusual in Ophidia where most of the inhabitants were swarthy and broad. The women were curiously dressed in white gowns that swept down from one shoulder and left one breast exposed. Their nipples were daubed with red dye, and some were adorned with sunbursts and moons. The men went barebreasted with coarse leggings and leather thongs strapped to their lower limbs. Bold images of horns decorated their torsos and many were pierced with thin bones through the flesh of their pectoral muscles. These men clutched short broad-barbed spears whereas the others carried thin pipes that Ceowulf eyed suspiciously. Despite their extraordinary attire and gruesome decorations, the most noticeable thing about them was the lack of emotion on their faces: calm, sombre, without fear or even curiosity.

'These people must have been very isolated for many generations to develop such distinct tribal characteristics,' Brid ventured. Her face had filled with wondrous curiosity at the sight of the people and she showed none of the anxious fear that Caspar knew was etched into the taut lines of his own face.

They were guided towards the central standing stones and Caspar realized how the whole valley was very much larger than it had at first appeared. The stones, which had seemed dwarfed by the basalt cliffs circling the crater, towered at least twenty feet above their heads and he wondered at the engineering that had enabled the stones to be manoeuvred into place. Most curiously they appeared to be of black granite rather than the dark brown basalt of the surrounding landscape. It amazed his sense of logic; the stones must have been imported from somewhere else – which meant from across the sea.

A broad flat slab of rock was placed centrally to the stones and it was covered in ominous dark brown stains that could be nothing other than old dried blood. Wicker hurdles were piled up just beyond the perimeter of the ring and Caspar frowned at them.

'I should think they block the spaces between the standing stones to create an enclosed arena within the circle,' Brid suggested.

Caspar swallowed hard. He was feeling very uncomfortable. The equine shriek squealed through the air again and a light-boned animal with a flowing mane and tail was led out from behind a tumble of giant fallen boulders. She was a magnificent cream almost the colour of polished silver though much of her coat was now flecked with red; her mane and tail were knotted with red ribbons and bells. She wore no bridle but was controlled like a bull by means of a ring through her nose.

As the young horse was dragged into the centre of the henge, the hurdles were moved into place, just as Brid had anticipated. The filly was let loose to buck and squeal, galloping round the inner perimeter of the ring with eyes wide and head held high. The hurdles were more than eight feet high and though the animal charged repeatedly at them, drawing blood on her velvet nose, it was impossible for her to break through. The five Belbidians and an astounded Pellam were ushered towards a boulder where an armed guard was placed around them and they were forced to watch the gruesome spectacle.

'Don't even think about trying to fight your way out of here,' Ceowulf growled at Hal. 'We don't know how many of these maniacs there are but those that haven't got spears are armed with blow pipes. I think you should bide your time and wait to see what's happening before you do anything rash.'

'I wasn't going to.'

'I'm not arguing, Hal,' the big mercenary asserted with authority. 'Just keep a check on your temper and keep that sword sheathed otherwise you'll see all of us dead for sure.'

By the time the islanders let the bull into the arena, the horse was sweated up and frightened. The man wearing the bull mask lunged into the circle and deftly struck his spear into the fleshy crest of muscle that arched over the bull's neck. The animal was not as big as a Jotunn oxen but was still a powerful beast, rippling with muscles. His heavy, coarse-browed skull was crowned by magnificent horns that curved forward into two needle-sharp points and he was white, almost as white as the filly. The ground seemed to shake as he heaved his heavy body into a cumbersome canter, horns lowered to charge the hurdles. A streak of red blood oozed from the spear wound.

The islanders stood on raised planks so they could reach over the barrier and they rattled their spears to goad the bull on. He tore strips of wood out of the hurdles and they stuck to his horns like so many pieces of a bird's nest. Beaten back by the stabbing points of spears, he soon tired of this mindless pursuit.

Caspar's throat was too tight to swallow. All he could be thankful for was that they had left their own horses behind and hadn't brought them here to smell the terror that filled the valley.

'Brid, what the hell is happening?' Hal demanded. 'What kind of paganism is this?'

The priestess was strangely dispassionate. 'It looks like some strange kind of bull cult that's taken over the ancient henge. This ritual appears to be some test to prove that the bull is superior to the horse.'

'How are they going to do that?' Cybillia asked naively.

Ceowulf lowered his voice. 'I don't think we need worry about that. It's just best not to look.'

Caspar was horrified. The two animals were not natural enemies and under normal circumstances would have grazed happily side by side but here they were both frightened and goaded. He didn't know at first how they had so scarred the shrieking filly until he saw a man with a long multi-corded whip. Knotted into the ends were metal spikes and he flayed the horse's hide with it whenever she came shakily to a halt. The flapping bright red ribbons and the jangling bells terrified the unbroken horse further. The bull, in turn, was goaded into anger with sharp spikes stabbed into its fleshy crest. Seeing nothing other than the shrieking horse, the bull lowered his horns and charged the animal.

Caspar couldn't look. He hoped the filly's end was swift but, judging by the squeals and shrieks, he hoped in vain. It was several minutes before only the heavy snorts of the bull filled the arena.

A low chant thumped out from the gathered islanders. No more than a whisper at first, it swelled into a heavy drone. The bull was prodded into a narrow pen and then hooked by a stick through the ring in its nose. Blood trickled from his nostrils and his big rolling eyes gaped from sagging eyelids. With lumbering strides, he ambled meekly after his keeper like some pet lamb.

'It's still three days till the shortest day of the year,' Brid muttered. 'This ceremony can only be a precursor to the main carnival. And if pitting a bull against a horse is their sport now, what in the Mother's name have they planned for the solstice?'

'Us?' Ceowulf asked with no surprise in his voice.

The priestess nodded.

The islanders had no intention of allowing their new-found, sacrificial victims to escape. They were held in a dark dank cave with a metal grid across its narrow entrance and it was guarded by five men armed with spears. Hal had not relinquished his sword without spitting many bitter words and, in the end, it was only Ceowulf's restraining arm and steady voice that convinced him they were far too outnumbered to fight their way out.

The shaman was delighted by the sword. He dragged his bull's skull off his head, revealing a disturbing face. One eye was a pale brown and the other white, with a scar cutting down from his forehead over the eyelid of the white eye and onto his cheek. The white tissue had been dramatically emphasized with blue woad outlining the scar and rimming the eye socket. He fell with delight on the sword, easing it out of its scabbard and peering closely at the runes. He gave the Belbidians a quick nervous glance, cradling the sword across both arms and carrying it to the central altar stone in the middle of the henge.

Hal ground his teeth and turned on Ceowulf. 'You cowardly fool, I could have killed him. If I'd got the leader, the rest would have quickly capitulated. I could have killed him. Now, he's got my sword.'

Ceowulf was unmoved by this outburst and merely put his heavy hands on the boy's shoulders, pressing him down. 'Just think about it, Hal. We're not going to get out of here without a plan and we've got two days to think of one.'

Pellam sat cross-legged on the floor, muttering away in Ophidian. A look of betrayal darkened his face. 'Why didn't you say it was dangerous? You're not hunting for treasure and you've been talking to Brid as if she were some sort of witch.'

'I am some sort of witch,' the Maiden patiently explained, which brought no comfort to the man. He looked at her not as if she were evil, as any Belbidian would have done, but as if she were mad. 'I'm a high priestess to the Great Mother, One of the Three, and She's not about to let me get sacrificed by a bunch of semi-possessed priests from a bull cult. As Ceowulf says, we have two days to think of a plan.'

'You expect me, an Ophidian, to believe in such nonsense?' Pellam looked at her edgily, his eyes clearly stating that he thought her deranged.

But they didn't have two days. They languished fretfully for that night and the next morning until the man with the white eye returned. He pointed at Brid and Cybillia, gabbling quickly in singing Ophidian. The Belbidians turned expectantly on Pellam.

'When the moon rises the two girls must enter the arena with their finest mare at the same time as a bull. The rest of us will go tomorrow with the stallions as this will be a greater contest for the bull at the dying of the year. I think Hal was right; he should have used his sword while he still had it.'

In the dark of the cave, Cybillia's face looked moonishly pallid with fear but Brid was still defiantly untroubled. 'It's just a lot of superstitious nonsense. At least I get the chance to sort this all out before you four make idiots of yourselves.'

She tucked herself away in the corner, muttering charms and crushing herbs in her palm while refusing to talk to the others. By the time the sun dipped away behind the crater walls, even Ceowulf had run out of reassuring platitudes.

When White Eye returned, he came with an armed guard. He swaggered as he walked, the runesword now tied to his back.

Brid stood up to greet him. 'I serve a far more powerful deity than you. Prepare to tremble, shaman, before my power.'

Caspar felt a tremor of awe run through his body as he sensed the power in her voice. The shaman may not have understood her words but he understood her tone and movements. He took a step back in surprise but then grinned and flicked his head towards his men.

Cybillia squealed as they gripped her arms and Ceowulf bristled with anger. Five knives were pressed to his throat. Brid, too, was roughly grasped and led away before the rest of the Belbidians and Pellam were dragged from the cave and bound tightly. They were hauled to the edge of the arena and up onto the stands.

First a wraith-white mare, goaded with the cruel whip and with a ring through her nose, was loosed into the arena. She was a beautiful animal, like Firecracker in form with long lean legs, a full deep chest, high arching neck and muscled quarters. She paced the arena, snorting and dancing, the silver bells jangling around her belly, but she showed none of the fear of the filly from the day before.

Despite his crushing fears for what might happen to Brid, Caspar couldn't help yearning for the magnificent horse. She plunged into a headlong gallop across the width of the arena, turning deftly away from the barriers at the very last minute with all the balanced grace and speed of action of a tournament horse. She's an Oriaxian purebred just like Cracker, he thought with amazement. For a brief second his fears for the two maidens were distracted and he felt a deep plunge of grief for this magnificent beast. Her death would be such a terrible waste.

A black bull snorted into the arena, crescents of turf kicking up from his cloven hooves. A spear hurtled across the arena and struck the bull in the flesh of its crest. Its back stiffened and, for a moment, it looked startled. Quivering, it let out a high-pitched squeal then lowered its horns and circled slowly about its huge back quarters, searching for its attacker. Short powerful legs flexed beneath its solid body and it tore at the ground with its cloven hooves. In response the mare reared up and flayed the air with her pale hooves, more in defiance than in anger, her jangling bells frustrating and startling the bull.

The priests began a low murmuring chant as Brid and

Cybillia were shoved roughly into the arena and left alone and defenceless. The sweating bull swung its horned head. Black-brown eyes stared out from its coarse face.

'You must keep still,' Ceowulf shouted encouragement across the arena.

Caspar found the chanting disturbing, frightening and goading at the same time. He was sure it would have driven Firecracker completely berserk by now. Suddenly the chanting stopped and his nerves tightened.

Brid was standing on the low bloodstained altar slab, arms outspread, the glowing orb of the moonstone in one upheld palm, its light casting a ghostly glow over the umbral scene. The scarlet fire-drake was coiled around her arm like a torc, its tongue flickering greedily towards the iridescent light. The orb drew the bull's gaze just as it drew the gaze of everyone else in the crater. For a moment Caspar thought it had worked. But the power of the orb was not as mesmeric on the animal as it was on the fearful hearts of the superstitious humans.

The huge black bull backed up, made a brief spurt forward and then backed up again. At the first charge even Brid visibly faltered. Caspar wrenched at his bonds in desperation, knowing that the slightest show of weakness in Brid's movement would draw the animal to her.

Cybillia suddenly slapped her thigh, making the bull turn his head in her direction. 'I've had enough of this,' she declared in an irritated voice, brushing down her tattered dress. 'Quite enough. It's only a bull. And he looks a damn sight smaller than the bulls I'm used to.'

'She's mad,' Pellam choked.

Caspar didn't dare breathe. The girl was marching straight towards the great beast, looking him straight in the eye.

'Don't do it, Cybillia,' Ceowulf implored in a hushed but urgent whisper.

'I've never heard so much nonsense in all my life,' the Jotunn noblewoman declared in rounded tones as if she were scolding a naughty puppy. She approached slowly and with steady purpose until she was twenty feet from the animal.

'Now you know you don't want to be any trouble,' she told the bull.

He backed up again threateningly, but she never took her eyes from his, continuing all the while to talk in steady tones without showing the least tremor of fear.

'I can't believe that's Cybillia behaving like that,' Hal muttered.

Caspar was laughing nervously. 'She's been brought up alongside oxen twice the size. I guess she must know how to handle them.' His chest muscles had loosened up enough for him to breathe, but the respite was only temporary. He snatched in another gasp of air as the cream mare screamed and bucked from the sting of a feathered dart that stung her rump. Bucking around the arena, she tore past Cybillia, who squealed in terror, breaking her concentration over the bull.

Brid however was not worried by the mare. 'Cybillia,' she commanded, 'keep talking to him. Don't worry about the horse; I'll deal with it.'

The mare stood on her hindlegs then bucked, twisted and kicked, trying to free the jangling tresses that caught hold of her legs. Cybillia looked anxiously over her shoulder, still more frightened by the horse than the bull, which she was gradually approaching.

Brid boldly stepped out in front of the horse. Caspar closed his eyes, certain that the mare would run her down. The crowd gasped and Caspar didn't know how she had done it, but there she was, up on the horse's back, her hands hooked into the cinch of ribbons that adorned the horse's neck. The mare bucked again but looked very much more pacified.

Cybillia swallowed hard and turned back to the bull. 'Now you're a mean old boy. I know that and you know that, but we both know you don't want to cause any more trouble.'

The bull seemed to agree with her and raised his head, relaxing his threatening stance. He waddled forward like a de-horned bullock. With natural ease, she scratched the broad flat expanse of his forehead. The bull took a deep breath before letting out a low rumbling sigh.

An awed gasp muffled the remaining uneasy chants from the island priests. Cybillia unhooked her belt from around her slender waist and looped it through the bull's nose-ring. Like a docile old cart-horse, the bull allowed her to lead him round the ring. She told him constantly that he was a fine animal and gently berated him for being such a troublemaker. Many of the islanders fell to their knees and Brid seized the opportunity to heighten their emotions.

'The Great Mother Goddess proclaims her power over all the beasts who inhabit Her body. We stand here midst the power of Her broken bones. Feel Her glory!'

She raised the moonstone up above her head and a single moonbeam fell from the sky and touched the globe. A burst of white light shone out from the orb, scattering to illuminate the black giant shapes of the twenty-one standing stones. Brid and her creamy mare were bathed in silver, a vision of hope and light standing in the circle of dark. Whether the priests of the Farthest Isles understood her words or not, Caspar didn't know, but they certainly understood her power. They fell to their knees in supplication.

Chapter 9

'Devils! Devils, leave me be!' Rosalind howled as she stabbed at thin air, her face a picture of terror.

May looked on in horror. Normally so placid and calm, the kitchen-maid was standing on the tables, pummelling thin air with frantic fists as though defending herself from some demonic attack. Her eyes were staring black pits as though she looked straight into the jaws of death.

Elaine clutched her daughter to her. It was late and they had been sleeping on the rough pallets around the edge of the lower hall, huddled closely together to stave off the deep midwinter cold. Rosalind's fit had startled them all wide awake. Now Maud, thick-set and practical, was struggling to restrain her.

But Rosalind was not the only one in distress. Another of the kitchen helpers, a nervous mousy woman called Frieda, was sobbing fitfully as she rocked back and forth, cradling one of May's rag dolls as though it were a baby. May hadn't looked at her once-treasured toys since the beginning of the siege and now they seemed so trivial to her. Had she really wanted to play with those dolls? She couldn't imagine it.

And then there was Isabel . . .

May's eyes were drawn towards the screens at the end of the hall as her ears were pierced by a series of long sorrowful shrieks, worse than the screams of an arrow-struck soldier, worse than the screams of a wolf caught in a trap. A young soldier stood outside the screens, wringing his hands, his face distorted in grief. It was Isabel's husband.

'I need water,' Morrigwen demanded, 'hot water. Cook, get

to the kitchens and bring boiling water. May, stop staring and help her. And, Maud, shut Rosalind up and keep her away from these screens. We've got enough trouble with Isabel without these women going into hysterics.' The old Crone turned towards May's mother and lowered her voice. 'Elaine, help me.'

May didn't know what was happening to Frieda and Rosalind. She wondered whether it was the cries from Isabel that had so disturbed them. Both seemed to be hallucinating. She couldn't believe that Isabel's plight had so unhinged them, not when they had seen so much of death in the past months. Funeral pyres burnt every night, crisping the brave honoured bodies, nearly a hundred of them now since the ruby was taken and the runes defiled.

As the protection from the runes of war dwindled, even the few who still clung to the New Faith could see just how much Torra Alta needed the guardianship of the Great Mother. Even the Captain had finally abandoned his worship in the chapel and stood with the others at dawn and sundown as they lifted their voices in prayer to the Goddess.

But it was as if the sun never set now. The funeral pyres kept a crimson glow in the sky over Torra Alta and the place stank of charred flesh and sizzling fat. Rosalind and the others had stayed calm throughout, silently accepting the tragedies around them, but today Isabel had been stricken and two of the other kitchen-maids had fallen prey to a distraught madness. Perhaps it was because they were women that they were so much more distressed by Isabel's plight than by the horrors of battle. Isabel was with child and that night she had cried out with a despair that had woken the rest of the keep. Morrigwen had hobbled over to her pallet but, when she emerged from tending the woman, her face had been saddened.

'I fear she will lose it. Something is wrong.'

The screens had quickly gone up around Isabel and for several hours there had been an uneasy silence except for Isabel's sobs, quiet sobs of a grief too painful to bear.

'Is it the lack of food?' Maud asked Morrigwen.

The Crone shrugged. 'I don't know. Sometimes these things just happen. She seemed so well.'

'But she hasn't lost it yet?'

'No,' Morrigwen agreed, 'but she will. There are signs. I have seen it too many times in my long years.'

For the first few hours of that night, the longest night of the year, Isabel had been painfully silent. In the candlelight May had caught a glimpse of her behind the screens. Her face was drawn, anxious, grieving. She didn't seem to be in pain but there was a haunted look in her eyes. Then in the small hours, she had begun to shriek from behind her screens as if her soul were being eaten by the Devil. May could still hear her as she and Cook struggled through the snowdrifts, carrying a small cauldron of boiled water across the frosty, starlit courtyard.

Isabel lay on her back, staring up at the ceiling, her arms cradled around her body. She had withdrawn into herself and May couldn't even begin to imagine the pain the woman felt. Morrigwen mopped her brow while the other women washed down the sleeping pallet and cleared away the bedding.

Elaine crept out from behind the screen. 'She lost the baby.'

'I know,' May said.

'Morrigwen's given her a draught to take away the pain. She'll sleep now.'

Elaine looked distracted and stared at the other two stricken women. One was being violently sick.

'Morrigwen,' Elaine's voice came out in a harsh whisper. 'Morrigwen!' She turned and ran back to the screens where the old woman rocked Isabel back and forth in her arms.

The ancient priestess looked up, immediately aware of the urgency in the young widow's voice. 'Speak, woman.'

'It suddenly struck me. The three of them, Isabel, Rosalind and Frieda . . . Last thing yesterday evening Cook set them to baking wheatcakes specially for the midwinter festival. Just the three of them. The men will be handed the cakes first thing at dawn. Neither I nor Cook nor any of the others touched them. It was just those three.'

'Oh, Mother mercy,' Morrigwen whispered. 'Cook, get to the kitchens. Don't let an ounce of food out of there. It'll be dawn soon. Elaine, you had best go with her.'

Morrigwen turned towards the spiral staircase at the far edge of the lower hall that would take her to the Baron's chambers but she stumbled awkwardly and May ran to support her. The Crone barely lifted the corner of her mouth to smile but it was enough for May to know that she appreciated her help. Breathlessly, the woman reached the top of the stairs, her hands shaking with the effort, though she beat on the door to the Baron's chamber with surprising force. Without waiting for his reply, she swung the door open and hobbled into the room.

'Branwolf!'

Barely dressed, he came stumbling from his solar with his breeches and his shirt still unfastened. The sight of the old woman halted him in his tracks.

'Bad news?'

'I have two women struck with hallucinations and fever and another has just lost her baby,' the Crone started.

'You trouble me with –' Branwolf began but Morrigwen raised her hand in an imperious gesture that not even the Baron could ignore.

'No, Branwolf, I trouble you with news of plague. Ergot plague. We have contaminated wheat in our stores. We must burn it now.'

Branwolf stiffened and slowly buttoned his shirt. 'You're surely mistaken.'

'We will only know that when we examine the grain,' Morrigwen replied unshaken.

The Baron was past them and out of sight long before Morrigwen had made it down the first steps. May patiently steadied the old woman's arm as she hobbled out into the courtyard. The shadows were long and grey as a sombre dawn light washed over the castle.

The Baron had already ordered two soldiers off the night watch to stand sentry over the stores. As Morrigwen approached, he flung the doors wide and advanced on the sacks of grain. He slit the first one open with a knife. Scooping out a handful of wheat, he examined it closely before turning to Morrigwen.

Their eyes met and she nodded silently. 'That's it; a purplish coating of ergot mould over the corn. It causes hallucinations, will loosen a child from its mother's womb and can cause gangrene and death if enough is ingested. Three women baked cakes yesterday and they must all have tried one. The cakes would have gone out to all the men this morning.'

The realization of what might have happened hit May like a stone on the temple. She caught just the smallest echo of her emotion veiled in the faces of the adults. Branwolf stared for just a moment too long at the poison in his hands while Morrigwen's eyes searched beyond him to the stacks of grain piled high. The Baron flung the fistful of wheat to the ground in restrained fury and very, very slowly turned and punched the door in one slow deliberate movement to demonstrate his frustration. Quietly he turned to one of the guards.

'Fetch the storemaster for me, will you, lad.' There was a lightness to his tone that only served to emphasize the serious-ness of his mood.

'My lord?' the storemaster greeted the Baron a short while later. His face was expectant as he awaited the Baron's command.

'I want you to go through each and every sack,' the Baron ordered.

The storemaster's eyes opened wide at the immensity of the task but he said nothing.

'You're looking for this,' the nobleman informed him sol-emnly, opening the sack and exposing the moulded grain.

'Dog's teeth,' the storemaster groaned. 'Ergot. How? How could anyone have done this to us?'

Branwolf didn't seem to hear the question but Morrigwen shuffled forward and cut open another sack with a small golden sickle that she took from her girdle. 'There must be a farmer in the heartland who has fallen on poor times. He's obviously slipped in his rotten harvest for fear of losing all the money it could earn him – money that he no doubt sorely needs to pay the Church Taxes.'

'Go through each sack,' the Baron ordered. 'Restack the good ones just outside the door and have the contaminated ones loaded to a cart and taken to the trebuchet on the north wall. If we can't eat it, we may as well use it as ammunition. When the store-room's empty, scrub it clean and restack the good grain.'

'Yes, sir.' The storemaster saluted and Branwolf nodded in acknowledgement before stepping through into the kitchens.

Knife in one hand, rolling pin in the other, the broad-girthed cook was standing braced before a crate of wheatcakes. The few remaining kitchen staff were quietly lined up against the far wall. The determination in the cook's eyes clearly forbade anyone from touching one particle of kitchen fare before the Baron had given his orders. The woman curtsied with a very brief and rather stiff bend of her knee as the Baron entered.

'My lord,' she welcomed him loudly into her domain.

He nodded. 'Everything that has even touched the flour must go,' he told her. 'We can take no risks. I'll have a cart put outside the kitchen doors. Throw out all these cakes and anything else, be it flour, puddings, breads, everything that contains wheat. I want the lot thrown into the cart. Then spend the day scrubbing from top to bottom. I'll get you more hands. This is a priority. May, for one, will stay.'

The Baron left with Morrigwen hobbling after him. The small chestnut-haired girl from the Boarchase Forest looked in despair at the heaped cakes – a thousand of them, breakfast for the starving men, all to be thrown away.

'Well, look sharp about it, May and you knaves.' Cook indicated the two young boys who had been allocated to the kitchens, both about Pip's age. 'You three can clear the cakes out. That's a nice simple task.' She came over and looked them sternly in the eye like some vast rhinoceros preparing to charge them down. Cook had been vastly rotund before the siege but even now could still be described as corpulent. She took her rolling pin and tapped the younger of the two boys on the head. 'And don't you eat one tiny crumb of it, you hear, boy. I don't care that your hungry belly feels like a thousand ants are stinging inside it. You heed me or you'll die.'

She turned and fixed the other kitchen-boy in the eye. He looked quite terrified of her, possibly even more terrified of her than of the Baron himself. Cook, within her kitchen, was an empress.

'May, keep an eye on them. I know you understand, so make sure they don't even lick their fingers.'

May nodded. She did understand, though it felt peculiar being put in charge. People seemed always to be giving her responsibilities lately and she wondered at it. Before the siege she had just been another child but now . . . she didn't know what was different. She was useful, she guessed. She turned and picked up the first basket of cakes and trundled towards the door where she tipped them into the waiting wagon. There would be no food today. Water, yes. Several of the women took it in turns to bring it out to the men, who nodded brief thanks and looked despairingly at the dingy, clouded water. The new Wellmaster was still learning his trade.

May knew how they felt. It was very difficult to concentrate on anything but her stomach. The distraction was as basic as being unable to breathe and produced a dull apathy which permeated the castle, a feeling made far worse as they watched the freshly baked wheatcakes being catapulted from the walls.

May led the cart-horse across the snow-covered cobbles towards the men on the north wall. One of them turned to greet her.

'Now, here's a sight for sore eyes,' he said amicably. 'Don't I wish I were twenty years younger.' He winked at her and May blushed with uncertain embarrassment. She knew what the man said wasn't really polite but she was pleased nevertheless because they all seemed in such good spirits.

'Brock, leave the poor lass alone. She's still too young to

understand your teasing,' objected a younger archer standing duty beside him.

'I'm sorry.' Brock smiled more gently. 'We see quite a lot of you, young lass, now don't we? Mark my words, you'll be running the castle one day the way you boss all the sergeants around.'

'But I don't . . .' May protested and the men laughed.

'Another few years and your ma will be worried sick about you running around in a castle like this,' Brock teased.

Not knowing how to reply, May gave him an innocent smile and changed the subject. 'What are they doing today?' she asked.

The soldiers grinned and the older archer lifted her up to look over the broad crenellations. May quickly realized what had caused their newly raised spirits. Splotches of white covered several rocks where several bags of flour had burst open around the base of the Tor. Further out, speck-like men could be seen busily scurrying back and forth amongst the foundations of the unfinished cathedral. They were foraging for the contaminated sacks of grain that the Torra Altan trebuchet had catapulted over the walls.

'Can you hit them from here?' she asked.

Brock patted his bow and nodded. 'Oh, yes, I could hit them but just for now we'll let the barbarous curs live. We don't want to deprive them of sampling our generously offered supplies.'

'Well, we can only hope that they take it back and gorge themselves silly.' The younger archer laughed with one of the men as he loaded another pile of cakes onto the trebuchet. 'Flour and cakes; it's a funny weapon to be throwing but maybe some good will come of this tragedy.'

'But they won't eat it surely?' May asked Brock. 'They must know we wouldn't fire good food at them?'

'Oh sure, they'll worry about it a lot, but they're ill-disciplined troops and I doubt Northmen understand ergot. After all they don't grow any crops, do they?' He gripped his bow and glowered down at the canyon floor, which seethed with enemy camps, before continuing. 'Besides there's a madness in these people and however brutal their leaders, I doubt they have much discipline over the men. They'll umm and ahh a bit over this flour that's fallen out of the sky but they'll eat it in the end.'

His companion nodded in agreement.

'They've got food though,' May protested. 'When the north wind blows you can smell the reindeer herds.'

Brock nodded. 'Aye, missy, but there's a lot of men down there.'

There was no denying that. May knew that they were supposed to number more than a hundred thousand though how many were in the canyon and how many still struggled through the snowbound north, no one knew. All she did know was that the noise rising up out of the canyon was terrible. It was a constant hum and rattle and the entire canyon seemed to stir and shift with the movements of the over-crowded enemy.

May left the men to their idle banter and returned to the cart-horse. He nudged her in the back with a playful nuzzle and picked up her plait in his mouth, playing with it as if it were a wisp of straw. Distractedly May led him back to the stables and as she walked past the stores on her way back to the kitchens, she looked in. Men with brushes, water and soda cakes scrubbed at the floors.

The kitchens were already scrubbed clean and, before she knew it, May found herself with a big ladle in her hands stirring a pot of simmering broth. One minute Cook had given her a cake of harsh soap and a coarse brush to scrub her hands and the next she was set to work in a whirlwind of hustle. May suddenly had sympathy for her younger brother, kept in the confines of the well-room every day, scraping out the sulphur barrels. Even through the coldest spells of the winter he had complained of the sweltering heat. Now the steam brought colour to her cheeks as she stood over the cauldron.

When the day's work was finally done, May trudged wearily after her mother towards the keep. They stopped outside the stores where the storemaster was still organizing the last sacks of good grain into place. The food supplies were depleted by well over half and his expression was grim with worry, though he managed to smile weakly as Elaine and her daughter approached.

'It's sure a sorry sight, Mistress Elaine. Wheat was our main store here by far.'

Elaine nodded grimly, acknowledging the loss, and gripped her daughter's hand tightly as they entered the keep.

That evening the refectory halls were sombre. The men seemed more tired than usual, the bleak despair of hunger gnawing at their spirits.

'Fine fare for the midwinter festival,' an archer grumbled in disgust as he dipped dry bread into his murky broth. He was immediately cowed by the disapproving looks of his fellow men.

'At least it's food,' one of the sergeants snapped back. 'At least we're still here to eat it.'

Elaine had saved her supper yet again and refused to eat it, saying she would give it to the dogs if Pip and May didn't share it.

'But, Ma,' Pip began, even though his eyes never strayed from the tough strip of salted venison that she held out to him.

'If I've told you once, I've told you a hundred times, don't you "but Ma" me. If I say you'll eat it, you'll eat it,' she ordered.

'I will not.'

'I'll give it to the dogs,' she threatened.

'Give it then.'

'If your father were here, he would make you eat it.'

'But he's not, Ma. And I don't believe he would. He would make you eat it and since he's not here to do that anymore I'll have to make you eat it instead.' Pip pouted and stamped his foot.

Elaine looked at her children in despair. Finally she dropped her hands. 'Listen and try to understand. Wystan is dead. All I have left in the world is the two of you. That's all that matters to me, *all*, you understand.'

The two children nodded.

'I'll be fine,' Elaine said bravely. 'You're still growing and need far more food than I do. I'm not going to die.'

'Pa died,' Pip said as if contradicting her.

Elaine nodded, her fiery red hair dancing loosely around her shoulders. 'Yes, Pa died,' she conceded. 'I know you two have seen so much now, so many shocking things around you and you've grown up so quickly. You're no longer the troublesome little tearaways that you used to be.' She smiled affectionately. 'But listen, even if I do die, and of course I will one day, you must keep on living. You are what I live for and you must live for me.'

'But Ma,' Pip's eyes suddenly brimmed with tears, 'we cannot live without you.'

She laughed. 'Oh what foolishness. Of course you can.'

May looked at her doubtfully.

Elaine's expression suddenly turned to one of seriousness. 'You must, May. You might miss me but you'll manage. The Baron has promised he will look after you and a Torra Altan is a man of his word.'

Tears suddenly brimmed over the woman's eyelids and she looked at her son and then at her daughter. 'Please, you must understand you're doing this for me.'

Pip suddenly relented and took the meat and May finally reached out and took the other half. She broke it in half again and gave the rest back to her mother.

'I'll eat this bit for you, if you'll eat that for me.'

Chapter 10

Caspar couldn't take his gaze off Brid as her blinding presence captured the eyes of all those around the henge. Bathed in the light of the moonstone, she exuded an ethereal radiance. He hardly noticed as his bonds were cut by the cowered priests of the bull cult, though he galvanized his stiff muscles into action as Ceowulf slipped the muzzle from Trog's straining neck. The terrier bolted straight for the heels of the cream horse, evidently blaming the animal for Brid's previous distress in the arena.

Caspar took a headlong dive into the dirt but failed to get more than a finger to the dog's tail. Peace was eventually restored to the scene only when Brid dropped lithely down from the horse and whistled the Ophidian snake-catcher to her side.

As Caspar sat on the ground, brushing the dust from his jacket and rubbing his wrists where the rope had frayed his skin, he felt strangely happy, strangely at one with his surroundings.

Brid's presence was electrifying and she drew everyone's gaze to her. As the priesthood shuffled closer, he could feel invisible bonds of empathy unite the people as more and more figures stepped into the circle. Animal masks were shed from their bodies and spears dropped. Caspar had the wondrous feeling that they all understood each other without speaking, in the way brothers and sisters could speak volumes to each other by the merest inflection of their head or dart of their eyes. But then Keridwen's words loomed large in his mind and he knew something was wrong.

'Brid, you must put the moonstone away,' he warned her. 'Keridwen told me not to use it.'

'Don't worry, Spar,' Brid smiled reassuringly. 'I'm not delving into the channels of magic, only letting its light flow out to unite us within the circle. It's only dangerous if I let my mind slip into the ethereal world of the orb. But you were right to warn me.' She lifted her head and looked into the shadows. 'Now, I need to talk to these people.'

She called Pellam. In the dim light, his eyes were black and his step faltered but Caspar gave the man credit. Thrown into these bizarre events, he kept his head well. 'You must be my voice. Step into the circle. Hal, Ceowulf,' Brid ordered.

'My God,' Pellam whispered as he walked between the vast shoulders of two obelisks. He looked eerily around him. 'What is this place? I can feel . . .'

His voice trailed away as if he were unable to describe the emotions that flooded into him. His fear, however, turned to wonderment as he stepped into the confines of the ancient circle bathed in the pure white light of the moonstone.

'You feel Her power.' The priestess stretched out her slender arm and spun slowly round, beckoning all into the henge. 'Tell them, Pellam. Explain what I'm saying.'

In stutters the young man repeated her words to the silent priesthood.

'You can feel the power of the Goddess in this ancient circle. You can feel the magic of life. You can feel the closeness of the unity we share. We are all the children of the Great Mother. So often we walk across Her bare earth and forget our origins and we forget the timeless order of things. But here, where Her power is concentrated, here within the circle at this great confluence of energy, even the most insensitive of us can feel Her glory. We are Her children. Tomorrow is the sacred day that marks the rebirth of the Sun and tomorrow we will all join together to perform the true rites that belong to this circle.'

For Caspar it was a long night. He was uneasy at the sudden

change in the islanders' emotions. Initially, he found comfort in the strange unifying power he had felt within the circle of stones, but these people were just too quick to change, switching their worship from the bull to Brid and Cybillia whom they lifted to their shoulders and carried reverently aloft to the stone altar. It all seemed so unreliable and he prayed that Brid's spell over them would last.

Through Pellam, Brid explained that it was the power of the Primal Gods, whose stellate symbol was stamped into Cybillia's skin, that enabled her to control the ferocious bull.

Caspar felt considerably better when White Eye anxiously returned their weapons to them and he had his bow firmly clasped in his hand. As his concerns seeped away, he was overcome once more by the enthralling sense of power trembling through the earth at his feet.

'Amazing, isn't it?' Hal said in his ear.

'Mmm,' Caspar nodded, aware of the thrilling energy he could feel welling up from the earth.

'All these men completely awe-struck just because Cybillia knows how to handle a cow and Brid has that glowing pebble. Superstitious fear does such incredible things. There are hundreds of them here and they all fall flat at Brid's feet because they believe they can feel the power of the Goddess. How does she do it?'

'But . . .' Caspar frowned blankly at his uncle. 'You can't feel it, can you?'

'Feel what?'

'The power, the magic in this place. It's like uniting with your life source.'

Hal grinned. 'I'll never understand you, Spar. I can't feel any of those things. No, of all the things Brid goes on about, the only one that I can really feel is the magical craftsmanship in this blade.' He drew the sword and the pure silver light of the moonstone kissed the surface of the white metal. The blood-red runes danced with energy as the light played on its surface.

'Put it away,' Caspar breathed. 'Sheathe it. You must not

expose it. Not here in this magical concentration of energy. Its power sings.'

The light of the moonstone deepened, concentrating the energy of the moon through its crystalline structure and reflecting it onto the sword. Jagged bursts of white energy sizzled like lightning bolts from the tip of the blade, spraying out in radiating shafts of blue-white light to strike each of the twenty-one stones.

'Mother!' Brid turned on Hal. 'Put it away. Put it back in its sheath,' she ordered, her voice so full of urgent concern that the words came out in a hoarse whisper.

For a fleeting instant Caspar felt them: huge, heavy faces with drooping jowls and thick brows. Time seemed to move so very slowly and he wondered whether his eyes deceived him as he saw twenty-one giant figures stir in their circle. Seams and shadows on the stones moulded into ogreish faces. Some had thick long beards and some had the soft expressions of women. Were they moving closer? Caspar felt very small and vulnerable as they leered over him. They were looking at him, he was certain they were looking deep within his soul. He fancied that the stone giants wanted to break open his skull as though it were a locked casket to probe for the secret of the Druid's Egg.

'Cover the sword!' he cried urgently.

Hal fumbled to slip the blade back into its scabbard. Finally it was sheathed and Caspar could breathe. The circle of twenty-one stones was back as it had been: lifeless lumps of solid rock.

Brid released her pent-up breath. 'We are at a point of intense power where energy lines convene and concentrate. When you drew the sword and exposed the runes of sorcery, they touched on the spirits within the rock. The waves of energy, the after shock of the magic within the runes, will have rippled out along the lines of energy that radiate through the earth's crust.' She looked intensely worried.

'Another confluence of power,' Caspar murmured.

Brid nodded, 'Just like the cairn where Keridwen is trapped within the ice.'

'I saw them,' Caspar continued. His voice felt tight in his throat. 'I saw their faces. Giant men and women of stone. They wanted me.'

Brid drew her thick plait protectively round her neck and looked up at the dark stone monoliths. 'They want you to lead them to the Egg. The runes on the sword awoke their spirit but only the Egg can bring back their form.'

'There's no harm done then,' Hal said brightly, exonerating himself.

Brid's face remained tense and she tugged nervously at her plait. 'Starting here at a confluence of power, a surge of magic can be felt all across the earth. Anyone, anything sensitive to the magic will know that something important has happened here, particularly on such a sacred day.'

Hal shrugged. 'Well no one could possibly link the magic to us nor our search for the Egg. It's just not possible.'

Brid tossed her plait back over her shoulder and lifted her head in a bright optimistic smile. 'No, I'm sure you're right. No one could.'

It was already light long before the sun broke over the high crater walls that formed their immediate horizon.

Brid looked perplexed. 'It's only a henge. I thought I would be able to understand its patterns like I might any other henge. I thought I would need to line up the rising sun with the stones but the sun won't climb above that wall of the crater until mid-morning.'

Ceowulf studied the rocks around him and the flat grassy surface of the extinct interior of the volcano. 'The stones must be arranged so that their significance can be understood when the sun breaks into the crater. I suppose that won't technically be dawn but it'll be dawn for this valley.'

Brid nodded. 'You're right. And we've got a few hours yet to take a look.'

Caspar now felt uncomfortable within the circle. The shadows of the twenty-one standing stones seemed to form the outline of faces and wherever he moved he was certain their eyes were following him. Brid stood to the east of the circle and looked west. 'The sun will rise behind those eastern cliffs and touch the capital of one of those western stones first – which one in particular I'm not sure, but we will have to follow its shadow as it points us westwards. Somewhere before us there must be a clue to the whereabouts of the Egg.'

She walked from east to west across the circle, stopping to examine the altar stone, and then continued on and passed through the huge obelisks and out of the henge. Littering the ground before her were thousands of fallen boulders that had tumbled from the crater rim. Many were daubed with woad or had the horns of bulls carved on them and several were covered in layers of moss with bracken skirting their bases.

'This might be interesting,' Cybillia suddenly called out.

Brid hurried to her with Trog skipping and leaping at her heels. The men drew to a halt and left the women to their hunt.

Ceowulf fondly shook his head at the two girls. 'I didn't think Cybillia would cope last night.'

'You mean with the bull?' Hal asked.

'Mmm.'

The dark youth laughed. 'Yes, she certainly came into her own.'

But Hal's eyes weren't following the knight's gaze that lingered on Cybillia. He quietly studied Brid instead.

The two girls were overflowing with exuberance as they hurried back to rejoin the Belbidians. Brid looked around for Pellam but, when her eye fell on the mousy-haired young man talking earnestly to a small group of islanders, she relaxed.

'At least half of the rocks scattered across the valley bear a runic message: mostly simple well-known adages, some so dated that they seem completely meaningless. One or two describe the purpose behind each of the fire festivals but most of them carry a sort of riddle or instruction, like "follow the North Star", or "from the land of fire go north until the next sign comes to meet you".'

Ceowulf and the two Torra Altans looked at her blankly.

'Brid,' Hal said with a touch of exasperation, 'can't you just say what it means?'

'Well, this is the way I see it: when the sun rises over the rim of the crater it will be directly behind one of those standing stones there.' She pointed westwards. 'Its rays will touch the westerly stones first because it will already be so high in the sky before its rays break over the crater rim. The head of that stone's shadow should touch one particular boulder lying in this crater. Then all we need do is read its inscription. I think the other messages are there to divert us away from the correct one, but once the sun points us in the right direction, we should find our next clue.'

The sound of crying and insistent voices distracted them.

Pellam was looking perplexed as several women lay sobbing at his feet. He raised his hands imploringly. 'They won't leave me alone. They say we saved them.'

'In what way?' Ceowulf asked.

'This woman –' He nodded at the tall islander kneeling at his feet. 'Her daughters were the chosen women for yesterday's sacrifice to the bull before Brid and Cybillia took their place. Since only I share their language, they've latched onto me as their saviour.'

The woman rose to stand almost as tall as Pellam and withdrew a chain from around her waist so that her robe billowed out into a loose sheet. Pellam politely but vainly tried not to look at her naked breast though the woman didn't seem to mind. She held the metal girdle out to him, muttering something in her own tongue.

Pellam looked at the Belbidians. 'She wants me to take it.'

'Well, lad, take it then. She's grateful and will not rest until she's done something to repay you. It's kinder to accept it graciously,' the broadly travelled free-lance advised.

Pellam bowed his head and allowed the woman to place the chain around his neck. The metal glinted in the soft grey light of morning. He looked at it with a grin. 'What's it made of? Some kind of bronze and gilt?'

Ceowulf laughed and examined the links of the chain

formed from three bands of different coloured metals. He supported a length of it in his hand, and smiled knowingly. 'I don't think you'll need to do any more roving the far seas to earn enough for your lobster boat.'

'I won't?'

'It's solid gold. Red gold from the distant deserts of Oriaxia, white gold from Glain and yellow gold from Ceolothia. Probably quite ancient too.'

Pellam's jaw dropped open in amazement. 'But it's not all mine; you'll want to share the money with me when we sell it. You came here on a treasure hunt after all.'

Hal and Ceowulf just laughed, making Pellam look utterly confused. Caspar couldn't bare to let the mousy-haired man continue to worry over the worth of his prize or about sharing it out.

'It's yours, Pellam. We're not looking for that sort of treasure.'

'Nobody turns down their rightful share in a prize. On board ship everyone takes their due share. We all need money to live, after all.'

'Take it, Pellam, for Dionella's sake,' Ceowulf urged and the Ophidian finally allowed a toothy smile to broaden his face.

'The sun!' Brid turned east, ready to greet the first welcome rays as the apex of the glorious globe of energy cast the eastern cliffs into deep relief. Clawing out between the boulders, the first shafts of light probed the sombre valley. She turned to follow the shadow. Stepping across the altar stone, she followed the black finger of shadow cast by the stone now crowned with the rising sun. The shadow led her to an unremarkable boulder standing amidst the thousands of similar ones that lay at random on the smooth grassy plain of the crater floor. Triumphant, she turned back to face the circle.

'Light the festival fires! Welcome the sun back; welcome the lengthening days. We will dance and rejoice in the warmth of that knowledge.'

Caspar felt the uplift in his own spirit. This form of worship was no more than outwardly expressing the joy of living. No soul-searching, no fears of dark forces or sinful deeds. This was about happiness and the well-being and love that come through the joy of living and sharing life with others. There was no ritualistic chanting or formal steps. The people of the Farthest Isles merely joined hands and danced and later, as darkness fell and the flames burnt high into the sky, they sang and laughed, and were united in their joy.

Caspar danced too. He couldn't help himself. He was caught up in an interweaving reel with a people with whom he shared no common language, but, within the circle, he shared their love of life and was united in their happiness.

'This,' cried Brid as she momentarily caught his arm and spun him around, 'this is the joy of the Great Mother. We are all Her children.'

Caspar laughed delightedly but then a sudden cloud dampened his spirits as he guiltily thought of home. There would be no midwinter feast this year. He had always loved the midwinter festival more than any other – though through his childhood the celebration of the winter solstice had been adapted to suit the worship of the one true God rather than the Goddess. Through the grim weeks of late autumn he had always looked forward to the festival when the weather finally turned from the insidious dampness of endless snowfall to bright crisp frosts. It was then that the snow packed down hard and they would go out to hunt. And when they returned, they would sit by the fires passing the long dark evenings by telling tales and singing ballads of the ancient heroes.

Pellam and Hal sat on a rock some distance from the festival, evidently disdainful of the pagan rite. Caspar also noted with a smile how Ceowulf and Cybillia had linked hands and danced their own dance a little way apart from everyone else. She would be beautiful again, he thought. Her hair was growing and thanks to Brid's herb lore, the ugly red scars on her cheeks were beginning to soften and pale. But what changed her countenance most of all was the smile growing on her lips. It brought a sparkle to her dusty blue eyes.

At last the moon rose and many of the dancers tired. Caspar

was tired and thirsty but felt deeply fulfilled. He slumped down next to Hal and lay back on the rock, looking up at the faraway stars, pointing out the North Star to his uncle.

Hal grunted in disapproval. 'We should be moving on. Why doesn't Brid stop this foolishness and tell us what she has found?'

Brid was flushed. A radiance shone through her body as she walked towards them with graceful energy. Her laughing eyes touched on Caspar. 'I don't look much like a priestess, do I?' she admitted. 'Not in these torn leathers and without my amulets and torcs but I've never felt more like one. To have a fire festival without fear of discovery . . .' She opened her arms wide, unable to express the magnitude of her joy. Caspar noticed how she studiously avoided looking at Hal, though he sensed that somehow her attention was on the dark youth and not on him.

Her smile dipped and she fixed the dark youth clear in the eye. 'You should have joined in.'

'I don't like the feeling within the circle.' He dismissed the idea rather than confronting Brid with a lecture about paganism and his fealties to the one true God as Caspar had expected. 'It makes me feel invaded. Besides, I'm worried about Torra Alta. I want to move on; I presume you now know where we are going.'

Brid's face fell to one of serious concern. 'Yes, of course I do. Do you think I would have danced with such rejoicing if I hadn't found the next part of the clue?'

'The next part? You mean we still don't know exactly where the Egg is?'

'Well, I probably would have if the parchment hadn't been ruined in the bog.'

Hal groaned. 'Tell us the worst then. What was written on the stone?'

She took a deep breath and recited solemnly:

> ' "East towards the burning fire
> Beyond the Gods' cold funeral pyre,

> *Deep in the black mouth, a golden shield,*
> *By runeseeker bold to be revealed."* '

' "Towards the burning fire" must mean towards the sun. That's not much of a clue,' Hal complained. 'That just means due east.'

'Yes,' Brid agreed, 'but then obviously we look for the Gods' cold funeral pyre and surely that refers to the Dead Gods, the old volcanoes in Glain. The funeral pyre could mean the flames from the volcanoes and of course they are cold because they are long since extinct.' She looked to Ceowulf for support. 'Wouldn't you agree?'

'It sounds probable,' the Caldean conceded reservedly.

'Well, it's a start. No doubt the rest of it, such as the bit about the mouth, will fall into place as we go but at least we will be moving in the right direction,' Brid told them brightly.

It took them longer to leave the island than Caspar anticipated. The islanders prepared a feast that lasted throughout the following day and into late evening. All the symbolic body markings of bulls were now washed away. In their stead, the chief priests, led by White Eye, had painted the sign of the pentagram on their left cheek in respectful mimicry of Cybillia. The dull chanting and the heavy faces of two days ago were replaced by songs and childlike laughter.

'They are an innocent people,' Brid murmured, 'having had little contact with the outside world for many generations. I don't know whether they have truly understood the love of the Great Mother but at least they are free from the slavery of the bull cult. Perhaps now they can learn to live without fear.'

Midst laughter and songs, they were escorted by torchlight down to the shore. A snaking procession, they wound out from the crater, through the open mouth of the stone bull and down the steep coiling track to the harbour. The schooner was hailed with long low blasts of a horn. As its lantern lights came into view, the islanders tugged at Pellam's arm.

He listened carefully and then turned to Brid and Cybillia.

'They are so very grateful that you've brought this joy into their lives. They cannot repay you except by giving you two gifts. The bull and the cream mare. They realize now that these animals are not gods and they want you to have them as a mark of their gratitude for helping them find the love of the Great Mother again.'

Brid was delighted.

'The mare's beautiful,' Caspar immediately leapt at this gift, 'but how on earth are we going to get a bull onto the schooner?'

Brid winked knowingly and patted her herb scrip. 'If we managed with Cracker I'm sure we can manage a silly little bull. Besides Cybillia has a magic touch with him.' The Maiden searched through her scrip. 'He's a big animal but a few mouthfuls of the Ovissian camomile and Gortan wild lettuce should keep him quiet.'

The owner of the schooner was very doubtful about having the two beasts on board but, when Ceowulf pressed a gold coin into his hand, he nodded practically. 'So long as you keep them quiet.'

Luckily there were enough experienced bull handlers amongst the islanders to help them coax the sedated animal across the broad gangplank and onto the schooner.

'The trick of course,' Cybillia told everybody once they had penned the animals between makeshift hurdles, 'is never to alarm or frighten them. Any bull can be dangerous but they are not naturally aggressive unless they are defending their herd. Once they know you're not having any nonsense they become quite peaceable.'

'Just like horses,' Caspar agreed.

'Do you think it works with wyverns?' Ceowulf asked with fake sincerity. 'I never tried to stare one down. Perhaps I could have saved myself some effort and a few good javelins.'

'Wyverns?' Pellam's voice rose in excitement. 'You've killed wyverns?'

'Now, don't get excited; wyvern hunting is not for you. You're going home to Dionella and then you're going to buy a lobster boat, and don't you forget it,' the knight reminded him with a patronly squeeze of the young man's shoulder. 'Dionella's relying on you.'

'Besides, you don't ride well enough to kill wyverns,' Hal teased.

'Not yet maybe.' Pellam appeared to be taking him seriously.

Ceowulf put a calm hand back on the young man's shoulder. 'You're a brave fellow, there's no denying that, but don't rise to Hal. He has a way of saying things that fools you into thinking he's an expert. But he's never even seen a wyvern and he certainly doesn't have the first clue about how to bring one down.'

The schooner's owner was a skilled seaman and he was not at all worried about sailing into Porta d'Oc at night. Caspar reflected that it was probably a good thing since the townsmen might have raised a few eyebrows at the sight of a fully grown bull coming off a fishing schooner. It was certainly a most unusual catch. The Belbidians decided that the best thing was to go straight to the ostlery and sneak the two animals into a barn.

Caspar volunteered to sleep with them in the straw in case there was any trouble, while the others found comfortable beds. Hal looked longingly towards the light of the inn and sighed. 'I'm sure I can sleep well enough in the straw too. I'll keep you company, nephew.'

'Thanks,' Caspar replied laconically, trying to sound as if he didn't care whether Hal stayed or not, but secretly he was worried about the bull and glad of his uncle's company. When the others had gone, he was more effusive. 'Don't you think the mare's lovely? She's like Cracker, only smaller and a little more biddable though clearly unbroken. But the sooner we can get rid of this bull the better. What if he goes berserk in the middle of the night?'

Hal looked at the animal's drooping head and listened to the slow deep contented breaths. 'I think Brid's given him enough of those herbs to last the week. I reckon sometimes she thinks she can solve all the world's problems with just a few sprigs of a herb.'

* * *

Caspar was sharply awoken. Blinking in the light that flooded through the old barn doors, he saw the ostler armed with a pitchfork. The man was frowning at the great horned beast munching contentedly at his manger. Caspar jumped to his feet.

'Don't worry, he's ours and he's properly tied through the nose.'

The Ophidian lowered his pitchfork. 'I thought I was seeing demons. Nice young mare you've picked up. She looks like a purebred from Oriaxia, from the desert plains beyond Lonis – just like your red roan. Now I never thought I'd live to see the day when I saw two of those animals at once, not in my stables at any rate. It's been fifteen years since last I clapped eyes on a purebred.'

It wasn't long before the others were up and Ceowulf was busy making enquiries about where he could sell the bull. The ostler was undoubtedly well connected in the livestock trade and by mid-morning quite a large gathering of farmers had come to inspect it.

Cybillia pouted sulkily.

'Whatever's the matter, Cybillia?' Brid asked her distractedly. She was petting the cream mare and teasing out wisps of straw from her mane.

'I don't want to sell him. He was a gift. Can't we please take him with us?'

'If you think that bull's going another inch with us we'll put you straight back on a boat to your father,' Hal declared.

Cybillia clapped her hand to her cheek and stared at him with wide tearful eyes. Caspar thought she was going to sob but she swallowed hard and looked quietly away. It was the first time for several days that she had worried about the scars on her face and the auburn-haired youth was furious with Hal for being so callous. Brid too scowled at Hal and drew Cybillia towards her.

'You can't ride a bull. We'll sell him and get you a nice sensible horse instead.'

Two of the farmers were very keen on the bull, having prodded his muscly quarters and inspected his mouth. Evidently rivals, they bid probably more than the animal was worth, far more in Hal's opinion, though Cybillia wasn't overly impressed.

'Father would get at least double the price for any one of his bulls.'

'Mmm, I dare say, but it'll buy us two saddle-horses,' Ceowulf argued.

'But we don't need two,' Hal started to object.

The knight nodded towards Pellam. 'We're going back towards Cocklebay, aren't we? Pellam's got enough money for his lobster boat now and, if I have anything to do with it – which I do – he's going straight back to Dionella. Katalin won't need to worry anymore.'

Pellam leapt at the plan. Caspar thought that the young Ophidian would still yearn for adventure, after all he was very young to settle down. But the mousy-haired sailor patted his shirt beneath which he had wisely concealed the fabulous gold chain.

'My father will be proud. A lobster boat of my own is all he ever wanted for me and at last we can hold up the family name.'

'And Dionella?' Ceowulf sounded concerned

'She's the most beautiful girl in the world. Now I'll be able to look after her as she deserves.'

Ceowulf grunted in deep satisfaction.

Leaving Ceowulf to conclude the negotiations, Hal and Caspar set off to fetch their horses from the pasture. Hal tossed back his head and flicked his black fringe away from his eyes.

'If I were Pellam, I'd have gone to sail the seas in search of adventure for a few more years. No, I'll correct myself there. Nothing would entice me willingly to sea. I'd have gone to the deserts in search of wyverns – anything rather than settle down so young.'

'Even if it was with Brid? You'd rather venture abroad than have Brid?'

'Oh, she'd wait for me.'

'Hal!' Caspar was speechless.

Fortunately the ostler was able to sell them two of his own saddle-horses, a chestnut and a bay. Caspar examined them critically and was fully satisfied though the ostler didn't have a side-saddle for Cybillia.

'Very few women in Ophidia ride,' he explained. 'The fine ladies tend to go by carriage and very few of the normal folk ride so we don't have much call for them.'

'She'll manage,' Brid reassured the ostler before the flaxen-haired girl had a chance to complain.

Then when Brid announced that she would be riding the cream mare Caspar protested. He wasn't too sure of the priestess's ability to manage the animal. It had clearly never been saddled and as they were in the company of such inexperienced riders as Pellam and Cybillia it just wasn't the right time or place to break her in. The bucks and plunges tended to worry the other horses and Firecracker snatched anxiously at the bit, certain that the cream mare was game for a race.

Brid, however, was quite stubborn. 'There's no way I'm leaving her behind and I've broken in lots of horses before. It'll only take a couple of days to settle her and then she'll be magnificent. Like a star streaking across the heavens,' she declared. 'Like a comet.'

'Comet,' Caspar repeated. 'That sounds good.'

Brid was delighted with the name.

'I bet you've never broken in one like her before though,' Hal challenged the Maiden.

'Well, maybe not,' Brid admitted, 'but that doesn't mean I can't.'

They set out eastwards, following the directions uncovered at the henge. A few hours later Brid was beginning to look tired. Hot from her exertions, she removed her thick brown bearskin cloak and stuffed it into her pack.

'What type of fur is that?' Pellam asked Hal and Caspar who both wore the same fur cloaks.

'It's brown bear,' Hal informed him. 'All Torra Altans wear

them. It's the only thing that keeps out the winter weather. Only the Yellow Mountains in the north of Belbidia have brown bears. They're fur is much warmer than wolf-skin.'

Caspar suspected Brid's resolve was finally failing as she pitched towards Comet's ears. The young unbroken mare was shying violently at a stick that had shifted in the winter breeze. Cybillia squealed, dropping her reins to fling her arms round the chestnut's neck as Comet thumped into the rump of her horse. Ceowulf quickly snatched the chestnut's bridle, so averting any disaster, and reassured Cybillia that there really was no problem.

The spiky-haired girl looked unconvinced and whimpered at the priestess. 'Oh please, Brid, give her to one of the men to handle.'

Brid went stiff with indignation at the suggestion. 'Ceowulf would squash her and Hal would ruin her mouth.'

'I'd manage,' Pellam enthusiastically offered, which brought a burst of laughter from Hal and Ceowulf and a wry grin to Caspar's face. He looked at the young man with his elbows out, his toes pointing down and with a twist of mane wound round his fingers for security. He was doing very well for someone who had only just learnt to ride but was still blind with the confidence born of ignorance.

'But Brid's not been thrown yet and she's only a girl,' Pellam protested. 'Surely any man can manage a horse better?'

Cybillia nodded enthusiastically at this pronouncement, as Comet half-reared and plunged her head forward against Brid's restraining grip on the reins.

'Pellam, I'm sorely tempted to take up your offer,' the priestess grimaced, 'if only to prove –'

'Don't even think of it,' Ceowulf warned quite sternly, adding the first mature level-headedness to the youngsters' display of bravado. 'Pellam, believe me, you don't want to ride Comet. I've been riding all my life and trained to the highest levels in the tournament field and I know she'd be a handful. The others are just teasing you.'

Caspar was worried that Brid's arms would be pulled from

their sockets and sidled up alongside her. 'Come on, Brid, you've proved your point. I know you're doing a marvellous job and you're certainly doing better than Hal would, but you're tiring yourself out and it's a long journey. I'll swap with you. You'd like to ride Cracker after all, wouldn't you?'

Brid grinned from ear to ear as if she'd been waiting for the suggestion. 'I'd love to ride Cracker.'

After several days on the road through the green pastures of northern Ophidia, they all realized that Pellam would shortly be leaving them. Cocklebay lay just two days' ride to the north.

Ceowulf repeatedly warned him that he must get a fair price for his gold chain and Pellam promised never to repeat to a living soul the events that had befallen them in the Farthest Isles.

'I couldn't, could I? Not just for my own sake but for Dionella's. All that hocus-pocus and witchcraft, I'd become a laughing stock. I wouldn't bring such disgrace on my friends or my family.'

When they finally reached the cross-roads that would take Pellam north and the Belbidians east, the Caldean knight tucked a letter addressed to Katalin into the man's breast pocket. Cybillia scowled at the note but quickly rearranged her face into one of dignified disinterest when she caught Caspar's eye.

'I'll have a fleet of lobster boats by the time you come to Cocklebay next and, with the money I earn, I'm going to buy a horse as fine as Cracker.' Pellam looked more comfortable now on the bay, and sat deeper into the dip of its back, finally relinquishing his grip on the animal's mane. He turned to wave farewell. 'I hope you find your treasure.'

Chapter 11

With the windy marsh flats and pastures of Ophidia now far
behind them the group wearily approached the dusty lands of
Glain. Dirt scratched at their eyes and filled their lungs as the
breeze whipped up the red sand. Caspar coughed uncomfortably.

'The main sweep of the desert lies miles to the south,'
Ceowulf explained, his eyes wrinkling against the windblown
sand. 'But to get to the Dead Gods we have to cross this
tongue of desert that licks up towards the spit of Glain.'

Patches of thrift and silver-eared marram grasses lay crisp
and sunburnt like seaweed thrown up above the high water
mark. Deep rooted olive trees shaded the occasional village
but otherwise the soil was bare.

'To think this was all green grass and wheat before the
farmers of Glain stripped it bare,' Brid complained bitterly.

As the road dipped and curved between fluted dunes Caspar
heard the faint tinkle of bells drifting on the breeze. Firecracker
snorted and Comet plunged against her bit in alarm.

Ceowulf's voice was strained with tension. 'Camel bells,
which means nomads. Horses can't bear the stink of camels.'

'Should we be afraid of them?' Hal asked doubtfully, not
looking in the least afraid. 'They're only merchants, after all.'

Ceowulf glanced quickly at Brid and Cybillia then stiffened
his face into a troubled smile. 'Of course not but all the same
we should avoid drawing attention to ourselves.'

They travelled on through the blaring heat of the day and,
except for the faintest sound of jangling bells carrying across
the dunes, there was no further evidence of the nomads.

Though Comet and Firecracker looked quite at home in the sand the group's overall progress was laboured and slow because the three heavier horses tired quickly in the loose footing. Caspar was vastly relieved when the cool of evening hugged the land and as the beating sun finally dropped below the horizon, they curled up under their cloaks for the cold desert night ahead.

It was Trog who woke them.

Caspar tried to leap to his feet but he found himself tied and gagged. He stumbled head first into the sand before rolling upright, shaking the grit from his eyes. A dizzy sickness thumped within his temples and he was certain he must have been coshed in his sleep.

The dog's violent growls and snarls were rapidly fading into the distance and in the dark Caspar could just make out Trog's white shape streaking over the dune. A frayed rope showed where the terrier had chewed through his tethers. Though Hal and Ceowulf were still tied and thrashing, he couldn't see Cybillia, Brid or the horses. A desperate panic rose in his throat and he wrenched at the bonds while trying not to choke on the foul-tasting rag that had been stuffed in his mouth.

At last Ceowulf managed to fumble for a knife and sawed at his ropes. Within seconds he was free. Spitting out his rag, he slashed through his ankle bonds and quickly released Hal and Caspar. Glumly they turned south towards the dune and their last glimpse of the baying dog.

'Slave traders?' Hal asked heavily, stopping only to retrieve his sword before beginning to run. Ceowulf snatched up a water canister and sprinted after him. With his bow bumping on his back, Caspar was at his heels, relieved that at least their attackers had left them their weapons.

The haunting stillness of the desert night added to his fears as they struggled through the undulating landscape, the eerie starlight reflecting off the pale sands. They slipped, rolled and stumbled down the far side of each dune before attacking the exhausting climbs. At each demoralizing step the loose sands seeped away from their feet, stealing their progress and forcing them to a steadier but firmer pace. As they reached the top of a dune they paused for breath and looked down the far side. Trog had long since been lost from sight.

Apart from Ceowulf's heavy breathing, a deathly hush hung over the empty arid wasteland. To the east a pink dome of light was feeling its way over the horizon and at least now it would shortly be dawn. At last the light was strong enough to cast shadows over the wind-rippled dunes, defining a trail of hoof prints, though the breeze stirred by the rising sun was already beginning to blow whispering sands into the hollows.

'They're riding abreast,' Caspar commented, frowning.

Hal agreed with a nod.

'But there's no more than five tracks,' Ceowulf added flatly. They stared at each other blankly before tripping down the side of the next dune and stumbling through the disturbed sands, battling ever southward.

'Wouldn't camels leave tracks?' Caspar asked. 'Shouldn't there be more tracks?'

'There should.' Ceowulf looked disturbed.

'Wyverns wouldn't leave tracks; they'd fly,' Hal ventured.

'That's right, lad, but they don't tie people up and they wouldn't steal horses. They'd just eat them.' Ceowulf spoke in short bursts between heavy breaths. He was still not fully fit after his injuries and the arduous pace was beginning to take its toll.

A little further on the hoof prints were crossed by camel tracks travelling east.

'The nomads,' Ceowulf grunted.

Caspar was slowing in the rising heat of the sun, sweat prickling his back, and Hal was drawing gradually ahead, striding to the top of a dune. Suddenly he stopped, dropping onto his haunches as if he had seen something, before waving the other two on. Panting, Caspar clawed his way up the last few paces. Something small and white lay in the bottom of the next valley.

His heart pumped in his throat as he hurled himself down

the far side of the slope and flung himself to the ground by the faithful dog. Trog's thick tongue filled his gaping mouth and his huge lungs bellowed in and out in desperation to cool his overheated body.

'Trog,' Caspar mumbled. 'Trog, you stupid dog.'

Ceowulf fumbled for his water canister and dribbled the cooling liquid over the dog's head before forcing it down his throat. At first Trog did nothing but gasp until at last his eyes opened. He gulped at the liquid, squirting as much out of the sides of his mouth as he managed to swallow. Finally he stood up on shaky legs and, with just a quick look at Caspar and a thump of his tail, stumbled southward again at a subdued plod.

The Belbidians couldn't force themselves to move at more than a limping march, runnels of sweat stinging their eyes. Caspar's throat rasped with thirst but at last the monotony of the rolling landscape was broken by a splash of green cresting the next dune.

'An oasis,' Ceowulf whispered, taking another swig from the canister. Caspar quenched his own rasping thirst before trickling more of the water into Trog's panting mouth. The animal drank eagerly before sniffing the air and pricking his ears up at the valley below. Caspar put a hand on his collar to hold him back. In the shade of the palm trees, he could see their five tethered horses, swishing their tails against the heat.

'Where are they?' Hal whispered. 'They surely wouldn't abandon the horses.'

Caspar studied the sandy valley. Apart from the five exhausted horses standing with drooping heads, there was no sign of habitation. He slipped his belt through Trog's collar and they crawled warily down towards the oasis.

Firecracker gave a gentle whicker as they approached, his hide matted in a crust of dried sweat, though he looked in a better state than the others. Fortunately they were tethered within reach of a steep-sided pool that bubbled up from white rocks coated in mosses and silver-stemmed plants.

After several minutes searching, they only found two sets of footprints.

'This is ridiculous. You don't suppose the girls simply went mad and took themselves and the horses off, leaving us behind?' Hal suggested half in jest. 'There's no trace of an attacker.'

They were distracted by Trog, whose hackles sprang up to ridge his spine, his tail bristling and rodlike as he suspiciously sniffed at the sand.

'Slip him off the lead,' Hal suggested.

The dog traced backwards and forwards across the earth, snuffling and scratching and running between the horses and a needle-shaped sandstone rock that rested on the far side of the oasis. He whined pitifully at the ground and looked back and forth between the humans. A look of confusion wrinkled his thick-boned forehead. Traces of the girls' footprints led towards the sandstone rock and then disappeared.

'He can clearly smell something,' Caspar muttered, suddenly feeling cold despite the garish heat from the sun. 'Perhaps it's that thing again, the thing we felt in the yew forest mist.'

Hal's face was set hard with cold reasoning. 'Stop being over-dramatic. There has to be a reasonable explanation as to why their captors don't leave any marks in the sand.'

Trog suddenly started to dig and the three noble Belbidians stared dumbfounded at the ground. The terrier cocked his head as if listening and then started to dig more furiously again, kicking out sprays of sand behind his back legs. Ceowulf dropped to his knees and pressed his ear to the ground, frowning. 'Keep that dog still; I'm trying to listen.'

Hal dragged at Trog's collar while Caspar knelt down next to the knight. 'What is it?'

Ceowulf shrugged. 'You listen.'

At first Caspar could hear nothing but the beat of his heart and the dog's panting. He concentrated his mind and strained his ears. Was it running water? Or perhaps the sound of burrowing rodents? He listened harder. No, it was more like chattering voices. He looked bleakly up at his two companions. The knight nodded in reply to his aghast expression.

'Yes, voices. There's some kind of underground dwelling.'

'There has to be an entrance.' Hal looked at the girls' foot-prints leading to the sandstone rock. They sprang to their feet, brushing through the rushes that skirted the edge of the pool, and hurried to re-examine the stone. 'It must move,' Hal insisted, shouldering the rock but to no avail. 'It must be some kind of entrance.'

He grunted as he rammed his shoulder repeatedly against the rock but finally gave up as he watched Trog sniffing excitedly at the spot, blowing clogs of sand from his snuffling nostrils. A tiny speck of something dark emerged from beneath the soil. Caspar plucked it up. A limp and shrivelled stem of a plant lay in the palm of his hand. 'It's loosestrife, isn't it? It must be Brid's.'

He plunged to his knees, scooping aside the hot, surface sand and digging furiously alongside the dog. 'There has to be an entrance down here. A covered trap-door perhaps.'

He didn't have time to scream. As a scaly three-clawed hand wormed out of the soil and grasped his wrist he didn't even have time to think. He was horrified, fearing that they had disturbed some burial ground and the dead were now creeping up out of the earth to devour him. The hand jerked his wrist downwards and only when he felt himself being sucked into the sand did he begin to scream.

The hot sand pressed around his body as he was pulled down into entombment. He tried to squirm free, terrified that he would suffocate beneath the earth, but the cooling sand held him too firmly. He felt his lungs would burst as he was dragged deeper and deeper. He could hear Hal's desperate yells and then quite suddenly nothing.

His world went black.

Trog was already gone. Hal gripped onto Caspar's disappearing legs, digging his feet into the soft sand to give himself purchase, and heaved with every sinew in his body. Though he shook with effort, Caspar's legs still slipped through his fingers to be swallowed by the sand.

'No, Spar, no!' he screamed as the sand rippled and then smoothed over as if it had never even been disturbed. 'Spar!'

He thumped the ground furiously with his fists before rocking back onto his ankles, looking up despairingly into the blinding sky. Ceowulf pulled him upright and dragged him away from the rock. 'Get your head together otherwise we'll all be swallowed.'

Hal looked forlornly at the spot where he had last seen his nephew's feet disappearing into the hot ground. Angrily he pushed the knight's restraining grip off his arm and stood up. 'It's not your kinsman buried alive in the sand!'

'Believe me, I care,' Ceowulf replied with self-restraint, 'and for Brid and Cybillia too. But we can't help them if we get grabbed ourselves.'

Hal couldn't think. All he wanted to do was kill something, someone, whoever it was that had taken his nephew and Brid. Without thinking, he drew the great runesword and let his finger run down the groove of the central fuller, tracing out the blood-red runes. He ignored the new runes of sorcery that fringed the outside of the pattern and concentrated on the runes of war. These runes commanded necessity, lordship and battle-craft but Brid had pointed out one in particular: Tiw's rune, dedicated only to war. And this was war! Someone threatened what he held most dear in all the world.

'They can't take Brid,' he cried. 'Nor Spar. Great Mother, we stand here on your bare skin and implore your mercy. This is the only rune I know. If I draw it here in the soil will you help me find your priestess?'

Carefully he used the point of his sword to draw Tiw's rune into the sand, forming the sigil: $\uparrow$. As he inscribed the rune, a great hot swell of furious bloodlust rose up from his heart, girding his mind with a sense of godly invincibility. He was thrilled with a need to vanquish, to conquer, to be the warlord. He was aware of nothing else around him except his own presence gathering strength.

Somewhere a small voice was whispering in his ear. 'Hal, talk to me; listen to me.'

It took him a few moments to realize that the voice belonged to Ceowulf. He gripped the runesword tighter. He wanted to swat this irritating voice aside with a quick flick of the blade but his own faraway conscience squeezed into his bloated thoughts. *It's Ceowulf; you need him.* He dropped the sword, appalled at how his mind had been swamped by the power of the runespells.

'Such dreadful power,' he murmured, awe-struck by the force that had possessed him.

Ceowulf gave him a fleeting look of bewilderment. 'Hal, you'd better drink some water. The heat of the sun is getting to you.'

He shook his head. 'No, the power of the Goddess. I felt it. I wrote the one rune that I know and suddenly I felt this unbelievable strength.'

'A rune?'

'Yes, a rune. What do you think that is?' Hal demanded, pointing at the sand.

'An arrow.'

Hal studied the shape for a second and wondered whether the Goddess had guided his hand. An arrow ... Surely it meant something. Surely it pointed the way. Sceptically the two noblemen followed its direction, which led them to the edge of the water. The pool shone silvery white as the dazzling sun reflected off its surface. They both squinted.

Ceowulf shook his head. 'There must be another way. I never did hold much store in Brid's runes.'

'Nor I,' Hal agreed, 'but I definitely felt something, a terrible power. And that arrow didn't happen by accident.'

'But it's only led us to the water.'

'I know,' the dark youth replied glumly. 'I must sound like Spar gibbering about magic but I felt it. I felt the power and I know it means something.'

He dipped his hand into the water. He was surprised by its coolness until he realized that it must lead deeper underground, protected from the shrivelling heat. To clear his head, he plunged his face into the pool and blinked, washing the dust from his eyes. He flicked up his head and smoothed back his raven-black hair. Staring down at his reflection in the bright surface, he tried to empty his thoughts, hoping that an answer would suddenly spring to mind. The dazzling sun burnt his eyes where it glinted on the water.

He plunged his head back into the pool. Below the glinting surface, the water was clear and he could easily see to the sandy bottom, where the darkening waters probed the black of an underwater cave. He wrenched his head up and blinked in the sunlight.

'There's a cave down there.' Quickly he began stripping off his shirt and boots and handed his sword to Ceowulf. 'I'll take a look.' Without further hesitation he dived in. The cool of the water punched him, stunning his senses. He struck downwards, swimming towards the murk of the cave, and as the visibility dimmed, he felt his way across the grainy rocks and swam on into the dark. The cave walls closed in about him. Fearful of running out of air, he was about to turn back when he saw a dancing red light playing on the surface of the water above him. He let his body drift upwards and slipped his mouth out of the water to draw in a controlled silent breath.

It took a moment for his eyes to adjust and he soon realized that the light came from torches, pinpoints of glowing colour in the darkened space. Hundreds of faces leapt out from the surrounding curved walls, all eyes seemingly turned on him, and it was a second before he realized they were trophy heads hung on walls. He appeared to be in some sort of chamber hollowed out beneath the sand. Ahead of him a stone pillar rose out of the floor and obstructed his view, so he swam silently to his right to see beyond it.

The ground appeared to be moving. Trying to focus on the shapes, he kept low in the water with only the tuft of his black hair and his eyes showing over the brim of the pool. The shapes muttered and chattered in shrill screaming tongues that hissed and slithered over their sibilant words. But still he couldn't see them. They were like shadows. They were coming closer, dragging something that thumped lifelessly along the ground. Spar! It had to be Spar!

Then at last the creatures moved into the ring of torches and he could make out the outline of their wispy bodies. They had lizardlike faces and translucent gossamer-thin skin, as if the sun had beaten straight through their bodies, hammering away the substance to leave only this fragile casing. They were thin and stood upright like men, with long arms and legs sprouting from short round bodies. Their hands were long and slender and their feet webbed and spread. So light a body on such wide flat feet, Hal thought. No wonder they left no mark on the sand. And their bodies were so narrow. They could move like sand lizards burrowing straight through the soil. They had large dished faces with only four eye-teeth to fill their mouths. And their eyes! Huge round bulging froglike eyes with lower lids that blinked upwards.

Hal looked hurriedly about him, noting the squirming numbers of these creatures, most of which bore spears and short swords. One of the lizardlike creatures was moving uncomfortably close so he filled his lungs with air and plunged back into the water to swim back the way he had come.

As soon as he was bathed by the dappled light of the desert sun streaking through the palm leaves, he kicked upwards, splashing towards Ceowulf's anxious feet. The knight bent down to take his arm and pulled him bodily from the water.

'There's more . . . than forty of them!' Hal spluttered incoherently. 'All . . . armed.'

'Steady. Calm down. Breathe first and then talk,' the knight advised.

Hal took three breaths and reached for his clothes to protect himself from the searing heat. 'The cave leads to some underground dwelling, a huge burrow. They have Spar bound but I saw no sign of the girls. There were at least thirty of them, probably forty.'

'Forty what?'

Quickly Hal realized that he was gabbling and steadied himself to explain more clearly and succinctly. 'They look vaguely like men, but more like lizards. Thin but very strong, able to burrow straight through the sand, they're armed and belligerent.'

'Forty or so all armed?'

Hal nodded.

'If we could meet them out in the open we might stand a better chance but with only the two of us we can hardly storm the place.' The big man sucked at his lip.

Hal was infuriated by his silence. He marched forward for his sword but Ceowulf pushed him back. 'For God's sake, it's my nephew down there. I can kill all of them with the runesword.'

'Forty?' Ceowulf held off the youth with one hand as Hal kicked and struggled.

'Give me my sword! I can do it.'

'Listen, lad, you'll just get yourself killed. I've got a better idea. Those nomads will help us.'

'Nomads?' Hal thought him mad. Ceowulf had told them many stories of the treachery of the desert nomads. But at least they would be armed and right now they needed armed men.

There was no time for further thought; the two Belbidians ran to the horses, snatching up Comet and Firecracker since they would be far fleeter over the loose sands.

Ceowulf lurched back in the saddle, taken unawares as Firecracker spurted up the dune. With the wind rushing past his ears, Hal raced after him and they quickly breached the crest of the next dune, turning east to catch the caravan of nomads.

Ceowulf was more out of breath than the stamping red roan when he hauled on his reins, calling out in greeting to the desert travellers. Firecracker shied and danced, making it difficult for the red-faced knight to control him.

'How does Spar manage him?' he growled through gritted teeth.

'Who knows?' Hal shrugged, deciding it was better to dismount than to try and make the horses approach the foul-breathed camels.

The train of twenty camels swaggered to a halt and several men draped in loose white robes turned their sallow faces towards them. Their mouths were covered with silk cloth to protect them from the air-blown dust and only their dark eyes gave any clues to their emotions. Long, curving scimitars flashed against their sides and there was a relaxed confidence about them.

'Belbidians,' one of them rasped in an obviously despising tone, his grumbling accent deep and stilted.

Ceowulf brushed aside all attempts at formality. 'Our party has fallen prey to strange devilish creatures. We need help. We've lost two young ladies and a boy.'

The leading nomad, who wore a purple sash around his draped head, looked haughtily down from his camel. 'What care we if you're fools enough to bring innocents into the desert? There are always raiders. A girl here . . . a girl there . . .'

'These are not raiders,' the knight hurriedly explained, 'but strange men with lizardlike skins living beneath the dunes.'

'Dunedancers?' The man's eyes narrowed with revulsion, warily fingering the hilt of his scimitar. 'Slaying dunedancers is quite a different matter; it is an honourable matter for a man of the desert.'

'Dunedancers,' Ceowulf confirmed. 'They dragged my companions down into the sand. About forty of them, all armed.'

'Forty,' the nomad echoed more warily than sympathetically. 'I'm sorry for your plight, foreigner, but I have a valuable caravan and very little incentive above honour to endanger my men. With so many dunedancers, honour is not enough. What reward can I expect for this help?'

'By thunder, man, these are young helpless girls and a boy,' Hal exploded.

To his chagrin the desert trader merely laughed. 'The desert is a place of death. Many bones have paled and powdered in these sands. What does it matter if a few more skeletons are added to the pile? I need payment.'

Hal looked at the tall Caldean knight for guidance, hoping that Ceowulf's long experience in these southern lands had taught him one or two things about bargaining with these ruthless men.

'We have a little gold,' the knight ventured, 'but we appeal more to your souls as good men.'

Hal was disappointed; this approach would never work.

'A little gold,' the merchant sneered. 'I have a caravan laden with treasures.'

'You have to help us,' Ceowulf repeated. 'We have only a little gold now but we have many friends, many kinsmen, and I will repay you a thousand times over for your action.'

'Stranger, I have only your word for that.'

'You do, but it is the word of a Belbidian.'

The coppery-skinned men fell to their own private discussion, looking back and forth at the Belbidians.

'Will they help us?' Hal demanded under his breath.

Ceowulf nodded. 'Yes, but for a price. It's a matter of offering the right thing.'

'We will take your word, Belbidian, but we will also have your two horses. Two purebreds – a mare and a stallion at that! The blessed Father smiles on us today. That is the price for our help.'

'Firecracker!' Hal exclaimed. 'Firecracker is worth a kingdom. Spar would kill us.'

Ceowulf ignored him and held out his hand to the nomad. 'The horses for your help.'

Three-fingered claws sank into Caspar's flesh, dragging him down into the cool dampness of the underworld. His flesh crawled as shapes squirmed snake-like out of the walls and ceiling to flop lightly down into the burrow beside him. They stank insipidly of fresh fish and the light from their torches shone through their partially clothed bodies. They squirmed and wriggled like ghostly lizards.

He flinched as the faces of exotic savage beasts struck out at him but he quickly realized that they were merely stuffed trophies hanging on the walls of the hollowed-out chamber. He was flung to the ground next to Trog and blurrily focused on the upright pedestal beneath a rough white slab of marble reminiscent of an altar table. It was strung with smooth skulls, mainly of horses and lizards but some were quite clearly human. Above it hung a vast bestial head, twice the size of an ox's and with a long beaky snout tapering sharply to a savage point. Its eyes had been gouged out leaving black craters and its skin was a withered greenish-brown, like shreds of dried seaweed, peeling off the white bones beneath.

Beyond the altar the chamber narrowed and from somewhere far down this tunnel came a rumbling roar. A putrid stench hung in the air.

A woman screamed.

Caspar lifted his head with difficulty and strained to look over Trog's tightly bound body. Brid and Cybillia were roped by the wrists to an iron ring set into the floor. The Jotunn maiden was wailing uncontrollably. 'Brid!' he gasped.

'Spar! Where are the others?'

'They were right with me before . . .' His voice trailed away as the grumbling noise grew louder. 'What is that?' he asked, trying to hide his fear.

'Judging by the size of this burrow it can only be a wyvern.'

Cybillia redoubled her wailing.

While the rumbling grunts and snorts from the side-tunnel gradually drew nearer, Caspar struggled frantically, almost dislocating his shoulder joints in his effort to free his bonds. He knew there was a little give in the ropes around his wrists and he just needed to struggle hard enough. At last he managed to worm his wrist free. Quickly he worried at the bonds on his feet and reached for his knife.

He scrambled over to the two girls and deftly sliced through their tethers before seeing to the dog. Trog flung himself furiously at the lizardlike men behind them but was repelled by aggressive stabs from their spears. Cybillia had at least stopped screaming and was now only sobbing softly.

The lizard men began a slow hissing chant to accompany a rhythmic jerky dance, their long thin hands flicking out in perfect time with each other. The ground beneath their feet shuddered at the approach of heavy, lumbering footfalls as the dance drew the beast from its lair.

Cybillia fled behind the altar and curled up into a terrified ball while Brid stood beside the red-haired youth. The moonstone in one hand and her sacramental sickle in the other, she stooped to hastily scratch a circle of runes around them. 'The runes of protection. Cybillia, get into the circle. Stand with us.'

The stubbly-haired girl only whimpered pitifully and buried her head in her lap, hugging her knees to her chest.

'Fetch her, Spar,' the priestess commanded as she drew in a deep breath and placed both hands on the moonstone. 'Great Mother, protect us.'

As Caspar stepped out of the circle to reach Cybillia, he instantly felt the cold tide of fear well up from his leaden feet. Fiercely he gripped Cybillia's hand. 'You've got to get to the circle. You'll be safer there.'

Frozen in terror, she clung more fervently to the altar and resisted the youth's tugs. He didn't know what to do. He tried to drag her but her terror increased her strength and, sobbing pitifully, she clung rigidly to the marble. He yanked harder and harder until finally her grip gave and he dragged her, struggling and kicking, towards the circle. He was nearly there when he froze in his tracks. His hands went limp and Cybillia pulled away from him.

Eyes burnt through his skin.

He turned very, very slowly, his mouth sagging open in limp terror, and looked straight into vast ocean-green eyes that swam and swirled in a massive head.

The beast's earless head was like that of a monstrous featherless fledgling. Smaller than a dragon and with only two legs, it had stubby but powerful wings and a grotesquely vast head set on a short neck rimmed with spines. Oily green and black scales covered its back but its underbelly was wrinkled and leathery. It belched no fire, only a shrieking roar from its huge beaky jaws.

It rocked forward on its giant birdlike legs and stretched out its leathery wings, revealing hooked talons at its shoulders. A barbed tongue, unravelling like a lizard's, flickered out from the gaping jaw and its huge bulging eyes swivelled forward in their sockets. One fixed on Cybillia and the other on Brid. The creature ignored the boy.

'Get into the circle,' Brid spoke with a tremble in her voice though her tone was very soft and low so as not to alert the devilish beast to her fear. 'Both of you, get in here. Spar, now.'

Caspar couldn't. He couldn't leave Cybillia whimpering out there on the beaten floor. He reached for her hand and tried to drag her towards him.

The priestess crouched to the floor, gripping Trog, and stood her ground. The wyvern, looking like a giant scaly hawk, strutted forward, its long tongue unravelling and coiling through the air, probing first towards Brid and then Cybillia.

Caspar had his feet on the edge of the circle and, as he felt the love of the Great Mother rise up through the sand, his strength returned. He heaved Cybillia half into the circle just as, with one heavy step that shuddered the burrow, the creature towered over them. It let its tongue slide leisurely over Cybillia's calf and wrapped, tentacle-like, around her ankle. The girl screamed high and long. Fitful sobs burst from her lungs. 'Father, save me! Father!'

The animal's eyes widened in delight. It moved forward, placing a proprietorial claw on the girl's thigh. The scream stopped instantly and Cybillia's body went limp as she swooned.

The wyvern swivelled its bulging eyes towards Caspar. Again he froze and, as if falling into a whirlpool, found himself dragged deeper and deeper into the oblivion of the animal's mind.

'Don't look at it,' Brid yelled at him and he jerked his eyes away.

The Maiden snatched at Cybillia's arm just as the wyvern

stooped and gently plucked the blonde-haired girl up in its beak, its serrated teeth closing on her dress almost tenderly, without even nipping her skin. Caspar slid helplessly over the ground and his grasp was broken by one slash of its clawed wing, which hurled him to the ground.

In seconds, the two-legged creature had disappeared down the tunnel towards its nest, leaving only the sound of its swishing tail thudding against the side of its burrow. A noise, like the cry from some monstrous crow, screeched out of the tunnel. Caspar and Brid clutched at each other for comfort.

'Cybillia,' Caspar murmured helplessly.

The chanting moans of the lizard men abruptly stopped. From behind the altar came the sound of splashing water and angry warlike cries. Bare to their waist and with hair dripping wet, a dozen men rushed forward brandishing scimitars. The lizard men surged forward, spitting viciously.

Caspar grabbed Brid and yanked her to the side of the chamber, fearful that she might be caught up in the battle. Trog burst forward, raking his teeth into the gossamer skin of the nearest reptilian beast. Bewildered for a second, Caspar stared into the fray. There was Hal, half-naked, dripping water onto the sandy floor, his black hair smeared to his cheeks. Both his hands gripped the runesword as he stood at Ceowulf's side.

'Spar,' Hal yelled into the mêlée, his eyes searching through the interweaving network of clashing weapons.

'Over here!'

Hal and Ceowulf cut their way across the chamber, cleaving through the long-limbed creatures in their way.

'It's taken Cybillia,' Caspar yelled over the sound of crashing steel.

'What's taken her?' Ceowulf seemed to cut out all thought of the lizard men from his mind. He suddenly stiffened as he sniffed the foul air of the burrow. 'Wyvern!' he exclaimed, his face taut with horror. He swivelled on his heels. 'Hal, get Brid and Spar to the surface. I'm going after her.' He reached up for one of the flickering torches that burnt in a bracket on the wall of the chamber.

Caspar didn't try to argue but ran after Ceowulf, grabbing a short spear from a fallen lizard man as he went. 'This way,' he said. 'Down here.'

'Get back and stay with Hal!' Ceowulf bellowed at him, but didn't bother to argue as Caspar stubbornly disobeyed.

They left the noise of combat behind as they coiled back and forth through the tunnel, its sandy walls glowing a deep red in the light of the firebrand. It was like scurrying through the entrails of a snake, Caspar thought fearfully.

When they curved around the next twist in the burrow, Ceowulf halted and pushed Caspar behind him. Chattering, high-pitched squeaks and sighs came from ahead, interspersed with a deeper more satisfied clucking. A splintering cracking noise, a little like the sound of walking over shingle and dried seaweed, filtered back down the tunnel. Caspar could hear sobbing.

'Cybillia!' Her name caught in the knight's throat. He turned towards Caspar. 'Keep back out of the way and, whatever happens, don't look at its eyes.'

'Yes,' Caspar replied, letting the knight take a few paces forward before following, keeping himself pressed close to the tunnel walls. The knight pressed himself to the far wall, then sprang forward, sword in one hand, firebrand in the other, flooding the nest with torchlight.

Lying in the centre of the floor was a cluster of enormous green eggs each about a foot across. Scattered around them were the jagged remains of broken shells and crawling through these were the tiny offspring of the wyvern. The gruesome infants, half-reptile and half-man like the creatures that had attacked them, chirruped like birds and threw back their heads, screaming for food. Bile burst up Caspar's throat and into his mouth.

Behind the scatter of eggs, a huddle of three women rocked themselves back and forth; maddened creatures absorbed in their own private worlds. Two were inky skinned and the last was fair with mousy hair. One of the dark women was beating her head persistently against the wall as if trying to wake herself from a nightmare and all three had enormously swollen bellies. Caspar looked at them and at the eggs and could hardly bear to imagine what horror they had suffered.

The wyvern had its back to them, its long thick tail twitching back and forth, raking across the broken eggshells, as it stooped over Cybillia's tightly curled body. It stiffened and flicked up its heavy head as Ceowulf sprang forward, the beaky mouth snapping open into a screech. Ceowulf lowered his gaze, deliberately avoiding the animal's eyes, apparently judging its approach by sound and the movement of its claws alone.

Lacking the knight's experience and self-control, Caspar took several faltering steps backwards. His gaze was sucked into the whirlpool of green fear as the creature's bulging eyes drank at his courage. His knees went weak with terror and the grip on his weapon loosened. He snatched his eyes away and, remembering Brid's actions, dragged his foot through the sandy floor to form a circle. He didn't know which runes the priestess had used but he knew only one: the rune of the Great Mother. Hastily he drew the three radiating lines within the circle and the rune was complete. ⊕: the rune of the Mother.

He was suddenly overwhelmed with the reassuring conviction that the Great Mother would protect his soul and he had the strength to raise his head. The wyvern's swivelling eyes were focused on the tanned knight who, apart from his leather leggings, was entirely naked. The angry purple wound, where the mercenary's axe had sliced into his collarbone, puckered painfully on his bare chest. Then, with sword held high in one hand, he swung the torchlight in a slow circle with the other. The wyvern's head moved to trace the swirling patterns of light.

Eggshells ground and crunched underfoot as it advanced on the armed intruder. It swept into the midst of the unhatched eggs, bursting them open and spilling yellow yolk and wriggling, partly-formed embryos onto the floor. Arms and grossly underdeveloped legs writhed feebly for a few brief seconds in a squirming pottage of aborted life.

Ceowulf watched only the wyvern's approaching claws as he unflinchingly held his stance. Again the giant legs took another pace forward, crushing a screaming infant beneath it. It was now only four or five feet from the knight and still he didn't move, keeping his head firmly down to shield his eyes from the creature's terrifying glare.

Caspar very slowly readjusted the grip on his sword, thinking that he could hurl the blade at the wyvern's throat if Ceowulf faltered. For the moment, however, he knew he must wait for the knight to make the first move. Ceowulf had told them of his time in the deserts and how his friends had called him Wyvernbane; it would be far wiser to bow to the ex-mercenary's greater experience.

The wyvern paused and blinked as if uncertain of this dauntless man who dared stand before him. A muscle twitched on Ceowulf's back as he very slightly shifted his pose before stabbing upwards with the torch in his left arm to blind the wyvern's eyes. The knight leapt aside as the creature screeched in alarm, its long tongue coiling out with lightning speed to slice the air where the man had just stood.

Ceowulf slashed sideways, severing the tongue and, without pause, twisted the blade, thrusting straight up into the creature's ribcage. The wyvern tottered on its clawed feet, its wings unfurling in an attempt to steady itself before its great weight crashed to the ground. Its severed tongue lay like a length of bullwhip on the ground and Caspar tentatively picked his way round it, breathing heavily with relief.

Ceowulf was already hurrying towards Cybillia through the spill of yolky gelatinous fluid that oozed across the floor. She was trembling on her feet, her mouth moving up and down as if trying to call for help. The knight caught her in his solid embrace, holding her tight before he swept her up in his arms and carried her back over the eggs to Caspar. The young boy tried to comfort her but she kept looking towards Ceowulf.

'I've got to help the other women,' he told her calmly, 'and then we'll be out of here.'

One by one, he carried the three women out of the nest and delivered them to Caspar. They stared at him with unseeing eyes as if the terror of their miserable existence had destroyed their grip on reality. Cybillia's look of fear gradually dissolved as she gazed at their maddened faces and, very gently, she raised her hand and stroked their cheeks. 'We'll take you home,' she murmured.

Two of them seemed unable to hear her, though the mousy-haired woman finally started to cry. 'Home,' she echoed softly before continuing in a foreign language.

Cybillia's concern for the women seemed to fortify her own courage. She dragged the sobbing woman firmly by the hand, while Ceowulf carried another and Caspar struggled with the last. Her eyes were white and rolled back into her head. She seemed to have no realization of their presence and staggered after them as if dispossessed of her soul.

They wound back through the tunnels and were met by Hal's anxious eyes. Beheaded corpses and severed limbs lay all around him and the few remaining lizard men were hastily retreating by slithering out through the sandy walls.

The fair-skinned woman looked down sorrowfully at the dead creatures. 'My babies,' she mumbled and clutched her arms around her with a shudder.

Hal stared with horror at the three women and then at their swollen bellies. 'My God,' he muttered, taking a step back in revulsion just as Brid stepped forward to offer her hand to one of the ebony-skinned women.

'Is the wyvern dead?' she demanded of Ceowulf.

'Yes, very much so.'

'I'll catch up with you then,' she told him. 'Get the others to the surface.' Taking Ceowulf's torch she silently ran back towards the wyvern's nest.

'This way,' Hal ordered. 'We've opened up the roof where they dragged Spar through. It's the easiest way out. Oh, and, Spar, I found your bow.'

'Thanks,' Caspar muttered. He struggled to lead the maddened woman forward along the tunnel and blinked up into the shaft of dazzling sunlight that fell into the pit. A ring of reddish-brown faces looked down at him and several hands reached in to haul the women up into the midday heat of the oasis. They only had to wait a very short time for Brid, who appeared carrying a cloth bundle.

'What's that?' Caspar demanded.

Brid covered her mouth conspiratorially with a finger. 'Don't ask.'

Once on the surface, Caspar took a deep breath of fresh air, air free of the stench of wyvern, and looked suspiciously at the desert merchants. Two of them were standing around Comet, feeling her legs for soundness, while a third was trying to approach Firecracker.

'Hey, that's my horse,' he yelled, hurrying forwards, but Hal caught his arm.

'There's something I need to tell you, Spar.'

Suspiciously Caspar turned to face his uncle. 'Oh?'

'It's about Cracker. You see, we needed help and we had nothing to bargain with except –'

'Except my horse!' Caspar's voice came out as a thin shriek.

He couldn't think. His mind reeled with fury. Firecracker was his very finest possession. Furiously he shoved past his uncle and stormed towards the desert nomads. 'The deal's off. That horse wasn't his to bargain with. You can have anything, but not my horse.'

The men closed in around him, bristling with indignation, their hands resting lightly on the hilts of their scimitars, but the youth barely noticed.

'Nobody breaks confidence with a man of the desert.' The tall nomad with a purple sash around his head towered over Caspar.

'I didn't give my word. That horse is mine! They had no right to bargain with him.'

Caspar found a big, hard hand gripping his shoulder. 'The bargain stands,' came Ceowulf's determined voice. 'Despite his churlish behaviour, we still value the boy's life more than his horse.'

Caspar thought he would cry. He couldn't bear to think of abandoning Firecracker to these traders.

'Home.' The fair-skinned woman looked imploringly into Caspar's eyes. 'Please, home.'

'Spar,' Brid gently took Caspar's hand, tugging him away from the nomads, 'come and help me. I've got to free these women from their terror.'

Half-blinded by hazy tears Caspar numbly followed her as she gathered some dried palm leaves and stones to hold a fire.

'Hops and root of Caballan valerian,' she said, crumbling the conical hops and horny root into a small pot filled with water. She lit the palm leaves and placed the pot over the fire, studiously watching the mixture until it began to simmer gently.

Cybillia steered the women to the fire and gently pressed them down to sit. The two darker women rocked to and fro, wailing, but the light-skinned woman sat quiescently, staring into the flames. Occasionally she cast her questioning eyes around the rest of the group as if some flicker of reality still lingered in her mind.

Brid poured three cupfuls of her brew and, with Cybillia's help, tried to get the women to drink it. 'There,' she said with satisfaction when they finally succeeded. 'Now we just have to wait for it to work.'

The women had helped distract Caspar's mind from Firecracker but now, with nothing to do but wait, he watched bitterly as one nomad tried to mount his stallion. Predictably Firecracker would not stand still. Eventually the man got a foot to the stirrup but before he could swing his leg over the back of the saddle, Firecracker was away, bucking and leaping. The man was flung to the ground and the lean red roan reared over him, squealing like a demon.

Three more men approached but could get nowhere near the stallion's hooves. Caspar grinned to himself. The desert nomads stank of camel and Firecracker would have none of it.

The nomad leader was furious. 'You have cheated in your bargain. You promised us a horse but he is not a horse; he's a devil of the desert winds. And the mare will be worth far less to us without the stallion. I demand a new bargain.'

'You do?' Caspar ran straight to his horse, flinging his arms around the animal's neck.

'Fifty barrels of Caldea's finest wine, a dozen caskets of boar tusks from Torra Alta and ten prize Jotunn bulls. I'll send for them at the next port,' Ceowulf promised, solemnly shaking hands with the chief nomad.

Chapter 12

The Crab and Lobster was stuffy and crowded, far more crowded than was usual even in the long winter evenings of Horning. Pellam was slapped on the back and jovially welcomed by a great many more friends than he knew he had. Some of them he hadn't spoken to for years. It had taken him nearly a month to find a reputable dealer who would buy his gold chain for a fair sum but now at last he had the money and his purse was full.

All the men of Cocklebay wished to drink his good health on Ophidia's finest golden brew and he found himself dipping into his bulging purse with alarming frequency. Of course it was right and proper for a sailor to share his good fortune with his friends. But so many friends! He looked round eagerly for Dionella but he couldn't see her for the press of singing, swaying sailors.

Someone slapped him hard on the back and his frothy drink sloshed over the top of his tankard and spilt down the front of his new doublet.

'It looked too fine on you anyhow,' the sailor laughed mockingly and turned to his fellows. 'Our young Pellam runs off to sea in a plain boat and comes a-riding home on the back of a fine saddle-horse and what's he carrying? Aye, he's carrying treasure! Aye, treasure, me lads, can you imagine? And what's he going to spend it on? Wine? Fine clothes? Women?'

'Women!' the chorus went up as tankards were raised to the heavens.

'Now that's what I'd do. But this young lad, he wants to

buy a lobster boat so he can settle and have a few wee Pellams with the fair maid over there.'

'A toast, a toast to Dionella,' one of Cocklebay's ruddy-faced townsmen cried.

'No, no! A toast to the *Lady* Dionella now it must be. But I ask you, with all that money would you buy a lobster boat?'

'And what's so wrong with buying a lobster boat?' Pellam demanded. 'Besides I'll not even have enough money left for that if you drink on the way you are.'

'Now, it's fair inviting bad luck not to share your good fortune. Every sailor out of Cocklebay knows that.' The man slammed his emptied skin on the wooden table. 'Here, land-lord, another full goblet to toast Pellam's good fortune.'

Pellam groaned. Raising both his hands in surrender, he retreated to a quiet corner, wishing he had never bragged about his fortune. It seemed as if the whole town had come to the tavern, and a swarm of people were now clustered around Dionella. He didn't like that at all. He grabbed her roughly by the arm and pulled her towards him.

'Here, just leave my girl alone, will you?'

Dionella shook him off but smiled gratefully. 'Thanks,' she said and nodded towards a secluded table that crouched unoccupied in a dimly lit recess. A single smoking lantern cast swaying shadows across the scrubbed board. 'I wouldn't be serving here anymore only the landlord begged me to help out since his missus is ill.'

'Well, you shan't do it now,' Pellam proudly declared.

'No, now I'll learn to mend nets and gut fish.' She made a face but her eyes twinkled as she teased her beloved.

'As if there's not a girl in Cocklebay that didn't know how.'

'May I join you?' Their conversation was abruptly halted by a wiry little man with a strange stilted accent. Despite the heat of the stuffy tavern he kept his brown bearskin cloak clasped to his shoulders.

Pellam looked at the cloak and then at the man's thin face

and smoky blue eyes. 'You don't speak Ophidian too well, my good man.' He hooked his foot under a chair and pushed it back, nodding for the stranger to sit.

'No, I'm from Belbidia,' the stranger returned. 'The inn is crowded out and you seem to have the only free space at your table. If I buy you both a drink will you allow me to share your company?'

Dionella smiled. 'Why yes, of course, but you needn't buy the drinks.'

'No, no, I insist.'

'Well it would make a fair change from the rest of the day,' the young mousy-haired Ophidian remarked somewhat ungraciously.

'Pellam!' Dionella flashed him a chastening look, forcing him to smile more good-naturedly.

'Some good fortune then?' the stranger asked, turning to fetch the drinks without waiting for an answer. He returned shortly, precariously juggling three tall goblets, and repeated his question.

'Oh, you could say that.' Pellam sipped at his blood-red drink. 'Caldean wine?'

'I thought it more appropriate for the young lady,' the small man nodded towards Dionella. 'It's lighter than the bitter Ophidian ale and more special.'

Dionella tilted her head graciously and Pellam couldn't help thinking she was lovely and how, at last, he had the chance to make her happy. Never once in his life had he thought any other girl pretty in comparison to Dionella. Well, he thought guiltily, perhaps that wasn't quite true. The young lady with the dazzling eyes from Belbidia was in truth more beautiful than Dionella though he couldn't think exactly why. There was a certain magic about her, a certain beauty from within. So much promise of life.

Dionella smiled sweetly at Pellam's silence. 'We have friends from Belbidia, one from Caldea and the others from Torra Alta. Where might you be from?'

Dismissively, the foreigner spread his hands across the table, small nimble hands that twitched and moved as if his thoughts worked with them.

'Ah, my mother could never tell me for sure,' he said with a self-effacing smile. 'We moved all over, a family of bards and storytellers. And now I travel across the world in search of new tales with which to delight the courtiers' ears when I return home.'

He stretched his arms wide to illustrate the enormity of his travels and the cloak slid from his back revealing a wolf-pelt jacket. The sleeve of the jacket had crept slightly up his arms and Pellam caught a glimpse of thin black scars striping the pale freckled skin of one forearm.

'Indeed,' the Ophidian observed rather coldly. 'I would think there were tales enough in Belbidia already. Troubles in the north, so I hear.'

The storyteller twitched his hand away in disgust. 'Those will soon blow over. There have always been raids along the northern border. It's been going on for years. Anyway, that's just where every other travelling minstrel will be going and I'll be the only one with a new tale. A different tale might bring a bit of life to the bored ears of the nobles and maybe the odd extra silver coin for me as well. Now tell me, fine sir; it seems you've been on an adventure. Perhaps it would make a good tale. The ballad of Pellam of Cocklebay town.'

'He went to sea and found treasure,' Dionella delighted in telling the stranger. 'And he's going to buy a lobster boat and we're to be wed.'

Pellam somehow wasn't sure that they should be telling a stranger about his good fortune. He remembered the furtive looks that Ceowulf and Brid continually cast around them. On reflection, Pellam decided that from the start he had known they were pretending to be people they were not. He wasn't sure if they were up to any good or not, but he was used to that. After all how many of his fellow shipmates were up to their dangling earrings in mischief? As long as the mischief wasn't aimed at him or his own, he didn't think it too much of his business.

At first he had little liked the Belbidians but now he considered them friends and he wasn't about to land them in any trouble. He tapped his purse surreptitiously under the table. After all, thanks to them he could now buy a lobster boat and that deserved his loyalty.

'Aren't you a little young to be getting married?' the minstrel asked, making Dionella blush.

Pellam relaxed. The stranger didn't seem unduly interested in Dionella's revelations of treasure and was no doubt looking for a tale with some emotional interest. These bards liked the softer emotions. After all, the courts were full of young ladies. Perhaps he was harmless after all.

'I would rather marry him now and keep him here than let him sail away into those seas again for another year. If he went away again, he might never come back at all. There's talk of monsters sighted off the coast.'

'So I've heard,' the stranger nodded towards the bustle of the smoky tavern. 'They've been telling me how the sea from Caldea and out through the Teeth was simply writhing with monsters for several days.'

'Well, maybe not quite writhing,' Pellam laughed. 'But we've seen krakens.'

'Krakens!' The man's pale, reddish eyebrows rose up on his forehead. 'Now I thought they were only to be found in story books.'

'Well so did I,' Pellam admitted. He felt quite warm now as he lazily sipped at the sweet-tasting wine. He wondered that it wasn't a little too sweet but he had never tasted much wine and decided not to display his ignorance by commenting on it. 'But they were krakens all right. There were plenty of sightings right from the time when our friends landed in Cocklebay till we reached our destination on the other side of the Teeth.'

The stranger nodded into his tankard. Pellam wondered if he was digesting his words or was lost in thought. The man's expression was so difficult to read.

'Your friends, merchants or sailors perhaps?'

Dionella frowned and replied guardedly. 'One of them is an old friend of my mother's.'

Pellam found the stranger's questioning eyes pressing him for more and without knowing why, he found himself adding, 'A mercenary I think. From Caldea.'

He didn't know why he had said it and felt certain that he should not have done so but the stranger's disconcerting lupine eyes had seemed to compel him to speak. Pellam frowned. This man's eyes were very like Spar's, though Spar's were brilliantly blue and alive like the deepest blue of the sea. The stranger's eyes were pale and faded as if from long illness.

'A mercenary?' The stranger sounded impressed. 'And the krakens hunted you until you got all the way to ... Where did you say?'

'The Farthest Isles.'

'You went through the Teeth in midwinter!' The wiry Belbidian whistled.

Despite himself Pellam couldn't help feeling proud; the stranger was obviously impressed.

'Oh yes. The seas were high and the young girl had to drug the horses, especially that young red stallion, because he had a temper on him you'd never guess of in a horse.'

The stranger nodded again, his thin lips smiling very faintly. The expression looked curiously out of place on his taut features, creating new lines that had never been etched onto his face. His hair was curious too. The tips were a dull flat brown and yet the roots were gingery. Very strange, the sailor thought lazily. Perhaps it was the fashion for Belbidian minstrels to wear brightly coloured hair of different shades. Perhaps they were much like jesters who wore brightly coloured suits all in clashing colours. How was he to know? He was just a sailor from the small port of Cocklebay.

'And, so the locals tell me, you found treasure there on the Farthest Isles. Odd place to find treasure though. I thought the islands deserted.'

'Oh no, not deserted,' Pellam continued drowsily.

'I wonder, did your friends find treasure too?' the Belbidian asked, but not too curiously. He seemed to be studying the lantern above their heads. Pellam felt that the light was beginning to pulse and he pressed at his temples. He felt strangely distracted. He looked hard at the stranger. Perhaps it was a trick of the smoky light but his eyes seemed to be swirling. The man's accent, though stilted, had a silky warm quality that soothed away troubles. Pellam relaxed and leant his chair back against the wall, feeling lulled and distant from his surroundings.

He shrugged uncertainly. 'I don't think so. They turned back east to continue their search.'

The minstrel stood up. 'Let me buy you another drink?' A velvety, compelling tone edged his voice.

Pellam found he could hardly hold his head up as it was, and Dionella had already flopped onto the table, her dark, almost black hair swirling in a thick coil across the ale-blanched surface. Guiltily he thought of what Katalin would say if he brought her home like that. But she had only had one glass of wine. In fact she had only drunk half of it and was now soundly asleep. He had a nagging feeling that the wine was not quite right; the landlord must have shipped in an inferior case.

He was about to refuse the stranger's offer of another drink when he realized the man had already left their table and was talking to a strange-looking group of men who had just entered the tavern, big thick-set men who wore hooded cloaks. The Crab and Lobster suddenly seemed quieter. He nudged Dionella but she wouldn't wake up and he looked thoughtfully after the minstrel. Strange, he thought suddenly. Why didn't the stranger say where he came from when he was clearly wearing a bearskin cloak? Hal had made a point of saying that the thick brown heavy cloaks were only worn by Torra Altans.

He thought back over everything he had said. None of their conversation could possibly trouble his Belbidian friends. No, he was certain of that, so he dismissed the thought from his mind and let his head sag down on the table. His mind aimlessly wondered around thoughts of buying a lobster boat. He now had more than enough money for several boats but one would do. Katalin had always thought of him as irresponsible and he wanted to prove to her that she was wrong. Maybe in a year or so he would think of something else to spend his fortune on.

Chapter 13

Brid unwrapped the mysterious bundle that she had taken from the wyvern's nest and the three women they had rescued shrank back in horror.

Two green spheres, as mysterious and threatening as the dark angry sea above the Crest of Ophidia, glinted in the firelight, tentacles of red blood vessels and globules of yellow fat clinging to their undersides. Caspar feared that some monster would leap out of the dead eyes that swirled and stared as if the wyvern's evil spirit were still alive within them. The three women whimpered, covering their eyes, and Cybillia's breathing became fast and shallow.

Brid held up one of the gelatinous balls in the palm of her hand. 'I'm going to prove to you there are no demons inside. The Book of Names says that the terrifying glint of a wyvern's eye comes from a crystal within it.'

Caspar bit hard on his tongue for fear of gagging, as she gouged the point of her sickle into the gelatinous orb. She sliced into the white spongy tissue behind the iris and finally her sickle ground against something solid. Cybillia covered her mouth as Brid plunged her thumbs into the gory matter and tore the eye open, juices squirting out onto her face.

'Look at that!' Ceowulf exclaimed. 'Brid, you're right!'

'Of course I'm right,' she replied with deliberate smugness, sloshing water from her cooking pot to clean off the last tatters of slimy tissue clinging to a dazzling gemstone. 'It's really quite beautiful. It is believed that when wyverns are first born there are tiny grains of sand in their eyes and as they grow the crystals grow within them. They're quite priceless.' She handed the crystal to the three women. 'Look, this is all you fear.'

Carefully she hid the intact eye from sight, tossing aside the shredded remains of the one she had torn open. Trog leapt at the discarded tissue and hurried away with it before anyone could stop him. Carefully she wrapped the whole eye in palm leaves and replaced it in the cloth, while the three women stared at the crystal. It was an intense green threaded with thin lines of black. At last their eyes blinked and one of the inky-skinned women looked up and gave the hint of a nervous smile. She muttered something incomprehensible.

The fair-skinned woman looked in disbelief at the crystal. 'It's quite beautiful,' she spoke in a deep breathy accent, the words slurring together. 'How can I ever repay you for rescuing us? I thought I'd never see daylight again.' Sorrowfully she dropped her eyes and glared in disgust at her swollen belly. 'But I can never go home to Laverna; look at me.'

Caspar couldn't bear to contemplate how long the women had suffered their terrible nightmare.

'If I went home and they saw the eggs . . . It would be better to die here.'

Brid patted her hand before reaching for her herb scrip. Momentarily the fire-drake poked its red snout out from beneath her shirt and blinked at them before snapping its head back down to resettle alongside the moonstone. The priestess selected a straight slender black root from her pouch. 'Salisian poisoned winter hellebore,' she declared. 'Very poisonous so we must wait for the blessing of the moon to lend us her magic but I can rid you of your burden.' The woman began to sob and fell into Brid's arms, the tears of torment finally flooding out as she abandoned herself to relief.

Thus when the horn of the crescent moon scythed the peak of a dune Brid led the three women into the seclusion of night.

Caspar knew he would be haunted by their screams forever and the next morning he found it impossible to look them in the eye. The two black-skinned women moved with slow doubled-up actions, but at least they chatted to each other in a delightful-sounding language, full of clicks and squeaks between lullaby notes. It was clear they spoke not one word of Belbidian. The fair-skinned woman's eyes were at last bright with relief and she introduced herself as Avriana.

The following day, with the women well-rested and over the worst of their pain, the group decided to move on. Caspar felt his own sense of relief as they rode eastwards, leaving behind the worst of the red desert. Ahead, bursting out of the relentless sweep of coarse sands and shimmering in the mid-morning heat haze, rose the broken shoulders of two extinct volcanoes. Their dark ragged outlines dominated the horizon and marked the edge of the arid wilderness.

'The Dead Gods,' Brid declared. 'This must be it.'

Avriana looked at Brid in amazement. 'You've come all this way across the desert to look at two old volcanoes?'

'It's part of a riddle to a clue. I suppose you could say we are seeking an ancient treasure,' Caspar explained, sticking to the same story they had told Pellam.

Her eyes brightened. 'Really?'

From her enthusiastic response, Caspar thought she was interested in the treasure but, as she continued to chatter, he realized he was wrong.

'My father was a minstrel at the Camaalian court in the capital of Laverna. He spent many of his days making up riddles.' She sighed deeply and wiped at her eyes.

'Do you want to tell us what happened?' Brid asked gently.

The girl looked away. 'I fell in love. His name was Kynan, the son of the under-gardener to King Valerius of Camaalia. Kynan was a fine man with gentle ways, reliable and honest. We'd been courting many years but my father said, "No, Avriana, you cannot marry him. You should choose one of the fine young soldiers who will work his way up through the ranks and give you position."'

'But your heart was set on the gardener,' Ceowulf finished for her.

'Yes. And we'd waited so long I thought I would die an old maid. So I persuaded Kynan that we should elope to Ophidia, send word to my father and return after a few years, by which time I thought my father would have forgiven us.'

'But you didn't make it through the desert,' Caspar guessed.

Avriana nodded. 'I was stolen by the dunedancers who dragged me down into the soil while Kynan was asleep. He probably thought I ran away. But, maybe he looked for me. Maybe he is still looking for me. Who knows? He could be grief-stricken or happily married. But I like to think his love was as deep as mine.'

Cybillia was in tears. There was something about this Camaalian woman's lack of self-pity that made her tale all the more touching.

Later that day, as the first springy grasses feathered the edge of the desert, they fell under the broad cooling shadow of the Dead Gods. Looking up at the horned peaks draped in wisps of cloud, Avriana finally summoned the courage to ask Brid the words of the riddle.

Brid looked doubtfully at her then shrugged. 'Well, it can't do any harm.' Slowly she recited the verse.

They rode on, listening to the sound of Avriana's breathy Camaalian voice mulling over the verse time and time again. After some way, Ceowulf led them off the road and onto a black cinder path that wound up through tufted grasses towards the nearest of the two Dead Gods. Goat bells rang across the valley.

'The riddle tells of a mouth. The gaping hole of a cave in the mountainside would look much like a mouth,' Brid decided.

As the road steepened and the going became increasingly arduous, Ceowulf suggested that Brid, Caspar and Hal continue on alone while he remained to protect the others. The three readily agreed.

After watering the horses at a cool brook, the three Torra Altans made good time. They weaved along the track as it cut back and forth to the higher pastures on the flanks of the old volcano. Caspar rode with renewed vigour. Each step of the journey meant they were closer to finding the Egg and that meant closer to returning home. No longer hampered by the oppressive heat of the desert, they climbed higher, refreshed by the cool air.

After several hours of fruitless searching, Caspar was becoming very hungry and tired. They had finally reached the far side of the biggest of the two Dead Gods and, as the light of day faded fast, they became increasingly despondent. Darkness curtailed their search and, dispirited, they descended back towards the others. The slopes gradually levelled out and they crunched over the gritty soil to be met by the welcome sight of a spitted lamb crackling and sizzling over a well-tended fire.

'We met a shepherd,' Ceowulf explained cheerfully, 'and I bought a lamb from him. 'Anyone hungry?'

Caspar fell out of his saddle in his eagerness to eat.

'Did you have any luck?' the knight asked doubtfully as he studied Brid's crestfallen face.

'I want to think,' she muttered and walked away from the others, followed only by Trog. She took no more than an apple with her for supper.

'We searched everywhere,' Hal groaned, 'absolutely everywhere. And even if there is a cave, we might not find it in a hundred years because the higher slopes are so overgrown with moss and ground ivy. Tomorrow we'll take a look at the other mountain but I think if we're successful it will be more by luck than judgement.'

'We have to find it though,' Cybillia said brightly and blushed as the three Belbidians all turned and looked at her in surprise.

'That's the first time you've shown any concern for *it* – you know, the treasure,' Caspar blurted.

Cybillia shrugged and self-consciously stroked her slowly healing cheek.

'Um, I've been thinking and . . .' Avriana stuttered.

Hal ignored the Camaalian woman, calling over to Brid. 'You're idea of a search is hopeless. Women can never find anything. You should have listened to me.'

'You?!! If I'd listened to you, we'd –'

'Can you two just stop for a moment?' Ceowulf broke in, 'Avriana's trying to tell you something.'

Brid instantly flashed her eyes on the milky-skinned Camaalian woman as if sensing what she had to say was urgent. Hal clamped his mouth shut in silent indignation at being interrupted.

'It's the riddle – I've been thinking about it all day. I don't think it's here at all.'

For just a second there was a flash of anger across Brid's face but her expression quickly turned to hungry eagerness, anxious for anything that might enlighten them as to the whereabouts of the Egg.

'I think you've misinterpreted the riddle,' Avriana explained.

'I have?' Brid sounded quite incredulous at this news while Hal whooped with delight.

The priestess gave him a cool, dark stare.

'You say the riddle is thousands of years old,' the Camaalian woman continued.

Brid nodded.

'Well, when it says "East towards the burning fire" you've taken that just to mean "East towards the sun".'

'Yes, of course.'

'I think it means the volcanoes near Camaalia. You're meant to look "beyond" the Dead Gods, which is here, and then "towards" the fire. They only smoke now but legend has it that the Smokies once sent up great sheets of fire into the sky. I'm not saying I'm right of course,' Avriana humbly apologized for her suggestions. 'And I don't want to disrupt your plan but I really do quite enjoy puzzles.'

Brid sat down quite heavily and twiddled a bit of heather back and forth in her palm. 'Avriana,' she declared, 'you're a genius.'

The Camaalian woman smiled self-deprecatingly. 'I just like riddles.'

That night Brid's spirits were much raised after the frustration of the day and she busied herself with ointments and herbs, preparing shoots of dragonfire and Ophidian pennywort for Cybillia's scarred cheek. Hal, Caspar and Ceowulf grouped closely round the fire, trying to blot out Cybillia's gasps of pain as the mixture burnt into her cheek. Ceowulf couldn't help glancing anxiously over his shoulder towards her.

'I wish it didn't have to hurt her so much.'

For the first time Caspar realized that the Caldean knight was harbouring a slow-kindled desire for the girl. After all, the two of them had spent many days alone together while Cybillia nursed him through the worst of his convalescence.

For many days they rode steadily eastwards towards the Smokies and Caspar passed much of the long journey chatting idly to Avriana, pointing out anything of interest in the changing landscape. She became friendly company for the youth and told him much of her home life and how her family lived in the shadow of the Camaalian king. She was born the youngest of five, though one of her brothers and then her mother had died of plague when quite young. The others had all grown up and married. With heavy irony, she explained how she was her father's favourite and how he had always felt she was destined for higher things than Kynan.

'Higher things,' she laughed. 'He was a good man, my father Talmus, but I think he got airs and graces by spending so much time with the noblemen at court. Their lofty ideals and lack of understanding of the world rubbed off on him.'

Lack of understanding! Caspar was indignant. All noblemen in Belbidia could read and write and were well educated about the world around.

'Tell me about yourself,' the woman coaxed as she sat behind him on Firecracker. 'What would a strange band of Belbidians be doing so far from home without anything to sell? I've met many, many Belbidian merchants – the Camaalian court is awash with them – and they always have something to sell.'

'Not everyone in Belbidia is a merchant,' Caspar laughed. 'There are hunters, soldiers, farmers, cattlemen, fishermen, vine-dressers to name but a few.'

'So what do your family do?'

Caspar hesitated but then decided to tell the truth. There seemed no reason to lie. 'My father is the Baron of Torra Alta, the most northerly barony in Belbidia.'

Avriana laughed. 'It can't be as bad as all that. Why won't you tell me the truth? Smugglers perhaps?'

Caspar could see no reason why the young woman wouldn't believe him. 'No, really. Hal is my father's half-brother. Cybillia is the daughter of the Baron of Jotunn and Ceowulf is the son of the Baron of Caldea.'

'And Brid? I suppose she's the queen.'

'No, Brid is merely related to my mother,' Caspar sidestepped a direct answer on that point.

'Even if I believed the rest of your story I could never believe that. Whoever she is, she outranks all of you because when she says jump you jump.'

'We most certainly do not.'

'Oh, but you do,' Avriana laughed. 'It's the one thing I'm good at – watching people.'

Caspar fell silent at the alarming revelation.

The further east they rode, the more tense and taciturn the Camaalian woman became. 'Kynan,' she murmured once or twice on the wind and Caspar could only guess at her worst fears.

After several long weary days trudging through Glain, they reached an arched stone bridge which spanned a turgid river, choked with red mud. The two dark-skinned girls looked southwards along the red river and clucked and gasped at each other in their own incomprehensible language.

As the horses' hooves chimed on the cobbled bridge, Avriana pointed out the Old Smokies breaking the horizon, their fluted columns of smoke coiling lazily to darken the eastern skyline. Soon the volcanoes overshadowed the landscape where withered and stunted shrubs grew in soil not yet recovered from past eruptions. The horses' hooves crunched over black aerated rocks solidified from molten magma. These darkly smoking mountains that had erupted from the Earth's mantle were so very much more intimidating than the Dead

Gods, their devilish faces smouldering down on the people below.

A foul smell seeped up from the ground where side vents from the earth's broken crust allowed the excess gases to bubble out into the atmosphere. The area was littered by lone boulders as if a giant had scattered them over the ground in a game of marbles. A small stream ran towards them, trickling off the nearest slopes and winding between the ferns and coarse grasses. Bubbles squeezed out between the pebbles on the stream's bed as if some creature were breathing down there, buried beneath the rocks. Deep beneath the earth's crust the volcano was simmering away, emitting gases that percolated through the bedrock to heat the stream. Caspar shuddered and looked up at the Smokies' grey slopes.

'They're alive,' he whispered. 'Breathing like great brooding monsters.'

As before, Ceowulf remained behind to guard Cybillia and the three women while the others continued straight towards the nearest volcano. Rising before them were four volcanoes in all and they argued noisily over which to search first.

'The biggest one in the centre,' Hal insisted. 'You would naturally hide something in the biggest one.'

'No, the most easterly,' Brid insisted. 'It fits the riddle better.'

'Well, you didn't understand that properly from the start,' Hal grumbled. 'It took a jester's daughter to explain it to you. Someone whose mother tongue isn't even Belbidian.'

Caspar blocked their bickering from his mind, riding on alone into the foothills where the hot steam evaporated in clouds from the walls of the sleeping volcanoes. He somehow knew that Brid and Hal were both wrong, feeling himself drawn towards the most northerly peak, most thickly veiled in mist. The dun smoke seemed to puff rhythmically from its crater and its brooding presence made his skin prickle. Caspar was certain that it was somehow alive.

But Caspar was unable to convince the other two and finally they gave in to Hal, who insisted that they search the most westerly volcano first. In silence they began to skirt the mountain and, though they found many caves and crevices, nothing bore any resemblance to a mouth.

'I should have listened to you, Spar,' Brid admitted as they rested for lunch. 'I was too busy arguing with Hal to listen to my feelings but I know what you mean now. That volcano does have a certain presence.'

After they'd eaten, the trio dropped down into the next valley to start the steep ascent of the shaded northern mountain. Caspar felt uneasy as it swallowed him into its secluded world, even more so as Comet's cream coat seemed to disappear into the mist lapping the cooler ground. Caspar worried about losing contact with the others and as the fog thickened he became more and more disorientated. The tracks, which had been carved by sheep and goats scavenging for food, were narrow and disjointed. As the mist closed in and clamped out the sky, Caspar became uncertain whether they were climbing or descending. He kept Firecracker to a very slow steady pace and listened intently for any strange noises in the muffling fog.

'There'll be mists like this at home by now,' Hal sighed, 'but at least there we'd know every inch of the tracks around the Tor.'

'Like the backs of our hands,' Caspar supplied, 'as Old Catrik would say.'

Suddenly he thought someone was mocking him as a thin haunting refrain mimicked his voice but he quickly realized it was only an echo. 'Listen!' Caspar exclaimed only to have his voice drowned by the echo rebounding back and forth between the rocks, lifting and amplifying his words to a larger audience.

'It's a natural amphitheatre,' Brid whispered though even her soft words were projected loudly into the air. 'It's as if the mountain speaks to us.'

'With a mouth,' Hal concluded.

They stared thoughtfully into the gloom and followed the line of the hollowed valley whose sides slowly loomed out of the mist as it narrowed into a gorge. The sound of the horses' echoing hooves boomed out around them, swamping their senses until they reached the head of the valley where a narrow recess led them towards a cold vent in the side of the volcano.

Brid unfurled the moonstone and its white light chased into the cave's shadows, lighting a narrow passage that drew them into the heart of the volcano. Caspar jumped as he saw a bent old woman standing before them, her vividly expressive eyes filled with dark hatred. Like Brid, she was very small. Her long unbraided grey hair fell in a cape about her shoulders and she wore a white silken robe that no longer fitted her tired body. Her eyes were a pale shadowy green, vivid like Brid's but lacking in beauty. A twisted band of silver adorned her arm and a circlet swept back the hair from her face. Gathered behind her were several other women dressed in the same ancient style.

Brid blinked for a moment before exclaiming, 'The Keepers! So we have found you. It makes sense now.'

She hurried towards the woman as if to greet her with a warm embrace but Caspar felt none of Brid's elation. There was a stony cold glint to the Keepers' eyes that he didn't like. As Brid stepped forward with energetic delight, the woman gave a peculiar growl in her throat.

'But the Great Mother has sent me,' Brid stammered, as if totally thrown by this unexpected response. 'I am the Maiden, One of the Three. The Trinity is threatened. The Mother is trapped and dying. Only the power of the Egg can save her. The Great Mother Goddess has sent us to find the Druid's Egg.'

The woman's eyes blackened. In an instant Hal was next to Brid, his broadsword drawn and pushing her behind him.

'Speak, woman! Why do you threaten us so when Brid is one of your high priestesses? Speak.'

'She can't.' Brid's voice was thin with disappointment. 'They've no tongues.' She pushed Hal out of the way. 'This is not a time for force. I can't very well threaten people of my own faith. Of course they are wary of us; we seek the secret they have guarded for thousands of years.'

Caspar understood now. Since the Keepers could no longer safely guard the secret of the Druid's Egg in Belbidia, they must have abandoned the Mother Cauldron to protect the clues to the Egg's whereabouts elsewhere. He was wondering how they survived here alone when more than a dozen men crowded around the seven Keepers. All were brandishing swords though not one of them was even as tall as himself.

'Your weapons,' one man demanded. 'You are out-numbered.'

Brid raised her hand to try to diffuse the tension. 'We do not seek violence nor do we come to desecrate your shrine, but we come at the bidding of the Great Mother. You cannot defy the Great Goddess by denying us access to the knowledge of the Egg's whereabouts.'

The old matriarch merely growled in her throat and, without further warning, the men sprang forward in attack, swords slashing. Caspar nocked an arrow to his bow and loosed three in quick succession. His first shots hit their mark, piercing one of his attackers through the throat and embedding deep in another's chest. But his last arrow missed its target, skimming to the left of his assailant's ear. The man was still moving fast, charging with self-sacrificing bravery upon him. Caspar jerked his hand up for another arrow, fearing that he had no time left to him.

Hal was faring better. Thumping Brid to the ground, he swung round and hacked into a man's back, splitting him through his spine. The man fell heavily onto Caspar, pinning him against the wall, thick blood gobbing from his mouth. By the time Caspar had thrown off the body, Hal had cut another four to the ground, split in half like gutted pigs. A head was rolling away from the fountain of blood that spurted from a severed neck. The five remaining men turned and fled, aban-doning the women who retreated deeper into the cave.

Hal lowered his hand and pulled Brid to her feet. 'Are you all right?'

She shook him off. 'Yes, of course, I'm fine.' She seemed oblivious to the swill of blood around her feet as she stepped through the bodies and, with the ghostly light of the moonstone filling the cavern, strode towards the inner sanctum.

'I am Brid the Maiden and One of the Three and you will obey me,' she declared in fearless tones that echoed around her. 'You are the Keepers who guard the secret of the Egg for the Trinity and I will have it.'

The eyes of the old woman stabbed out of the darkness and glinted red in the light of the moonstone. A bestial growl erupted from her tongueless throat as she barred the way. The light of the orb swam past her and lit a circular shield set into the solid rock at the back of the cave. The moonstone's silvery light was reflected back in a golden sunburst as it touched the yellow metal. Four women were attacking the golden shield with palm-sized sickles, chipping away with frenzied determination.

'Get away from it!' Brid's voice cracked with cold anger.

Not one of the women looked round. Instead they redoubled their efforts as the bristling matriarch stood defiantly before Brid.

The Maiden wasted no time. 'Hal, Spar, stop them,' she urgently commanded as though she were a warrior queen midst the fray of battle. 'Stop them now.'

As they hurried forward, the wizened old woman sprang at Caspar, tearing maniacally at his eyes with her nails. The matriarch was small but still he had to fight determinedly to shake her off. He lunged at one of the other women and tried to drag her away from the shield only to find the blade of a sickle raking against his cheek; nails and teeth sliced into the flesh of his hands. For a second he struggled with his conscience.

These were women and it would be utterly unforgivable to hurt them yet they were behaving like maddened, savage animals and he had to stop them destroying the golden shield. Closing his mind against his conscience he lashed out, one fist connecting with the jaw of a small russet-haired priestess. She didn't immediately fold or collapse as he had expected but sprang back, spitting and kicking with renewed vigour.

Then quite suddenly they stopped as a chilling green light filled the chamber. Brid stood with both hands upheld, one fist grasping the moonstone and the other cupping the fearsome green globe of the wyvern's eye. Caspar tried not to look at it but found himself drawn into the terrifying patterns that froze his heart.

Hal, however, was still gripping the runesword and showed no concern. He pulled himself away from the tangle of women around his neck as they gibbered fearfully. Here in the dark of the cave, the moonstone's glow melded with the green of the wyvern's eye to imbue the Maiden with a terrifying presence.

'Stand away from the shield,' Brid ordered in a coldly calm voice. But the women could not respond. On quaking knees, their faces were fixed on the wyvern's eye. 'Hal, Spar, pull them away,' she ordered, with stern authority.

Hal grumbled in his throat as if resenting the girl's tone but nevertheless obeyed her, hooking his hand under the arm of one of the inert priestesses and dragging her aside. Once Caspar had wrenched his gaze away from the horror of the disembodied green eye, he felt his will return. Following his uncle's lead, he started to pull the women aside. Brid stepped regally forward but as she drew close to the golden shield, her presence seemed to dwindle as she was absorbed in the runic message inscribed in the metal. Her arms relaxed and lowered as she thoughtfully studied the radiant shield embedded in the wall.

'It looks like a sun,' she murmured to herself.

Caspar was following her gaze, tracing out the scuffed and scratched emblems around the rim of the shield, when a sudden movement caught the corner of his eye. The old matriarch staggered forward with blind rage, both hands clasping the hilt of her sickle, which she aimed to dive between Brid's shoulder blades.

Caspar yelled in warning, pulling Brid towards him and alerting Hal. The dark youth started to pivot and raise his runesword. With one swing, he slashed through the woman's thin neck and she sprawled to the ground.

Brid went white with horror. 'You've killed her!' she cried, turning her blazing eyes on Hal. 'She was a priestess, a part of the old ways, a part of us – and you killed her!'

'Brid, it was either you or her!'

'But you killed her,' the Maiden objected, numbly replacing the wyvern's eye in its bag. The remaining Keepers came wailing forward to drag at their matriarch's gory body. 'You've killed her. You've made me betray the Old Faith,' she moaned as the women retreated, mournfully bearing the small bleeding body of their elder from the cave.

Distractedly, she turned back to the golden shield, her eyes quickly intent on the patterns. She fumbled for her scrip and retrieved the crumpled piece of parchment on which was written the cauldron's smudged and ruined message.

Hal sheathed his sword in disgust and slung it across his back. His hand with its missing little finger was covered in blood and he wiped it disgustedly on the clothing of a slain man. 'I didn't make her do anything!'

Brid showed no sign of hearing him. Her fingers traced round the runes on the shield, muttering away to herself while her frown deepened.

'What's the matter?' Hal growled. 'Don't tell me that they've scratched the runes away.'

'No,' Brid still sounded distant as if her mind were struggling with the problem. 'No, we stopped them in time. The metal is very hard and the runes deeply scored so they've had little effect on them. It's just that they don't make much sense.'

'What do they say?' Caspar asked eagerly.

Brid read aloud:

' "From here, think on the door of stone.
Take up the challenge for the warriors' throne.
Learn cut of blade and turn of mount
And ready thyself to be first in account.

> Then on the day of the new crowned queen,
> When the field is arrayed for the battle scene,
> Heed what the runes on the cauldron say
> And only the victor can point the way."'

Brid looked disgusted. '"From here, think on the door of stone." It doesn't mean a thing to me.'

'"From here."' Caspar rubbed at his crooked nose. 'I think we should go outside and see what we can see from there.'

A trail of blood led down from the rock around the entrance of the cave and Brid looked anxiously about her for fear of attack from the remaining Keepers. But they were already swallowed by the mist.

'Where will they go?' Caspar asked, concerned for their plight.

'Where can they go?' Brid replied sadly. 'All we can do to help is find the Egg. If we succeed perhaps their time will come again.' She dismissed the subject with a wave of her hand. '". . . the door of stone . . ."'

The valley was still draped in mist so Brid decided they would have to climb up above it. At last they reached a crag that poked above the veil of mist and from this height they had a clear view over the surrounding plains. To the north-west, Caspar could see the blue-green sea where three ships were slanting in the wind. To the north-east, the sun caught the emerald olivenite towers and glistening copper-green domes of a city. Standing on a rise, it was surrounded on three sides by the quiet waters of an oxbow lake long since abandoned by the main course of the river, which snaked along the border between Glain and Camaalia.

Brid sighed heavily. 'A door! It's ridiculous! You'd never see a door from here. We'd better get back to the cave and destroy the shield in case anyone else finds it.'

'Gold set against rock? It won't shatter like the cauldron,' Hal asserted.

'No, but it should melt. If we collect enough wood to make

a bonfire beneath it we might at least soften it enough to smooth over the writing.'

Brid was right but the task of collecting the timber looked like it was going to be a long hard one. They were all relieved when Ceowulf appeared hurriedly following Trog, who launched himself delightedly at Brid.

'I heard strange echoes booming out from the mountain and was worried for you. It took Trog no time to pick up your scent, so here we are.' He nodded at the blood in the cave. 'No trouble I hope?'

Hal shook his head. 'Nothing we couldn't handle.'

'Huh! Don't be too sure of your skills, young man. It takes many years to train a knight and even then, however great your sword, one day you'll come across someone with more skill than you.'

Trog delighted in the task of building the bonfire. He dashed in and out of the undergrowth, exuberantly searching for his own branch to carry, showing great excitement every time he found one, and repeatedly scraping Caspar's shins with the end of his stick. Brid lit the piled branches and fanned the flames.

They retreated from the smoke to the outer cave and waited for the flames to lap at the shield and melt the gold. Brid was brooding so Caspar steered clear of her and slumped down by Hal who was examining his sword. Only Trog was brave enough to nuzzle up against Brid and she fondly put an arm round his thick neck.

'Are the women all right?' Caspar asked Ceowulf, remembering the rest of their party.

The knight nodded and grinned. 'It was Cybillia who insisted I came to check on you. She made me give her one of my throwing knives and I left her standing on duty with a fearsome look on her face.'

Caspar smiled. He was glad that Cybillia was regaining her confidence.

Hal grumbled moodily. 'Today she might just be feeling brave enough not to need your constant protection, but tomorrow she'll be ordering you around.'

'So you and Brid had another quarrel, did you?' Ceowulf sounded amused.

'It's not funny,' Hal growled. 'I had to deal with these maddened women and she ordered me to drag them aside as if she were a queen and then I was forced to kill one of them.'

'Oh.' Ceowulf immediately saw why Brid was upset. 'One of her own priestesses. I dare say she wasn't too pleased.'

Brid disappeared into the smoking cavern and returned shortly with her mouth buried in her sleeve and her eyes smarting. 'It's done,' she declared, casting a quick black look at Hal and marching stiffly ahead to the horses. As she rode she distractedly played with her hair. Each time she had it neatly plaited into a thick braid, she ran her fingers through the coppery strands to unwind them before starting the process anew.

' "From here think on the door of stone." ' She rolled the words repeatedly over her tongue, each time with some new intonation in her search for their meaning, while Trog snuffled contentedly around Comet's hooves. 'Of course we couldn't see a door; the riddle says *think* not *look*.'

As they approached the base of the volcano, Ceowulf spurred Sorcerer into a canter and the others rapidly chased him. 'Cybillia! What's happened?' he shouted as the girl stood up to greet him. 'Where are the other two?'

Caspar looked hurriedly around the camp. Avriana was calmly prodding the fire with a stick and watching them all, as she often did, through the corner of her eye. The other women were gone.

Cybillia deliberately smoothed out her skirts before answering. 'They just upped and left, that's all. I couldn't very well stop them. They waved their arms about and gabbled at me and in the end I guessed they knew where they were and just wanted to take themselves home.'

Ceowulf relaxed. 'But you're all right?'

The Jotunn noblewoman nodded and blushed, giving them all a warm smile. 'You've been a long time; I was worried.'

Caspar caught Avriana's bright expectant look as she

studied them closely, clearly eager to hear their story. 'We found another riddle,' he told her.

'You did?' she said enthusiastically though she was still too reserved to ask what it said.

'Read it to her, Brid,' Hal demanded sharply. 'She was much better than you at solving the last one.' His voice was abrupt and no doubt designed to wound though the priestess showed not the least concern.

'Avriana, of course! You're good at riddles.' Brid handed her the parchment.

A flicker of self-conscious doubt spread across the Camaalian woman's pale face. 'I can't read,' she admitted self-deprecatively.

Quickly Brid smiled and placed a reassuring hand on the woman's. 'That doesn't matter a bit. I was rude to presume.'

Avriana blushed, smiling warmly at this response, and listened intently as Brid slowly and carefully read aloud the inscription.

Avriana lowered her head as she listened and drew several meaningless circles in the dusty soil at her feet before finally venturing, 'Where it says, "Heed what the runes on the cauldron say" that must mean it's part of a larger riddle.'

'I'm afraid we know that. We have some of the first part but not all. The cauldron gave us the first in a series of clues that led us here and one other bit that says, "Climb above the weeping rocks, rise up above the sorrow," which I don't understand. But we know nothing else.'

Avriana nodded thoughtfully and fell silent for several minutes.

'Well?' Hal demanded. 'What does it mean? Can you solve it?'

'Maybe, I'm not sure, but any good riddle should take some time to solve. Usually the thoughts roll around in your head and then quite suddenly, when you're not thinking of it, the answer just comes to you.'

'But have you any idea?'

Avriana shrugged. 'No, but my father was wonderfully good

at riddles. Maybe if we can find him . . .' She paused in thought. 'His skill amused King Valerius who would have men come from all corners of the realm to challenge him to a contest but never once did anyone outwit him. Kynan, though, never saw the point to riddles.' She sighed heavily and Caspar could see the anxiety in her eyes as she looked eastward towards her home. 'I was just wondering what Kynan made of the riddle of my disappearance. He would have awoken in the desert to find me gone without trace. I wonder what happened to him – whether he's alive.'

Later, as the fire burnt low, Caspar sat and chewed on a bone of mutton, Trog slobbering at his shoulder, waiting for the last morsel. He begged the knight to tell them a story while Brid and Avriana continued to think on the puzzle.

The Caldean's tone mellowed and his eyes brightened as he began his story. 'Lonis is a very wet place with trees so tall and densely packed that men can live right up in the treetops. The Cagog Nomads, they're called. It's a strange land because it has two kingdoms that cover the same area, literally one on top of the other. The farmers, who live below on the land, and the Cagog Nomads, who live in the trees. One day there was a war. The farmers felled a tree because they wanted to clear an area for pasture but this tree had a Cagog dwelling in it. The tree people naturally took this to be an invasion.'

'I presume, then, that you went to fight on the side of the tree people,' Brid interrupted stiffly as if defying the man to contradict her.

'As a matter of fact we did, not because the Cagogs were necessarily in the right but simply because they offered to pay so very much more. I suspect, though, that they were offering money stolen from the Lonisians. But it didn't matter much where it came from. We just did as Gatto told us.'

'I just can't imagine fighting like that for no reason. There's no glory, no triumph,' Caspar blurted.

'No, there wasn't much glory but there was an awful lot of money especially since we were very good at what we did.

But, for our sins, our treasure was stolen from us by the sea on our way home.'

'I'm sure Catrik would have had something to say about that,' Hal laughed.

Ceowulf shrugged. 'I'm not saying I was right; I'm just saying what happened. You get used to the sour taste it leaves in your mouth, I suppose. But I was bitter with life and joining Gatto's mercenaries did much to satisfy my anger at the world. It wasn't until I saw them turn cold-heartedly against my own countrymen, namely your good selves, that I realized how insignificant my misfortunes really were. I mean, does it really matter that my brother will one day be a rich and powerful man while I will own nothing just because he was born a few minutes before me?'

'Minutes!' Caspar exclaimed. 'You mean you're twins.'

'Oh yes. I think that was why I was so bitter until I realized how much more to life there is than being jealous of my brother.'

A black look drew across Hal's face. He had unsheathed his sword and was busily polishing it with an oily rag, periodically testing the edge with his fingernail for sharpness. 'I'm not jealous of Spar,' he remarked pointedly, 'not one single bit. I would hate to be small and freckly.'

Caspar gritted his teeth against his rising temper, trying to will away the bright red glow that flooded over his face. Desperately searching for a retort, he glowered at Hal's smug smile but to add to his humiliation he could think of none.

Just as Caspar thought he could no longer control his rage Ceowulf intervened, positioning himself between the two youths to prevent further trouble. 'Now listen, lads, we were having a nice quiet conversation and then you two decide to make war with each other.'

Caspar moved sulkily away from the others and turned his back on the fire. After a moment, he felt Trog's wet nose snuffling at his arm and was grateful for the unjudgemental company, but he was even more grateful when Brid came and sat quietly next to him. She said nothing for a few minutes but Caspar sensed her breathing in unison with him as if sharing the same body and the same thoughts.

'You should stand up for yourself more. He'd give in if you were more positive about yourself.'

'Hal, give in! We're not talking about the same person here. You don't know him!'

'No, you're probably right,' she agreed. 'But then he doesn't quite know himself either.' She cast a look over her shoulder and studied Hal's brooding back, the light from the fire bathing his strong, growing body.

Caspar fell back into brooding, instinctively aware that Brid was thinking of Hal. It seemed so unfair. Brid's thoughts wandered so closely to his own through the maze of shared imagination and yet she wanted to share nothing more with him. Instead she hankered after the thrill of the unknown that lurked within Hal's mind.

Cybillia was laughing. He looked up with surprise, wondering if he had ever heard her laugh before.

'I'm telling you it's true,' Ceowulf protested. 'The King of the Cagogs, when he wanted to speak to us, was lowered down on ropes and swung backwards and forward in mid-air with his feet kicking and dangling – quite undignified. Then he got caught up in all the branches on the way back up again.'

'I don't believe it,' Cybillia continued to giggle, her eyes dancing as they sparkled with tears of laughter.

Caspar turned back to Brid as they sat alone away from the others, only to see that her eyes still covetously lingered on Hal. He thought to distract her by talking about the riddle on the golden shield. 'Somehow I can't help feeling that we've missed something in all these clues,' he told her.

She flicked her eyes towards him and frowned. 'Well, yes, of course we've missed something. I'm sure the message I copied down from the cauldron would have been very enlightening but it got ruined.'

'I didn't mean that. I was remembering the first clue about the twenty-one standing stones. Because of your knowledge of runes you quickly recognized which henge held the answers.

All together all but one henge formed the rune of rebirth. I can't help feeling that we've overlooked something that would lead us more directly to the answer, something that has more of a pattern, more design in it than these haphazard riddles. They're too cryptic, too complicated.'

'But they're meant to be complicated,' Brid told him patiently. 'The Druid didn't want just anyone to find the Egg.'

'You keep telling me that the laws of the Great Mother are the laws of nature,' Caspar tried to explain his hunch. 'Nature is full of symmetry and design. I know it's daft but I can't help feeling we're looking at a pattern somewhere in all this but haven't quite realized it.'

Brid sighed and rolled out the map. 'I can't see how we've missed anything.' She spread the parchment out in front of Caspar. 'What pattern is there to see other than the pattern of the henges?'

'I don't know,' Caspar despaired. 'It was just an instinct. Look, we started here at a confluence of power with Keridwen – my mother,' he faltered. 'From the Vaalakan glacier we moved south towards Torra Alta, then on to Farona where we thought the cauldron would be but it wasn't; it was in Ildros in Caldea. From there we went to the Farthest Isles, another confluence of power, and now we're tracking east again.' He traced out their journey with his finger. 'The more I look at it the more I'm sure that it's part of a pattern, but I just can't see it.'

Brid stared at the parchment for several long minutes but simply shook her head. 'If only the parchment hadn't been ruined then maybe it would be clear.'

Beneath the brightness of the southern stars it was difficult to sleep and the unresolved riddle of the golden shield played heavily on Caspar's mind. He decided that if he concentrated on the problem hard enough, an answer would eventually spring to mind – but nothing came; only sleep.

In the middle of the night they were all startled awake. The crescent moon, sharply defined in the clear night of Lenting, was full overhead, and bathed them in its fragile blue-white light.

Avriana was on her feet, laughing with delight.

'I've got it! I know what the first part of the riddle means.'

Chapter 14

Spurred on by Avriana's revelation they set out early in the cool of the next morning. But after only a couple of hours Caspar had to protect his head from the garish sun with a white cloth. He swished irritably at the flies buzzing around him. If it was this hot in early spring, what would it be like here in high summer?

'It's not far to Laverna now,' Avriana assured them. 'There's only two valleys between the Old Smokies and the Serpent, the river that divides Glain from Camaalia. It used to be very fertile, so they say, but even this far north you can see how it's drying out.'

Brid shook her head sadly.

They crossed the first valley and passed over a small range of rounded hills into the second. The ground was cracked and divided into hexagonal sections where the desiccated soil had shrunk and broken apart. The valley bottom was lined with sand and to either side the limestone rocks rose up in steps, scored by horizontal striations where the wind had lashed the bare rock face with grit from the desert. Fluted dunes skirted around blocks of stone, toppled pillars, arches and crumpled domes, where once a grand dwelling had stood. Avriana covered her head as well as her face with a makeshift veil created from one of Cybillia's petticoats. She explained that a Camaalian woman wouldn't dream of venturing out of doors without a veil; the sun was too stripping for their fair skins.

'Are these they?' Brid asked incredulously, as they entered a shallow valley.

Ceowulf nodded. 'The fabled gardens of Mesmera where

once violets, daphnia and jasmine filled the air with their heady scent, and women bathed in the shade of the sandalwood trees. Here the fairest princess ever born attended her father's court and greeted a thousand suitors every year. She lived in a castle of pearl and ebony with silver leafing on the floors and diamond-studded ceilings. It was set within a garden of fountains which showered its exotic plants in a dewy mist so fine that rainbows danced in the sunlight.'

'What happened to her?' Caspar asked, looking round at the cracked soil and the chipped masonry that littered the valley floor, half-buried in the fine dust.

'She needed to be absolutely sure of her choice of suitor because the future of her people depended on it. You see, she was the heir to the old kingdom of Astaria, which is now divided into Glain and Camaalia. She knew she was so beautiful that she could have the choice of any man in the world. But no one was ever quite perfect. Year in, year out they came and worshipped her beauty but she could never decide. Then one year they stopped coming.'

'Plague or pox?' Caspar asked.

'Oh no, neither. She had just become old and her beauty had withered. The young men finally realized that she wanted a perfection that no man could ever attain.'

Cybillia looked wide-eyed around her and absent-mindedly brushed at her cheek. Much of the skin had healed and the remaining red- and silver-streaked scars were only visible as feathery lines.

'And then what happened?' Caspar prompted, always eager for a tale.

'Well, according to the story,' Ceowulf continued, 'she had two younger sisters, both married with fine sons to carry on the family name. In the end old King Japheth decided to divide his great realm in half. He gave one half to his middle daughter and the other to his youngest, since they had husbands to oversee the people and sons to inherit their kingdoms. And that's how Camaalia and Glain came about.'

'But what about Princess Mesmera?' asked Cybillia.

'The garden around her withered as she too withered and, what was once beautiful, turned back to dust. But they say you can still see her tomb. If the desert storms haven't been blowing too strongly up from the south and buried it, we should be able to find it up by those big marble pillars.'

Cybillia insisted on finding it.

Ceowulf was right: the tomb, half-visible beneath the mounds of sand, lay in the shadow of the toppled pillars. The sand was so dry that it whispered as it flowed and filled Cybillia's footsteps long before she had climbed to the top of the tomb's entrance. The once proud portal was nearly covered but the tablet at the head of the architrave was still partially exposed. Kneeling, she swept aside the time-heaped sands to read the inscription:

> ' "My name is Princess Mesmera and my bones lie in the sand.
> Look, everyone, about you for this was once my land.
> Once it was a splendour, a wonder past compare
> But now, like me, it lies as dust where the wind has picked us bare.
> Listen to the moaning wind, listen to his song,
> For I lived but a very short while and the wind will be here long." '

Cybillia dabbed at her eyes as she brushed aside the sand from the inscription. Brid placed her hand on the girl's shoulder.

'It wasn't a sin for Mesmera to be beautiful. There is no sorrow in being beautiful, and no doubt it wasn't her fault that everyone spoilt her for it. But she alone holds the blame for her own plight. Her downfall was that year in, year out she made the same mistake but never learnt from it. She thought her beauty made her immortal but those who are blessed with it should know that like a plucked rose from the garden it quickly fades.'

'I was beautiful once,' Cybillia sighed. 'But I have lost it.'

'Well, no, not really,' Brid said sympathetically, 'though none of us exactly looks our best at the moment. Your hair's growing back and, in the right light, your cheek's hardly noticeable.'

They marched throughout that day, stopping only to water the horses at the infrequent streams that trickled out from underground springs. Caspar was shocked by the parched barren land so close to the Serpent river. The terracing and irrigation channels were still just visible and he easily imagined the once fertile landscape to have been lush with olive trees and vines. It had all now been ruined.

Avriana rode behind Ceowulf now, since Sorcerer was better able to bear the extra weight than the slender-boned Firecracker. Her eyes peeked over the top of her veil and fixed firmly on the horizon.

'Last time I rode through here,' Ceowulf explained, 'it was summer and we were wearing full armour. It was like being in a kettle and two men died from exhaustion, fried in their own sweat.'

'The last time I rode through here it was with Kynan,' Avriana said quietly. 'I'm not exactly sure how long ago it was. Two years maybe three. I wonder if he'll still be there when we get home to Laverna.'

No one could think of anything to say to ease the woman's pain. Hal coughed anxiously and drew attention to the buzzards that hung with lazy purpose above a crag. Cybillia turned her face away, biting at her lower lip. Brid, however, eased Comet alongside Ceowulf's heavy-boned destrier and reached out to Avriana to smooth her hand with a light touch.

'I'm so sorry, Avriana. I know there's nothing that we can say to stop you worrying. You can only wait till we get there to see what has happened and you must be brave. There is nothing else you can do.'

Avriana turned her veiled face towards the Maiden. There was the hint of a tremor in her husky voice. 'Thank you for your kindness. And thank you for not saying that you're sure everything will be fine and that he'll just be waiting there for me to come home, because I know that sort of thing just doesn't happen. It helps to be realistic and at least I have other things to occupy my mind,' she smiled bravely. 'This riddle is very perplexing.'

'Too perplexing?' Brid groaned.

Avriana seemed to rise to the challenge. 'But we solved the first part so there is hope. And it really wasn't that hard in the end,' she exclaimed delightedly.

Caspar smiled to himself, thinking that *they* had solved nothing and only Avriana's unusual mind had managed to probe the hidden meanings.

Hal raised his eyebrows at his nephew. 'Not hard, she says.'

'Well, now I agree, you could never have solved it because you don't speak Camaalian. The riddle may be written in Belbidian but, presumably because it was placed in Camaalia, it uses more of the Camaalian way of thinking. Since the Camaalian words for door and gate are identical, it should have been blindingly obvious. I'm obviously a little rusty. So what we are looking for is not the door of stone, which you imagine to be something quite small such as the entrance to a house or a cave. No, it should be the gateway and the most likely place for a gateway is one leading into a walled city and everyone knows where the gateway of stone is.'

'Of course. Sequicornum Castle,' Ceowulf supplied. 'The approach to the citadel is marked by two upright stones – two monoliths, I suppose you would call them, standing three times as high as a man. And then of course the middle part of the poem, "Learn cut of blade and turn of mount", becomes clear, because once you pass through the gates of stone, there before you lies Camaalia's famous training ground for knights.'

'And then what?' Caspar asked, watching Hal draw the runesword and examine the blade. The taller youth squared his shoulders and looked wistfully ahead at the mention of the acclaimed training school.

Ceowulf snorted condescendingly. 'I wouldn't get any ideas, about that, Hal. The contestants train for many years; you wouldn't last two seconds even during practice.'

Hal raised an unworried eyebrow. 'We'll just see about that.'

'But when we get there what do we look for next?' Caspar demanded though his mind wasn't fully focused on the riddle. Like Hal, he too felt his adrenaline surge at the thought of the great reputation of the Camaalian training grounds.

'We don't know,' Brid answered. 'We can only hope that something falls into place. If only Hal hadn't been so careless in the bogs around Nettleymarsh we would still have the whole inscription from the cauldron.'

'Of course,' Hal replied curtly. 'Blame everything on me.'

The capital city of Camaalia loomed large on the horizon and the weathered copper domes and fluted minarets brought a burst of colour to the dusty valleys. A vast cathedral with glittering emeralds studding its buttresses was set like a crown at the head of Camaalia's splendid capital. There was a geometry to the city radiating out from the central spike of the spire. To Caspar it was as if the sun had been caught in the heart of a cut emerald that now sparkled out its radiance over the surrounding land.

'Laverna was built by King Verdinand a thousand years ago,' Ceowulf explained as they waited for the ferry that would take them across the Serpent. 'It was Gatto's home city and he was very proud of it. King Verdinand apparently wanted to build something that would outshine the avaricious green of the wyvern's eye and he felt that the reflection from the cathedral would do something to shy away the creatures.'

'He must have built the city all in one go,' Brid surmised, staring up at the lines of the city's streets as the ferryman hauled them across the broad sluggish river. 'How else could he have created such uniformity?'

Avriana who had withdrawn into herself at the first sight of the city managed a small laugh. 'Oh no, Camaalians love uniformity. And elegance of course. Structure is very much part of our lives. That's why I like the riddles so much because they confound all the logically minded folk. Though actually Father loves them for exactly the opposite reason, claiming that it's a logical mind that solves them but I don't agree.' Her usual husky voice was high and shrill and a patch of crimson tingeing her cheekbones was just visible above the top of her veil.

The horses now struck firm paved road as they trotted towards the city and out of the desiccated landscape. Irrigation channels ran from springs at regular intervals, forming neat geometric designs as they moved out of the random patterns of nature and towards the sterilized world of civilization. As they reached Laverna's vast copper gates, whose scrolling metallic leaves belied the nature of the lands around them, Avriana raised her eyes. They were full of foreboding. Staring at the layout of the city before him, Caspar was amazed at the Camaalians' limitless capacity to recreate endless symmetry in every detail.

'It's like a spider's web,' he suddenly declared, gazing at the patterns ahead of him, 'with all these central roads leading in and linked by concentric circles of smaller roads. It's quite extraordinary.'

'No. It really is quite dull,' Avriana contradicted with feeling. 'All through my youth I longed for an unexpected twist in the road or an unprecedented curve to a building.'

The only things that were not uniformly placed were the circular ornate towers that appeared to be randomly dotted throughout the city. They looked like well-heads and each one had been decoratively finished as if with great reverence.

'They're ventilation shafts for the old copper and emerald mines,' Avriana reliably informed him.

Eagerly both Hal and Caspar peered into the nearest well and, leaning precariously from his mount, Caspar hooted into the hollow shaft, listening for the sound of his echo. Just as his echo died, the younger Torra Altan thought he heard some strange knocking sound. 'What was that?' he asked anxiously. 'I'm sure I heard something.'

'There's no one down there,' Avriana reassured him. 'They worked out the western section of the mine hundreds of years ago. It was probably just dripping water or something.'

It most certainly was not, Caspar thought, but didn't want to argue with the woman. The taut frown on her blushed face made it quite clear that she already had too much on her mind. As the beat of their horses' hooves echoed through the swept streets of Laverna, Avriana started to fidget and pluck at her filthy dress and sand-stained veil. Brid looked at her anxiously and called a halt.

'We can't possible bring Avriana home like that. Ceowulf, will you find an inn for us where we can all have a bath. Avriana can come with Cybillia and me to find some clothes.'

'Oh no, I couldn't possibly,' the Camaalian woman objected. 'I have no money.'

Brid dismissed her with a sweep of her hand. 'But Hal has.' She held out her open palm to the scowling youth.

He ground his teeth and looked blackly back at her. 'You overstep the mark,' he hissed and avoiding Brid's outstretched hand, he pressed several silver coins firmly into Avriana's palm. 'Look, it's nothing. Take it.' He gave her a broad, generous smile.

'I can't,' she insisted but her eyes kept flicking towards the money and then at her shabby clothes. Torn between the two emotions, she chewed her lip.

'All right then,' Hal said softly. 'Accept it as payment for helping us solve the riddle. Will you do that for us?'

Avriana relented and gratefully took the offered money. 'There's a quiet inn just up the street a little and to the right,' she told Ceowulf. 'We'll pass a dressmaker's on the way.'

Ceowulf looked around him at the Camaalian women hurrying about their business. The older women were dressed in drab black with knitted shawls. The younger women were fractionally more adventurous in subdued blues and greens but all of them, even the youngest girls, wore veils. He looked thoughtfully at Brid and Cybillia.

Just as they reached the dressmaker's, Ceowulf drew Brid aside from Avriana. 'It certainly wouldn't do any harm if you went native,' he suggested. 'The veils would be a very practical disguise, but you'd have to put a dress on too. You'd look pretty silly in hunting leathers and a veil.'

Brid agreed. The Camaalian veils were of finest silk and

hung from tiaras clipped into the wearer's hair. They would distract attention from her unusual eyes and hide the faint remains of Cybillia's scars.

'I know we're far from home and any threat of King Rewik's Inquisitors but Laverna's full of Belbidian merchants,' the knight reminded her. 'And besides the Camaalian men are staring at your exposed faces. They're obviously not used to seeing unveiled women.'

Hal was bristling indignantly at four youths who stopped to stare at the Belbidian maidens, his fingers drumming on the hilt of his sword. Only Ceowulf's quick reaction in placing a solid hand on his companion's shoulder prevented the youth from rashly drawing his weapon.

It took several hours before Avriana and the two Belbidian girls were finally washed, brushed and ready. Cybillia and Brid were almost unrecognizable in the repaired dresses they had long ago bought in Farona. The Jotunn noblewoman wore a decorative dress of soft pink with cream sashes and bows that fanned out from her hips. A constricting bodice squeezed her waist and her bosom was demurely veiled with lace. She looked the perfect lady. Brid was more simply dressed in the delicate folds of a pale blue robe that clung to her slender hips and swirled around her ankles. Nevertheless the coppery-haired priestess was immediately more engaging. The simple understated design exaggerated her blossoming curves, moulding in soft folds to her form and whispering against her graceful body.

Avriana had bought a sober green dress with very little embroidery or shaping but she seemed very pleased with it. She looked around at her rescuers. 'Thanks. It's all I can say though it sounds so little for everything you've done for me. You've all been so kind.' She turned towards Ceowulf. With a half-laugh that did little to disguise her stressed emotions, she teased, 'These four are so very understanding for ones so very young.' She then took a deep breath as if steeling her nerves. 'Nearly there now. Nearly home.'

Brid pressed her hand in support.

There was an orderly hush to the bustle of the city. Nobody

yelled their wares or haggled frantically as they might in Farona's grain markets. Instead the traders set about their business in orderly fashion, working earnestly hard throughout the middle of the day.

'As a man from Caldea, the very thought of working through lunch time makes me shudder.' Ceowulf looked disapprovingly around him. 'It's only right to have a solid meal and a long rest when the sun reaches its zenith. Just like Gatto, these people never rest till their day is done. He always said lunch interrupted the flow and the concentration.' For a moment the free-lance looked burdened with sorrow and Caspar suspected that he regretted the necessity of killing his former colleague. Despite the man's ruthlessness, Ceowulf had evidently held him in some regard.

'Well, so it does,' Hal argued. 'If you stop at lunch time you then have to continue into the chill hours of evening to get your work done.'

'There's no point arguing about it,' Brid interrupted. 'Torra Alta doesn't suffer the heat of Caldea's midday summer sun so that easily explains the difference. Mind you, we're further south than Caldea here and it surprises me that they have such northern customs.'

'Oh, not at all,' Avriana interrupted. 'You obviously don't know the full history of the city. Princess Mesmera's youngest sister inherited it. She married a baron from Belbidia, from Nattarda I believe, and he brought many of his customs with him.'

Cybillia made a face at the mention of Jotunn's neighbouring barony. She had often referred to her father's low regard for Baron Wiglaf of Nattarda.

The houses of each street were all painted a uniform colour but each street was subtly different from the last, hence the city was divided into bands of varying shades. At the head of every fourth row stood a larger house with a bright red door. Avriana explained these belonged to the prefect of each section.

Ceowulf led the way with Avriana giving directions.

Respectfully caught up in the tension of the woman's emotions, the rest rode behind in silence.

'Nearly there,' Avriana announced as they reached a broad street lined with fountains that led to a marble palace. 'King Valerius's,' she explained laconically before directing them around to the mews at the back of the palace. Several grooms looked up curiously at their approach, though they continued to brush vigorously at the gleaming dappled coats of six greys that stood in the courtyard.

Avriana led them wordlessly through the mews to a little back alley, set neatly at right angles to the main street, where a row of low terraced cottages cowered beneath the shadow of the palace.

'It's the third one on the left,' she muttered and briefly raised her veil to dab at her glistening eyes. Caspar could see her hands shaking as Ceowulf helped her down. She looked at them all in trepidation. 'I daren't go in.' Then she looked back with pleading. 'You won't say about the wyvern . . . You'll only say he held me prisoner. No more than that,' she begged.

'Of course not,' Brid assured her, stepping lightly forward to grasp her hand reassuringly while Cybillia took her other trembling arm. Ceowulf and the two youths hung back, wary of the emotional intensity.

'I can't go in,' Avriana stammered.

'You have to.' Brid was firm but kind. 'The longer you wait, the worse it will feel.'

She knocked purposefully at the door and they waited several long, heart-stopping minutes until they heard the approach of stumbling feet and an awkward scratching noise from within. Very slowly the bolt drew back, and the door opened to reveal a man standing in the shadow of the door. He was tall and quite certainly far too young to be Avriana's father. Caspar guessed despondently that the old man had either died or moved away from the house.

He studied the man whose tight skin was strangely mottled as if he had suffered terrible burns. Though wasted and gaunt, his broad frame made him look as if he had once been strong.

There was an anxiety about his movements and he held his hands awkwardly out from his body. His eyes were dead white. He demanded something in Camaalian and waited expectantly for an answer.

Caspar saw the horror and disbelief in Avriana's face and instinctively he knew that the blind man was Kynan. She staggered forward but then swooned into Brid's small arms.

The man repeated his words and then paused, finally reiterating in Belbidian, 'Who knocks at the house of Talmus? Who are you? Answer me?' he demanded, evidently unsure and displeased by the activity. He jerked his head and looked straight at Caspar and his companions as, with the heightened sensitivity of a blind man, he felt their presence. Firecracker snorted and stamped a hoof and the man started.

'Horses. What do horsed men want here at the house of Talmus? You know the old man is ill.'

Brid left Avriana to Cybillia's care and stepped lightly forward to take the Camaalian's hand. 'You are Kynan?'

The man nodded, tensing as if aware that she brought news of great import.

'We have come from afar and last moon we travelled through the deserts of Glain.' Her voice was gentle and calm. Reassuringly pressing the man's hand, she prepared him for the shock. 'We found her held prisoner by dunedancers and a wyvern. Avriana is well and we have brought her home.'

His mouth slowly caressed the woman's name as it slipped though his lips. 'Avriana,' he breathed incredulously. 'Where?'

'Here.' Brid led him forward to where the woman lay blinking in the sunlight. Her hand stretched upwards beseechingly for Kynan's touch and he knelt down beside her, wrapping her in his thin arms.

'Avriana, answer me.'

There was no word that could escape the woman's lips and only a sob cracked in her throat as she clung ever tighter to the man's body. The years of pain and anguish were too deeply scarred into her mind to be washed away in a single moment. She gasped back her sobs and they spoke softly to each other in their own tongue for several minutes before Avriana's tear-streaked face looked up at Brid.

'He's alive,' she choked. 'After all this time he's alive.'

Caspar found his tongue was thick in his throat and he prodded at the corner of his eye, which was beginning to prickle with hot tears. Hal hastily coughed.

'I looked for her,' Kynan sobbed, as though trying to excuse himself. 'I searched for years. Eventually I stumbled back to Camaalia, where her father found me weak and broken from grief. Talmus was frail with age and worry but still he cared for me out of loyalty to Avriana's memory. I could do nothing but stay and wait for her return. And now she is here.'

The two Camaalians stayed wrapped in each other's arms, Kynan rocking the woman to and fro like a baby. An old man, bent double and supporting himself on a stick, stumbled from the shadows within the cottage, grumbling and muttering.

'Kynan?' he questioned, obviously confused by the commotion but on seeing the woman enfolded in the blind man's arms he dropped his stick and fell on his knees beside her. 'Avriana,' he gasped.

The emotional reunions took several minutes and Cybillia and Brid withdrew and motioned that they should quietly slip away from the scene and return to the quest but Avriana turned towards them with tear-stained cheeks. 'No, you cannot leave without accepting our hospitality. We must in some way thank you for what you have done. Leave your horses in the mews and then come back so that we can offer you food and shelter for at least one night before you continue to the stone gates of Sequicornum. Please, it will soon be dark.'

They accepted with much pleasure since it was many days since any of them had slept in a real bed.

On returning from the mews, they were ushered into the parlour of the small cottage. Trog leapt into a chair by the fire and stared imperiously around him before scratching undignifiedly at his collar.

Avriana, too, looked curiously around her at the room. She lifted her veil and swept it back over her hair. There were several work benches lining the room and each was covered with carved pipes and flutes. A variety of chisels and gimlets lay neatly to one side. With expert hands, Kynan swung the kettle over the fire, refusing to allow Avriana to help him.

'The flutes?' she queried, speaking in Belbidian in deference to their guests.

The old man nodded towards Kynan. 'He came home, what was it, a year and a half ago now. He had searched for two years in the deserts, living off lizards till eventually his eyes were burnt away by the stripping sun. When he returned, he found me a man broken by grief for the loss of my daughter and no longer able to work. And in memory of you, he stayed here to care for me as would have been his duty if you had been married. Despite being unable to see, he taught himself to carve these flutes. He has great sensitivity in his hands.' The old man seemed to have straightened up a little. 'And now you are home, perhaps I will once more play them for the King because my heart is filled with happiness.'

Avriana beamed.

'You will be married,' the old man declared. 'As soon as you feel fit.'

Trog yipped excitedly as if he had understood the words. He leapt onto the floor and dashed madly about, scattering chairs as if he were hunting an imaginary rat.

'He senses our emotions and then gets over-excited,' Brid explained while everyone laughed at the dog's antics.

'I'd swear he's laughing too,' Avriana exclaimed.

After Avriana and her husband-to-be had prepared a full meal of pottage and hotpot, they ate contentedly and relaxed around the fire. Kynan and Avriana longingly touched hands across the hearth until it was time for them all to retire to their rooms for the night. The cottage was small with only two bedrooms. Brid and Cybillia left to sleep in the same room with Avriana while the two Camaalian men retired to the other. The three Belbidian men insisted they would be comfortable sleeping by the fire.

Avriana laughed. 'You know, these young men tried to tell

me their fathers were great Belbidian noblemen. But now I know they are not because they are happy to sleep on pallets by the hearth. Noblemen would demand to have proper beds and a room to themselves.'

Caspar drifted off to sleep almost immediately, content at least that they had united Avriana with her beloved Kynan. Later that night he woke suddenly as if some sixth sense had startled him awake. He sat bolt upright in the pitch dark. Alarmed and disorientated but certain that someone had woken him, he called out, 'Who's there?'

Heavy footsteps rushed down the stairs and a black shape appeared by the door. Ceowulf was already awake and quickly lit a candle. Kynan stood in the middle of the room, feeling anxiously about him.

'What's the matter?' Caspar demanded, already on his feet.

Kynan was staring blankly beyond him and slowly pulled the boy protectively towards him. Utterly unnerved by the fear in the man's expression, Caspar turned to study the room. Kynan's dead eyes appeared to be following the movements of something but, whatever he sensed, it was not visible to Caspar.

The Camaalian muttered something that sounded like a command. Met with stony silence he repeated it in Belbidian. 'I know you are there. Come out and show yourself.'

'But there's nothing there?' Hal objected. Nevertheless, the metal of his sword whispered across the sheepskin lining of his scabbard as he drew the blade.

'I might not be able to see but I know when there's a thief about,' Kynan growled. 'You get to sense things. There's someone here.'

The skin on Caspar's neck was beginning to prickle. He stared into the shadows as Ceowulf lit another candle and stoked up the fire. With his sword drawn, he roughly pulled aside the chairs from the edge of the room.

Light steps pattered down the stairs and Brid breathlessly alighted into the room. A pale white glow of luminescence shone around her as she held the moonstone above her head.

The light fingered into the crevices and niches, dipping behind the black kettle in the hearth and probing the chimney. A spray of light caught the runesword and then dived off it again, refocused as a single point of light. Just for a fleeting second Caspar caught the image of a face – a very human face though the eyes were big and the mouth and nose too small.

There was a greenish-brown hue to the creature's skin and, as it looked greedily into Caspar's eyes, its tongue slipped out between small pointed teeth to flicker at him. Brid ran forward and thrust the light of the moonstone aggressively into the creature's face. With a waifish shriek the image was gone, sliding out between the shutters and dissolving into the night.

'What was that?' Hal sounded almost nervous.

'I don't know,' Brid murmured. 'I've never seen one before. Maybe a goblin.'

The old man of the house, with Avriana at his shoulder, shuffled into the room and looked bewilderedly at the moonstone. 'What manner of witchcraft have you brought into my house?'

Kynan hurriedly said something in Camaalian and Talmus was pacified. 'A thief? Here in my house?'

'It was no ordinary thief,' Kynan continued. 'It smelt of evil and malice. I could feel it directed at the boy here.' As he spoke he never once took his eyes from the moonstone and his face took on a wondrous expression. 'I can see it. I can see the glow and I can see Brid's shadowy outline. I can see your light,' he gasped. 'It's so . . . so beautiful.'

The old man drew up a stool and sat by the fire. He calmly turned to Avriana and, as courtesy demanded, spoke in Belbidian so as not to exclude his guests. 'Get us all some warmed wine to bolster our spirits, child. Now tell me, what did you see in my house?'

Brid explained in great detail.

'By what you describe, I'd say it sounds like a knockerman,' he replied with a dismissive laugh, 'though I can't believe it. The city is built over a deep mine that penetrates far into the soil. In olden days when men crept down with pick and shovel to claim the minerals, they would occasionally come running back to the surface, shouting about the strange and peculiar knocking in the rock. So a story grew up around the mines that there were little green creatures living down there who made these strange noises that no one could trace; they called them the knockermen.'

'I didn't realize,' Brid answered. She looked anxiously towards Caspar and whispered, 'You shouldn't have called down into the mine.'

'Of course they now realize that it wasn't creatures at all but minute movements in the earth,' Talmus continued, not hearing the Maiden's softly spoken words, 'so I don't believe that's what you saw. It was no doubt just a trick of the light.' The old man looked uncertainly at the moonstone. 'It's quite extraordinary, a fascinating bauble. A luminescent gas, some phosphoric compound, I imagine, spontaneously igniting on exposure to the air.'

Brid snorted in disgust.

Hal turned and burnt his furious eyes into hers. Avriana looked at the Maiden reflectively, a spark of growing recognition in her eyes, and she smiled knowingly as if she sensed there was more to this than her father imagined.

Caspar wondered at the Camaalians' response. Quite unlike any Belbidian, Kynan and the old man were unafraid of the old magic. The Camaalians obviously dismissed witchery simply because they found it illogical. It had been hounded from their land many hundreds of years ago and since they had little memory of it they no longer believed in its existence.

The pragmatic Camaalians shortly took themselves off to bed, leaving the superstitious Belbidians alone, with their fears of the dark.

'I saw it as clearly as I see any of you.' Hal was quite positive. 'Much as I would like to agree with the old man, I know my eyes didn't deceive me.'

Brid solemnly put the moonstone away. 'The runes of sorcery have called up all the dark and sinister creatures who, wary of man, slither and creep through the dank shadows of this world. I fear that since they have raised these creatures they may also have drawn the beasts of power from the Otherworld. I fear that their spirits are following us to the Egg.'

Silently, she contemplated the glowing embers of the fire before continuing, 'He who holds the Druid's Egg commands these creatures. But for the moment it is the Egg that keeps them locked within the Otherworld, where they are forever trapped in limbo between this world and the bliss of Annwyn. If they get to it before Spar can hold it in his hands, they will control their own destiny. The weaker creatures that still lurk on the earth are not of so great consequence. But if the dragons, griffins, unicorns, winged-horses and sabre-toothed wolves are released from their exile to roam the earth once more, then there will be no place left for man.' Brid dropped her head for a moment, tugging at her plait.

'It's all my fault. I used the sword to stir the potion in the Mother Cauldron. The sword distorted the magic and the runes of sorcery were cast. They awoke these creatures before time. We should not have stirred them until we held the Egg and the power to control them.'

Caspar was disturbed by her words and couldn't sleep for the rest of the night. He feared the knockermen, but worse was his dread of the fearsome, shadowy creatures that sought to steal into his thoughts, scavenging for the secret location of the Egg.

Brid stayed down in the parlour for the remainder of the night, cradling the moonstone in her lap to ward off any more of the spirits. The throbbing power of the crystal cried out to Caspar, its restless energy fraying at his nerves. He knew he must try to resist the call but he desperately wanted to reach out and touch the globe so that he could delve for his mother whose soul was trapped inside the crystal.

'Some kind of phosphoric gas,' he sneered. No gas could produce images so vivid and compelling, with all the emotion and power of real people. The salamander had crawled out from Brid's clothing and sat basking in the warmth of the fire.

One claw was placed firmly on the orb. Caspar felt sure that the animal was paler and had lost much of its deep scarlet hue. He wondered if it would turn white like the mutant dragon.

With relief Caspar finally heard the first signs of movement from the waking streets. He opened the shutters and let the welcome light of daybreak flood into the musty room. He had one hand on the latch when he noticed a greasy hand-print on the wide expanse of windowsill. Involuntarily, he snatched back his hand. Slime from the imprint had eaten into the wood and the outline of the fingers was long and thin, too long and thin for a normal human hand. Caspar knew it was the mark of the knockerman.

His fears, however, were quickly dispelled by the smell of breakfast cooking over the hearth; spicy Camaalian sausage with savoury breads that Kynan had slipped out in the early morning to buy from the local baker's. Caspar ate hungrily, keeping a careful eye on the amount Hal was eating in case his uncle managed to wolf all the sausages before he had eaten his fair share.

'Avriana tells me you have a riddle,' the old man prompted, relaxing back in his rocking chair and sucking at a pipe of lungbane. 'I don't think I would be boasting if I told you I am very much respected throughout all Camaalia for my art of solving riddles. There's nothing I enjoy more. Would you humour an old man by telling me your puzzle?'

Brid rustled in her scrip and brought forth the battered piece of parchment.

Chapter 15

There was a smell of roasting meat that morning. It woke May with a start and at first she thought she must be dreaming but as she saw the faces around her, wide-eyed with expectation, she knew she was not. Dressing quickly, she hurried with her mother to the kitchens.

Despite basting a glorious sizzling carcass that twisted slowly before her on its spit, Cook looked grim. 'I've never heard such nonsense, Rosalind.'

The kitchen-maid was now recovered from the ergot poisoning and was back doing her usual duties, though at that moment she had an uncharacteristically sour expression on her now thin face.

'Are we really reduced to this, Cook?' she grumbled, as she used a wooden spoon to swipe at two young boys to keep them away from the fire. 'Never in my lifetime would I think to see the day!'

'Oh stop complaining,' Morrigwen snapped. She was grinding what appeared to be hay with a pestle and mortar and sprinkling it into a cauldron of water.

May looked at the sizzling carcass suspiciously as Cook basted it.

The tough-minded cook still glared at her scrawny helper. 'I don't want another word, Rosalind,' she scolded. 'Not a word. We should all be grateful for the meat.'

'But horse meat! Torra Altans have never eaten horse meat.'

'Would you rather we starved to death?' Cook threw up her coarse scrubbed-red hands in despair. 'No one else is grumbling.'

'I'm sure Torra Altans used to eat horse meat,' Morrigwen added to the conversation without emotion. 'And besides we haven't got enough grain left to feed the poor beasts and they're only going to starve. At least they'll keep us going a little longer. We just need a little more time, that's all. It's Lenting now. Brid will surely find the Egg soon. She must.'

May slid past Cook and pressed herself against the Crone's side. 'What are you doing?' she whispered, still keeping a wary eye on the cook, who was beating out her frustrations on a pudding mixture and grumbling about ungrateful women.

Morrigwen looked down at May for a moment as if taking in the changed picture of the girl. May knew that the once soft skin on her face was dry and her mouth was sore from ulcers. Her hair was brittle and her eyes sunken. She felt tired, terribly tired now, rather than simply hungry. Morrigwen raised a shaky arm, her bones as thin as the stick she supported herself with. She soothed the girl's shoulder. 'You're so young for all this. Too young.'

'And you're so old. Too old,' May retorted with a laugh.

Morrigwen smiled. 'You remind me of Brid. I miss her.'

May nodded understandingly and then looked back to the crushed seeds of hay and pulped stems. 'We can't eat that.'

'No, I know we can't eat it.' The old Crone flashed her an irritated look. 'Why do you young people always question? Why can't you just watch, listen and learn?'

'I don't believe you ever just sat and listened.' May was determined not to be intimidated by Morrigwen's stiff tone. She had long since got used to the bluntness of the woman's speech and knew that her acerbic tone veiled a certain softness towards her.

Morrigwen tilted her head and laughed in resignation, inducing a phlegmy cough. 'No, no, I don't suppose I did. But that doesn't mean to say I was right now, does it? Make yourself useful and help me.' She pulled the pestle towards her and broke up more hay with her gnarled fingers. 'Humans can get no nutrition directly from hay but if we boil it, some of its properties will seep into the water. Though it won't give us

264

strength or energy, it'll help keep away all these sores and boils. It won't stop you feeling hungry but it will keep you a little healthier.'

May nodded, absorbing the information readily.

'When will Brid get back?' the young girl asked, trying to talk above the battering sounds of rocks that suddenly showered down on the castle. The Vaalakans had managed to dig more and more of their siege-engines into the sides of the Tor. They were now close enough to cause real damage even to the castle's ten-foot thick whinstone walls.

'Brid will return as soon as she can. She won't let us down.'

'And Master Hal and Master Spar?'

Morrigwen's expression changed and she shrugged. 'They will do their best.'

'You know, I didn't like them at first,' May ventured, desperate for any conversation that would divert her mind from the gnawing hunger and the constant pounding shock of boulder after boulder slamming into the outer walls. 'I thought they were so arrogant and surly.'

'Ah well, I suppose Hal is,' Morrigwen agreed. 'But funnily enough not in an unpleasant way. It's just the uncertainty and over-enthusiasm of youth. No doubt he'll mellow like his brother did. He's just frustrated because of Spar.'

'But why?'

'Why?! They live like brothers and Hal is so much more the natural leader. But they're not brothers and it's Spar who will inherit Torra Alta and one day become his uncle's superior. It's very hard on him.'

'You didn't seem to have any sympathy for him on the journey here from the Boarchase,' May reminded her.

'No, I know. That's because he's too full of himself and needs to be kept in his place. Otherwise, before I knew where I was, he'd have had me at his beck-and-call just like he has Spar.' Morrigwen laughed in amusement at the idea. 'Anyway what's this sudden interest in Hal?'

'Oh, I'm not interested in Master Hal,' May blurted out, suddenly blushing.

'Ah well, that I'm glad to hear. You'd have a little too much competition I fear. Brid hardly takes her eyes off him.'

'But she argues with him all the time,' May protested.

'Brid's very headstrong. She couldn't really love someone like a woman should love a man if he worshipped her. Brid's very special; but she needs someone equally headstrong and determined. Someone who will love and respect her but not worship her like a lapdog worships its mistress. Hal's wayward, that's for sure, but he's just about as stubborn and awkward as she is. They'll never have a tranquil easy time but at least Brid won't be able to dominate him. She wouldn't really like that and she knows it.'

May fell silent again and felt Morrigwen's eyes burrowing into her head.

'So why don't you ask me what you really wanted to ask?' the old Crone teased.

May blushed and refused to look up. She could still feel Morrigwen's eyes on her and eventually she could bear the scrutiny no more.

'Don't look at me like that. You know I can't ask. It's not my place to talk about . . .'

'Someone like him when you're only a woodcutter's daughter from the Boarchase?'

May nodded.

'I don't think Spar would ever consider that. He's thoughtful, soft-hearted and . . .' The old Crone stopped and looked sideways at the girl, almost with pity. 'Too loyal.'

'You make that sound sinful.'

'Only that he's too loyal for his own good in his affection for Brid, worshipping the ground on which she walks, as they say. And I think having to compete with Hal only makes it worse.'

'Oh,' May dropped her head, feeling embarrassed and deflated. A few months ago she would never have felt like this. When Master Spar had been here, she thought with embarrassment, she had done nothing but scowl at him. She must have looked like a baby to him then. She had blamed him for her father's death but the months in the castle had changed that view. The Baron fought for his men and they respected and loved him for his inspiring determination. She had seen the way the men were prepared to fight against fearful odds and die for the Barony. And die they did.

Of course he didn't show it and seemed resolute and calm in all things, but May sensed his sorrow. Baron Branwolf loved his men, loved his Barony, and clearly they would do anything for him. Her father had only done what any one of these garrison soldiers would have done in the same circumstances. He had given his life for the love of the Barony. It hadn't been Master Spar's fault, just as it wasn't Baron Branwolf's fault, that the garrison men were dying at the hands of the Vaalakans.

She had also heard the men talking about the two noble youths – their concerns, fears and hopes for them. She had gradually learnt that the common soldiers were on very familiar terms with both youths. They had never kept themselves separate or aloof and were universally liked – except, she thought, by those with unmarried daughters. They were generally a little disapproving of Master Hal. The young maidens, however, didn't appear to share their parents' views and many a tear had been shed when the raven-haired noble youth had galloped from the castle.

She couldn't understand that at all. When Morrigwen had been gravely ill from the Vaalakan fang-nettle, she had felt Caspar's mind reach through the moonstone – a soft, soothing, reassuring touch. But Master Hal, no. He was arrogant and reckless and stubborn. What could Brid possibly see in him?

The outer door swung wide and Pip strolled nonchalantly into the room, unheeding of the cold blast of air he let swirl into the steamy kitchen. His job for the morning was to bring pitchers of purified water up from the well-room to replenish the kitchen's supply. The pitchers swung from each end of a yoke balanced across his shoulders and his pathway, back and forth across the courtyard, was covered with the evidence of his wayward progress.

'I see you've got the hard tasks again,' he muttered sarcastically at May as he nudged past Cook and plunged his grubby fingers into an unattended pudding. May suspected that Cook had seen but chose to ignore the act of thievery.

'Meat,' he sighed slobbering at the carcass as he trotted out with his empty pitchers.

Pip had been gone barely a minute when suddenly the doors burst inwards with a splintering crash. Broken panels and two soldiers were hurled into the kitchen. They lay soundlessly midst the splintered wood, their purpling flesh coated in masonry dust. The mayhem of the courtyard, where shouting soldiers fled from the hail of rocks that rained out of the sky, swept into the kitchens.

For a second, before the shock of the assault gripped May, she found she saw the scene through calmly dispassionate eyes. She could hear the confusion and turmoil, could see the archers as they ran for cover while those caught in the courtyard screamed out to the Great Mother. Aloof for only a moment, her mind could only puzzle over the thought that the attack came not from the north or west but from the south.

Then the reality of the scene hit her.

'Pip! Oh no, Pip!' she screamed.

Pip was out there in the courtyard. Morrigwen's arms wrapped around her, suddenly holding her back as she started to run forward. 'But Pip's out there!' she cried, flinging her arms towards the people trapped beneath the fallen south wall.

'You can't do any good until the men have repelled the attack. You'll only get hurt yourself,' Morrigwen shouted above the rain of mortar tumbling over the broken south wall. 'They've got through the Jaws of the Wolf. They've slipped beneath the white snow-capped teeth and crawled around the southern edge of the Yellow Mountains where they've built more of their monstrous siege-engines.'

It took what seemed like an age for the Torra Altans to unleash and drag the trebuchets from their station on the west side to defend the howling gap in the south wall. The cumbersome engines were hard to haul through the debris and bodies littering the courtyard, but nothing could be done for the injured or slain until they had countered the hail of missiles and driven back the attack.

Helped by Cook, Morrigwen clutched the struggling child in her arms. Her voice was calm and detached as she watched the jerking movements of the trapped men. 'They must have lost thousands of men trying to get through the snows high up in the Jaws of the Wolf. The snows hold in that pass well into Fallow.' Her eyes were fixed on the courtyard and the heaps of dusty rubble and yet she seemed to be talking without any thought for what she saw. 'Vaal-Peor has guided them through.'

At last the frenzied screams of action from the walls calmed and everyone in the castle turned to look in dismay at the ruin and broken bodies. Some were sobbing, some moaned softly but all too many lay in cold silence. Morrigwen swallowed hard and hobbled out into the open, supporting her crooked weight on her staff.

'Get the injured to the physician in the keep,' she ordered.

Elaine was already rushing into the courtyard, her eyes searching anxiously. She grasped at her daughter as the chestnut-haired girl fled from the kitchens, sobbing incoherently.

May dragged at her mother's arms. 'Pip! Pip! He was in the courtyard when the south wall collapsed.'

Elaine's rosy cheeks turned white and her hand limply fell away from her daughter as she stared at the tumble of rubble and broken limbs that protruded from the debris. The ruined wall lay heaped in haphazard piles like boulders tumbled from a scree slope. Legs and arms jutted out from beneath the rocks, some wriggling or kicking, others lying still in the dust.

'Pip!' Elaine screamed, flinging herself into the rubble.

May could no longer think. Her body seemed to work quite independently from her mind. She didn't notice the blood on her hands nor the splinters of stone that ground into the raw shredded skin of her palms. She had no notion that her arms ached or that her eyes were sore from the dust. She was unaware of the archers still sending flurries of arrows over the walls, while she stooped to fill the barrows with rubble.

They were still working when evening fell and the Vaalakan attacks had ceased. Teams of men poured off the walls and silently fell in alongside the women. The Baron moved amongst them and put his hand on May's shoulder.

'Rest for a moment, child, and drink some water.' He was looking across at Elaine, his eyes filled with sorrow. He moved alongside her and heaved at the rocks, dragging them aside with ease while she futilely tried to move a great slab. 'I'll get a pick,' he said softly.

He didn't tell her to stop working. There was no point.

Huge chunks of masonry, some slabs two or three feet across, had crashed to the middle of the courtyard. These were the last remaining blocks of debris and in all the rubble and shattered bodies there had not been one sign of Pip.

'A boot!' a dust-covered searcher yelled from the far side. Elaine scrabbled at the heap of rubble, but Branwolf finally lifted her up and placed her out of the way.

'Listen, I understand, but let me do this now. You're just not strong enough.'

Elaine slumped back and sobbed, holding out her arms to May who clung to her. 'I couldn't bear it,' she cried. 'Not Pip.' She kissed her daughter and hugged her possessively as if frightened that she might lose her too.

The soldiers cleared aside the top layer of the rubble and revealed three men heaped, one over the other, arms and legs twisted at impossible angles, backs broken and skulls crushed. And then May saw it: the shattered ewer and the tip of the yoke that Pip had been carrying on his shoulders. One by one the dead bodies were lifted reverently away. May was on her feet, staring, unable to do anything but wait and pray. Her mother's grip crushed her hand.

'Pip's boot. That's his boot,' she choked as a small black and tattered leather sole was pulled from the rubble. They dug deeper and uncovered a big, broad-shouldered man lying motionless, face down in the shattered masonry.

'It's Godric,' someone muttered sadly.

As Godric's body was eased out of the rubble the entire party gasped. Pip's wide eyes were blinking up at them from beneath his cropped fringe.

'Pip! Oh Pip!' Elaine was shrieking now, scrabbling through the rubble to get to her boy. She flung herself towards him but stopped short, too scared to touch him lest she worsened his injuries.

'Can you move?' Her voice was so very quiet.

Pip nodded but didn't speak. He reached out a hand and Branwolf scooped him up and carried him towards the keep. Elaine hurried alongside him.

Pip wouldn't speak for several hours but clung to his mother who never took her eyes off him. Finally the tears rolled off the boy's washed cheeks and he fell into his mother's embrace. May swallowed hard. She knew that Pip had tried to be brave but he was really so very young, not yet even eleven, and he couldn't keep his courage up any longer.

'Ma,' he sobbed. 'He saved me. Godric grabbed me and hurled me to the ground and covered me with his body. Ma!' The boy's slight body shuddered with choked-back tears. 'And he didn't die right away. He groaned for hours and told me to be brave. He said the Baron would come for me. That Baron Branwolf would never abandon one of his men. And then he told me his name and then he died, Ma. He died there right over me and I could hear the cries and moans of the other men and then there was nothing but silence. Silence for hours.'

Elaine rocked her son back and forth in her arms, smothering the top of his head with kisses.

Forty-two men had died that day. It was a terrible toll and not even the taste of the meat cheered anyone's spirits. It tasted sweet and perhaps a little dry compared to the more fatty beef but May welcomed it. She couldn't share Rosalind's view that it was wrong to eat horse, not while they were all wasting with starvation. But even Rosalind seemed to have relented now, as she was chewing hungrily away at her ration.

The Baron ate in the refectory hall with his men. He moved

round amongst them, nodding and talking solemnly. When it seemed that most had finished eating he stood on a chair and raised his hand, asking for volunteers to venture over the walls and flee south to beg King Rewik for reinforcements. The chances of making it through the enemy siege lines were slight.

Chapter 16

Brid took a deep breath and again recited the riddle from the golden shield.

'Very interesting,' Talmus mused, sucking toothlessly at his pipe. 'I hope my daughter has explained the first half because it's really very simple.'

'It took me a little while,' Avriana admitted, never once leaving go of Kynan's hand.

The old man nodded, seemingly rejoicing in his superior skill. 'Well, the door of stone quite clearly means the monoliths of Sequicornum's eastern gate. Then, once you have realized which city is referred to, "Take up the challenge for the warriors' throne" can only refer to the famous training ground for knights situated at the heart of Sequicornum Castle. The rest of the riddle requires a good deal of specialist knowledge about the area, which I doubt you would be able to decipher, so I guess that is where you came unstuck.'

Hal narrowed his eyes and fixed them on Caspar, silently warning him not to mention that they had been unable to solve a word of the riddle right from the beginning.

'Now the next part; tell it to me again, child,' the old man prompted Brid.

'"Then on the day of the new crowned queen/When the field is arrayed for the battle scene,"' she recited.

Talmus closed his eyes and chewed thoughtfully on his pipe for several moments before continuing. '"The new crowned queen" is difficult but I think I have it. At first, because I was thinking about castles and knights, I was put in mind of a real queen but of course it's not; it's a festival queen.'

Brid groaned as the realization struck her. 'Now, I really should have been able to see that,' she berated herself. 'But which festival?'

'Well, they don't have festival queens in Camaalia, not anymore at any rate. We're not what you would call an excitable people; we like our routines. Festivals do interfere with work so. But we're talking about Sequicornum here and they do have one festival each year. No doubt they used to have a festival queen but nowadays the day is marked only by the great jousting contest. It's held on the Feast of St Beonor. St Beonor lived in Camaalia about seven hundred years ago. He slew many wyverns and even a dragon, or so the tales go. His feast day superseded an earlier rite, performed on the second full moon after the vernal equinox. They keep the same date now of course, though I'm not sure when that falls this year.'

It took Brid no time to work it out.

'It's not until the twenty-first day of Merrymoon,' she groaned. 'If we have to wait until then to solve the riddle, we'll have under six weeks left to get back home before the end of Fallow,' she blurted.

'Virtually no time at all.' Caspar's heart was thumping in his chest at the thought. When they set off from Torra Alta they had had eight clear months ahead of them. That had seemed like an endless amount of time, but how quickly it was being swallowed up as they struggled on with their quest! It was already Lenting.

'What about the last bit?' Brid anxiously pressed the old man. 'Have you any ideas?'

'"And only the victor can point the way," suggests that whoever wishes to solve the riddle must be the victor of the challenge on St Beonor's day. I should think there's something specific about what happens in the private victory ceremony that will give you all the answers but personally I really have no idea so it's only a guess. Of course "Heed what the runes on the cauldron say" means exactly what it says and I assume refers to a previous riddle. No doubt it told you what the victor should look for. Now I imagine the only way you can solve it is to have your eyes, ears and wits about you when you become the victor on St Beonor's day.' The old Camaalian laughed at the absurdity of the idea. 'But of course that's impossible. Scores of the world's bravest and most skilled knights enter the prestigious competition, every one a master of their art.'

Later, as the Belbidians prepared to depart for Sequicornum, Avriana finally released Kynan's hand and took Brid conspiratorially by the arm. 'I'm a Camaalian and know little of the superstitions and old ways of Belbidia but I've overheard some of your whisperings and realized the arcane nature of the treasure you seek. I believe you to be a follower of the old ways, which are so long forgotten in Camaalia. I've seen the magic in your healing and felt the joy in your heart. You have brought me life again; how can I repay you?'

Brid smiled. 'Every morning you awake, give thanks to the Great Mother, and teach your children to do the same. If you do that, you will repay me a thousand times over.'

Avriana's expression was unreadable beneath her veil as she waved farewell but Caspar could sense her happiness.

They rode north towards Sequicornum. The weather cooled with a pleasant, fresh breeze blowing in from the west and the ground beneath the horses' hooves was softer and more relenting. Firecracker tossed his head and snorted with delight at the feel of the grassy plains and Hal quickly became irritated at the way the stallion continually bumped sideways into Magpie.

'For honour's sake, Spar, control that animal,' he growled. 'If you don't keep him in order you'll make complete fools out of all of us when we get to Sequicornum. Why couldn't you have chosen a war-horse for yourself?'

'Cracker is a war-horse.'

Even Ceowulf looked slightly doubtful at this pronouncement. 'I must say I wouldn't like to take him into battle and, besides, he doesn't look like he's got the substance to carry armour.'

'We don't wear armour in Torra Alta.'

'No, I suppose that does make a difference,' the Caldean conceded.

The ride north took them well into the long swaying grasses of central Camaalia's open steppes. Though the land was green there was barely a tree in sight except where crack willows huddled around the occasional stream. It took them several days to cross the steppes and Lenting had already yielded to the month of Ostara before they sighted the castle of Sequicornum.

Unlike Torra Alta, which towered above a canyon crowded by the spiky peaks of the Yellow Mountains, the castle of Sequicornum stretched broad and wide over a low hill, the only highland for many miles. The entire hill was encompassed within the castle walls, which were beaded with round turrets. The castle boasted no less than three concentric rings of curtain walls, not to mention the ramparts and abatis that surrounded the stern black structure. At the centre of the sprawling fortification squatted a vast circular keep with lesser towers satellited around it. A crush of tightly knit houses slotted themselves into the confined space between the fortified towers, their slanting roofs set at haphazard angles as they squeezed into the narrow streets. As the riders drew closer they could make out a clear moat that lapped around the outer walls and a wooden drawbridge that gave access to the castle.

'It's not a castle,' Caspar gasped in amazement at the sheer breadth. 'It's an entire fortified city. It's enormous.'

'Quite magnificent,' Hal breathed, his eyes dancing with wonder at the sheer magnitude of Sequicornum. Absent-mindedly he drew his sword and tested the keenness of its edge. A shadow crept across his face as he stroked the metal and looked covetously towards the castle. Caspar knew what was on his uncle's mind because the same excitement thrilled through his own. He too wanted to prove himself at the famous training ground for knights and show himself to be a man of battle-craft.

Ceowulf's dark eyes were laughing at them and Hal caught

the look. 'You think we are too young to be of any worth against the great knights of the Caballan Sea. Just because you have more experience doesn't mean that you're infinitely superior to us. We are from Torra Alta and our ways may be different because we live in mountainous terrain but the blood of warriors runs thick and hot in our veins.'

'I don't doubt it,' Ceowulf laughed, 'not for a minute. I just think you underestimate the skills that a knight must learn – and there are a very great number of them. Youth is so arrogant in its innocence.'

'Oh, laugh now, knight, but tomorrow you'll see that smile wiped from your face in the arena,' Hal taunted with a mock show of aggression.

Brid threw her eyes heavenward. 'We come here for a very important reason and all you can think about is your pride.'

'Honour, my lady, is everything,' Hal replied in a high courtly tone, giving her a flourishing bow and grinning at the scowl that swept over the Maiden's expression. The veil irritated her and she had swept it back off her face while they rode through the open countryside.

'This is not the time,' she replied stiffly.

Hal was unperturbed by her rebuff. 'Will I wear your colours, my lady, at the joust? Would you give me that honour, for I will do you proud?'

Despite herself Brid blushed, the faintest hint of pink tingeing her cheeks, and her eyes danced with delight.

Caspar was not at all pleased by this playful bantering. She must know Hal is only playing at these courtly gestures, he thought, grumbling to himself. Hal never seemed to take anything seriously and his frivolous behaviour seemed inappropriate when they were at last drawing close to finding the Egg.

Caspar halted suddenly and Comet thumped into the back of the roan stallion. 'But where's the door of stone? Where are these obelisks?'

'They're at the east gate,' Ceowulf explained.

'Shouldn't we enter from there then?' he asked.

'It's a long way round. What difference will it make? The

training grounds are in the centre of the castle,' the knight argued logically.

'I think Spar's right,' Brid decided. 'It might be a long way round but I think we should follow the clues step by step.'

At the east gate two vast monoliths stood just outside like two giant sentries. Their cold dark faces glared with disapproval at the travellers as they trotted beneath their shadow. Beyond the monoliths, the city's eastern approach was guarded by a drawbridge, portcullis and barbican. Caspar pulled his eyes away from the glowering needles of rock to study them. The huge toothed grill looked rusted as though it hadn't been lowered in centuries. Jutting out above the portcullis was a stone statue of a unicorn's head.

'The crest of Camaalia,' Ceowulf informed them. 'You have to watch out for anyone on a battlefield who has a unicorn's head displayed on his shield. These Camaalians are very efficient in the field.'

Caspar paused, pushed his auburn fringe back off his face and nudged at his nose. He sensed a strange tingling energy creeping up through his bones to ripple through him. At the same time, just for a second, he felt that the unicorn was scrutinizing him. He looked over to Brid who had also briefly halted to study the statue.

She shrugged uncertainly. 'We've just crossed a line of power running through the earth beneath our feet. Perhaps that's what gives the crest an eerie sense of life,' she suggested and urged Comet on into Sequicornum.

The soldiers on watch studied them incuriously as they swept past. There were so many other knights, wagoners and traders roaming in and out along the busy route that nobody paid any particular attention to them. Caspar had expected to encounter an efficient military atmosphere once they had crossed the drawbridge. Instead he found himself looking disapprovingly at the open verandas and well-tended potted gardens of a huddle of brightly coloured houses. This wasn't his idea of a citadel at all. Children played in the streets with hoops, sticks and marbles, and countless dogs scurried, yelping excitedly at their heels. Winding stone staircases led up to houses built over tumbled down sections of the ancient fortress and it was as if every dwelling scrambled for space.

As they spotted three men with hauberks and swords at their sides at the end of the street, Ceowulf brought them to a halt. 'It won't do us any harm if we show them our colours. It's always best to give the right impression.' He unfurled the chequered red and white caparison, spreading it over Sorcerer's back, and Caspar followed suit with his own blue and gold caparison bearing the Torra Altan dragon. The chequered knight gave a quick glance at Brid. 'I think you and Cybillia had better pull your veils down now. In a place like this you never know when you'll bump into a Belbidian merchant – particularly one from Ovissia. Those wool merchants seem to get everywhere and we don't want any of them muttering about witchcraft and drawing attention to us.'

'I'm glad we don't wear veils in Belbidia,' Cybillia remarked as she tied her veil into place. 'They look so old-fashioned.'

Ceowulf grunted as he fastened the straps that secured Sorcerer's caparison in place. 'I wouldn't normally make such an effort simply for appearance's sake but we need to be taken seriously in this citadel. Putting our best foot forward is of paramount importance from now on,' he explained. 'Much of a knight's success in a tournament is achieved through convincing his opponent that he's going to beat him long before he even lowers his lance. Confidence is everything.'

Hal looked quite satisfied when Brid shook out her skirts to brush off the dirt from the road and adjusted her veil to hide her dazzling eyes. He grinned cheekily at her. 'That should keep you in your place. No maiden can give orders through a veil. It'd be too comical; you'd just make everyone want to laugh.'

'I'm sure you're right,' she replied with dignified composure while manoeuvring Comet so that the mare's haunches reversed against Hal's thigh, pushing him uncomfortably up against the wall. 'Oh dear, did I do that?' she exclaimed in aghast tones. 'Oh silly me, these animals are so difficult for a mere damsel to control.'

Hal squinted at her through slitted eyes.

Ceowulf sat notably taller and made an effort to gather his horse under him so that the big black destrier lifted his feathered fetlocks and floated on each stride of his high-stepping trot.

Hal and Caspar looked at each other and grinned. With the Torra Altan colours rippling around his flanks, Firecracker was caught up in the atmosphere and beat out an excited rhythm with his hooves. Comet instinctively did the same and Brid laughed with delight at the display. Even Cybillia, after so many weeks in the saddle, managed to look comfortable, allowing some grace back into her horse's movements.

The streets emptied in front of them letting the party approach the central keep and pass beneath the ugly teeth of an inner portcullis undisturbed. But once through the gate, the atmosphere of the town changed completely. In the shadow of the vast circular keep and housed within a huge quadrangle of barracks and mews, were several open arenas.

Men on foot clashed swords in practice and horsemen tilted their lances at stuffed bags of straw while others weaved through poles or rode blindfold. They had entered a place of serious training where little noise of the bustle of everyday life could be heard above the drum of hooves and the clash of metal. Two soldiers dressed in the livery of the Camaalian guard, wearing green tabards with the white head of a unicorn embroidered over their hearts, stepped forward and lowered their pikestaffs to halt the Belbidians.

'We are noblemen of the fair land of Belbidia. We have come to make our challenge for the prize on St Beonor's day,' Ceowulf announced in loud clear tones.

The soldiers looked at him seriously and then grinned at Hal and Spar. 'You, Sir Knight, yes, but you are not serious about the young lads.'

'Not serious?' Hal growled, his reflexes sending his hand to the hilt of his sword. 'Do you dare to insult me?'

The older of the two soldiers stifled a laugh in his throat. 'You are of course entitled to enter so long as you pass the preliminary rounds but of course everyone must pay the fee of entry. Three hundred gold crowns for each man of noble birth. Two hundred gold crowns for those of lesser blood.'

Caspar could feel his noble blood draining from his cheeks. It was a very high sum of money indeed and he knew they didn't have that amount on them. Determinedly he set his face hard and tried to stare back with what he hoped was an inscrutable look with just a hint of self-confidence. However, he had a sinking feeling that they were about to make fools of themselves.

'We will escort you to the treasurer but until all dues are paid we can allow you no further than that.'

Ceowulf nodded. 'Lead on, man,' he said brightly.

'What are we going to do?' Caspar hissed under his breath. They dismounted and had a moment to wait before they could enrol themselves because of the number of applicants before them. 'How much do we have?'

'Four hundred,' Hal answered.

'Enough money to last us years,' Ceowulf grunted, 'except for the exorbitant cost of the entry fee. But this of course is how the city makes its money and the King of Camaalia maintains an unequalled standard of skill within his household guard by choosing the very best knights out of the winners. It's an extremely astute ploy to ensure that he has one of the most skilful armies in the world. In the circumstances I think that perhaps only I should enter.'

'Why you?' Hal was indignant. 'Perhaps it should just be me who enters. After all I wield the runesword.'

Ceowulf looked down at him and grinned. 'Oh come on, Hal, you've got to be realistic. You have no experience of arena combat and though you've filled out a bit since I've known you, you're still not much more than half my weight. You'd never be able to even touch one of these men and if you used that sword of yours you'll get us all burnt for witchcraft –

even in Camaalia. And even if they don't burn us they'd definitely consider it cheating.'

'Well, I don't see why you should enter; it's Torra Alta's money after all,' Hal argued.

'Where's Brid?' Caspar had distanced himself from the argument and had noticed that the priestess was no longer with them.

Ceowulf and Hal stopped in mid-argument and spun on their heels. Hal looked slightly worried.

'She went in there,' Cybillia informed them, nodding towards the low stone arch and the cloistered rooms of Sequicornum's treasury house. The three men looked at each other blankly. Shortly afterwards, Brid reappeared with Trog at her side. The self-satisfied smile on her face very much matched the grin on Trog's.

'What do you think you've been doing?' Hal demanded. 'Girls don't just wonder around a castle like this unattended.'

'I wasn't unattended; I took Trog,' she retorted. 'And he's undoubtedly a better escort than any of you. Virtually no one had seen an Ophidian snake-catcher before and they were really rather impressed, particularly by his snarl.'

Hal looked decidedly displeased. 'It's most unseemly. And anyway what were you doing in there?'

She uncurled her fist and revealed three metal brooches, each cast in the design of a knight with a couched lance. 'I was securing all three of you a place on the entry register,' she retorted with a grin. 'The officer told me we should report to the guardroom and then they would show us to our quarters.'

'But how?' Hal insisted on knowing, excitement smothering his indignation.

'The jewel from the wyvern's eye was easily worth nine hundred crowns and they accepted it quite readily.'

'Clever girl.' Ceowulf was pleased.

Hal, however, was furious. 'You've made us look complete idiots. A girl going in to pay for three men!'

'Three men?' she sniffed. 'The way you were carrying on it reminded me of three spoilt toddlers.'

'I wasn't carrying on,' Caspar objected.

Brid gave him a stony look. 'You see, you can't even stop squabbling now.'

There was no retort that would successfully better the Maiden's remark. Hal and Caspar immersed themselves into sulky silence until they were distracted by a knight on a bright chestnut gelding. He galloped straight towards them and skidded to a halt a hare's whisker from Cybillia before charging away again.

Cybillia squealed in dismay and Ceowulf hurriedly pulled her protectively towards him. 'I think we're a little too close to the practice ground,' he murmured reassuringly while glaring thunderously at the knight.

The man returned for a second time and drew his chestnut gelding to a snorting standstill inches from where they stood. Probably in his late twenties, he threw off his plumed helmet to reveal a handsome face, with sharp clean lines to the jaw, a neat but manly nose and arched arrogant eyebrows. Only, thought Caspar, he could never be truly handsome; beneath his fair hair, his dull greyish-green eyes were stony cold and appeared to be very much lacking in humour.

'Newcomers, I see,' he announced in what was most definitely a condescending tone. He raised an amused eyebrow at the brooches pinned to Hal and Caspar's jerkins. 'A little fresh from the nursery for this game, aren't we?'

Caspar could feel his temper boiling inside him, stripping away any sense of self-control. He only just managed to bridle his emotions, though Ceowulf had to snatch at Hal's arm and pull him back as he struggled to confront the mounted knight.

'Get a grip on yourself, Hal,' he growled. 'You'll have us thrown out before we've even got started.' Ceowulf pushed past the raven-haired youth who fretfully ground his teeth. He met the man's arrogant glare with a polite but understated bow, which was both dignified and courteous and went some way to confounding the man's attempts to put them down. 'I am pleased to make your acquaintance, knight. I am Ceowulf, son of Baron Cadros of Caldea, of the mighty country of Belbidia.'

The knight nodded and reciprocated the ceremony. 'I am Turquin, the eldest son of Dagonet, king of the mightiest realm in all the Caballan Sea.'

'Oh, and which country would that be?' Ceowulf asked with feigned innocence.

Caspar grinned inwardly to himself, knowing full well that Ceowulf couldn't fail to know that Dagonet was King of Ceolothia.

'I'm a prince of Ceolothia,' he replied quietly. 'Clearly there has been a slight neglect in your education, but that can always be remedied. I look forward to meeting you on the practice arena over the next few weeks. Though before you go there, I suggest you spend a night's vigil in St Beonor's chapel over there.' He nodded to the northern edge of the quadrangle where an arched building stood humbly beneath the towering walls of the keep. 'You'll need to make your peace with the good Lord first.' He bowed his head stiffly and then turned to let his eyes linger for just a moment longer than was polite, first on Brid and then on Cybillia. 'And I look forward to meeting you, young ladies, outside the practice ring.'

There was nothing exactly impolite in the way he spoke but Caspar understood the lecherous look in the man's eyes. He struggled to find a suitable riposte with which to subdue the arrogant man and thought they would have to leave with the Prince of Ceolothia scoring an oral victory over the Belbidians, when to everyone's surprise Cybillia stepped forward. Her head was demurely bowed beneath the veil that hid her scars.

'We look forward to that, Sir Knight. I'm sure it will be an honour.' Though the words were polite they held a touch of dismissiveness that reminded Caspar of the way Cybillia had spoken to her servants in her father's manor. 'Of course we will try to remember your face so that we don't completely overlook you in the crowd. What was your name again? Silly me, I've forgotten it already.'

'Turquin, Prince Turquin,' he muttered in disgust and with

a quick nod he yanked his horse's head around and galloped off back into the arena.

The Belbidians laughed in delight and Ceowulf gave Cybillia a firm slap on the back that sent her stumbling forward. Apologizing profusely, he hastily steadied her.

The entry fee secured them sleeping quarters, food and specialist training for the weeks leading up to St Beonor's day and, although the tournament was over six weeks away, there was already an earnest sense of competition building up within the castle barracks. For a military establishment there seemed to be a very large number of young maidens in evidence and four of them appeared to be studying Hal in particular as they approached their new quarters.

'I imagine they've accompanied their brothers, hoping to get themselves a worthy husband. After all, the most eligible knights in all the countries of the Caballan Sea will be here for the tournament,' Brid guessed. 'Those veils don't quite hide their predatory stares, do they?'

'Wait till the jousting begins.' Ceowulf gave Hal a knowing nudge with his elbow. 'Jousts are the traditional time for ladies to offer their favours.'

Brid stared stonily ahead, ignoring Hal's smirk.

The two Belbidian maidens were swallowed into the women's quarters, which were easily recognizable by the flower beds and ornamental fruit trees that guarded their cold stone cloisters. The entire area within the castle of Sequicornum was built in a quadrangle that surrounded twelve arenas. Ceowulf looked distinctly uncomfortable as he and Hal and Spar were ushered by a young Camaalian towards the pillared corridor fronting their cells.

'It reminds me of St Wulfstan's monastery in Caldea. I've spent half my life trying to escape from the memory.'

Ceowulf was given a chamber of his own but because of the Torra Altans' youth they were obliged to share. The soldier who showed them to their quarters explained that, since so many men of noble rank and differing customs came yearly to the great tournament and because they were restricted for space, the only possible way they could agree on a seniority system for private rooms was through age. The young men and any kin were always asked to share rooms.

Once they had settled their few belongings into their respective chambers and seen that the horses were fed and comfortable, Ceowulf and the two youths strode into town to find an armourer. They needed to purchase suitable swords for both the Torra Altans. Hal was still indignant at having to hide the runesword and wield an inferior weapon in its stead but Caspar was delighted with his new weapon. He knew he was far better skilled with a bow than a blade but all the same he felt several inches taller with a sword swinging from his belt as they marched back to their quarters.

Caspar couldn't sleep for the excitement of the next day when they would start their training. Hal was sitting up on his pallet, staring rather forlornly across the room at his runesword. 'It's not fair. Why can't I use my own sword?'

'Hal, we've been through it a hundred times. You know it would draw too much attention.'

'We need to win though.'

Caspar felt a rising worry fluttering in his stomach. Perhaps their earlier confidence really had been utterly misplaced. They had watched thirty men on the practice fields that evening and every one of them looked fully accomplished with horse and lance. Caspar had to admit that he had never even touched a lance.

He woke early the next morning and for a moment, as he caught sight of the sky squeezing in through the shutters, he imagined he was back in Torra Alta.

Hal was already pulling on his boots. There was a keen hungry look to his face and Caspar wondered whether his uncle felt as confident as he looked. Personally, he was sick to his stomach, fearing that he would let the honour of Torra Alta down by being outclassed in the arena.

There were six other new entrants that day and the captain of the guard came out to greet them. First he explained the rules of the tournament before dividing them up into suitable classes corresponding to their likely strength and experience.

He was a swarthy man probably not originally from Camaalia, Caspar guessed, and by his sing-songy accent Caspar finally decided he was undoubtedly Ophidian. He had long thin legs and a square jaw with thick lips that he pressed tightly together as he examined the entrants. He stopped ominously in front of Caspar and looked down his arched nose at the boy. 'A bit young and a bit too small really for this, aren't you, lad? Wouldn't you rather come back next year?'

Caspar stiffened with indignation. 'I can hold my own,' he replied determinedly.

'Well, you wear the brooch so you have the right to try,' the captain replied dismissively.

A blond-haired youth, probably just a little older than Hal but taller with a broad straight back, lifted half his mouth in a self-satisfied sneer. Caspar decided that he already hated the youth, whoever he was.

The captain grunted as he strode past Hal. 'How did you cut your own finger off like that? Did your hand slip while sharpening your father's sword perhaps? You'll need a few basic lessons, I can see.'

'Don't say a word,' Ceowulf hissed under his breath, nudging Sorcerer closer so that he bumped into Hal's tall piebald mare and distracted the youth.

Hal's fists clenched into angry knots.

The captain strolled on and merely nodded at Ceowulf in brief assessment. Then he turned smartly on his heels. 'You have all paid good money to enter this event. We will train you to the best of our ability and to that end we must divide you into smaller groups. It has to be understood that the younger ones will need more fundamental training and so we will separate you accordingly. Those of you not yet eighteen will join Tancred in the outer arena, number eight. You will not need your weapons today.'

Caspar, Hal and the blond-haired youth led their steeds across the quadrangle towards the allotted arena. Caspar could feel his heart beating fast. Hal stepped out confidently and turned to face the other newcomer who marched smartly beside him. 'Hal,' he said offering his hand. 'Hal from Torra Alta, Belbidia, and this is my kinsman, Spar.'

'Oh,' the youth observed with indifference, ignoring the Torra Altan's outstretched palm. 'I am Prince Tudwal, the second son of Dagonet, King of Ceolothia.' He emphasized the word *prince*.

Caspar's heart sank. Turquin's brother. How very disappointing.

'Do you bear any titles or are you merely opportunist yeomen?' Prince Tudwal asked with surly arrogance in the same flat Camaalian accent as his brother.

Hal was quick to retort, 'In Belbidia a man is judged by his worth, not his title.'

Tudwal led a large dappled mare with a high-stepping action and powerful quarters. Caspar was surprised by the thin, severe bit that snagged on the corner of the animal's mouth but guessed the choice had more to do with the rider than the mount.

The three of them presented themselves to the dark-skinned man in the centre of arena eight, who studied them with as much criticism as the captain of the guard had done. He was well into middle age with tufts of greying hair neatly cropped close to his scalp but he moved with the athletic grace and confident upright stance of a man in his early twenties. He had a small white crescent scar beneath his right eye and a faint red line that ran up from his left cheek into his hairline. He wore leather leggings, a sleeveless vest and jerkin, revealing deeply contoured bare arms, which were a rich brown from long exposure to the southern sun. Caspar imagined he had seen many battles.

'My name is Tancred,' he announced in a husky Camaalian accent, 'but you will call me Sir and I will call each of you by your given names, dropping any references to title. The arena is a great leveller of rank so we might as well start without any pretences.' At this point Prince Tudwal gave a loud snort. Tancred gave no indication that he had heard him and continued smoothly. 'This might be Camaalia but we use only Belbidian here to make ourselves clearly understood by all. Your job from now on is to say nothing unless I speak to you, listen well and forget your pride. Too large an ego is the biggest barrier to successful learning. The youth that thinks he already knows it all has little chance of improving his skills.'

Caspar nodded in agreement though he noticed the look of resentment in both Hal and Tudwal's eyes.

After the newcomers had introduced themselves, Tancred briefly introduced the three other members of their group. Philippe, the son of a minor baron from the north of Glain; Oswain, mousy-haired and leanly built with a cheeky glint in his eye, and Kay, a youth of medium height with a healthy degree of self-confidence.

'Now, Oswain,' Tancred addressed the mousy youth, 'will tell our newcomers the most important skill that a knight must possess?'

The boy bowed to his new audience and took an over-dramatic breath as if he thought Tancred was taking the whole thing too seriously. 'The cardinal rule, fellow knights, is to be one with the horse. You must have complete trust and faith in the animal because in the midst of combat you are utterly reliant on your noble steed.'

Caspar nodded. If that were the case he was going to enjoy this. Looking round at the youths on their mounts he had a feeling that none here could possibly better him on horseback.

'Thank you. Obedience is what is most required from a horse. Fearless unquestioning obedience,' Tancred emphasized.

At this point Firecracker threw up his head and squealed, managing to take a sideways bite at Tudwal's mare before Caspar could stop him. Oswain laughed raucously at the stallion's sense of timing, though the Ceolothian prince curled up his lip in an angry snarl.

'That animal needs a twitch.'

The instructor frowned. 'I suspect that purebred is too much of a handful for you, Spar.'

Shamefaced, Caspar scowled. But there was nothing he could say to defend himself without sounding churlish. He wanted to ask the man whether he thought he could do any better, knowing that he most certainly could not, but sagely decided against it.

They were set to riding around the outside of the arena in a controlled trot while Tancred's inscrutable eyes studied them for several minutes.

When Caspar sensed the man's critical gaze studying his movements, he felt himself stiffen with anxiety. But he knew Firecracker was moving well underneath him despite the occasional buck that the red roan injected to break his stride. Tudwal was right behind him and growled angrily under his breath, 'If you can't even control your horse, you shouldn't be here.'

By the end of the day, Hal looked extremely bored and irritated. 'I thought we were going to actually learn something. All he did was watch us ride and moan at me for not having a supple enough back. I don't need someone to teach me how to ride. I could ride before I could walk. I thought we were here to learn battle skills,' he confided in Ceowulf.

The Caldean knight smiled patiently at the youth's complaints. 'I thought you would find this hard,' he pronounced enigmatically. 'Did you not listen to what your instructor had to say to start off with?'

'Something about total obedience from your horse,' he muttered. 'But he didn't give Spar such a hard time despite Cracker behaving like some young bull snorting and kicking. Some kind of obedience that was!'

Caspar thought it best to say nothing. Only he and Kay, with the quiet self-confidence, had escaped heavy criticism on the way they handled their horses and neither Hal nor Tudwal took well to Tancred's comments about their riding. Tancred had nodded at Spar, not so much with approval, more with acceptance, when he had watched him ride for a while though he had on more than one occasion questioned his choice of mount.

Hal stormed off to the far side of the quadrangle where he gloomily sat on a wall and studied the older knights who fought with sword and mace, clashing in brutal combat. Tudwal's elder brother, Turquin, was hooting with delight as he split another opponent's sword in half.

Caspar looked over at his uncle. Two young maidens had just approached and were now standing either side of the dark youth, chatting delightedly. Caspar shook his head, wondering how on earth Hal managed it. His uncle sat there looking like thunder yet within minutes the young noble girls were already flocking to him. Women seemed so contrary.

Both Brid and Cybillia gracefully emerged from their quarters and simultaneously noticed Hal's new company. Brid visibly faltered in her step but Cybillia lifted her face quite happily as she caught sight of Caspar and Ceowulf. Caspar suspected this had more to do with Ceowulf than himself. Brid, however, was moody. She seemed very irritated with the veil that she had to wear over her face.

'We're too far from Belbidia to worry about Inquisitors out here and I can't see properly. Why do women have to be so encumbered with such ridiculous attire? Can you imagine going into battle with a veil over your face?'

Ceowulf laughed. 'No, not exactly. I agree it seems quite ridiculous especially to hide such fair faces as yours and Cybillia's.'

Brid tutted. 'Ceowulf, that was too pat to be meaningful.'

Cybillia, however, clearly relished the words and, though she had previously always been totally at ease with the knight, she was now showing signs of nervousness. She swished her skirts back and forth as if overcome with shyness.

'Well, how was the first day?' Brid asked, deliberately turning so that she presented her back to Hal.

'Mixed, I think,' the Caldean knight replied. 'Hal is smarting a bit from what he considers unjust criticism.'

Brid snorted delightedly at this comment. 'And what about you, Spar?'

'It was interesting. Tancred's just trying to change the

emphasis of our riding to allow us to feel totally confident without the use of our hands to quiet the horse. He says we must feel what we are doing and learn to rely on our own feedback rather than being told all the time.'

'I think I like this Tancred,' Brid answered. 'His advice applies to so many things in life.'

Chapter 17

Perhaps it was because he had been cursing his new sword that Hal found himself on the floor. Tancred had caught him out in one of his nasty little devious tricks and he was face down in the dirt – yet again. Worse still Tudwal was laughing at him.

He thumped the ground in frustration. They had been training for three weeks now and he had begun to hate every minute of it.

Firecracker charged at the target; a sack of straw dangling from the crossbeam on a post. Two paces away, as Caspar stretched out wide with his new sword, Tancred reached in his pocket and scattered flares of camphor powder around the stallion's hooves. As the powder flashed and crackled the red roan lurched sideways but, even though Caspar was leaning out an arm's length from his saddle, he caught his balance and regathered his mount. Though he missed his target, he was able to turn on a groat and slash the sack on his second attempt. Tancred was impressed.

At least Caspar upheld the honour of Torra Alta, Hal thought as he began to push himself up off the floor. The small youth was so light, agile and flexible that nothing could unseat him, despite Tancred's most devious attempts.

Tudwal wrenched his dappled mare round by the reins and smirked down at Hal as he pushed himself to his bruised knees. 'In the dirt again, eh, Belbidian?'

Hal launched himself at the Ceolothian's smug face. For a second he had him round the neck and was dragging him from the saddle where he could pummel that sour face of his with his fists but he was being hauled off. Tancred was standing over him, the point of his sword at his throat.

'If you want to hurt someone, lad, get up on your horse and do it, but through skill and not temper. If you'd been in the battlefield thirty yeomen would have hacked your legs off by now. You have a fine battle-horse, far better than your temper deserves. Why don't you use her?'

Hal couldn't think for the temper thudding in his head. His entire vision seemed rimmed in red as he kicked himself back up into the saddle and growled with dissatisfaction.

'Come on, at it again, lad. I want to see you cut down the enemy.' He pointed his sword at the harmless-looking sack.

Determined to prove his skill, Hal thumped his heels into Magpie's sides, imagining the stuffed sack as Tancred's stomach. He held the reins firmly in his left hand and craned out over the saddle to thrust at the swinging sack. Suddenly the earth smacked him in the mouth; Magpie's hoof caught his shin as he rolled over, and the wind was knocked from his lungs, leaving him gasping helplessly. Slowly he sat up, trying to piece together what had happened. Magpie's saddle lay in a heap two yards from him and he groaned in despair. Tancred had loosened the girth while he'd been fighting with Tudwal and he had never noticed.

'You could have killed me,' he yelled at the instructor.

'Listen, lad, I'm not trying to teach you to sew neat stitches in a tapestry. This game is all about killing, after all. You know what your problem is?'

Hal groaned rather than look the man in the eye. He didn't want to hear it. Tancred thought he knew everybody backwards. Tancred thought he was so damn clever.

'I said at the beginning that a knight's downfall is most often his ego, and in your case it's a blind shame.'

Hal pulled himself to his feet and winced as he stooped for his saddle. Kay, a congenial youth, quietly confident with his horse and weapons, was thoughtfully holding Magpie for him. 'Your brother, Spar, is doing well, though,' he commented.

Hal struggled to hide his scowl. It irked to have to speak to anyone after his failure.

'He's not my brother,' he explained petulantly as Caspar charged the length of the field and retrieved a hoop from the ground by somehow dangling around Firecracker's knees. Spar got himself up in the saddle and still managed to side-step Tancred as the instructor produced a pikestaff from nowhere and lunged at the boy's outside foot, trying to lever him from his horse.

Hal nodded with satisfaction. Spar was doing well. 'Where are you from?' he asked Kay, to divert the subject from the practice ring, the place of his humiliation.

'Lonis. My father, Grinwal, has been trying for five years to win the tournament and this is my second year here. Our king sent my father to win the tournament for the honour of our country. No one from Lonis has ever won and Father was promised a manor if he did. He made the finals for the first time last year.'

Tancred allowed all but Hal and Tudwal to take brief turns with a mock ance and at the end of the day finally permitted the Ceolothian prince to handle one. The instructor, however, still refused to let Hal do anything other than continue the tedious practice of riding without reins or stirrups. Hal scowled at the others, barely noticing that, though Caspar was undoubtedly exceptionally comfortable on horseback, he was struggling with the weight of the lance.

After the day's practice sessions, Hal slipped quietly away, avoiding Caspar's cheerful smile. He simply couldn't face him graciously. He crept over to the far side of the quadrangle and watched Ceowulf unhorse a black knight, with expert ease. He sighed gloomily, remembering what he'd said to the knight when they'd first approached Sequicornum, and how the Caldean had laughed at his innocent arrogance. And it *was* laughable! He realized now just how many years of hard training it must have taken Ceowulf to reach such levels of accuracy with his lance. Hal wasn't the only one watching the display. Along with many other maidens, Cybillia's veiled head followed every movement of the Caldean knight who looked like the crowned champion at a spring festival, fluttering with flags, buntings and coloured garlands. Alongside Cybillia's purple token hung a host of other bright scarves and, judging by the way she suddenly spun round and marched away, Hal guessed she was offended that the knight had accepted them.

Ceowulf's mount, Sorcerer, moved with supreme confidence, charging down the lists and remaining firmly in line as the knights clashed. Though the lance tips were wrapped in cloth and covered with leather to prevent serious injury, they punched into the raised shields with the force of a battering ram. The knight unseated three opponents but finally was knocked to the ground by a big man on a heavy chestnut. The victor pulled off his helmet and Hal's heart sank. It was Turquin and he had the same gloating look as his blond-haired brother.

Broodily, Hal turned his back on the arena and stared towards the bustling citadel. He jumped as he felt a light touch on his hand. Looking round he saw Brid's deep, mysterious eyes fathoming his own.

'I've been watching you,' she said softly.

Hal didn't know what to say. He felt ashamed. The only way to save any of his dignity was to be honest. He took a deep breath. 'I'm sorry. I feel like I've let you all down. I've just made a fool of myself, thinking that I would naturally be good at all this and it turns out I'm hopeless. He's let all the others carry a lance, even Tudwal, so why not me?'

'The others have learnt as much as they're going to learn this year. And though Tudwal's a strong youth who's evidently handled a lance before, he does everything with rough strength rather than technique. Giving him a lance won't undo any of his new-found balance or skills because he hasn't acquired any. He's never once listened to Tancred. My guess is that Tancred's delaying giving you a lance until the last second so that you learn to rely on balance and skill rather than strength. A lance may upset your newly acquired skills. You handle a horse as well as Kay but Tancred's still hoping you'll break through to a higher level.'

'Break through!' Hal sniffed sceptically. 'I've been trying my hardest.'

'I know. That's the trouble. Your fear of failure makes you angry and then you lose concentration and revert to all your old bad habits so that Tancred has little difficulty seeing you unhorsed. He's trying to make you understand that it's your temper that's your enemy.'

Hal let his head flop onto his arms and groaned in despair. 'You think that's it then. If I didn't lose my temper I would be able to get it right?'

'Hasn't everyone been telling you that for years?' Brid laughed.

'I've been wasting so much time,' Hal groaned. 'The month of Ostara's almost over and, with Merrymoon nearly on us, it's only just over three weeks till St Beonor's day. I must practise.'

Despite his determined words he was filled with foreboding. In his heart he knew that, however much he trained, Ceowulf had been right. Both he and Spar lacked the strength and the skill to succeed against any of the more experienced knights here at Sequicornum. Their only hope lay with Ceowulf.

The next day, he cleared his mind of every thought other than the task at hand. Tancred had created some nasty obstacles for them to overcome. Flapping sheets billowed in the wind to startle the horses. A dead pig, rotting and half-decayed, had been dragged out into the centre of the arena and a forest of flagged poles was planted at random over the pitch. This meant they could no longer set a straight charge at the target. Again the target was a stuffed sack but this time it was on a rotating arm. As they swung a cudgel at the sack, it spun away and a heavy club on the opposite end of the arm spun round from behind. If they weren't quick enough to dodge it, they were thumped hard in the back of the head. Just beyond the swinging arm, a deep pit had been dug and soaked in water to make a squelchy bog. It was some fifteen foot across and the horses needed to be moving on at a good pace to clear it.

'If I remember from last year this isn't your favourite, is it, Kay?' Tancred laughed huskily at the young knight.

'A little tricky,' the youth agreed with an amiable grin.

Tudwal was first to charge, making a surprisingly good run through the obstacles and gripping his weapon, ready to swipe at the sack. As he rose out of the saddle and reached upwards, he also pulled back on the reins to balance himself. The mare obediently checked in her stride and, as the youth clobbered the target, the arm swung round hard and hit him hard on the back of the head. Somehow he found the strength to cling on.

Hal wasn't worried by the obstacles. For the first time in five weeks he was enjoying himself. He was only lightly grazed by the swinging arm and Magpie was a little slow over the last leap, splattering him in mud, but Tancred was pleased with him. 'Tomorrow we will all practise with real lances,' Tancred concluded.

Tomorrow couldn't come quickly enough for Hal. The lance felt good in his grip, though he was dismayed by its weight. Tudwal was powerfully built and heaved it up into position, stoically holding it firmly in place. Kay had evidently done this before and had learnt the balance points of the cumbersome weapon, swinging it around its centre an easily placing it in its couched position. He slotted the butt of the weapon into a pocket in the saddle so that most of the weight was borne by the horse.

Hal found himself heaving it into place, much as Tudwal had done. He gritted his teeth as he felt the weight of the weapon throwing him off balance. His joints stiffened to compensate and now he found himself jolted by Magpie's stride.

Worse, Tancred was back to his old tricks again. As Hal trotted round the arena, thumping heavily in the saddle, Tancred thwacked Magpie in the rear and the piebald jumped forward. Hal found the weight of the weapon dragged him back as the heavy tip lagged behind the momentum of the horse's movement. He gritted his teeth as he hauled it back upright, concentrating hard as he anticipated the next trick. His foot was lifted from his blind side by one of Tancred's helpers as the instructor yelled out his name to attract his attention. Hal found himself lurching forward but he flung his body to the outside to regain his balance and prepare himself for the next trick rather than growling with anger. The strap supporting his lance suddenly snapped and he grunted as he caught the weight of the weapon when it dragged on his shoulder blades.

'Still in the saddle, eh, Hal?' Tancred boomed delightedly.

Hal grinned. Had it really taken him so many long harsh weeks to understand what Tancred had been trying to tell him?

He was enjoying himself and he looked round the edge of the arena, aware that they had drawn an admiring crowd of young ladies. He was gratified when several veiled girls clamoured for him to come close, eager to tie their favours to Magpie's bridle. He was very pleased with himself when he had collected more favours than Tudwal but piqued that Brid showed no inclination to offer him her token. Instead she seemed unable to drag her eyes away from Caspar, he noted resentfully.

With jealousy souring his thoughts, it was some while before he guiltily noticed that Caspar had been struggling all day and clearly wasn't big enough to handle a lance. The long weapon toppled and swung precariously in his nephew's white-knuckled grip. Caspar's face reddened with humiliation as the lance swung off balance again and he simply didn't have the strength to hold it. It crashed heavily to the ground and Firecracker reared and danced away.

While Tudwal laughed loudly, Tancred took Caspar's bridle and led him aside. Hal couldn't hear the conversation but he could see Caspar's face: he was blinking fast and looked utterly dismayed. He kept his head bowed, not daring to meet the others' expressions as they studied him, wondering with avid curiosity what was being said.

Tudwal had just the hint of a smile on his face, his arrogant chin jutting forward and his eyes glinting with satisfaction. 'He's saying he must retire, I know it.'

When they were dismissed for the end of practice, Hal rushed sympathetically towards his kinsman, anxious to hear what Tancred had said, but Caspar pushed him away and walked despondently towards the west walls of the inner courtyard. Evidently he wanted to be alone, so Hal stared after him for a moment before hurrying to tell Brid and Ceowulf what had happened.

Caspar gazed broodily over the shadowy citadel and out towards the setting sun that dipped into the waters of the Caballan Sea, trying to lose his thoughts in the brilliant blush of the sky. I've failed, he despaired. Nothing will make me big enough to carry those huge lances.

Gradually he was aware of light footsteps behind him and he turned to meet Brid's questioning eyes. She must already know, he thought, prodding at his nose as he admitted his shame. 'Tancred has told me that if I don't carry a lance onto the tournament field I can't enter.'

'You have to enter, Spar. The Great Mother may need you in Her purpose.'

'I can't, Brid. I've failed and it's not for want of trying.' He looked despairingly at his small hands and felt the pain in his right shoulder as he tried to raise his arm. 'I tried until I thought the blood vessels inside my head would burst, but I couldn't wield the thing. I just couldn't, Brid.'

'Is there any rule about exactly what type of lance you have to carry?' she asked pensively. 'Could we not have a lighter, smaller one made up for you instead?'

'But I'd be a laughing stock,' Caspar began to protest indignantly but his face was already turning to a hopeful smile.

'Come on,' she said practically. 'Let's go and see the swordsmith.'

But by the next day his confidence had totally evaporated as he wilted under Prince Tudwal's condescending sneer. The lance he held was crudely fashioned with unfinished edges and was at least three foot shorter than anyone else's. Hal looked humiliated by his kinsman's appearance; ready humour was curling up on the others' faces and Tudwal was snickering loudly. Only Kay gave Caspar a nod of support.

Tancred came forward and stared him levelly in the eye. 'I admire your front, Spar, but I think it will only delay the inevitable. A lance like that will splinter almost immediately.'

'You said I could stay with the course if I could carry a lance and I'm carrying one,' Caspar tried to say calmly but he could feel the skin burning on his cheeks.

Tudwal snorted, unable to contain his mirth any longer.

The next two weeks brought more bruises, cuts and strains to Caspar's body than he could possibly imagine. As the smith had predicted, the lances lasted very little time but he disapprovingly made up more for him. Caspar bore the insults thanks to Brid's constant support. She stood at the barrier throughout the training sessions, her one thought to encourage him.

His opponents' blunt lance tips smacked into his shield long before his own could reach them and he was knocked from Firecracker's back countless time. But he never gave up; he hauled himself back into the saddle, helped every time by a smile of encouragement from Brid – and by the pastes and poultices of Yellow Mountain arnica and oil of wintergreen that eased the bruises and muscle strains of all three Belbidian entrants.

Ceowulf's old injury was plainly causing him some distress, though he bravely hid his discomfort behind a forced smile. Caspar took the cruel punishment bravely but at least his morale was bolstered by Hal's growing skills. His uncle seemed to have found a new resolve, and Caspar nodded his approval as Hal knocked Kay clean out of the saddle. The raven-haired youth hurried to help his new Lonisian friend from the ground to make sure he was unhurt and Kay grinned at him.

'You fooled me with that feint.'

Hal grinned back. 'Well, I was getting back at you for last time.'

Kay, Tudwal and Hal were now outstripping the rest of them in strength, skill and determination and Tancred split the group in half. His explanation was that they would learn more in small groups, but Caspar guessed that he had other motives. Philippe, Oswain and he lacked either the strength, concentration or skill to compete and he knew Tancred must fear that they would be injured too readily.

Caspar squared his shoulders and decided that the very best way of dealing with this humiliating situation was to pretend that it didn't exist. Like Oswain, he fixed a cheerful smile on his face and concentrated on doing his very best to throw his two sparring partners to the ground. But he was still aware that he was considered to be hopeless at the art of jousting. The only thing that kept his spirits up was Brid cheering him on from the railings.

Hal glowered at him sourly. Caspar slumped back into his saddle, crestfallen. Was he really such an embarrassment?

Chapter 18

On the morning of the tournament Cybillia was more radiant and far more distracting than the red, yellow, blue and green buntings that cascaded from every turret and were looped between the barbicans. As the trumpets blared she lifted her step, raised her head and finally flung off her veil. There was a general gasp at this unseemly act. None of the high-born women were ever to be seen exposing their complexions to the harsh, stripping heat of Camaalia's spring sun, but she could bear it no longer.

Caspar flushed a bright crimson as she skipped up to him and kissed him fulsomely on the lips. Once he had overcome his embarrassment, hiding his eyes from the hooting cheers of the young knights around, he was again stunned by her appearance. The last time he had seen her spiky cropped hair it had been dulled by the desert sands, but now the rich golden lustre coiled in pretty ringlets around her ears. Though it was still unfashionably short, the colour and curl were becomingly feminine. Her cheek was now so smooth and creamy as to be almost unnoticeable except for the finest of silvery lines visible when the sun glanced sideways across her face. The faintest sign of the pentagram gave her an almost mystical appearance and did nothing to detract from her beauty.

Her thin willowy figure had filled a little during their days of comfort at the castle. It gave her face a softly rounded appearance that contrasted starkly with the gaunt despair-ridden lines of the noblewoman who had accompanied them during their departure from Belbidia.

For a moment Caspar forgot all his misgivings for the day

ahead and grinned at her, delighted that she now found pleasure in life again. Brid was close on her heels looking very much more serious, though, to Caspar's eyes, a thousand times more beautiful. Brid had an inner beauty, a serenity, a feminine magic that could not be accounted for simply by her graceful curves and wide vivid eyes. A hint of a smile showed through her veil.

'So?' Caspar asked, 'Why is the noble daughter of Baron Bullback so very radiant this morning?'

'Ah, you'll see in a moment,' she whispered. 'Now, are you ready?'

'Ready, yes, but I don't know what difference it will make.'

Brid had insisted that today, the twenty-first day of Merrymoon, he turn himself out in the very best possible manner. He had spent all the previous day grooming Firecracker and Brid had repaired and washed the blue and gold caparison that declared the boy's noble lineage. His leather breeches and jerkin looked plain and unprofessional compared to the gleaming armour of the other knights. He had shunned the offer of any loans of mail and also declined to wrap himself in extra layers of clothing or padded leathers for fear of restricting his movement. Tancred had been furious, saying he couldn't enter completely unprotected and a fleece beneath an extra leather jacket would make all the difference. But there had been nothing in the rules against Caspar entering as he was and he had insisted. He had more trust in Firecracker's speed than in armour.

Many of the younger knights had as yet no armour of their own. Ceowulf had lent Hal a mail-shirt, breastplate, gauntlets and a helm. They were decidedly oversized but Hal stuffed out the spaces with fleece to make them more comfortable, though a little hot.

Those that had no armour generously padded themselves under their leather jerkins, though Tancred seemed unworried by the danger to his other young protégés. He explained that it wasn't until the last rounds that the lances would be used bare and before that they would be safely padded and blunted to avoid serious injuries to the less skilled entrants. He added that since all the younger ones would undoubtedly be knocked out in the first rounds little harm would come to any of them.

Hal looked really quite gallant except for the hard, determined expression on his face. Magpie gleamed and hopeful maidens were tying even more ribbons to the ones already pinned to her purple saddlecloth. Hal smiled at them indulgently and they tittered and fled.

Firecracker had only one ribbon, a silk scarf woven through his mane. It was plain white with a blue pattern that could no longer be read now that the scarf was knotted. Before Brid had secured it firmly in place, Caspar had studied the potent sigils that decorated the scarf.

ᚱᚾᛏ☉

'I've spent weeks making it,' she explained. 'I tried to think of the most appropriate runespells for the occasion.' Her fingertips were still blue with the last of the woad she had used to daub on the letters. 'Here is Rad's rune, the rune of the seeker, which represents you. Also Ur, the rune of strength, Nyd's rune of necessity and finally the rune of the Mother to show that you do this in Her name and with Her blessing. Belief in the Great Mother; that is your strongest weapon.'

She kissed him lingeringly on the forehead and Caspar felt his heart flutter with the thrill of it. He wanted to catch her up and kiss her back properly but she had already slipped back into the crowd to find the best position from which to view the tournament.

Caspar joined the ranks of competitors as the opening ceremonies began. King Valerius, a big fat man with a curling beard, took his seat in the royal enclosure. He looked wholly bored though the finely dressed woman beside him leant keenly forward, studying the faces of the crowd.

'That's his daughter, Princess Delfina,' Oswain whispered. 'She's an old maid now but they say she comes here every year, searching for the face of one knight. They say he used to be highly ranked in the King's guard but he left in disgrace and became a mercenary. She is supposedly frail from the long years of waiting for her lost love to return.'

And he never will, thought Caspar, realizing the tragedy of the situation. Surely this was the princess who had been the cause of Gatto's downfall. Ceowulf had told them how the mercenary leader had once held a position of rank in the Camaalian guard and trained King Valerius's men here at the famous castle of Sequicornum. He had greatly displeased the King by daring to fall in love with his daughter. Forced to leave Camaalia, Gatto had become a bitter, twisted man, selling his services as a free-lance and gathering a band of men to ride with him. Ceowulf had been one such man but, in defending his fellow countrymen, the Caldean nobleman had been forced to kill his former colleague.

'Read aloud the rules,' the King ordered in a somewhat bored voice before turning eagerly to a servant who carried a tray with silver goblets and an ornate jug of wine. The monarch was clearly too old and fat to take an active interest in knightly skill though, from his attitude, Caspar doubted that he ever had.

'The rules of the tournament are very simple,' the marshal declared in almost perfect Belbidian though his accent was a little clipped. 'The contestants will be divided into four heats by the drawing of lots and there will be sixteen competitors in each heat. To commence, you will each draw, without benefit of sight, a coloured straw from the table. Its colour will dictate which heat you will compete in. For instance, draw a green straw and you will prepare yourself to compete in the green arena, a yellow straw, the yellow arena, and so forth.'

He pointed out the green arena, which fluttered with green flags and strings of green bunting at the northern edge of the practice ground, and then the yellow arena alongside it.

'Each straw is etched with between one and sixteen notches. The number you draw dictates where in order you are placed within the lists of your heat.' He paused for a moment to allow the competitors time to digest the instructions. 'You will retire from the tournament when eliminated in the arena and the two left in each heat will enter the final lists. If you are successful in the arena but are unable to meet the next challenge you may name a second to take your place. All lances will be bound in padded leather for the initial rounds but the final heat will be fought with uncovered weapons. You will draw lots and may the best man win.'

A chorus of trumpets sent a cloud of startled white doves into the air. Caspar made his way to the table and reached under the cloth to retrieve a straw. It was green with three nicks in it. Solemnly, he led Firecracker over to the green arena at the north of the quadrangle and surveyed his opponents. He, Hal and Ceowulf had all drawn different lots so at least they wouldn't be competing against each other, Caspar thought with relief. But as he studied the fifteen other contestants who had also drawn green straws, he didn't have much faith in his ability to get through the first round.

Well, so much for Brid's runes, he thought, disheartened, as he fingered the silk cloth that was woven into Firecracker's mane. As they lined up in order, he noted that three of the men had come from Ceowulf's class. Tudwal had drawn straw number one and the only stroke of luck in his favour was that Oswain had drawn lot four, which paired them together. Oswain was the only person in the entire arena that he had a hope of unseating with a lance. They had drawn lots one after the other and Caspar wasn't sure that the straws had been terribly well shuffled.

He gritted his teeth and through a haze of anxiety, he watched as the first two pairings battled in the arena. It took Tudwal three tilts to unseat his opponent. With an arrogant jut to his chin, the prince smirked at Caspar as he nudged Firecracker towards the head of the arena ready to compete.

'Good luck, young squire,' Tudwal sneered. 'You'll need it even to beat Oswain but I really do hope you win because then I will have the pleasure of knocking you from the saddle in the next round. I've waited many weeks for this moment.'

Caspar found it hard to focus with Tudwal's voice ringing in his ears. The anticipated humiliation made it difficult to concentrate but the sight of Oswain's anxious face, as he readjusted his borrowed helm on his mousy-haired head, raised his hopes just a little. Oswain's front of humour and bravado had cracked under the pressure of the competition and he appeared even more nervous than Caspar felt.

Oswain's fidgety anxiety spread to his horse who crabbed sideways as they made the first charge, making it impossible for either one to place a blow on their opponent. Caspar turned Firecracker speedily on his haunches and was far better prepared than his opponent who was still struggling to wheel his horse at the top of the field.

Caspar was making his second charge before Oswain had lowered his lance and the Belbidian youth felt a pang of remorse as the young knight crashed to the ground, though he was thankful that he wasn't himself eliminated in the very first round. Oswain, however, looked relieved and shook the Torra Altan's hand.

'If I were going to lose to anyone I would rather lose to you,' he confided. 'At least you're not going to brag.'

Caspar, however, could hardly take in his words. He would have to face Tudwal next.

The following two sets of sparring partners competed with ferocious determination, exhausting their mounts with their repeated charges, but in spite of their protracted bout, his next turn was coming round with alarming rapidity. The three experienced knights from Ceowulf's class quickly felled their opponents in a dramatic and chilling display of skill, and soon it was time for the second round. Oswain remained on his horse in line next to Caspar as courtesy dictated that he should, watching the entire heat through. He spoke with delighted animation, apparently glad that it was all over and he need no longer fear the arena again that year.

'The first rounds are usually very quick because it's rare for two equally skilled knights to meet each other though the last rounds have been known to go on for several hours.'

Caspar tried to look over his shoulder to see how Ceowulf and Hal fared in the yellow and blue arenas but it was impossible to see through the wooden stands and banners. Before he knew it, the second round of the first heat was upon him.

As he squared Firecracker up, ready to meet Tudwal's charge, he prayed that Hal and Ceowulf would fare better than he would. Abruptly all thoughts of his own pride were swept away. He no longer cared how much of a fool he made of himself or how well he represented the honour of Torra Alta. All that mattered was that either he, Hal or Ceowulf won.

'Please, Great Mother let Hal and Ceowulf make it through to the final heats,' he begged as he spurred Firecracker on, already accepting his own defeat and neglecting to pray for himself.

The lance glanced off his shield and brushed against his waist, sending him reeling against the support of the high cantle at the back of his saddle. It jarred his spine and for a moment his entire world went red. He could hear nothing except the thunder of hooves, a few disappointed gasps and Brid's voice cutting through the crowd.

'Spar, you can do it, you can do it.'

Somehow he managed to retain his grip on his lance and hauled himself back up into balance. He focused again, bravely determined to make a better effort as, for a second time, he thundered towards the point of Tudwal's lance. With a quick nudge of Spar's right heel into Firecracker's ribs, the horse leapt to the left and he ducked underneath the point of Tudwal's lance, so gaining the extra feet he needed. His arm jolted back into his shoulder socket, twisting his body off balance as he made contact with Tudwal's ornate breastplate. For a second the Prince of Ceolothia lurched backwards in the saddle but then Caspar's lance splintered and the stolid youth hauled himself upright by the reins.

Caspar collected a new lance as he turned to charge again, but he had little faith in it. He knew it would splinter as easily as the first and he found himself charging the Ceolothian without conviction. Suddenly Tudwal's padded lance knocked aside his shield, compressed his chest and sent him tumbling over the back of his horse.

He was out of the tournament.

Still trying to suck in even breaths, he took his place next to Oswain. Without registering any more of the heat, he let his eyes follow the galloping chargers as they clashed against each other. He was vaguely aware of the cheers and shouts of encouragement that beat the air around him but most of it was drowned out by the screaming of his own conscience.

You failed, Spar, he berated himself. You failed because you didn't believe in yourself. You dodged Tudwal's lance once; why couldn't you do it again? Because you gave up. You just thought that Hal or Ceowulf would win, so you gave up. He was disgusted with himself. He should have had more conviction. Surely he knew that winning a fight was as much about conviction as it was about skill. He bit his trembling lip, fearing the consequence of his defeat. If they failed now, what then? What other possible clue did they have to the whereabouts of the Egg?

Finally the heats drew to a conclusion. Only one of the experienced men in their group had made it through to the final, since he had knocked the other two out. He was an Ophidian nobleman by name of Joaquin, quite unassuming and with few words. His face was covered with scars as if he'd spent his entire life in battle. To Caspar's disgust the other knight to qualify was Tudwal, who through the luck of the draw had managed to avoid competing against the more experienced knights.

Now that the heats were over, Caspar was free to watch from the comfort of the stands, only he didn't dare look round. What if both Hal and Ceowulf had been knocked out as well?

Trumpet blasts announced the arrival of the eight finalists to the central arena. Caspar tied Firecracker to a shaded stall, making sure he had water, and then sauntered to the stands where the eliminated knights could watch the final proceedings. He was grateful at least that Kay sought him out from the crowd and wriggled into the tight space on the bench.

He grinned at Caspar. 'Well, that brother of yours got me

in the end. He had a lucky strike and managed to get himself through to the final.'

'He did?' Caspar was delighted.

Kay nodded. 'You must be proud having an elder brother like that?'

'Hmm,' Caspar commented doubtfully. 'Actually, he's not my brother; he's my uncle.'

'Oh.' Kay sounded uninterested. He was already scanning the eight finalists as they paraded round the ring.

A fanfare blast drew the entrants to a halt and they each dismounted to draw a notched straw before arranging themselves in position.

'Marshal, read aloud the lists,' the King demanded with a dismissive wave of the hand.

The marshal approached the arena. Dressed in the green tabard embroidered with a unicorn's head, he wore the King's colours of the Camaalian guard. Standing on a box, the middle-aged, cleanly shaven man with thin legs made a great display of puffing out his narrow chest and filling his lungs.

'The first pair to fight will be Grinwal, from Lonis of yeoman stock. If he wins the title here today the King of Lonis has promised him a lordship.' There was a whisper of excitement amongst the crowd. Caspar felt Kay tense up with nervous anticipation. 'Pitched against him is Sir Taimon of Tutivillus. This is his third time here at Sequicornum and his first time to reach the finals.'

'I didn't think Tutivillus really existed,' Caspar whispered.

'Oh, no, the country exists. It's beyond Salise, but nobody believed it existed until recently. No, the peculiar thing about that is they don't have kings or queens. They elect three men to rule jointly. They once had a queen because there were no male heirs at the time and she chose three husbands. They all jointly ruled in her stead and the country prospered under the system.'

'How extraordinary,' Caspar declared. 'I can't think of anything worse.'

The fanfare blast silenced their words and the marshal announced the next pair.

'Prince Turquin of Ceolothia, the defending champion, is first pitched against Lord Joaquin, Baron of Midverda, Ophidia.'

'Well, that one's a foregone conclusion,' Kay muttered. 'Prince Turquin was unbearable last year when he won.'

'Lord Hal, brother to the Baron of Torra Alta, Belbidia, will compete against Sir Tylot of Salixa, Horsemaster of the Salisian Guard,' the marshal announced and Caspar swallowed hard, his heart beating fearfully. 'The last sparring partners are Lord Ceowulf, younger son of the Baron of Caldea of Belbidia, pitched against Prince Tudwal of Ceolothia, younger brother of last year's winner, the heir apparent.'

Ceowulf looked striking on his black charger draped in the red and white chequered caparison of the Caldean colours. Gone from his harness were all the ribbons and garlands of the previous weeks and only a single bright purple sash decorated his bridle. The purple colours of Jotunn; Caspar recognized them instantly. He looked around the faces in the crowd, and at last he saw them. Brid was sitting with one hand on Trog's collar while Cybillia had her eyes fixed on Ceowulf as she clutched her hands together across her bosom. She looked as though she would faint when Ceowulf's name was announced and the bold knight turned and bowed in her direction.

Brid jabbed her with her elbow as if firmly reminding her to keep her head.

'My lords, unbind your lances and prepare to do battle,' the marshal boomed in rounded tones.

Caspar winced as Grinwal and Taimon impacted. With visors down and war-cloths dancing around the horses' feet each knight and his destrier looked more like one mythical beast than two entities. They thundered with pure violence at each other, lances tilted, shields braced for the impact. Both reeled painfully back, smacking into their high-cantled saddles.

They charged eight or nine times, taking brutal blows to

their torsos before Taimon's lance broke and both discarded lance and shield in favour of sword and mace.

Kay's fingers were white where they gripped the edge of the bench.

'Come on, Father, come on,' he hissed through clenched teeth.

Caspar could only think that the power and might of either of these men would crush Hal to a pulp and he dreaded the moment that his kinsman took his place in the arena. As Kay had said, Hal and Tudwal were both lucky in their draws to get through to the final. It wasn't resentment on the Lonisian's part but purely an observation of fact. Even after all the weeks of practice they were not prepared for this.

Grinwal threw his lance aside and dragged a long thin blade of black steel from his scabbard. 'Hardened in the fires of the old Smokies,' Kay murmured without taking his eyes off his father. 'You can do it, Father! You can do it,' he willed Grinwal to succeed.

It was a long and arduous battle and the strain was beginning to show in both knights and horses as they wheeled and clashed, struggling to unhorse one another. Taimon's helmet was ripped from his head by a slashing blow from Grinwal's left. Taimon had ducked too late to avoid the hammering blow of the mace in Grinwal's other hand and, while still recovering, exposed himself to the cutting edge of the blade.

With the other man's cheeks bared and unprotected by the metal of his visor, Grinwal thrust a quick jab with his sword and nicked the Tutivillun's face just beneath his eye. The movement was beautifully executed and clearly demonstrated that he could have inflicted a severe injury if he had wished. Taimon of course was entitled to fight on, but Grinwal had already proved himself the better knight and the Tutivillun graciously acknowledged it, midst loud cheers from all parties. He chivalrously shook Grinwal's offered hand and wiped the blood from his cheek.

The crowd approved. It was not necessary for either of them to risk further injury and Taimon, by not utterly exhausting

Grinwal, left his opponent with a better chance for the next round. Kay was on his feet, cheering loudly long after all the other cheers had died down and his voice alone filled the arena. Looking slightly embarrassed but still grinning from ear to ear he sat down, breathing hard.

'You'll do yourself an injury cheering like that, young Kay,' a gruff voice behind them laughed. 'Well, I bet you two lads aren't so sorry to be eliminated before you had to face this. If both knights weren't such gentlemen that could have become very bloody.'

It was Tancred. Now that he was no longer their instructor much of his mystique seemed to have vanished. He looked smaller and older without his trainer's hauberk.

'You know, there is a great deal of pain and suffering to be had before skills are as finally honed as that. But the hardest task I have in training you young lads is instilling that battle is not all glory. You all come here with your heads stuffed with legends and heroic ballads. You think that, just because a watered-down trickle of some hero's blood still pumps in your veins, you'll be able to fight like a born warrior. But it's not a natural skill. Every bit of it has to be learnt.'

Caspar nodded in agreement. 'I'm sure you're right, sir. I don't think we believed a word of what you said to us for the first few weeks. It's not until now that I've realized just how good a real knight is.'

'Well, you were a good pupil.' He put a hand on Caspar's shoulder. 'And I hope your brother does well today.'

After Tancred left them for the more comfortable stands nearer to the King, Caspar demanded petulantly, 'Why does everyone always assume Hal's my brother, even after the marshal has correctly announced him? We don't look a bit like one another.'

'Because you treat him like an older brother, the way you argue and the way you always look after each other, even though Hal is still annoyed with you.'

Caspar shook his head. 'I haven't done anything to annoy him apart from not being big enough to handle a lance.'

'Oh, I don't think that worried him,' Kay disagreed. 'He seemed very concerned for you. No, it wasn't that at all.' He nodded over to the stands where Brid and Cybillia sat alongside Kay's sister, watching the activities. But his next words were lost in the fanfare as Turquin and Joaquin cantered around the arena, preparing to take up their positions.

Redolent of majesty, brilliant in his gold, red and blue colours, Turquin fought with a conviction that bordered on hatred. He was a much more accomplished knight than his younger brother and his broad-backed gelding, standing almost as tall as Magpie, stamped and snorted like a demon. A harsh thin bit held him in check until Turquin's long pointed spurs stabbed into the animal's sides. Caspar could feel the ground shake as both horses hammered across the turf.

The battle was bloody. Turquin showed no mercy. Though his lance broke first and neither was able to unseat the other, the prince showed the better skill. With sword in one hand, he beat mercilessly against Joaquin's shoulder with a mace in the other. The crowd booed as he swung forward and brought the mace upwards, catching Joaquin's horse beneath the chin. The animal reared and staggered backwards. The weight of the armoured knight on his back pulled him over and he toppled, crushing one of Joaquin's legs beneath him.

The man yelled with pain as Turquin circled the arena, punching the air with his fists.

'You could get to really hate the Ceolothians,' Kay muttered.

'But that's not fair. That's just not fair,' Caspar yelled as two stretcher-bearers trotted into the arena and bundled Joaquin away. 'Do something. It's not fair,' he yelled at the marshal.

'All is fair in war. And this is war at its purest,' Kay replied solemnly, tugging him back down onto the bench. 'It's the first motto a knight should learn. Joaquin should have expected nothing less from the prince.'

'It's a horrible thing to do.'

Kay nodded. 'And he's up against Father in the next round.'

His voice trailed away and he gave Caspar an anxious look. 'It's Hal's turn now though.'

Hal sternly avoided looking towards the red and white striped hospital tent that had swallowed Joaquin and fixed his eyes on his opponent across the arena. A sallow-skinned man from Salise, Sir Tylot, however, looked long and hard towards the hospital tent and was slow to place his helmet. Caspar decided this was a good omen. If Tylot lacked concentration then maybe Hal stood a chance. The dark youth looked as keen as an arrow. Magpie responded quickly to his touch and, as Hal tilted his lance, the animal's even stride barely altered. Hal had learnt to balance himself well.

'He's come a long way,' Kay muttered as the clash of metal rang through the air.

Caspar could only peek through his fingers. Tylot's lance tip had snagged Hal's arm and wrenched his wrist backwards, ripping his gauntlet from his hand.

Unflustered and without breaking Magpie's stride, Hal discarded his lance and reached for his sword, proving to Caspar that he was thinking with clear-headed logic, untroubled by his temper. Tylot, though, had long since anticipated him, having already turned his horse. Hal was not yet fully prepared and had no time to raise his shield arm in defence as the Salisian's mace hacked down through the air and smashed against his helm.

The follow-through of the blow scored across Magpie's bare shoulder, drawing furrows of blood in the white patch of hide. The horse shied sideways and without showing any sign of trying to recover his balance, Hal fell heavily from his saddle. Caspar found himself shoving and trampling over the men in front of him, focused only on getting to the arena. The stretcher-bearers were lifting Hal onto their canvas and carrying him towards the red and white tent. He was as white as a shroud and a trickle of blood oozed from his ear.

Brid was beside him. The minute they were within the tent, she ripped the scrip from her neck and angrily pushed the physician aside as he was in the process of shaking three leeches from a gourd. 'Spar, keep that man away,' she commanded threateningly as she stooped over Hal's body.

'I know what I'm doing,' the man retorted. 'I've been a field physician for fifteen years and I've seen many head wounds.'

Brid ripped the veil from her face. The force of her dragon-green eyes startled the man and without more ado he retreated to re-examine Joaquin's crushed leg.

'Hal,' Caspar murmured helplessly. 'Brid, do something for him.'

'That knight didn't have to do that.' Kay was there beside them. 'He knew he could beaten Hal without having to hurt him so badly. It wasn't necessary.'

Hal groaned and Caspar could see the relief on Brid's face.

'Will he be all right?' he murmured.

Brid's voice was high and tense as she eased the dented helmet from the youth's head.

'I thought at first that the blood from his ear was coming from within his skull but it's not,' she sighed. 'Look, he's cut just above the ear.'

'Is that a good sign, then?' Caspar asked, trying to keep his voice steady. He held Hal's hand tightly in his.

Brid nodded and pulled back Hal's eyelids. The pupils instantly contracted in the light.

'Yes, it's a good sign. The helmet's thick leather and cork cushioning has done its job well. He'll come round shortly but with a worse head than you could ever imagine.' She was smiling though her hand trembled with visible relief and she dabbed quickly at her eyes.

'You go out there and watch the rest,' she ordered. 'There's nothing you can do here anyway and he needs rest and quiet.'

Caspar nodded.

'Don't you think you should get the field physician to look at him?' Kay suggested anxiously as Caspar reappeared outside the field tent.

The Torra Altan shook his head. 'No, Brid knows exactly what she's doing.'

'She has extraordinary green eyes,' Kay whispered. 'No

wonder Hal was cross when she watched you and not him all this last month.'

Ceowulf and Tudwal were already pitched against each other. Tudwal was slow to turn his cream mare and Ceowulf, who had already swung Sorcerer round, chivalrously gave Tudwal a moment to organize himself and get his gauntlet disentangled from his reins. There was a murmur of approval from the crowd.

Ceowulf's chivalrous gesture induced Kay to mutter, 'That Tudwal doesn't deserve such courtesy. He should have just knocked him straight out of the saddle.'

Not once did Tudwal's lance even get near to Ceowulf and at each tilt, the big Caldean averted his lance from the prince's body at the last second, showing plainly that he could strike the younger man at will, but chose not to. Finally Ceowulf signalled to one of the squires who hovered attentively at each end of the field. A leather pad was strapped to the end of Ceowulf's lance by the time Tudwal had turned to make his next charge. This time, without any hesitation, Ceowulf spurred Sorcerer straight at the young Prince of Ceolothia and punched him full in the chest with the protected wadding of the blunt lance. Tudwal was lifted clean from the saddle and deposited on the ground where he had to scramble on hands and knees to avoid the tearing hooves of his horse.

The crowd laughed delightedly. Ceowulf had long since captured their hearts and this act of chivalry further stoked the fires in their breasts. Caspar reflected that when he had first met the Caldean he had considered him to be an ignoble treacherous man simply because he was a mercenary. He had long since reconsidered.

Tudwal was the only one not amused by Ceowulf's kindness. He stormed off in the direction of his older brother, his face red with humiliation.

'You'd think he'd rather have been badly wounded,' Kay muttered in despair. 'Ceowulf could have turned that into a blood bath if he had wished, like Tylot did with Hal. You'd think Tudwal would be grateful. There is never any disgrace in losing here. These are the finest fighting men in all the countries of the Caballan Sea.'

There was a long interval before the next round was due to begin and Cybillia dipped into the tent which housed Hal and Brid before running over towards Ceowulf and Caspar.

Caspar had never seen Cybillia run. When they first met her she would have considered it too unseemly, but now there was an unmistakable bounce to her steps as she eagerly wound her way through the crowd. Once she saw Kay and Caspar she seemed to suddenly remember herself, bowed her head and brushed out her skirts before trying to walk forward more serenely. However, she still could not disguise her eagerness to greet Ceowulf.

The knight bowed low. 'My lady.'

Cybillia's eyes flickered with embarrassment towards Caspar and then rose very slowly back towards Ceowulf.

Caspar was intrigued and studied them intently until he felt a tug on his arm.

'Spar, you're staring,' Kay muttered. 'I think they want to be left alone. Let's go and see how Hal is.'

Hal looked pale. His head was bandaged and he was propped up on a couch with a look of self-reproach on his face. As they entered he looked up, shook his head and grimaced.

'I was stupid. I should have come straight at him, making it difficult for him to place the lance. It was his blow to my hand that ruined me. I should have been able to avoid that. I might as well have been blindfolded,' he berated himself.

Kay sat by the edge of the bed and went through the fight blow by blow with the dark youth, while Caspar sought out Brid at the far end of the tent.

The priestess sighed more with annoyance than despair. 'All he's worried about is why he failed and how he could have succeeded and how next time he could do better. Next time!' She was fiercely grinding woundwort in a pestle. 'Now there's only Ceowulf and if he fails there'll never be a next time. Not for any Belbidian.'

Caspar saw the seriousness of the situation. They had been

so caught up in the tournament at Sequicornum that the reality of the outside world had withdrawn into insignificance. But what was this tournament other than a game to prepare these men for real battles? For too many of them the game had become more real than the mortal wars pitched against foreign invaders. Only for the Belbidians was it not a game. One of them had to win and only Ceowulf was left in the competition.

'I hope Ceowulf is ready,' Brid fretted, still looking towards Hal who was talking animatedly to Kay.

'He's with Cybillia,' Caspar replied, trying to import some meaning into his words.

Brid grinned at Caspar. 'Good. After everything that's happened, it's the one good thing to happen today.'

'Well, I'm not staying here any longer,' Hal announced. 'I'm going out there to cheer Ceowulf on.' Swinging his legs over the side of the couch, he flung himself to his feet only to take one step before crumpling to his knees. Kay quickly caught him before he hit the hard ground.

Hal's face was suddenly a greenish tinge.

'You've had a bad knock to the head, Hal. You need to take it very easy,' Brid fussed.

'I've got to watch the lists,' he protested though he didn't seem to have the energy to stop Brid from pressing him back onto the couch.

'You're staying here. We'll move you nearer to the entrance and peel open the tent flaps so you can see, but you've got to stay out of the sun and rest. You're more injured than you allow yourself to think.'

'I suppose you're going to watch with Spar then,' he announced rather bitterly.

Brid's nose tilted upwards as she pulled aside the tent flaps, ready to depart for the stands again. 'Yes, and why shouldn't I?'

Kay sat at the edge of his seat as he waited for the next round to begin. Turquin's bright chestnut gelding, finely arrayed in the prince's colours, circled at the far end of the arena, stamping and squealing like a bull. The prince's armour shone dazzling white as the hot sun reflected off its burnished surface. Draped in resplendent gold, red and blue and with his helm adorned with a coronet, he certainly looked the part of the heir apparent to the whole of Ceolothia. He rode skilfully, not with grace or subtlety but with a determined arrogance that nevertheless dominated the mind of his horse.

Closer to where they sat, Grinwal was preparing his bay mare. With no glorious colours to proclaim a noble birth, the animal was clad only in crupper and breastplate. Grinwal's armour was of plain steel and though no doubt as tough as Turquin's it would be very much heavier for his horse and more cumbersome for the knight.

'If he wins, the King of Lonis has promised to make him a lord,' Kay said eagerly.

'I know, but does he really want to be a lord?' Caspar replied.

'Doesn't everyone?'

Caspar wasn't sure. 'There's a certain loss of freedom that goes with responsibility. People start expecting things from you.'

Kay wasn't listening. He kept perfectly still like a panther preparing to pounce, taut with tension and anticipation, every muscle twitching for the moment of release. The two knights tilted their lances and urged their mounts forward. They fought long and hard, charging twelve times in all before either one of them found a chink in their opponent's defence. Finally Turquin's lance caught Grinwal's thigh. The Lonisian's bay mare was thrown to the left, momentarily unsettling him, but Grinwal was still able to swing his shield to hammer into Turquin's shoulder. For a moment Turquin swayed but spurred his horse on and out of danger to turn successfully at the end of the lists, ready to charge again.

Both horses were beginning to tire long before any useful blow was struck, and after the twentieth tilt they were instructed at the King's behest to abandon their lances. King Valerius was evidently finding the protracted bout too tedious for his tastes. At the next charge, Turquin swung his mace across Grinwal's saddle, belting it down onto the man's thigh. The weapon acted like a grappling hook, snagging into the Lonisian's armour, and Turquin swung his horse away, using the animal's strength to lever his opponent from the saddle.

Grinwal seemed instantly to sense that he would be unable to remain horsed. Reaching for his sword, he launched himself straight at the prince, thereby turning the position to his advantage and knocking the man to the ground with the weight of his own body. The men rolled apart and both were quickly to their feet. Caspar wondered how they managed to get upright under the weight of so much metal.

Once no longer on horseback, however, Turquin rapidly gained the upper hand. Grinwal's right thigh was clearly paining him and he was slow to lunge off that foot.

Turquin's power drove the older man steadily backwards. Still feeling that the Lonisian's skills were greater, Caspar wondered if Grinwal was only on the defensive to make Turquin tire himself out as much as possible until he could return the attack. The longer Turquin continued to slash with such extravagant broad strokes, the quicker he would tire. Grinwal's defence was economical and understated by comparison.

Kay grinned at Spar. 'He's going to do it. He's just wearing him out.'

There was an expectant hush muffling the crowd, though very gradually the chant of 'Grinwal! Grinwal!' rippled through the excited stands. Clearly they appreciated his skill.

Turquin turned his sword so that it swung upwards, aiming at his opponent's head, though Grinwal was clearly ready for this. What he wasn't prepared for was the sheer force of the knight's stroke as it slashed upwards. Grinwal's raised blade splintered, leaving only a broken hilt. Kay sat back in defeat, no longer wanting to look as if he knew from that moment on that it was over. With only his mace to defend himself, the Lonisian was caught again and again by slashing blows to his sides.

There was, though, a hint of forbearance in the Ceolothian's attack as Grinwal left his naked side exposed. A gap in his armour left him vulnerable to severe injury and Grinwal acknowledged the Ceolothian's courteous move and lowered his mace.

'You could have taken me, knight, and I declare I have lost to your greater skill.'

Kay slumped forward onto his arms.

'He should have fought on,' one of the younger knights murmured.

'There was no point. In truth, he had lost and why inflict injury in the tournament field when it can be avoided?' another retorted.

As soon as the fight was over, Kay ran to join his father. Brid and Caspar were left alone until a very anxious Cybillia finally dragged herself away from the Caldean knight and came to join them.

'Doth the fair lady blush from the sweet delight of yonder knight's eloquence?' Brid teased

'Oh shut up,' Cybillia giggled with embarrassment. She pulled Brid aside and, glancing shyly at Caspar, whispered, 'I'll tell you what he said later – when we're alone.'

There was evidently a strong friendship growing up between the two young women now that any rivalry for Hal had finally been removed. Embarrassed, Caspar looked away, not wanting to intrude on their womanly gossip. Cybillia fell silent, however, as the trumpet fanfare announced the next contestants.

Tylot, with his tilting helm firmly in place, snatched at his horse's reins as the animal danced sideways.

'He's seen Ceowulf fight many times before and he's worried,' Brid said. 'His horse didn't play up like that when he faced Hal. Now he's worried and his charger won't listen to his anxious commands.'

To everyone's delight, they were right. Whereas Sorcerer charged straight, the heavy strawberry roan facing him crabbed sideways with little speed. Ceowulf's lance thumped hard into the centre of Tylot's shield, knocking it backwards into his breastplate. Cybillia's hand leapt to her face, however, as she heard a stifled grunt coming from the Caldean's mouth.

Though Tylot was bowled straight out of the saddle and lay winded on the ground, Ceowulf dropped his lance as if it pained him.

'It's his old shoulder wound,' Brid groaned.

But with only the weight of a sword in his hand, Ceowulf seemed quite capable of fighting on. He had little trouble in repeatedly dodging Tylot's attacks, finally knocking the sword from his hand with a well-placed blow from his mace. But Caspar still noted a degree of stiffness in the Caldean's movement.

'I thought his shoulder was fully healed,' Brid murmured, 'but the repeated usage seems to have damaged it again.'

The red knight knocked the helm from Tylot's head and held the point of this sword against the man's throat.

Tylot dropped his mace.

'I yield, sir,' he said gallantly. There was disappointment in the man's face but now that he had lost, he offered his hand in friendship. Ceowulf took it reservedly, evidently remembering the injury Tylot had inflicted on Hal.

Brid studied the knight's shoulder in the hospital tent where Hal was still lying. The youth had tried to get up several times but was persistently overcome with sick giddiness. He smiled at Ceowulf. 'The day will belong to Belbidia, knight. You're a match for Turquin any day.'

'Oh how I admire the innocence of youth,' Ceowulf sighed, slowly rotating his shoulder as Brid applied a poultice of wintergreen and Yellow Mountain arnica.

'Does it hurt a lot?' she asked more out of necessity than sympathy. 'I'll give you some willow bark and bandage it to give some support. The muscles are still weak from your injury.'

'It doesn't hurt a lot. But if it didn't hurt at all I'd fight better.'

Brid grinned. 'You don't have to be brave.' She offered him a scroll of greyish willow bark. 'Now, chew on this and get some rest. At least you've got two hours until the final round.'

'I can't; I've still –' Ceowulf began reluctantly.

'I'll see to Sorcerer,' Caspar offered without hesitation. 'You go and take a rest.'

The man nodded gratefully. 'I'll stroll into the city and get right away from all the ceremony,' he said. 'It'll help clear my head for the last fight.'

The knight bowed gracefully towards Cybillia and lightly kissed her hand before marching from the tent. Caspar watched him stride out beneath the portcullis and into the busy town.

Chapter 19

'Try to stop her,' the Baron ordered.

'I can't.' Elaine's words were stiff and resolute though May could still sense the underlying fear.

Branwolf paced towards where the old woman stood on Torra Alta's central heartstone. About her were candles, chalice and a sickle – the sacraments of her holy office. One scrawny forearm oozed blood from three deep gashes. All about her roared the blue flames of consecrating fire.

'Stay back,' the Crone spat at the Baron. 'Stay back or I'll fling myself on the flames. Mother! Great Mother, hear me. For the sake of these people, accept my sacrifice.'

'Morrigwen, you must stop. You will die.'

'Only if the Great Mother wishes it. She does not believe that the people of Torra Alta truly love her. I must prove that we do; I must show her the depth of our love. Mother, accept this gift, accept my sacrifice. Accept that I love and worship you beyond all else. Accept my life and save these people; for I believe in their goodness.'

'You, soldier,' Branwolf spun on his heel. 'Fetch water and put these flames out.'

He kicked at the circle of flames himself, covering his face from the smoke. The man returned quickly and doused enough of the flames for the broad-chested noblemen to stride into Morrigwen's consecrated circle. But as he set foot on the heartstone, he shrank back in pain, his hands clutching at his temples. Doubled over and still pressing his hands to his head, he seemed to be battling with an invisible enemy but he struggled on and grasped the old woman by the arms, dragging her out of the circle.

'You don't know what you're doing. You don't have the right!' the old woman screamed.

May couldn't believe that Morrigwen still had the strength to shriek and struggle. Rage contorted her skeletal features and her eyes bulged from their sagging sockets. Elaine hurried ahead to prepare a settle while the Baron forcibly carried Morrigwen into the shelter of the keep and away from the pelting missiles that bombarded the courtyard. Branwolf's men were spread thinly now. Many had fallen from the waves of trolls that had breached the walls over the last weeks. The shored-up south wall was barely holding and the north tower was hanging at a precarious angle where the bombardment had undercut the roots of the structure.

The reinforcements never came. Volunteers had ventured over the wall throughout Lenting and Ostara but there had been no hint of reinforcements. It was now Merrymoon and no one spoke of it anymore. At first May had believed, like everyone else, that any day the King's men would appear on the southern horizon, but they never arrived. The only thing that appeared to the south was a troupe of more Vaalakans. The archers argued over the details but they all now knew Morbak's plan was clear. He would risk sending only a few men through the hazardous terrain of the Jaws of the Wolf, but it was enough to man the siege-engines that pounded the south walls. With Torra Alta under attack from all sides, Branwolf could no longer concentrate his men on the west and north walls. Their falling numbers were thinly spread and all knew it was only a matter of time now.

Either the King could not respond as he tried to defend the southern mouth of the Jaws of the Wolf or the messengers never got through. May never learnt the answer. All she knew was that Branwolf ceased to ask for volunteers and the assault on the castle thickened.

The chestnut-haired girl from the Boarchase Forest looked sadly around her at the glistening castle. The whinstone walls and cobbled courtyards were gleaming and slippery from thawing icicles and the sound of melting snow dripping through its last slushy stages of decomposition drummed within the castle's enclosed spaces. Spring had arrived late that year but now its heartening smell sweetened the air and its warmth spurred the last slabs of slushy snow from the sloping roof of the store-rooms to cascade into the courtyard below.

Normally May was cheered by the brief rains and brilliant sunshine of Merrymoon; after all it was her month. But this year there was no joy in the change of season. The Northmen had taken to bombarding them with troll carcasses riddled with poison and disease and their bodies crashed over the walls and splattered the courtyard at regular intervals. The putrid stench was sickening, morale low.

Not only the Vaalakan bombardment took its toll now. Four young children had died from malnutrition. Morrigwen had said that it would hit the young and the old first. How the old woman herself was still living nobody knew. Six of the old retainers had died, their hearts failing under the strain. At the last count six hundred men defended the castle but that was the day before yesterday. They hadn't had time to count the dwindling numbers since then.

The Vaalakans had come in waves, suicide waves at first. Those following had shielded themselves behind the wall of their own dead, thousands of them banked up, filling the ditches and smothering the earthworks that protected the Tor. Hour by hour they claimed more ground and with each yard tightened their throttling hold on the ancient castle that nobly held its head above the writhing storm. But they all knew that they would eventually sink under the tide of barbaric Northmen. There was a terrible sadness overlying the castle and yet in the brave Torra Altan hearts a stubborn resolve still burnt fiercely. May believed with conviction that the garrison would hold the castle and maintain its protection over the rest of Belbidia to the very last man.

Contemplating these things, she watched quietly as her

mother struggled to hold down Morrigwen. 'You of all must live,' Elaine beseeched her.

'But the runes have failed,' the priestess argued. 'It's near the end of Merrymoon already and Brid has not returned. I must make a sacrifice so that the Mother will hear me. If the castle is to stand until Brid returns the Great Mother must come to our aid once more, even though we do not yet have the Druid's Egg.'

'But if you die the Trinity is lost,' Elaine said softly. 'Then the worship of the Mother cannot be restored.'

'I would only die if the Mother wishes it. I have to offer the sacrifice. It is for Her to decide whether She takes my life or not. But I must offer.' She looked furiously at the Baron. 'You don't know what you've done or what you're doing, foolish man.' She redoubled her struggling.

Branwolf stepped aside, nodding to the castle physician to restrain her. The physician had little of the Crone's knowledge of herb lore, though he was skilled in field dressings and leeching. He moved forward to hold the priestess down while Branwolf pulled Elaine aside.

'We cannot let her die. We cannot let her weaken herself.'

'She does this for us,' Elaine said with tears in her eyes. 'Brid has not returned. There is so very little time left. Without the runes of war we will be overrun. She is our high priestess; we should let her do as she sees right.'

'But there is still time. We still have men, the finest archers in all the Caballan Sea, and though the outer walls are crumbling, the keep will stand on its own merits. Its walls are twenty foot thick and have stood for a thousand years. It will stand even without the runes of war for a few days yet. Not till the Vaalakans breach the outer walls and pound on the keep doors with their axes will I admit that our time has run out,' the Baron argued wearily. 'But while there is still time we must ensure that she lives. In preventing her self-sacrifice we prove our devotion. Perhaps at the end, we must prove that the Great Mother and Her Trinity means more to us than all else. More than Torra Alta. And in the end it is not Morrigwen's sacrifice that She wants, but Torra Alta's.'

May sucked in her breath, aware of the gravity of the man's words. They were heavy, ponderous and slow, but they were also profound as if many sleepless nights had gone into the labour of thought.

May looked at the impossibly thin old woman.

She knew that Branwolf had continually ordered that his own food should be given to her but the woman's thinness was not just the wastage of malnutrition. It was the wastage of age.

'The worship of the Great Mother was here long before Torra Alta and in the end it is the Old Faith and not Torra Alta that must prevail,' the Baron pronounced heavily.

Elaine looked at Branwolf and then at Morrigwen who was still being held down by Maud and the castle physician.

'I must offer the Great Mother my sacrifice,' the high priestess croaked. 'It is up to the Great Mother whether she accepts my life or not. You cannot hold me down like this. Elaine, do something!'

The red-haired woman looked at her in stony silence.

'We can't let you do it,' the Baron insisted.

'Merrymoon, my Merrymoon, you at least must let me do this,' Morrigwen begged the small chestnut-haired girl.

May found that she was sobbing. She held Morrigwen's hand. 'I'm sorry. I know you think you are doing the right thing but perhaps this is what the Great Mother wants. Perhaps she is stopping you through us.'

'Have you got nothing that will calm her?' The Baron turned to the physician. 'If she cuts herself again she will surely die and we cannot let her.'

The man shook his head.

Elaine searched Morrigwen's table that was littered with pestle and mortars, phials and powders where she had worked tirelessly through the siege, preparing her medicines. She sifted through them and held up two phials of ground powder. 'Gortan wild lettuce and Caballan valerian root,' she whispered.

'She gives it to soothe those that are dying. Perhaps it will help.'

'What if it does harm?'

'It won't. She assured me of that. It just soothes and quiets them to ease them on their journey.'

Branwolf nodded. 'Give it to her then.' His voice was stern and gruff as he took the responsibility on himself. 'She must live.' He looked at Elaine and gripped her arm. 'It's our duty and you will see to it.'

Elaine nodded. 'My Lord, with all my heart.'

That night the trolls broke over the walls. It was the first time they had attacked by night and the watch was slaughtered before the men could be roused from their beds. The pitiful remains of the kitchen stores, and any weapons, ropes and tackle along with two dozen kegs of brimstone powder from the well-room, were moved to the keep. The few men left retreated into the blocky tower of the central fortification. In ragged bands, they had pulled back from the curtain walls, and as the last of them passed inside, the masons and carpenters sealed up the entrance. A hundred souls huddled together and prayed, trying to block out the relentless thump, thump as the keep's vast oak doors were pounded from outside.

A great thunderous crash shook the walls of the keep and May clutched tighter to her mother.

'The north tower,' she gasped. 'It's finally fallen.'

Vast steel girders were slotted over the entrance to the keep. All knew without saying that it was now only a matter of time. Only a matter of hours.

Pip found himself a sword. He had prised the oversized weapon from the moribund grip of one of the many fallen soldiers and now he stood grimly before his mother. 'I won't let them harm you,' he declared bravely.

It was no longer a question of if the Vaalakans would tear down the keep, only when. May could see that even the youngest of them knew what would happen when they were finally overrun. They had all seen the terrible agony of death as the men were disembowelled and shredded by the trolls' fangs. Pip focused on the great steel door that took the hammering blows from the Vaalakans, never once taking his eyes from the shuddering panels that bowed under the impact of their axes. Morrigwen lay still now and most of the women gathered round her for comfort.

The lower keep was devoid of men. May had watched them climb to the top storeys of the fortification and had sent her prayers with them. She knew they were up on the toothed battlements at the top of the blocky tower grouped around the Dragon Standard, spending the last of their arrows in a desperate bid to drive the barbarians back from the lower doors. Every last arrow mattered. It bought one more precious moment in which Brid, Master Hal and Master Spar might return with the power of the Druid's Egg.

They could no longer get to the water, and the supplies were limited, but still the vast walls of the keep held out throughout the day. The hammering on the keep doors ceased at nightfall and the few Torra Altans who were left slept restlessly. Elaine, however, would not sleep. She held her two children and rocked them back and forth in her arms, stroking their hair and murmuring softly.

'Do you remember how happy we all were when we lived in the village with all the other woodcutters' families and Pa used to take you for rides on his shoulders?'

May nodded, holding her mother's hand and looking deep into her eyes. She knew that Elaine was trying to tell them that she loved them, trying to ease their fear as they waited through the darkest hours of the night. They feared the sunrise and the onslaught it would bring; but dawn would come and no amount of praying would stop it.

'Ma,' she whispered.

Elaine nodded, a flicker of firelight caught the points of her red hair. She turned her soft blue eyes on her daughter.

'Yes, May.'

'I love you, Ma. I just wanted to say that, in case –' she faltered. 'I just wanted you to know.'

Chapter 20

'Why isn't he back yet?' Cybillia fretted. 'He's been gone over an hour.'

Even Brid was beginning to worry and Caspar marched up and down, snapping his fingers distractedly. 'He should be here, Brid. He really should be here by now,' he found himself saying and suddenly realized that he was waiting for the priestess to tell him what to do next.

He stiffened up. As the future Baron of Torra Alta it was his place to decide the next action. With Hal still too confused to think straight, there was no one left but himself to take charge.

'We'll give him five more minutes and then I'll find Kay and go and look for him,' Caspar resolved.

'No, go now.' Brid's tone was decisive. 'He's been gone too long.'

He and Kay trotted quickly into the town. They met several knights sauntering back after a cooling drink of light ale in the local taverns but none of them had seen Ceowulf. Then Caspar caught sight of Tylot's sallow face.

'Sir, have you seen Ceowulf?' he demanded, trying not to think of how the Salisian had so brutally cudgelled his uncle.

The knight took in the boy's anxious frown with one glance. 'About half an hour ago,' he said with surprising pleasantry. 'Why? Is anything the matter? I saw him, Prince Tudwal and a few of the young prince's squires –'

'Tudwal!' Caspar exclaimed. It seemed so unlikely. The Ceolothian would be the last person Ceowulf would spend time with. 'Nothing's the matter, it's just that he's been a long time,' Caspar explained.

Tylot shrugged. 'I'm sure Ceowulf can look after himself but, just to calm your nerves a little, I'll accompany you while you look for him.' The man was more pleasant and relaxed now that, for him at least, the competition was over. He talked jovially, ignorant of the apprehension in Caspar's mind.

Ceowulf was always reliable. He couldn't possibly be late. Now if Hal were missing it would be a different matter. Hal was easily distracted. Caspar had a horrible cold feeling tightening around his heart.

They found him, eventually, down in the western quarter of the town. He was slumped against a wall, cradling his right arm and shoulder. A trickle of blood ran across his forehead, mingling with the sweat that beaded his ashen skin.

'Ceowulf!' Caspar cried, running towards him.

'Don't touch my arm,' the Caldean warned sharply.

Caspar noted that the shoulder looked agonizingly distorted where it should have been smoothly rounded.

'They jumped me from behind. They put a sack over my head, clubbed me and then did this to my shoulder,' the knight groaned.

'Who?' Tylot demanded.

'Some cheap opportunist, no doubt. I don't know. I never saw them. They just attacked me from behind and fled.'

'They didn't try to rob you then?' Tylot queried in surprise, peeling back Ceowulf's jerkin to examine his shoulder. 'That's a nasty dislocation. I'll find someone with a cart to get you back to the castle.'

'No, they didn't try to rob me,' Ceowulf muttered. 'They just did this to my sword-arm.'

'Hmm,' Tylot muttered suspiciously as he went to borrow a low open wagon from a passing trader.

'Someone was deliberately trying to prevent you from . . .' Caspar began falteringly. 'But not even Turquin would do that. Not just for the honour of winning.'

'Turquin wouldn't,' Ceowulf affirmed. 'He beat Grinwal

without stepping one toe beyond the boundaries of chivalry.'

'No, not Turquin,' Kay agreed. 'But Tudwal might. He might consider it his revenge for the way you beat him. Humiliation does not sit well on his princely shoulders.'

Ceowulf didn't look as if he cared. 'I didn't see who it was. It could just have been ruffians. I'm not going to go round making vain accusations.'

He didn't say any more until they got him back to the hospital tent. Brid deigned to let the field physician help her relocate the joint. The muscles were clearly torn and heavy black bruising masked his shoulder. Gloom hung heavily over the Torra Altans. No one said it but Caspar knew what they were all thinking. They had failed. After all their effort, after all those months, they had failed. He had never really considered the possibility but now it struck him like a blacksmith's hammer and he felt crushed beneath the blow.

After Brid and the field physician had finally levered Ceowulf's shoulder joint back into its socket, it was some minutes before Ceowulf was comfortable enough to speak. By that time the marshal of the ceremonies had entered the hospital tent.

'There seem to be a few too many Belbidians in here today,' he muttered, looking at Ceowulf's bloodless face. 'You were injured outside the tournament ring. By the rules of chivalry you may choose a second to take your place in the arena. There will be many brave knights out there today prepared to fight for your name.'

'I for one,' Tylot offered.

Ceowulf looked defeated and his voice cracked. 'Would I receive the award at the presentation ceremonies if Tylot wins for me?'

The marshal shook his head. 'No. If he wins he cannot keep the prize money – that of course will go to you – but otherwise he takes your stead throughout the entire ceremony. It is an extremely ancient sacred ritual and these rules have always been upheld – though it's five hundred years since the last time such an incident occurred.'

Ceowulf looked from Hal, still lying weakly on the couch, to Caspar and then at Brid.

Brid saw the man's dilemma. 'It has to be Spar,' she said softly. 'There's no alternative.'

Caspar's throat tightened.

The injured knight shook his head at the Maiden. 'I just don't see the point of putting the boy through it. He could never beat Turquin. Look what the man did to Grinwal. It's just not possible. He can't hope to inflict any harm on the prince without a full-sized lance; it's preposterous. Turquin will crush him.'

'Is there any rule to say that I must carry a lance?' Caspar said, the trepidation suddenly easing out of him.

The marshal shook his head. 'You must enter the arena bearing a lance but you don't have to use it of course. There's nothing to say you can't drop it.'

'Well then, that's what I shall do,' he said firmly.

The marshal raised his eyebrows and then looked back at Ceowulf. 'Sir, for the boy's sake this is not a wise choice. Sir Tylot here is very happy –'

'I said I'll do it,' Caspar boomed and for the first time a hint of authority girded his voice. He had to do it. He didn't know how he was going to do it but he had to. The imperative nature of the situation added strength of will to his voice.

Hal struggled upright on his couch and groaned.

'Don't be ridiculous, Spar. You'll get yourself killed.' He heaved himself onto his feet only to turn a sickly shade of green and slump back. 'I'll be fine in just a minute. I'll do it. I can't let you . . .' he insisted as Brid very gently pushed him back down onto the couch. 'Brid, I can't let him do it. Not Spar. He's my responsibility. Branwolf –'

'Hal, you've done your best,' she assured him.

Hal looked utterly conquered. He lay back groaning.

Caspar stepped towards his uncle and gripped his hand. 'It's only right, Hal. Torra Alta is my responsibility and I must do everything I can to defend the castle.'

Hal shut his eyes. 'I'm not going to watch.'

*   *   *

The only son of Baron Branwolf Lord of Torra Alta looked at his Oriaxian purebred and smiled. Firecracker's coat shone like burnished bronze in the sultry sunlight of Camaalia's spring. Philippe was offering him his fine armour. It was only a little too large for the auburn-haired youth but Caspar shook his head all the same. 'No, I'm no good with a lance and armour. I must use the skills I have to their best advantage.'

He saddled and bridled Firecracker and, slipping off his halter, led him out into the courtyard. The horse wore no armour and Caspar even left off the Torra Altan caparison, knowing that the animal would move more freely without the cloth flapping around his legs. Declining Ceowulf's offer of the loan of his sword, he carried only his familiar practice sword, fearing that the strange weapon might distract him. Even Brid's pleading eyes wouldn't persuade him to wear a visored helm.

'Pray for me,' he whispered as she reknotted her silken token through Firecracker's mane.

'I have and I will,' she replied. 'But I have also added two more runes to the scarf. Evidently I didn't put quite the right ones on before. They are the rune of Ehwaz, which represents the horse, and Sigel's rune, which represents victory. You see, I believe that victory lies in your horsemanship.'

Caspar nodded appreciatively as he contemplated the new arrangement of runes.

ᚱᚾᛏᛗᛋ⊕

His thoughts were so intent that even the raucous sound of the trumpet fanfare became little more than a muffled echo to his ears. He relaxed his mind, thinking only of the movements of the horse, trying to become one with the animal's energy. He felt they were floating on air as Firecracker danced up on his toes.

Dipping back into the saddle, he tightened the tension on the reins, asking the horse to curtsy onto his haunches and wheel round, stepping high with his forelegs. He focused on Turquin's bright chestnut gelding, resplendent in its rich colours of gold, red and blue, at the far end of the lists.

Standing solidly four-square on legs like tree-trunks, the animal must have weighed over a ton even without the heavily clad knight astride him.

Caspar could feel a nervous smile curling up on his lips. There was something quite preposterous about all of this and he couldn't help but see the humour in it. Here he was, a small youth on a light horse with only a sword while his opponent was encased in a fortune of plate steel. For just a moment, he ceased to be fearful.

But as the marshal gave the signal to begin, Caspar's heart plunged to his feet. All he could focus on was the point of the lance steaming towards him, driven by the force of a vast plunging war-horse. If the bare lance connected with his unprotected body he would be impaled on the point, quickly becoming little more than a red-haired pennon on the tip of Prince Turquin's lance.

He wrenched his mind away from his fear. Fear would do nothing to save him. 'Great Mother,' he prayed though he thought of the image of his own mother captured in the heart of the moonstone. 'Great Mother, help me.' The prayer gave him enough fortitude to pull away from his fears and sense the courage in his horse. The stallion's only intent was on sprinting at a heart-stopping pace towards the thundering red, blue and gold demon. Caspar, however, sat deep into the saddle and steadied the young horse, feeling for the bit to contain the pace. He needed to keep a very direct line, keeping Turquin's lance fixed towards his heart until the very last possible second.

The point of the long weapon seemed to swell before his eyes and the entire crowd held its breath. Less than a pace from impact, Caspar dug his right heel into Firecracker's ribs. The horse dipped its shoulder and swung sideways. The lance glanced over his thigh, missing its target. The big chestnut destrier puffed from the combined effort of its last sprint and the prince's vast weight on its back and was slow to turn. With a steel plate shaffron armouring its head and shining flanchards protecting its sides, the hefty beast clanked and jangled as he made a wide cumbersome turn at the head of the lists. At the opposite end, the young hot-bloodied stallion dipped elegantly on his haunches, pirouetted round and stood waiting.

Caspar could hear the cheers now. They were cheers for Ceowulf of course, whose place he was taking, but there were cheers for him as well. Gone were the mocking faces and their ridicule.

Again and again they charged, Turquin's language becoming more violent and abusive with each pass. His heavy chestnut charger was perceptibly slower now, its stride flat and listless as it heaved back down the field.

Caspar of course knew the man was no fool. Turquin would be anticipating each feint or side-step and Caspar feared that he might be becoming too predictable. He positioned Firecracker several paces too far to the left this time so that, as Turquin charged, he was forced to come out at an angle towards him. Caspar knew what he wanted to do though it was asking a lot of any horse.

He held Firecracker in until he was virtually cantering on the spot, allowing Turquin to make all the speed. Rather than dodge away this time he was determined to swerve in front of his opponent. With his reins in his left hand, he raised himself out of the saddle. He feinted to the left unexpectedly early, drawing Turquin even further out towards him, but then he turned Firecracker's head away to the right. For a moment his heart stopped as he felt the stallion's hooves slip away from him in the soft soil. He cursed, thinking he had swerved too quickly and his horse would fall sideways.

But Firecracker grunted and somehow managed to get his balance as he darted to the right, cutting directly underneath the breastplate of the chestnut gelding.

The prince tried to follow. He turned his horse sharply towards Firecracker but at such speed and with his heavy weight it was impossible. Caspar heard the squeal as the hefty destrier lost his footing, stumbled to his knees and rolled. Turquin would have been horseman enough to leap clear but for the encumbering weight of his armour. As the huge bulk of his heavy horse fell sideways, his leg was pinned beneath the animal's girth.

The tremendous roar from the crowd nearly drowned out Turquin's cry as his thigh-bone snapped. The gelding thrashed and kicked in an effort to rise but its legs were entangled in the reins and straps that secured its caparison. Its armoured tonnage pressed down on Turquin's broken leg. Caspar quickly turned Firecracker and leapt from the saddle. He grabbed the charger's bridle and disentangled the reins from its forelegs before steadying the animal as it heaved upright away from the groaning knight.

Carried from the field, Prince Turquin turned his head and moaned in humiliation, 'Felled by the smallest knight in the competition.'

'No, felled by the fastest horse,' Caspar said graciously. He almost felt sorry for the man.

The Torra Altan youth found himself hoisted aloft onto the shoulders of several jubilant knights. Garlands of white campion were thrown at him and he caught them delightedly. Winding them round his neck, he felt himself swelling with pride. He had done it. He was supreme! A twinge of guilt filled his mind. No, he hadn't done it. Ceowulf had done most of it, fighting round after round, beating so many knights and leaving him only one to conqueror. It was only because Turquin's hefty horse had been so unwieldy and the knight so heavily clad, that his victory had been possible. No, it had been Ceowulf's skill and Firecracker's speed and finally luck ... or was it luck? He thought of Brid's runespells and his prayer asking the Goddess for help.

'Thank you, Great Mother,' he whispered beneath his breath, suddenly humbled and afraid that his own arrogance might displease her.

The court assembled for the victor's ceremony. Caspar's mind sobered as he thought of the riddle. 'And only the victor can point the way.' He walked solemnly up to the royal box where the King of Camaalia rose from his throne.

King Valerius was grinning from ear to ear. 'Well, young knight, I've come here every year of my life, as is my duty, and to be honest, these knightly games have bored me stiff. The predictability and the painful clash of steel! But to see a young sprite like you win and without a single strike with a weapon ... I've not had so much fun in years. Anyway, it gives me great pleasure to give you the award, which of course you receive in the name of Lord Ceowulf.'

Caspar smiled and bowed, fixing his face into an expression of extreme gratitude though in truth he was completely dismayed. The purse of gold felt generously heavy, and he was grateful for it on Ceowulf's behalf, but how could it possibly explain where the Egg lay?

'You fought so well that I'm sorry you yourself get no share in the reward but every aspect of the tournament is one of tradition.' He looked towards his empty silver goblet. 'Fortunately the wine is also part of the customary festivities otherwise it really would be tedious. Anyhow, I'm afraid no second can be given a prize because the rules of the tournament forbid it, as the prize money and even the denomination of coins has always remained fixed. It's the only festival that we Camaalians really celebrate and we like to keep it traditional.'

Caspar felt sure that this information must be significant but he couldn't think how and he felt the dismay blush all over his open face. Quickly he raised his hand and prodded at his crooked nose.

'You look quite overcome,' the King commented. 'Well, chin up, young knight. You can't look so dismayed after such a victory. You'd best take a moment's solitary prayer before you formally sign the victors' register in the chapel of St Beonor. We don't want our winning knight to have shaky handwriting, now do we?' He laughed at his own joke but Caspar didn't find it the least bit amusing.

'Is signing the register just as traditional as the amount of the reward?' Caspar asked abruptly.

King Valerius looked at him askance. 'Why, yes, of course. The rules of the ceremony are sacred.'

Caspar's heart thumped. If the tradition were as old as the ceremony then it couldn't have been St Beonor's chapel where the knights of old originally prayed. No, not even in Camaalia. Over a thousand years ago, the new God had not been worshipped here and the chapel must have originally been built for the glorification of the Goddess. There was still hope.

Solemnly he followed the marshal and King Valerius's bishop into the small chapel set to the north of the castle. Inside, the chapel was very similar to any Belbidian church. The usual brass candelabras and incense burners hung overhead and set to the east were the altar and offertory plates. Caspar proceeded solemnly down the aisle, his eyes hunting for any difference that might direct him to the whereabouts of the Druid's Egg. Where the light from a stained glass window fell in a perfect circle just before the altar, he knelt as if in prayer while his eyes searched the building, studying the pulpit, lectern and reredos.

But he knew the answer wouldn't be there in the structure of the building. Brid and Cybillia had searched the chapel time and time again over the previous weeks and had discovered nothing. Brid had said there was nothing there except gargoyles and blasphemous scenes from the scriptures. She had lectured on for days about how men could have the audacity to think they controlled nature.

Caspar frowned. Kneeling on the cold floor, he tried to think. There had to be something that only the victor was privy to on this day. Since the rest of the ceremony was public, the answer had to lie somewhere within this private time allotted to him within the chapel. But where?

He started suddenly as he realized that the bishop was coughing to attract his attention. He had obviously kept the churchman waiting patiently for many more minutes than was normal.

'Your piety and righteousness are highly commendable but there is a time for all things and you must sign the register now,' he announced and led him to the side altar. The bishop knelt briefly and when he rose he held before him a large iron case. It was padlocked in three places and rusted at its hinges. Very carefully he removed a key from around his neck and gently released the locks.

'It's only here on the day of the tournament. The rest of the year it's locked in King Valerius's treasury for safekeeping,' he explained. 'It's so ancient that only the good Father knows how old it is.'

He opened the iron case to reveal a crumbling leather tome. Touching the delicate pages with only a silken glove, he opened it near the centre. The right-hand page was empty but the left-hand page was inscribed with a score of names scrawled onto the parchment. In big bold letters with ostentatious underlining, the bottom one read, 'Turquin, Prince of Ceolothia.'

The bishop produced an ink pot and quill before stepping back respectfully. Caspar carefully wrote his name in small neat letters though somehow he managed to blot the ink halfway through and smear it. He was fascinated by the tome. There were hundreds upon hundreds of names and he began to slowly turn back the pages, looking to the bishop for permission.

'May I?' he asked and the man nodded.

'A man is entitled to know in whose footsteps he treads.'

He turned the pages back from where the bishop had laid the book open for him to sign. After two thousand or so names the lettering slowly changed, becoming more ornate, difficult to read and increasingly foreign in appearance. As he turned the pages further and further back through time Caspar realized the writing had changed yet again and he was staring, mystified, at pages and pages of runes. Supposedly these were names but for all he knew they could be instructions. This had to be the last part to the clue and this was his one and only chance to understand it; but he couldn't read the runes.

The druid who had devised the chain of riddles had ensured through the tournament that the Egg could only be uncovered by a runeseeker of great worthiness. The seeker had to prove his bravery and skill in the tournament field to decipher the riddles, which at least meant that no common pirate could unwittingly stumble on the answer. But a runeseeker would be able to read the runes and now he stood here alone, the victor on St Beonor's day, not knowing a single rune. Well, only one: the rune of the Mother.

At last he closed the tome and stared at the brown leather covering with its peeling gold leaf lettering. It showed only the crest of Camaalia: the head of a unicorn. He sighed in defeat, staring blankly at the gold lettering. There seemed to be something slightly wrong, though, with the crest.

He thought hard but couldn't think what it would be and at last it hit him. It was the animal's eye. It was too circular for an eye. Some of the leafing had been rubbed away. As he peered closer to examine it in more detail, he realized that there were still very thin traces of gold and, though very faint, it was possible to trace out their original design. Three gossamer strands of gold radiated out from its centre and divided the eye into three segments. The rune of the Mother. Surely it meant something.

The bishop tugged at his arm. 'I really must lock it away now and arrange for it to be returned to the King's treasury until next year. It's time for you to make an appearance.'

Caspar saw the crowd only as a blur. He knew his smile was a feeble attempt at gratitude as they cheered him on. All he could do was try to spot Brid amongst the crowd of veiled spectators. He wanted to look into her eyes and seek out her strength. He needed her. He had failed. He knew he had looked at the answer and had been unable to understand its meaning. The ceremony seemed to go on for hours and he knew that he should have enjoyed the praise. He was only grateful that Ceowulf, with his shoulder firmly bandaged, was now at least comfortable enough to join him on the stand.

As Caspar handed over the prize money, the cheers went up for a speech from Ceowulf. The young Torra Altan gratefully stood back as the knight took a deep breath and filled his lungs.

'My friends, I am sorry, of course, that I missed the opportunity to win this prize for myself but then I would have deprived you of the inspiring spectacle that we witnessed today. As we watched this young knight defeat the most worthy of opponents, I think many of us realized there were two lessons to be learnt. However strong and powerful we may become, we can still be felled from the most unexpected of angles and however daunted we are by impossible odds our bravery makes all things possible.'

These thoughtful words were very much appreciated by the virtuous Camaalians but Caspar's mind strayed only fleetingly to the crowd before returning to the heavy tome. He knew the answer was there somewhere in all those runes but it was too late.

At last their ceremonial duties were completed and, exhausted, the Belbidians withdrew from the festivities. Hal's injuries allowed him to be excused from the revelries that would go on late into the night, though the younger competitors were still very disappointed when Caspar, the hero of the day, also slipped away to join his countrymen. Caspar trailed after Hal as he was carried to their room where Ceowulf and the two girls eagerly awaited their arrival.

Brid looked at him solemnly. 'You didn't find anything, did you?'

Caspar slumped down on the couch and pushed Trog away. Immediately disobedient, the terrier sprang onto his lap, excitedly licking his face. Caspar wasn't in the mood for such frivolities.

'I did find it. I know I found it,' he sighed in frustration, 'but I didn't understand any of it and, because I didn't understand it, how can I possibly describe what I saw?' He paused and, seeing little empathy in their expressions, shrugged and told them about the book in the chapel. 'There was a big book and I had to write my name in it but the earliest pages were covered in runes. At first I presumed they were names, just like the later entries but, for all I know, the first page could have been a list of instructions.' He picked up the heavy bag of gold that Ceowulf had deposited on the central table and chinked it in his lap. The knight was reclined on Caspar's pallet, nursing his injured shoulder. 'All we have to go on are these coins and a list of runes that I have no way of describing to you.'

'You can't describe a single one?' Brid looked almost angry.

Caspar shook his head. 'No, not a single one. Brid, why didn't you ever teach me the runes? The only one I recognized out of thousands of them was the rune of the Mother on the front cover of the register.'

Brid suddenly lit up. 'The rune of the Mother! It is the most sacred rune and only used for very special reasons, like in the ruby that Branwolf placed in the centre of Torra Alta's heartstone. Describe exactly where it was.'

'It was set in the very front of the tome. It was placed centrally within the Camaalian crest,' he explained.

Brid frowned. 'That's meaningless to me.'

Hal laughed humourlessly. 'You're not very good at riddles, are you, Brid? What we really need is Avriana.' He still looked rather green as he lay gloomily back on his pallet.

'Well, we haven't got time to go all the way back to Laverna. Time is running out fast. We just have to think harder.'

Caspar stared at Trog who was looking dolefully at him through black narrow slit eyes. The youth shook his head, thinking of the dog's eyes. 'No, we don't have to *think* harder, we need to *look* harder or at least use our eyes. The crest of Camaalia, of course –'

'Is a unicorn,' Hal interrupted irritably, 'but it's meaningless as Brid said. And don't yell so, Spar. My head's thumping.'

'No, but the rune of the Mother replaced its eye,' Caspar hastily explained more softly.

'There's something special, something significant about the unicorn's eye,' Brid mused.

'The unicorn is looking at something. The unicorn's looking at the Egg,' Cybillia suggested. She had been very quiet for several minutes and they all turned to stare at her.

Brid grinned. 'That wouldn't make sense. That book is movable and so where the unicorn looks is changing all the time.'

'No, but it's not the only unicorn. There's another in Sequicornum. The head of the unicorn hanging over the eastern gate by the two obelisks is always looking in one direction,' the noblewoman insisted.

'East,' Brid declared brightly as a look of revelation swept over her face.

There was a stony silence for several minutes as they all thought about the idea. 'Well, isn't someone going to look at it while Ceowulf and I recover?' Hal demanded. 'We have a direction but we need to know how far east. There must be something that tells us on the crest.'

Caspar was out of the door before Cybillia and Brid were on their feet. They crept around the edge of the quadrangle, trying not to attract any attention, though most of the castle inhabitants were still within the festival marquees, enjoying Caldea's strongest export wine.

'In another hour no one will be in a fit state to notice anything,' Brid remarked, quickening her step. 'They won't think it odd if we examine the unicorn's horn because no doubt they'll shortly be examining grains of earth or knots in the table themselves.'

In the evening light the unicorn's head was a dark grey stony mass, its black eyes just visible. Caspar had always imagined the beasts to be gentle doleful creatures but the sculptor had captured something sinister in this animal's expression. There was a devilish power malingering in its eyes. He had thought that, apart from the horn, a unicorn would look much like a horse but this creature had the intense eyes of a predator.

'Not even Cracker looks that devilish,' Cybillia laughed nervously.

Caspar considered the unicorn doubtfully. 'It's just the crest of Camaalia. There's nothing significant about it. We didn't need to win the tournament to look at it and, besides, we could follow that horn forever.'

'There might be something significant about the horn. Something else written on it,' Brid suggested. 'Something that might tell us how far east we need to go. That would be helpful,' she sighed with heavy understatement.

She moved impetuously towards the winding gear of the portcullis and put her hand on the chain, ready to haul herself up towards the unicorn twenty feet above their heads. 'If I can get to the top of the chain, I could swing along the bottom of the portcullis to take a look.'

Caspar laughed. 'They'd be quite shocked to see a young maiden swinging above the portcullis. A young lady would have to be very drunk to do that sort of thing. No, we'll attract less attention if I go. Anyone seeing me would put it down to high spirits.'

Brid made a face. 'I suppose you're right.'

Caspar hooked his legs through the struts of the portcullis and climbed up to sit astride the statue's neck. About a foot out from the head, he spotted a tiny pearly white mark glinting in the stonework. Frowning, he peered at it more closely. The masonry seemed to be peeling away. With difficulty he reached for his knife and flaked away at the patch. He uncovered a smooth surface with a mysterious patina of swirling white that reminded him of the moonstone. He flaked away more of the masonry to clear a patch about the size of his palm. He stared at the spiralling pattern. 'It's real,' he whispered in awe.

'What?' Brid called up from below.

'There's nothing written here.' He raised his voice. 'There's nothing at all, but this horn is real. It's been caked in daub to make it look like stone. But it's most definitely real.' Suddenly he felt a sense of danger up there on the beast. It seemed uncontrollably wild.

'Get down,' Brid warned urgently and in his hurry Caspar skinned his hands as he slithered down the chain of the winding gear.

'It sensed me,' he shuddered.

'But it's dead, Spar,' Cybillia murmured. 'It has to be dead. It's been there thousands of years.'

'It's dead,' Brid affirmed, 'but its spirit is only sleeping. The runes of sorcery on the sword have stirred its spirit.' She looked deeply concerned for a moment and then seemed to brush away the thought as she turned her gaze to follow the trajectory

348

of the unicorn's horn. A single evening star blinked just above a ridge of distant peaks thrusting up from the Camaalian plain.

'Without any hint of the distance involved, we can't do anything else other than follow the unicorn's gaze,' Brid sighed as they hurried back towards the castle quadrangle.

Caspar wasn't listening. He couldn't rid himself of the sinister feeling that the unicorn had instilled in him. 'It was real. A real unicorn,' he exclaimed as he threw open the door to their chamber.

Hal was unimpressed by their fruitless search. 'So we follow the horn, but for how long? For a day's ride, till we reach Lonis, or till we fall off the edge of the world? It's meaningless.'

Brid looked hurt.

Ceowulf shifted uncomfortably to relieve the stress on his shoulder. 'It's treacherous terrain that way. The peaks are cruel places. We don't want to travel through them if the Egg is beyond. It could take days just to climb the first few peaks and what if the direct line leads us straight over a cliff? What do we do if we have to deviate from the path? We might miss the Egg completely. There must be something else here that we've overlooked.'

'But there's nothing,' Caspar objected. 'The only significant thing was the ancient tome with all the names in it. Oh, stop that!' he shouted petulantly at Trog who was growling at the heavy purse of coins. Rather than desisting, the terrier leapt at his quarry and closed his jaws with a snap. His sharp teeth cut straight through the leather pouch and gold coins rolled out across the floor. Ceowulf stooped to pick one up with his good arm and frowned at the design.

'Well, King Valerius has put on weight since this likeness was made,' he joked and turned the small thin coin over. 'Hello, I've not seen this design on the back before, have you?'

'No,' Caspar agreed, straining to look at the outline of three archers with their bows drawn and ready to fire. He was distracted by Trog as he wrestled the white terrier for the pouch, realizing with frustration that he was losing the battle. 'King

Valerius said it was a traditional coin used for the ceremony. They always use this coin and there are always the same number of them.'

Everyone's eyes leapt to the coin in Ceowulf's hand.

'There has to be something significant about it then,' Brid announced firmly, taking up one of the coins that rolled from the pouch as Trog shook it in his powerful jaws. Hal was suddenly alert and snatched it out of her hand.

'Let me look. You'll never work it out.'

'Your head is obviously feeling better,' she said archly, reaching for another coin. 'Spar, can't you control that dog. He's ruining my concentration.'

Cybillia obligingly produced a biscuit. 'Here, Trog,' she said sweetly.

The dog's eyes focused greedily on the biscuit and he dropped the purse, drooling expectantly at Cybillia.

Caspar placed the bag on the table and gently shook out the contents.

'It has to be the design on the back,' Brid insisted.

Caspar studied the three archers.

'But there's nothing that relates to distance,' he objected but reconsidered as he spoke. 'Of course!'

'A bowshot. The length of the flight of an arrow,' Hal declared, obviously catching on at exactly the same time as his nephew. 'Three archers means three bowshots. We simply multiply that by the number of coins.'

There was a flurry of activity as they carefully piled them into heaps of ten to count them.

'Four hundred and twenty-four coins,' Hal announced on the third recount. 'So if I multiply that by three for each archer, that gives us the number of bowshots. So that's, um, about . . .' He scratched away with a quill for several minutes and made many crossings out before explaining his working. 'So that's one thousand two hundred and seventy-two bowshots. And at fifty-three bowshots to a league, I end up with about twenty-four leagues in total.'

'Hmm.' Ceowulf sounded uncertain.

'It is. Look! You can check my numbers,' he defended himself, pushing the paper towards Ceowulf.

'I don't doubt that,' he muttered. 'But look at the bows on the coin, lad. Do they look like ones that would fire the standard hundred yards?'

Hal grunted in acquiescence. 'No, I was thinking of the Torra Altan war bow. You're right, they're old-fashioned short bows and will only fire half the distance. So if I halve the final figure that should be right: twelve leagues.'

Brid was carefully unravelling a tired piece of parchment, revealing on its mottled surface the messages she had copied from the cauldron, the henge and the golden shield. She had written on the back of the ancient map that Caspar had secreted away from the library in Farona and, delicately, she turned the parchment over to study the chart. She spread it out on the table only to be nudged aside by Hal.

'We're here,' he announced, using his thumbnail to mark the map and then trace out a straight line due east. 'And that would be about twelve leagues.' He prodded the map just a little way beyond the Frosted Peaks.

Brid pulled his finger back and pointed it straight at the centre of the mountain range. 'No, you've not measured right. It's here by this lake.'

As Brid's hand stroked the lettering across the range of mountains Caspar felt a nervous tingling shudder his spine. 'The Lake of Tears,' he read the ornate characters aloud. 'Of course, the last part you deciphered from the cauldron! '"Climb above the weeping rocks, rise up above the sorrow." It all becomes obvious.'

Chapter 21

From afar, the Frosted Peaks looked as if they had been painted on the horizon. It just didn't seem possible that they could rise so abruptly and so high out of the Camaalian plain. Rather than beginning as smooth rounded hills they rose like inverted icicles, their sheer, menacing sides tapering ever upwards until their heads were lost from view in a veil of wispy clouds.

The road running east was little used and petered out into deltas of deer and goat tracks that were quickly swallowed by gorges and ravines. The range soared far higher than even the tallest Belbidian mountains. The sheer windswept sides and narrow overshadowed valleys gave a sense of being trapped down in their depths, imprisoned beneath the great stakes of the rising cliffs, unable to see further than the nearest rise. Caspar longed to climb out of the valley and into the peaks so that he could see across the savage vista.

Ceowulf was strangely quiet. Though Caspar knew the knight's shoulder was still paining him, he suspected that the real problem was that they had left Cybillia behind in the care of Kay's sister. The Caldean nobleman had decided that the high mountains were too dangerous a place for her. Now, he clearly missed her.

After the rigours of the tournament, they had been forced to wait until Ceowulf and Hal were fit before they could travel. Now as they began the hard climb into the silver-tipped crests of the Frosted Peaks, Caspar ruefully reflected that the long sunny days of Fallow were already upon them. They had precious little time left until the runes of war, engraved in Torra Alta's heartstone, would finally fade away. He swept back his curling fringe from his face as if trying to wipe away his troubles and focused on the arduous climb ahead.

The mountain air lifted his spirits, reminding him of home and the heights of the Yellow Mountains. For a moment, as he looked around at the untamed, weather-worn landscape, he forgot all else except the timelessness of nature. His sense of freedom was quickly swept aside, however, by a wariness that darkened his spirits. He felt as if his shadow was being stalked and the feeling seemed to be gradually intensifying. He told himself that it was only his imagination but nevertheless his nerves tingled with anxious anticipation.

Brid was breathing deeply now as they moved up into the thinner air of high altitude. Caspar smiled tightly at her. She had cast off her blue silk dress and was once more garbed in her ancient hunting jacket and shredded leather leggings. Her long coppery-brown hair floated loosely about her shoulders as Comet danced close to Firecracker and flirtatiously nipped the stallion's neck.

Hal gave them a supercilious glare.

Brid was looking anxiously about her. 'The power in the bones of the Great Mother is intensifying. We must be drawing close to a confluence of energy lines where the force of the Goddess is strongest.'

'Surely that's a good omen, though.'

'Yes,' the priestess replied uncertainly. 'Only that when Hal unsheathed the sword in the henge in the Farthest Isles, the runes of sorcery were cast into the air. The spell will be at its strongest along the lines of energy radiating out from that point.'

Trog was beginning to lag as the climb steepened so, while the others moved ahead, Caspar strapped him to the cantle of his saddle. The landscape around him was lifeless and yet he was sure that something had stirred and was now watching him.

The steep valley sides soared upwards, lined with black rocks and the occasional waterfall tumbling down from higher valleys. Splintered rocks, sheared from the cliff faces, lay broken on the valley bottom and rents in the upturned bedrock bore testament to how the earth's crust had buckled and heaved under immense elemental stresses. To Caspar it looked as if some raging giant with a great axe had uprooted the Camaalian plain and heaved it onto its side.

A buzzard lifted his line of sight as it took to the wing, skimming along the edge of the rock faces, its shadow darkening the cliffs. Apart from the wind soughing around the cliff tops there was barely a sound but still Caspar was certain he had heard or seen something other than the bird. Ever since Brid had put her finger on the map and pointed to the Lake of Tears, the hairs at the back of his neck had constantly tingled. He was convinced they were being followed.

He nudged Firecracker forward. The sharp clip of the stallion's hooves on the rocky goat track echoed back and forth between the enclosing valley walls. The uneasy atmosphere urged him to a faster pace. The higher they climbed, the cooler the air became and Caspar finally reached for his cloak and slung it round his shoulders. Even though it was late spring, patches of snow still lay in the grey mountain's deep hollows and dark ravines. The river to their right was a boiling torrent, filled by the meltwater from the winter snows off the highest peaks. Chunks of ice tossed and danced in the frothy water as it boiled around the jagged rocks.

'We're further south than Torra Alta, yet there's still snow on these mountains,' Hal observed. 'We must be even higher than the peaks of the Yellow Mountains.'

'They seem so old,' Brid murmured. Her eyes scanned up from the valley floor, darting from one boulder to the next and examining every juniper bush and twisted birch that dared to grow in this hostile land. 'I don't think man has ever lived here. There's no pasture, no trees and precious little shelter. It's like a land forgotten by the rest of Camaalia.'

Ceowulf craned his neck upwards at the stark peaks. 'I don't like them. They're too tall and they look like they're brooding.'

The other three laughed. 'Lowlanders!' Hal despaired derisively.

'I didn't mean that,' the knight protested. 'There are too many places for someone to hide.'

'So someone's hiding in them.' Hal shrugged. 'They can't possibly worry about us. Besides we have in our company Lord Caspar of Torra Alta, the bravest, invincible and most skilful knight in all the countries of the Caballan Sea – if not beyond.'

Caspar made a face, protesting at the jarring note of sarcasm.

'We don't need the Egg,' Hal continued. 'We have the great Lord Caspar who can defend Torra Alta single-handed. Well, at least his horse can.'

'Oh shut up,' Brid snapped. 'Leave him alone. Haven't you got anything else to worry about other than your pride?'

'I suppose you would have to stick up for him, wouldn't you? Your little protégé.'

Brid kicked Comet on and cantered ahead of the rest.

'Did I say something to offend her?' Hal asked innocently, throwing a dark look in Caspar's direction.

The tension between them was broken by the tinkle of rocks as somewhere high above them a slide of scree scuttled down a couloir. Ceowulf's hand went to his sword.

Hal merely laughed at the hollow echo bounding back and forth between the valley walls. 'Don't be so nervous, old man; it'll be a mountain hare or a fox. No man would be skulking around up there, it's far too difficult. The goat track we're on is the only feasible path I've seen all day. If there's anyone else up here they'll be on this track or very close to it.'

'What if it's not a man? What if it's that thing again?' Caspar pointed out with a shudder.

'Huh? What thing?' Hal asked.

'The thing in the mist in Caldea.' Caspar couldn't believe that Hal had forgotten.

'Oh that. That was nothing. We were all so spooked after the excitement in the yew forest, it was probably just imagination.' Hal dismissed the memory. But despite his denial, the raven-haired youth drew his sword.

Brid turned her head as the white steel of the blade breathed into the air. The workmanship of the blade was so fine that it caught and turned the sunlight as if the sword were made of cut diamond. The buzzard overhead screamed out a single, high piercing screech that made the hairs on the back of Caspar's head stand upright. Trog growled.

They rode on more warily now, each with a growing sense that something was wrong. Everything was too quiet, too still, the air too expectant.

The horses were beginning to labour and as they climbed higher, the air gradually thinned around them. After many months at sea-level Caspar's body was no longer acclimatized to altitude; his head ached, his mouth was dry and he was beginning to feel breathless.

'We should rest the horses,' he declared. His voice cut through the air like an icy breeze blowing into the heat of a stifling room in midsummer. The echo rolled on and on and the entire world seemed to be holding its breath, listening intently to the sound of his voice. They dismounted and sat back against a smooth boulder. The horses nibbled at the dry grass that was still yellow after the long winter, sealed away from sunlight by a layer of deep snow that had only recently melted. In patches the ground was still soggy underfoot.

After freeing Trog from Firecracker's back, Caspar chewed thoughtfully on a thick slice of bread spread with a traditional Camaalian meat compote though he was very uncertain of the taste. It was apparently made of camel meat and he couldn't quite get used to the idea of eating such a foul-smelling animal. He was busy watching Hal who in turn was watching Brid. This absorbed much of his concentration and he noticed little of the surrounding landscape except the soothing noise of a nearby river.

Brid was looking wistfully towards a white peak that clawed so high towards the heavens that its summit faded away into the grey and white clouds that rose in plumes around it. She raised her hand as if to speak when she suddenly ducked and shielded her head as if from attack. Trog leapt to his feet, growling ferociously, his hackles as stiff as a scrubbing brush along the length of his spine. Hal looked bewildered though he was already standing protectively over Brid, his sword drawn.

'What's the matter?' he demanded.

Brid had no time to reply and this time Caspar felt it too: the rush of cold air and the deafening beat of wings above him. But there was nothing in the sky. For a moment they held their breath, swamped by the chilling atmosphere, and stared into the sky as if a malevolent ghost had swept overhead.

The moment passed.

Brid shook herself and rose defiantly. 'We'll move on,' she said too decisively as though she were forcing herself to conquer her fears. Her hand was on her breast, feeling for the moonstone. 'We must get there quickly. We must find the Egg before anything else does. I felt their spirits. I felt the presence of the creatures of the Otherworld. They might not have slipped through the chasm that separates the parallel universes yet but, like a waking dream, they are very close. How long before their manifestation is real?'

'The beasts of power,' Caspar murmured in an awe-struck whisper, drawing his brown bearskin cloak tightly around him before strapping Trog to the back of Firecracker's saddle.

'I can smell wyvern,' Ceowulf muttered as he remounted. 'A rancid fishy smell.' He wrinkled his nose in disgust.

Caspar could feel his heart pounding in his chest. Shying and skittering, Firecracker was becoming increasingly jittery beneath him, so making Trog whimper and wriggle in discomfort. He released the dog and lowered him to the ground. The terrier's ears were pinned back and he walked protectively alongside Comet, on stiff alert legs. Even Magpie's step was uneven.

Caspar patted his horse's neck. 'Steady there, Cracker. There's nothing to worry about.' But he could sense it too. As the wind swept down through the valley, he heard the faintest echo of what he thought was a wild shriek lingering on the mountains' breath and then thundering hooves. He could hear the sound of galloping horses! Firecracker raised his head and squealed, then darted sideways, flinging out his heels.

It came with a rush, the sound of fast and furious galloping. A shadow passed between them, the drum-roll of galloping hooves thundering in their ears. Their horses screamed in terror. Comet reared and plunged at her bridle and Caspar was too slow to block her path. Suddenly the cream mare bolted, running with the wild raw energy of the hurricane of fear that swept through their midst.

Caspar spurred his heels into Firecracker's sides but the red roan refused to advance, fearing the atmospheric forces that were jostling them from either side. Ahead the young barely trained horse, terrified by the spirits around her, bucked and weaved along the narrow path. Caspar could see the mare was being buffeted from side to side, but by what? He thumped his heels repeatedly into Firecracker's side, aware of what would happen if Brid were thrown. Suddenly, as if released by a giant hand, the stallion leapt forward.

Firecracker's neck was at full stretch and his long lean legs reached out like a hare's, sweeping over the ground in elegant strides. Caspar quickly drew level with the panicked mare. Her head plunged between her knees as she threw up her heels. Abandoning the idea of taking the mare's reins, Caspar did the only thing he could and grabbed for Brid. The Maiden clung to his outstretched arm and pulled herself athletically round behind him. Comet shrieked like an animal tormented by a swarm of bees and galloped off with the invisible presence still storming around her.

Caspar couldn't turn. He was being buffeted from side to side by the unseen forces but his trained war-horse remained steady and galloped straight rather than bucking wildly like the young mare. Something hard and spiky stabbed at his hand and Brid let out a suppressed yell. He pulled hard at Firecracker's reins and gradually he was able to slow his stallion down.

The raging storm swept ahead of them. The valley narrowed and the path twisted into a deep shadowy ravine, where craggy overhangs peered down disdainfully from the cliff tops to either side. As they moved forward into the umbral passage, Caspar saw the storm for the first time. Gossamer outlines galloped before them, like tall lean horses, silvery in colour but with cloven hooves. A single spiralling horn spiked from the forehead of each majestic beast.

The silver shadows drove Comet on. Caspar reined to a halt, unable to do anything else as Comet, in her terror, galloped blindly into the head of the ravine where a wall of ugly black boulders blocked her path. The terror in the atmosphere dissolved. The sound of thundering hooves was absorbed by the wind and a cloud swept away from the face of the sun. Brighter light fell into the gully and the spirits were gone.

Brid's breathing was fast and anxious.

'We'd better take a look at her,' she said doubtfully, clutching at her arm.

'Are you hurt?' the youth demanded with concern.

She shook her head bravely. 'It was just a graze.'

Comet's skull was crushed. A splinter of bone pushed out through her forehead, weeping tears of blood onto her perfect opal coat. She had bled from several tears in her flank and her eyes gaped with terror but she would never again know fear. Brid slid from Firecracker's back and sorrowfully examined Comet's sides.

'They are gaining power. We must get to the Egg first.' She drew in a deep shuddering breath.

'What were they?' Caspar asked nervously, pushing his grief from his mind and reaching a hand down to Brid to help her up behind him.

'The spirits of unicorns.'

'I sensed such evil. Such malice.' He shuddered at the memory.

'No, not evil. Just untamed, like the power within the Egg,' she explained as they hurried back to where they had left the others.

Caspar was perplexed. Ceowulf and Hal should have been galloping to greet them as they rode back out of the ravine and into the wider valley – but they were not. A little way off Magpie and Sorcerer stood tethered to a rowan but there was no sign of Hal nor Ceowulf. Trog stood on a boulder, barking furiously at the steep scree slope on the opposite side of the valley.

Caspar wheeled Firecracker round and round, searching the rocks and scanning the couloirs. 'Hal!' he yelled only to be bombarded by his own shrill echo.

'If they had continued along the valley bottom, they would have stayed on horseback,' Brid shouted above the sound of Trog's barking. 'They must have gone up there.' She looked up at the sheer slope walling the valley side.

Caspar raised his eyes but could see nothing save the movement of a stag skirting along the top of the valley wall. Coated with scree and scarred by deep couloirs, the valley sides were far too steep for any horse to scale. Somehow the rocks and coarse vegetation that clung precariously to the sheer slope had swallowed their companions. Caspar felt both fearful for Hal and betrayed by him. Why had he and Ceowulf gone off and left them? Brid gripped tightly to his back. He could feel her tension.

'Something else must have attacked,' she presumed. 'But how then did they have time to tether the horses?'

'Mmm.' Caspar was worried. 'Unless they've gone after something instead.' It didn't make sense and he stared at the two heavy war-horses who were contentedly nuzzling at the ground, searching for wisps of grass.

'We haven't got time to wait. We'll just have to go on without them,' Brid decided firmly.

'But we can't.'

'We have to. There are too many things up here in these wild mountains that we can't explain, too many creatures. The runes of sorcery have awoken many spirits and they all seek the Egg. If they find it, their powers will be unleashed and the Earth will once more be dominated by the beasts of legend. They are wild, savage, creatures with no tolerance for man's existence.'

Caspar nodded and turned Firecracker's head into the cold east wind. The steep valley sides and craggy overhangs made it impossible to see what lay ahead. All they knew was that they were moving steadily upwards. Trog trooped anxiously at Firecracker's heels and Caspar tried to keep their spirits up by chatting, but he knew Brid wasn't listening.

The shadow of a cloud scudded over the ground and Caspar thought he heard the clap of wings. The wind moulded the cloud until it resembled two vast bat-like wings hovering above them. Then the wind backed momentarily and the image was gone. Firecracker half-reared and snorted nervously.

'A dragon?' Caspar whispered in question. 'I could feel its eyes on me.'

Brid shrugged and anxiously scanned the narrow strip of sky that roofed the valley.

Firecracker dropped his head down beneath his knees in his effort to struggle up the steadily steepening path. Trog was lagging far behind and every time Caspar looked round, the dog sat down and looked at them pleadingly with his head on one side and his thick tongue lolling sideways.

At last they reached the head of the valley and looked out at the opening landscape, where rank upon rising rank of peaks climbed into the mauve distance. In the darkly defined foreground and to one side, a conical peak stabbed up towards the rich blue sky. To the other side, a solid block of rock with sheer walls and a flat plateau above overshadowed the head of the valley. It looked almost like the square keep of a castle. With one beat of its wings, an eagle launched itself from an outcrop of basalt that spat like a tongue from the strata of the blocky heights. The bird glided effortlessly through the thin air to the conical peak that stood sentry over the pass on the opposite side of the valley.

The wind rushed through the pass and Caspar recognized that sudden change in climate associated with moving from one valley to the next. His hair was swept back off his face as he took in the scene ahead. A circular nest of crags like the points of a crown, rose up around a lake, its deep black waters reflecting only the icy tips of the snow-capped peaks above.

Ribbons of white water cascaded from the heights and tumbled down the lower slopes to fill the lake. It was a lonely desolate scene. There was a foreboding silence.

At home in the Yellow Mountains there was silence too, but a tranquil peace that raised the spirits. The hunched shoulders of the Yellow Mountains were like those of dozing old men, the wind that coiled around them like their sighing breaths. Here the silence was of sorrow, the silent sorrow of a tragedy long past. It was as if the mountains wept and sent their tears dripping from rock to rock to fill the black lake with them.

'The Lake of Tears?'

'Yes! The Lake of Tears!' Brid exclaimed. 'It was the one bit left of the cauldron's riddle. '"Climb above the weeping rocks, rise up above the sorrow,"' she quoted. 'We're looking across at the lake at the moment so we need to go up.'

She pointed across the water to a high crag, a sharply pointed summit that rose like an ox horn above the tarn. Mist shrouded its shoulders and rising gusts of wind swept the snow off its left flank into spiralling eddies like white feathers rising from the side of a witch's hat. They picked their way carefully around the boggy marshes that satellited the lake, the rich spongy mosses providing a soft cushion for Firecracker's nimble hooves.

'We are nearing a confluence of power. I sense the energy lines in the Mother's mantel intensifying. We must be drawing close,' Brid said with excitement.

'I hope there's nothing in this bog, like that lindworm in Caldea,' Caspar remarked soberly. 'If we are so close to the energy lines the runes of sorcery may have disturbed them.'

Brid didn't reply. She was too intent on the peak ahead of them. Once they had crossed the mossy plateau that separated them from the horn-like summit, the last of the meandering goat tracks vanished into the wilderness. They were faced with chunks of broken scree at the foot of a couloir.

'We'll have to leave Cracker,' Caspar said rather unnecessarily as Brid slid from the horse's back. Looking up at the taxing climb, he decided to leave his sword as well. He knew he was no master with the weapon and his light holly and stagbone bow would serve him far better. He knew from experience that the climb would be arduous. The boulders rolled and knocked beneath their feet as they clambered breathlessly over them. For the first time Trog skipped ahead, nimbly hopping from one rock to the next, just as he would on the boulders at the head of a beach.

Caspar's legs ached and the blood in his head pounded against his temples. This climb seemed far harder on his muscles than any other he had attempted and he realized for the first time what it was like to suffer a sudden move up to altitude. He remembered guiltily how he and Hal had often scoffed at lowlanders for their frailty when visiting Torra Alta. But now, after so long at sea-level, he too was breathlessly weak and giddy, strained by the effects of the thin air. At first they rested every hundred yards but quickly the stops became more frequent.

'This is awful,' Brid groaned as she leant against a rock, her hand pressed to her chest in a vain attempt to steady her racing heart.

'Yes, it is, isn't it?' a voice agreed.

Caspar flung up his head and looked above him in astonishment. At first he thought the effect of the altitude was playing with his brain, but Brid was also staring.

'You've changed, little nephew.'

'Who ... how ... ?' Caspar stammered as he looked up at the sprightly figure of a man wearing black leather leggings, a wolf's pelt jacket and a brown bearskin cloak. His hair was cropped short but was the same fiery auburn as his own. In one hand he held a thin sabre with a dog-toothed edge. With mocking laughter and deliberate emphasis, he tossed something red and sparkling up into the air and caught it again.

Caspar looked at the man's thin face and the wide, ghostly blue, loveless eyes. With his dull brown hair now red and without his shaven pate or black cowl of office, he was almost unrecognizable.

'Uncle Gwion?' Caspar muttered, too stupefied to think. 'What are you doing here?'

The man laughed, a humourless cackle filled with long-festered hatred.

'You don't know how I've yearned for this.' Gwion's face contorted into lines of pure hatred. 'How long I've waited to destroy my dear sister's precious little son. You have the moonstone of course.' A harsh laugh rasped through his dry throat. 'I will make you summon her. And then, dear kinsman, oh great and mighty nobleman, she will watch your death.' His dark red tongue relished the words. 'Think of her torment! And then at last I will have the Druid's Egg. I will have it, you hear.'

Caspar couldn't take the words in. What on earth could Gwion possible want with the Egg? He was a man of the New Faith, a man of the one true God. He had preached avidly the merciful ways of forgiveness and peace that were the basis of civilization but now he was cackling at him like a madman.

'But your hair,' Caspar said dumbly, still unable to understand what was happening.

'My hair?' the priest echoed in ridicule. 'It's always been this colour but it's not very seemly in a priest.'

'Blackroot,' Brid muttered. 'He's been dyeing it with blackroot, that's all.' Brid was looking anxiously around her, though Caspar was still so stunned by his uncle's unexplained presence that he couldn't think.

'Did Father send you to help us?' he asked innocently.

Brid tugged at his arm. 'Spar, you're not thinking. This man is evil. And Branwolf couldn't possibly have sent him because he has no idea where the Egg is. Get your bow ready.'

'Would you listen to the sibilant hissing of a witch or to your own uncle?' Gwion continued more smoothly. 'Now come to me, my boy, and we will see an end to this.'

Caspar was uncomfortably aware of several horned helmets rising up out of the cracks in the broken landscape around them. Gwion was not alone. Of the eight men approaching, Caspar focused on one alone. He had a bear-like figure and his fierce lupine eyes were cold with hatred. With his white-blond hair in war knots and a row of weasel skulls hanging on a string around his shoulders, he thumped his heavy war axe into his palm. The top half of both his ears were missing. Caspar could never forget that face. Numbly, he stared at the Vaalakan warrior Scragg.

'Master,' the blond warrior addressed Gwion in harsh guttural tones. 'I kills them now?'

'No! No, not yet. I want to see my sister's face one last time and only the boy can summon her. Bring them to me.'

More than eight Vaalakans advanced. Caspar struggled for his bow, fumbling for a second before loosing three arrows in quick succession. He hit one Northman through the mouth, shattering his teeth before the barb penetrated his brain, another through the lung and one through the gut. The last was still screaming and groaning in agony as Caspar was forced to lower his bow. Another growling Vaalakan was on top of Brid, holding a knife at her throat. He was smaller and darker than the others and Caspar instantly knew him for their shaman Kullak.

The priestess didn't scream or kick but remained perfectly still as Caspar lowered his weapon in defeat. Kullak ripped open the Maiden's shirt and pulled the moonstone from around her neck. He offered the orb to the viper-eyed priest and flung aside the salamander as it hissed and bit. Gwion looked longingly at the incandescent orb.

'My dear beloved Keridwen,' he hissed with icy hatred in his voice. 'At last your final defeat.' He pushed up his sleeves and Caspar sucked in his breath at the sight of the black striations that marked his uncle's arms. Some of them were recent and still red and angry, but others much older, blackened by frostbite where pleading nails had clawed at his arm – where his mother's hands had begged for her life.

It was Gwion who had held her under the freezing waters running off the Vaalakan tundra. It had been his mother's brother who had forced her half-drowned body under the freezing waters as they froze to form the Vaalakan glacier. But to what end? He couldn't believe it; he couldn't understand it. Gwion was her brother: how could he do such a heinous thing?

'Uncle Gwion,' he cried, 'but you loved her. You mourned for her for over twelve years. Besides me, she was your only kin.'

The man's face pulsed. Caspar could see the angry veins on his neck furiously pumping blood to his tense muscles.

'I've hated Keridwen from the moment she was born,' he hissed icily through clenched teeth. 'She killed my mother. She killed her with witchcraft. She had to kill her so that she could become a high priestess. Only an orphan can become One of the Three so she killed her. And you know why she wanted to be One of the Three?'

Caspar couldn't believe what he was hearing.

'She wanted to be more powerful than me. Anything to be more powerful than her brother so she killed our mother. Then she patronized me further by so graciously looking after me. I am her elder brother and I am a man and she gloated in her domination over me. She married that sneering, self-satisfied Branwolf and became the Baron's wife and then mother to the future Baron just to increase her power over me.' Gwion's reedy voice rose to a shriek and a stain of angry blood rose like a purple flood up from his neck to darken his face. 'I tried to gain position but even when I had rid the world of her evil, by entombing her in the glacier, still she held me down. I could not be recognized even within the New Faith because of the stigma of being the brother of a witch. Don't you see? She has to be punished. All she wanted was sinful power. She killed my mother to be more powerful than me.'

'Gwion, your mother died in childbirth,' Brid said quickly, smoothly and gently. 'Morrigwen told me. Keridwen didn't kill her. She couldn't have; she wasn't more than half an hour old.'

'She killed her! She killed her to gain dominion over me! She killed my mother and now I'm going to punish her by killing her child!' Gwion was sobbing. Maddened tears of rage ran hot and steaming on his purple cheeks. He flashed his rolling eyes at the big Vaalakan warrior. 'Make him summon his evil witch-mother. Make him do it.'

Scragg grabbed Caspar's hands and thrust them onto the moonstone, pressing his palms onto the surface of the white orb. The seething white pain of energy jolted up through the boy's palms. He tried to wrench his hands away but the bullish muscles of the huge warrior were impossible to oppose.

'Fight it. Don't summon her,' Brid shrieked but her words were silenced by a slashing blow across the mouth. Gwion's hand bled where he struck her.

Laughing maniacally, the priest jerked away from her and wheeled round on the auburn-haired youth, digging his sharp nails into the boy's wrists and pressing Caspar's palms tighter against the skin of the Druid's Eye. 'I will kill you, boy, but only before your mother's precious eyes, and when you are dead the girl will lead me to the Egg. I know it's close.'

'It's nowhere close,' Caspar shrieked. 'Brid knows only half the directions and I the other.' He played for time, struggling to think of anything he could say to save them. 'If you kill either one of us you'll never find it,' he yelled, concentrating his energy on Gwion and not the probing light of white energy that snagged across his brain.

The deranged priest sniggered. 'Ah, but I know it's here, very precisely here. We are near a confluence of power. The shameful blood of the Old Tribes runs pure in my veins and I can sense the power. It's near, almost certainly on this peak above us, and, since you're heading for it, I feel my theory is already proven.'

'The peak is only part of the clue. We have to move on a long way beyond it,' Brid said determinedly, as Caspar's face screwed up in agony. He was trying to fight back the power in the orb but it was drawing him inexorably towards his mother's mind. He tried to wrench away. He couldn't let Keridwen see this. He couldn't let her suffer anymore.

Gwion suddenly released Caspar, his face contorted into

evil laughter. 'Your lies are wasted. You've been all round the Caballan Sea, seeking the Druid's Egg, when all along Branwolf had the answer in his hand.' The priest reached inside his pocket for the bright red jewel and held it out on the flat of his palm.

Caspar blanched. It was the ruby Branwolf had set in the centre of Torra Alta's heartstone. Within the jewel, he could see a pattern of silver threads that formed the rune of the Mother.

'That would have told you nothing,' Brid scoffed.

'Ah, but wouldn't it? It took me a while at first, but when that old hag Morrigwen said that my beloved sister survived because she was entombed at a confluence of power – well, I began to see a pattern. And Keridwen was the first point in it.'

A pattern. Caspar's mind was reeling. He too had sensed there was a pattern but he had been unable to uncover it.

Gwion's diatribe continued. He seemed to enjoy the expressions of dismay that dragged at his captives' mouths. 'The cauldron of course was central to the clue. It was so intrinsic to finding the Egg that it had to be central to the pattern. You found that in Ildros. Kullak and Scragg waited for me and showed me the place and I had my second point in the pattern. Then you so kindly traced out the next point on the pattern for me. You left such a trail of happenings, with tall stories wagging from Caldea to Ophidia about mythical krakens, that not even a fool could have missed it.'

He drew breath and smiled smugly, seeing how the youth and the young Maiden were stunned by this revelation. 'And you thought you were so clever,' he sneered. 'The tales of kraken led me to the little Ophidian port of Cocklebay. When I arrived, the place was buzzing with talk that revolved around a very pompous young lad called Pellam. He was very informative.'

'But Pellam wouldn't . . .' Caspar stammered. He couldn't believe that Pellam would betray them.

'Oh don't fret, precious nephew.' Gwion's voice was full of

mock concern. 'The young man uttered not one word to condemn you, only he innocently let slip news of a fiery red horse, and anyone who knows Firecracker would never mistake him in conversation. He said he and his friends sailed to the Farthest Isles and that you then turned east. But I already knew you had reached the Farthest Isles. On midwinter's day I felt a huge surge of energy ripple through the earth's crust, emanating from those isles. You must have exposed a very powerful runespell right there at the confluence of power. That was very foolish of you. The confluence of power in the Farthest Isles gave me a third point and I didn't even need to waste time travelling there.'

Caspar looked at Gwion's clenched fist and glimpsed the sparkle of the ruby. He bit his lip in despair. The pattern was gradually becoming obvious.

The priest followed the boy's stare and laughed, tossing the ruby up into the air again. 'It's so neat when you finally have the answer, but don't feel too bad; I didn't see it at first either. I was confused because I took the central point of the pattern to be at Ildros where the cauldron was, but of course the cauldron had been moved from Farona, the ancient sacred city. Farona, not Ildros, was the central point. I had three of the four points needed to complete the pattern. With those first three points – Keridwen, Farona and the Farthest Isles – I could find the last point just by tracing out the rest of the pattern on a map. All I needed was a map.'

He riffled around inside his cloak and produced a neatly scrolled parchment, which he unravelled. 'Look. With Farona as the central point, Keridwen in the north and the Farthest Isles to the south-west that gives me three out of the four points needed to form the Mother's rune.' He circled them to prove his point. 'To complete the sacred rune, the last point has to be here at the Frosted Peaks.' His voice sounded almost rational as he calmly pointed out the various locations. 'And I know I'm right because, now I'm here, I can feel the intensifying energy in the bones of the earth. I experienced great satisfaction in discovering something that the rest of you so clearly couldn't,' he preened, his voice ridiculously serene, grossly belying his twisted and degenerate soul.

Brid was speechless.

Caspar's mind reeled.

They had wasted months. How much suffering had befallen the men at Torra Alta while they had dithered at Sequicornum? They could have been here months ago if only they had thought about the ruby. The Great Mother had placed the answer right into their hands and yet they had not seen it.

Gwion slipped the gem back into his pocket and snatched up Caspar's hand. The boy felt defeated and helpless, unable to resist the will of the moonstone as it swept his thoughts over the sea. His mind was rushed past the vast wastelands of the Dragon Scorch to the white crystalline plains of Vaalaka's tundra.

A screaming face leapt at him out of the ice, her eyes glazed and dead, a deathly blue-white hue tingeing her distorted cheeks. Caspar willed the warmth of his body into hers. She was nearing death. In these long months, they had not given her enough heat and now her body had shrivelled.

'Not much of a priestess, anymore, is she?' Gwion leered into the crystal. 'Little sister, wake up, little sister. Keridwen, hear me, it's your loving brother, Gwion.'

Her eyes flickered open and, though they were still a dazzling violet, like a twilight sky in midsummer, they no longer had the vibrancy or the strength of a few months ago.

'You are dying, little sister,' Gwion laughed gleefully. 'At last you are dying. But before you do, I want you to see your little son die and know that soon I will have the Druid's Egg. Morbak is already leading his army through the Pass and into Belbidia and when I have the Egg, I will lead them beyond. Soon all the people of the Caballan Sea will worship Vaal-Peor and I will be His arch-priest. I have been spurned by the Great Mother and the New Faith but Vaal-Peor welcomes me as the spiritual leader of his people. When Lord Morbak bows before me, I will hold dominion over the world. I am the Master.'

There was a salivary lust to his voice as he rejoiced in his words. 'I am the Master.'

'You lie! Morbak cannot get past Torra Alta. Branwolf will stop him. The runes of war will stop him! They will hold fast until the end of Fallow,' Caspar shrieked.

'The runes of war!' Gwion threw back his thin neck and crowed like a cockerel. 'Poor innocent child, did you really believe they would work when I was there in the heart of the castle? Did you really still hope you had time to find the Druid's Egg and so save your precious homeland? Oh, dear nephew, I am sorry but you are far, far too late. I destroyed the runes of war months ago. Nothing stands in my way now, not even Torra Alta.'

'He's lying,' Brid said coldly. 'The man has lost his mind. The Great Mother promised protection through the runes of war for nine months and they will hold.'

'Such innocence,' Gwion berated her. 'The Great Goddess only said they would hold until they were worn away, which would naturally happen with the spring rains. But of course they could be worn away by a mason's chisel too. I destroyed them!' he proclaimed triumphantly.

Scragg was throttling Caspar so tightly that he could barely hear the words as Gwion grabbed his palms and pressed them onto the moonstone. While the bear-like warrior gripped Caspar, the shaman thrust Brid into the stranglehold of another Vaalakan and approached the youth. Hissing chants and murmuring the name of his Ice-God, Kullak stalked with ice-cold eyes towards the choking youth.

'Do it, Kullak. While my dear sister is watching,' Gwion ordered. 'Do it. I know you've waited a long time for this.' Gwion slid his tongue over his lips, his eyes widening in blood-lust. 'Do it slowly so that he feels it, so that Vaal-Peor can rejoice in the sacrifice.'

Seeing only the glinting blade of the knife, Caspar's eyes bulged as he fought for breath. Scragg's icy hands squeezed around his neck and the edge of Kullak's knife pressed deep against his throat.

'In the name of Vaal-Peor,' the shaman chanted.

Caspar could feel the first trickle of blood running down his neck.

'Mother,' he pleaded. 'Mother.' He didn't know whether he was begging for his own life or for the end of his mother's suffering as she lay in torture, her weeping eyes fixed on his. Her hands were desperately reaching out to pull him towards her.

His thoughts swept deep into the moonstone. Sinking into unconsciousness, his mind was spiralling inwards. His body felt deathly cold though his neck burnt with a fiery pain where the blade pricked at his skin. His mind was filled with the chant, 'Vaal-Peor!'

Chapter 22

'Brid!' Hal wheeled Magpie, urgently lurching to snatch at the cream mare's bridle.

The powerful energy buffeted and jostled him but his thoughts were only on Brid. Together they wrestled against Comet's wild panic. But the horse's fear was greater than her training and with a lunge she ripped the reins from his hand and bolted.

In an instant Hal's eyes took in the jagged rocks that littered the valley floor and his imagination saw Brid being hurled from the bucking mare, smashed on the flints and trampled underfoot. Caspar was already in hot pursuit, strips of turf slicing off the red roan's hooves. Magpie was slower to respond and, as Hal turned her head to follow, Ceowulf grabbed her reins.

'Up there,' the knight shouted above the sound of thundering hooves, pointing urgently up the steep sides of the valley that overshadowed the gorge.

'I've got to get Brid,' Hal protested furiously.

'Let Spar do it; you'll never catch her and I saw something up there.' The urgency in Ceowulf's voice made Hal stop and look. A few branches of juniper and myrtle bushes shifted in the breeze but nothing else stirred. 'Up there!' Ceowulf pointed fiercely.

Hal caught a glimpse of something moving. It stirred again and he glimpsed two horns lurking behind a protruding boulder. 'It's only an ibex,' he muttered, but then he saw it move again. The motion was uncharacteristic of stag or ibex; it was too rapid, too jerky. Instantly he understood Ceowulf's urgency. 'Have they seen us?'

The knight moved closer to the foot of the ravine where they would be swallowed from sight. 'They're watching Spar and Brid,' Ceowulf guessed. 'I think we should sneak up and jump them from behind before they try anything on us.'

They slid from their horses and tethered them to a rowan bush before starting the climb. Hal hauled himself up from one tree root to the next, thankful for the tough juniper stems, which eased his climb, though the fresh spring shoots scratched over his arms. He was dismayed at how quickly he tired. Thinking how hard he had trained over the last few months, he couldn't believe his weakness. His heart pounded furiously with the effort of pumping his thin blood around his body. Born and bred in the mountains, it came as a shock to find the heights so debilitating.

At last he crested the valley wall only to see more swelling mountains rising above them. Wave upon wave of saw-toothed peaks stood in ever rising ranks before him, entire valleys hidden from sight by the giant cradle of spined peaks. He craned back his head to look anxiously at the clouds. Here in the lower valleys the wind was no more than a gentle refreshing breeze but around the higher crags, the clouds whisked by. Billowing plumes of white streamed out from the leeward side of each peak, like the plumed helmets of an army of giants storming into battle. The weather was already vicious higher up and he hoped it wouldn't descend to engulf them here on the lower slopes.

He was still waiting for Ceowulf to join him. Lighter and more used to climbing, Hal had quickly outpaced the older man but he thought it unwise to move on without him. He crawled forward and crouched low behind a boulder to assess the new terrain.

'Which way do you think they went?' Ceowulf whispered as he crept up behind him. His voice rasped in his gasping throat.

'I'm not sure,' Hal shrugged. 'They'd vanished by the time I got here.'

Ceowulf motioned him forward. 'They were moving in that direction.'

The knight's chain-mail ground and clinked as he moved but the wind was blowing in their faces and Hal was sure that the sound would be swept away behind them. They progressed slowly along the ridge overlooking the valley, which was at least easier on their muscles than the direct climb. He could see across to the far side of the valley but where the mountainside fell away from his feet, he could no longer look down on where they had left the horses. As the last sign of the valley floor slowly sank away into a grey haze he felt he had climbed into a different world. They were now isolated from the tame world of man, at the mercy of the mountains and their capricious climate. He chanced climbing onto a boulder to gain a better view and, just for a moment, he caught a glimpse of Brid and Spar both riding Firecracker. His heart beat a little more smoothly. He didn't care what had happened to Comet; at least Brid was safe.

He found himself quite shocked by the thought. How could he be more worried about Brid than Spar? He was still furious with her for her behaviour in Sequicornum, where she had done nothing but fawn over his nephew. But he couldn't remain angry with someone who made him feel so alive. He had to admit to himself that when she was not there, close to him, it was as if the world became flat, the colours of life dull and uninspiring as if a pall of grey cloud had draped itself over a summer sky.

Yet he could not say these things to her. She was too strong, too powerful and if he declared his position, he would become her puppet. Hal, a girl's puppet: it was unthinkable!

He laughed, thinking of Caspar's helpless devotion to the beautiful priestess. Brid was far too powerful for his little nephew and Spar too much like a faithful hound. Hal feared that this was what might become of him if he openly declared his affections. He had been quite content to brazen it out and wait for her to crack. But she hadn't succumbed. No, she had spent the last few months mooning over Spar, even giving him, and only him, her favour to wear in the tournament. That really rankled. In all that time she hadn't paid him the least bit of attention.

But he feared for her now.

'Footprints,' Ceowulf announced as the ground dipped and became more marshy. 'We should be close now.'

Keeping low, they moved forward until eventually they caught sight of the horned helmets once more. With a shudder, Hal recognized the blond plaits that dangled from beneath their peaked helms. Black bearskins covered naked, taut-muscled torsos. Reindeer skins were bandaged to their legs and only soft-soled skins sufficed as footwear.

'They've abandoned their disguises and adorned their battle gear,' Hal warned. 'They're expecting trouble.'

'They couldn't possibly be expecting us, though.' Ceowulf sounded perplexed. 'Nobody could know we would be here. It just isn't conceivable.'

'It is a horrible coincidence though,' Hal argued. 'I mean, Vaalakans here in the Frosted Peaks! There has to be a reason.' His breath chilled in his throat and he fell silent as the Northmen climbed above a dip in the uneven terrain. 'I count ten,' he murmured. 'But there may be more.'

'We'll follow until we can find a suitable place to jump one or two from behind,' Ceowulf told him.

There was little chance of being heard in the mountains. Noise was quickly swallowed into ravines and gullies and every boulder and twist in the terrain distorted the sound. The Vaalakans were looking down into the valley and evidently didn't suspect that anyone was following them. Hal wondered if they were watching Spar and Brid. Gradually the Northmen spread out and Ceowulf indicated with his hands that they should move to the right onto higher ground.

At last one Vaalakan split off from the rest, lagging just a little behind the others. He was scanning the crescent-shaped formation of high-pointed peaks that rose vertically before them.

Ceowulf waved the raven-haired youth down and then

pointed at himself, gesticulating that he would make the first move. Hal nodded in agreement. The ex-mercenary had more experience of these stealthy forms of warfare and he wasn't about to contradict the man. The Caldean skirted quickly uphill and pounced. The gash across the man's throat cut the cry from his mouth but he continued to struggle for what seemed to Hal like an eternity. At last Ceowulf lowered the limp body to the ground and signalled for Hal to follow.

'Nice work,' the youth muttered as they crouched behind a boulder, waiting for two further Vaalakans to come into view. Hal hated the Northmen's white faces and the dull washed-out blue of their cold eyes. His only relief was that neither Kullak nor Scragg was in their number.

'Ready?' Ceowulf hissed.

Hal didn't have time to think. With his broadsword drawn, he ran straight for the nearest man. The force of his charge drove the runesword clean through the man's belly. Hal yanked the blade upwards, cleaving through the ribcage towards the heart. Thick purplish blood and a coil of white gut burst through the gaping wound as Hal twisted the blade. The Vaalakan's mouth and eyes dropped in disbelief. He stared first at Hal and then at his open chest. Gurgling, he fell to his knees.

Ceowulf's first cut had missed his man's shoulder but his second sliced across the Northman's face and hacked down into his upper ribcage. Another quick thrust had him stabbed cleanly through the heart but not before the barbarian had given out an agonized scream. Overhead the circling eagle tipped its wings and gradually spiralled down towards the fresh kills.

'Quickly!' he urged as the knight struggled to withdraw his blade. 'It'll be easier to take them if we have the higher ground.'

Keeping low to the ground, he scurried away, his thigh muscles protesting as he led Ceowulf up the untracked slope. He was breathless by the time he reached the ridge and peered over the top. Seven Vaalakans were climbing towards them.

'I'll draw them off,' Ceowulf told him without waiting for argument. Crouching to keep his big frame from view, the Caldean ran along the ridge until he was a hundred yards from Hal. He deliberately tossed a stone so that it struck a boulder and then raised his head into view. The Vaalakans wheeled towards him and Hal advanced on their rear.

As Ceowulf leapt out and ran screaming towards the Vaalakans, Hal charged silently from behind. Two of them stood slightly back from their companions and he felled them expertly. One sideways swing severed the nearest's head as easily as slicing through a soft pear and, following the stroke through, he hacked into the shoulder of the next. The man spun round, half his arm dangling from only a thread of sinew where the runesword had sliced clean through the bone. Before the wounded Vaalakan could raise his sabre, Hal plunged the blade straight through his chest, feeling the sword twist and rasp as its point bored through the ribs and stabbed into the soft tissues beneath. The runesword seemed to revel in the glory. For the first time he thought he heard its glorious victory song wailing out into the channels of magic. A magnificent sense of satisfaction welled up into his heart.

He felt invincible, god-like; the world bowed at his feet. He could destroy everything and anybody in his path. Only five Vaalakans lay ahead of him now. Two turned towards him. He approached them confidently while the rest parried strokes with Ceowulf who was being beaten back by the force of their combined axe blows.

Raging bloodlust stormed through his mind. He spun in on them, hacking indiscriminately to left and right, but then a voice yelled in his ear. It was Tancred's, warning him to control his frenzy; that his rage would bring defeat by clouding his senses. He took a pace back and drew a deep steadying breath. Only then did he notice an eighth Vaalakan, whom they had not spotted previously, slinking up to attack from behind. He spun on his heel and braced himself, just in time to avoid a stroke that would have cut straight through his left hand. As it was, the blade skinned the flesh off the back of his hand.

Hal was caught slightly off balance and let the runesword drop to the floor to steady himself. As the Vaalakan raised his axe to beat down on him, he jerked his own blade upwards with all his might. It caught into the man's groin and split him open as high as his belly button. His innards cascaded down through the deep gash in a stinking, snake-like mass of gut.

Hal turned again, this time more wary of his emotions. *Slow down and keep your head*, Tancred's words rang through his mind. Coolly, he feinted left, stooped and, swinging the runesword in a wide arc, cut the legs out from under his two remaining assailants. Ceowulf had already brought two men down and now quickly dispatched the last warrior with an angled blow across the chest. A pool of blood, thick with gory tissue, oozed wetly around their feet. The Caldean nobleman looked down unemotionally at the broken bodies slumped on the marshy ground. A host of black ravens fell from the sky and flapped jealously around the carrion.

Ceowulf leant on his sword, drawing sharp breaths. His hand automatically reached for his wounded shoulder as if the pain constantly nagged him. He looked down again at the mutilated bodies. 'I still don't see how they got here. I can only think they followed us,' he decided.

'All the way from Caldea?' Hal was doubtful. 'It doesn't seem possible. There were no ships travelling through the Teeth other than the *Moonshadow* when we left Cocklebay.'

Ceowulf froze and cupped his ear. 'Listen, there's more of them!' He pointed towards the circle of sharp-toothed mountains that rose like a giant claw out of the earth's crust. Its vicious nails, ragged and torn like those of an ancient hag, hooked at the sky.

'How many of these devilish bastards are there?' Hal swore, loping after Ceowulf. He hardly noticed the gruelling climb. With his sword drawn, he was infused with the hungry desire to kill.

A peaty burn wound its way towards them across an open area at the foot of the mountains that continued to soar, peak after peak, above them. They followed the stream's course into a bowled valley sheltered by a horse-shoe formation of jagged crags crested in a veil of bluish-white snow. Hal barely took in the details. All he knew was that across the lake stood another knot of Vaalakans and they had Brid and Spar!

His throat was dry. Ceowulf snatched at the impulsive youth as Hal lurched towards the Northmen. The knight gripped his wrist and yanked him back.

'Steady, lad, we've got to be careful now. One slip and . . .'

It didn't bear saying. Even from here he could see that both Caspar and Brid had knives at their throats. Trog was nowhere in sight. Hal could hardly think for the blood pumping through his head. He wanted to charge but he knew Ceowulf was right. He bit his lip, trying to think of a plan.

Caspar fought back as his mother's mind reached towards him, trying to cradle him in her embrace, shielding him with her own body. But he knew it was only her spirit guarding his; her flesh could not reach out through the moonstone. Whatever his mother did, the knife was still free to cut his jugular. All sound around him was becoming indistinct. Only a strange whirring filled his ears as he balanced on the verge of unconsciousness, bathed in a brilliant white light.

His mind sank deeper into the magical, insubstantial universe of the moonstone, aware that Gwion's mind piggy-backed on his. His mother's presence was vivid around him, her voice strong, and when her words rang through the ghostly world of the orb it was as if the mountains themselves had spoken.

'Gwion, leave my son. He has never harmed you.'

'No?' The priest's voice was sickeningly cold. 'His face has harmed me every day for twelve years, reminding me of you.'

'Gwion, I forgive you. Just let my son go. You are my brother and I forgive you.'

'Who are you to forgive me? I am the Master now. Your

death means I am the Master. I have all the power. The worship of the Great Mother will be gone forever and never again will a woman rise above her kinsman.'

'I never humiliated you. I tried to get everything for you,' she protested.

Caspar felt as if he were nested in her breast. Though still fearful of the raging madness festering within his embittered uncle, he was soothed by his mother's embrace. Like a small child, he revelled in the ultimate security of her comfort.

They continued to argue and very gradually the boy realized that Keridwen was distracting the priest, drawing him away from his goal, but still Kullak's knife was snatched tight at his neck.

He was no longer sure if it was part of the magic or not, as he heard a bestial roar bellow out round his head. A salivary gnashing of teeth and a fiendish deep-chested snarl filled his ears. There was blood everywhere. Caspar couldn't move for the knife at his throat but he could feel the fresh hot liquid smothering his face. He didn't know if it was his or someone else's, only that it filled his eyes and trickled round into his mouth, bringing with it a distinctive salty, metallic taste. He was choking on it, unable to breathe properly, and then someone flung him aside. He tumbled over and over, gasping for air, but he still clutched the moonstone.

'Run, Run!' Someone was yelling at him to run, but he couldn't. He couldn't leave Brid. The voice was compelling. He didn't know where it was coming from until he looked down at the orb still firmly held in his hands. 'Run, child, run. You have to. You must get to the Egg before they stop you.' It was his mother. He could not disobey her and yet he could not abandon Brid.

He faltered and turned back. Brid had vanished. Midst the carnage, all that could be seen were the flash of white teeth and a spinning hound screaming and shrieking as he tore at flesh. With the expert skill that had allowed him to kill the sand vipers on the beach, the frenzied animal was snatching at arms and crushing bones in his gnashing jaws.

But Brid was gone. He couldn't see her against the dull dun colours of the mountainside. All he could make out was Kullak rolling on the ground, clutching at his arm where Trog had ripped the flesh clean off the bone.

The Ophidian snake-catcher spun in mid-air and leapt again at the Vaalakans. They slashed back and forth with their blades but they were too slow for him. Though he was a cumbersome beast with little staying power over long distances, Trog was a killer, bred over generations for his speed in dispatching the sand snakes that troubled Ophidia's coastline. If he could outmanoeuvre a darting snake, he could easily outmanoeuvre a human hand.

Suddenly Brid was beside him. With the practised ease of one so harmonized with nature, she had slunk away from the Northmen to blend with the colours and folds of the mountainside. As she folded back her hood, he saw that her face was scratched and she was covered in blood but otherwise she was whole.

'Run,' she commanded as if repeating Keridwen's orders.

They sprinted for the higher slopes, Caspar slinging the moonstone around his neck.

As Trog launched his attack Hal charged, focusing on the tangle of people before him. The Vaalakans were turning in startled horror at the ferocity of the dog's attack. Brid was already free and, in that uncanny way of hers, had melted into the background, becoming like a shadow around the base of a boulder. As Gwion looked up in alarm, he released his grip on the moonstone. With great relief Hal saw Caspar wrench his arms backwards, ducking down and wriggling free from the grip of the enemy like a squirming lizard.

With Caspar out of the way, Hal charged to slash at the back of the nearest Vaalakan. But the man ducked down, avoiding the blow, and kicked backwards, catching him hard in the ribs with his foot. Hal felt the wind wheeze out of him and as he sucked in the cold mountain air a far more violent punch sank into the soft tissue of his belly. A small rat-like face with vapid blue eyes leered into his and he knew in an instant it was Gwion.

Hal couldn't believe it – nor could he believe the force of the punch. The priest hit him again, this time on his temple, and the dark youth felt his grasp weaken on the hilt of his sword. Suddenly he had lost his weapon. Speechless, he looked up into Gwion's leering face. The man opened his fist and Hal looked down at the open palm and at a shard of bright white steel. He knew instantly it was the splinter of blade that had broken from the runesword when he had struck the cauldron.

Gwion hit him one last time. The strength bestowed by the energy of the metal sent the youth sprawling. When his breath returned, he felt numbly weak and vulnerable as if stripped naked. His sword was gone. Without his sword he was helpless.

'Get up, Hal!' someone was shouting as he floundered amongst the boggy mosses. A pair of black boots stood astride his body and the furious clash of metal on metal rang in his ears. 'Get up. We've got to hold back these barbarians so Brid and Spar can get clear.' It was Ceowulf's voice and Hal was flooded with relief. The great knight stood over him as he struggled for breath. Spar and Brid must have escaped, he thought quickly, but his relief quickly evaporated. His sword was gone.

A spurt of blood gushed down from above.

'Hal, grab a sword, any sword,' Ceowulf was shouting urgently.

The raven-haired Torra Altan grappled midst the bodies and wrenched a curved sabre from a Northman's spasming grasp. He had never used one before but was quickly on his feet, trying to clear his head, trying to let his training ring through his scrambled emotions. Cut, parry, thrust and block.

The two Belbidians were surrounded. Hal was cruelly aware of the violent force of the Vaalakan axes that he blocked time after time, the joints in his arms and wrists jarring with each massive impact. Where was his sword? His sword was gone.

He needed it. How could he fight these huge bear-like men without his sword?

Instinctively he leapt into the air as an axe swept under his feet. His legs shook. He was tiring, he knew he was tiring, and, too accustomed to a double-edged sword, he had to think to rotate the sabre onto its keen single-edged blade. He could almost laugh at his own lack of skill. He had believed himself invincible, all powerful. But it wasn't him, it wasn't him at all: it was the sword. Now it was gone; but where?

He couldn't take his eyes off the enemy for an instant. Scragg was hacking determinedly towards him, his war knots rattling around his blond head. Without his sword he would be hacked to pieces by the vast axe-wielding warrior. *Let him tire*, a calm voice urged within his head. Again it was Tancred's. *If your opponent is bigger and stronger than you, use your energies to avoid his blows. Think only of defending yourself and don't attempt to challenge his power until he shows signs of tiring.*

Hal gritted his teeth and stuck to this tactic. He allowed nothing else to fill his mind. His concentration became so honed that the distracting sounds around him were silenced and he cut out the vision of the other Vaalakans, concentrating solely on Scragg. The barbarian was intent on nothing more than killing him.

'Belbidian weakling, you dies. We have power of the Master and you dies. I chop off your ears, then nose, then fingers, then hands and you dies. Dies slowly. Master has total power.'

The words scrambled Hal's concentration as his mind jarred on the title of the Master.

And what was Gwion doing here? Was it really Gwion who had punched him with such monumental force, the force of a charging bull?

A seething pain jerked his body round. A wetness leaked along his left arm. He had momentarily lost concentration. His arm . . . He knew something was wrong. Scragg's expression changed to one of sneering contempt.

'I cut you slowly, bit by bit.'

With his hand hanging limply at his side, Hal fought on

with renewed focus, thinking of nothing but his own actions and the skill of battle-craft. His was numb to the pain in his left arm. He blocked it from his mind. He had to think of every stroke he had ever been taught and clear his mind of all else.

Only in the back of his mind did he hear the screams of the dying. He hacked on and on, finding himself stepping further and further back until he was pressed up against Ceowulf's back.

'Well done, friend,' the big knight grunted, raising his arm for another stroke. 'We must hold fast.' His words were broken by grunts of effort and the clash of steel. 'We have to give them time.'

Hal felt Ceowulf drop to his knees behind him but there was nothing he could do. All his energies were absorbed in holding off Scragg. For a moment Ceowulf was back up, pressing his shoulder against Hal, but then he faltered again and dropped back down to his knees.

Chapter 23

Side by side, Brid and Caspar began to run upwards. After fifty paces the Baron's son hesitated for a moment and snatched for his bow but it was impossible to make a safe shot. He could hit Hal or Ceowulf as easily as one of the enemy. They were outnumbered but Hal had the runesword and would hold his own; there was no need to worry. Obeying the moonstone's command, he tore up the slope after Brid and into the mist that descended towards them.

'Run! Run!' it shrieked at him. 'Get the Egg before it's too late.'

Brid grabbed his arm and together they scrambled on. They were quickly out of breath and, as the mountain steepened, they hauled themselves upwards hand over hand. Some way behind, Trog was struggling after them.

Fallen scree made the climb difficult and Caspar instinctively veered towards the sound of running water, knowing that the stream would have carved the most direct route. Keeping just to the edge of the water, he used the natural cascade as a staircase and climbed towards the next crest.

The tumbling stream gushed from a narrowing ravine and the walls of the valley closed tighter and tighter around them as they were funnelled towards its head. The ground steepened, showing less vegetation and more exposed blocks of rock. They were forced to climb from ledge to ledge, Caspar reaching down one hand to haul Brid up the higher steps.

'It's like a giant's staircase,' she complained as they stopped to draw breath. Caspar didn't know how much further his legs would carry him.

Ice trapped in the rock fissures made the going more treacherous and their hands turned a purplish red from the cold and from scrambling over the harsh rocks. The surrounding valley sides closed in, trapping them in the ravine, and the stream was now no more than a trickle as it played over the sheer steps of a frozen waterfall. The sloping rocks to either side rose into a near vertical slab of featureless basalt. The youth cast around him for an alternative route.

'We'll have to go down again and cut to one side or the other,' he groaned. 'It would be longer but not so steep.'

Brid put her hand on her chest, which rose and fell with her sharp breaths. Still too flushed and breathless to speak, she waved him upwards. After a moment she fought for some words. 'I'm not going down. It was too much hard work getting here. We'll get over that. We're Torra Altans after all.'

Caspar smiled at her confidence and turned to study the sheer slab of rock. Only one small sprig of heather broke its barren uniformity but it was beyond his reach.

'I'll push you up towards it,' Brid suggested. 'If I can get you to the top, then you can pull me up. Our belts should make a long enough rope for you to reach me.'

Caspar looked at her doubtfully as she gave him her belt and crouched down, offering her shoulder as a step up.

'But –' the youth started to object, afraid that he might hurt her but, with one look at her determined face, thought better of it. Without further thought, he put his boot on her shoulders and scrabbled for a handhold in the rock. The sprig of heather was just beyond his reach but as Brid grunted and straightened her back to push him higher, he finally got his fingernails into a crack in the rock.

'Sorry,' he yelled, feeling his boot slip on her hand but she only grunted.

Reaching up with his other hand, he found himself fighting for space with the roots of the heather, but eventually his fingers were at last firmly slotted into the rock. The top of the basalt slab would have been just out of reach of his upstretched fingers but as Brid stood up she was able to push him a little higher. Now he could reach the tips of coarse spring heather that dangled from the ledge above. The rough plant slipped through his fingertips as he grabbed for it but he flung his other hand upwards and gained a good enough hold to swing one leg up onto the ledge. Flopping his chest onto the flat rock, he swung his other leg over the lip and spun round on his belly to lower the belts for Brid. Breathlessly, he hauled her the few feet needed to reach the crack in the basalt while she scrabbled for a handhold. Finally, grunting with the effort, he dragged her over the scratchy overhang to slump beside him. Breathing hard, they both looked round at the plateau before them.

The ground stretched out for several hundred yards in a mass of bogs and peat levels before rising again into a series of rocky crags that stretched up into the clouds.

Looking back down the way they had come, they could see beyond the foothills, which had previously obscured the view of the Camaalian plains. The perspectives seemed to have changed, giving the sense that if they slipped they would fall right off the mountain to the miniature world of the flatlands below. The overhang beneath their feet hid all the mounds and hollows and their line of sight was unbroken directly to sea-level.

Far below they could make out the white speck of Trog struggling after them. All around they could hear the clash of metal ringing out over the mountains, echoing back and forth between the ravines, tossing the sound of battle from one peak to the next as if two entire armies clashed within the Frosted Peaks. But they could no longer see Hal nor Ceowulf.

Caspar was panting so hard that he needed time to catch his breath. He was hot despite the icy cold wind but they couldn't delay. There was precious little time left. Both Gwion and the insubstantial ghosts of the beasts of power sought the Egg. He had to get there first.

It was a relief to cross the plateau of high pasture as it gave them time to settle their breathing. Ahead of them lay a path, probably cut by ibex, their sharp cloven hooves slicing through the heather stems and scraping through the thin soil to the bare rock beneath. Caspar caught Brid's hand and pulled her on.

'Quickly.'

She seemed distracted. 'Hal,' she murmured anxiously. 'The runesword ... I can't hear its song and yet I can still hear the clash of battle.' She turned and hurried with increased determination towards the next climb. 'We must get the Egg before it's too late for Hal.'

The mist was stifling and Caspar quickly began to feel disorientated. He had experienced this uncanny sensation many times before and was well aware of the bewildering sense of isolation that mountain fog instilled – but that was in terrain he knew well: here, he was a stranger to these high, ragged peaks. The mist had quickly become a thick stifling fog, heavy and oppressive, a soup of curdled grey that smoothed the contours around them. Caspar knew it would snow any minute. He halted and waited for Brid, catching her arm as she drew close.

'Stay with me,' he warned her.

The path beneath their feet was swallowed into creamy greyness and only the black points of the nearest boulders were visible. They stooped low, following the path, hoping their instincts would draw them upwards. Caspar felt the first wet snowflake land and melt on his cheek. At first the snow fell in docile, drifting flakes like soft downy feathers sifting out of the sky but the higher they climbed the more the wind gave them bite. Soon the flakes were coming thick and fast, stinging his lips and slashing against his face, finally falling as hard pellets, nipping his smarting eyes and raw skin.

Brid looked at him with concern. 'I hope we don't have to go any higher.'

Caspar agreed. They were mountain people and, anyone who understood mountains knew that the weather on the peaks was always dangerously vicious compared to the climate in the valleys below. As they climbed higher, he imagined that they were intruding into the threshold of the gods; it was a place too vast, too immense, too overstated for mere mortals. This was the weather of giants.

He pulled his cloak over his head and clutched it tightly but the biting cold still sliced into his forehead. His scalp tightened and constricted the blood vessels on his temples. His head ached, his fingers were swollen, his face smarted, his eyes stung – everything hurt. The wind drove the wet snow through his torn breeches and his legs had chafed where the damp freezing leather clung to his thighs.

He tried to block the discomfort from his mind and concentrated on the climb. They must be heading towards a pass. He was sure of that because the wind seemed to be funnelling towards them, winding and churning through the natural path.

He bent double and shouldered himself into the wind but Brid, both lighter and smaller, was struggling. With numb fingers, he grabbed for her hand and hauled her closer behind him as he battled upwards. The wind was strengthening, whipping the snow horizontally into his face, and he could see no more than a few feet. But worse, he couldn't breathe. Snow choked his windpipe, making him splutter and cough. The sheer ferocity of the biting gale stole away his breath and he could sense his lungs clenching up against the freezing cold. His hands were now two balls of painfully clenched bones and the only blessing was that they were beginning to go numb. He lowered his head to protect his face and covered his mouth with his cloak so that he could suck in air through its protective layers.

The ground levelled out and narrowed into a thin track that curled away to the left, precariously cutting into the edge of the mountain. The visibility was better now and they could see that the track ahead skirted the brim of a dramatic precipice that fell a thousand feet and formed the back wall of another mountain tarn. Caspar carefully picked his way forward, always keeping a concerned hand held out for Brid.

He knew she was shouting at him but the wind strangled her words. The path was widening, leading them away from the head of the cliff to flatter terrain where the snow was piled in drifts. It dragged at their feet and soon Caspar was wading through deep layers that sapped more and more of his strength. Brid waved ahead again, shouting, and Caspar looked up, squinting to protect his eyes from the onslaught of biting snow.

There was a light ahead. It didn't seem possible. But it was there, a thin wand of white brightness gleaming through the snow. With renewed vigour, Caspar surged forward, dragging Brid behind him. Thigh deep in the snow-field, he laboured through the heavy layers, heaving one foot and then the other out of each deep crater created by his boots. This had to be it. If it wasn't, they would soon die from cold and exhaustion. No one could last long in exposed conditions like this, not in the mountains.

A shape, black against the stormy grey of the snow clouds, condensed into human form, holding the beam of light. Caspar hooked his frozen hands forward and tried to clutch at a boulder for support as he dragged himself forward towards the figure. Was this a guardian druid or a statue bearing a light to guide them on the very last stretch of their quest? He wasn't sure, but hope was growing within him. They had to be close.

The wind howled and swept a ferocious curl of twisting snow towards them and in an instant Caspar knew he was mistaken. The figure was charging them, brandishing a bright sword. Caspar focused on the sword. It wasn't just any sword. There was no mistaking the cold, graceful resonance of the great runesword as it wailed and sliced through the thick atmosphere.

Hal! Caspar thought in stupefied disbelief. His mind charged through the possibilities. What was Hal doing there? Why was he attacking them? But then this man was too small and light and his voice was high and strained with the terror of madness eating into his brain. With a rising sense of relief – and horror – he realized it wasn't Hal, but Gwion. But what of Hal? If Gwion had his sword was Hal slain?

Exhausted and frozen, the youth had no time to think. His deranged uncle was moving too fast and his own hands were too stiff with the pain of frostbite to allow him to reach for his bow. He let go of Brid and felt her stagger back onto the rock, her light frame flung backwards by the wind.

With nothing to protect himself, he looked up in horror at the blade of white steel that was whirring towards his skull. He knew it could slice through flesh as easily as cut through lard. It was a cruel hard weapon designed only for killing – and now it was in the hands of a madman. Facing death in the jaws, Caspar's mind moved quickly so that it seemed minutes before the blade began to bear down on him.

Without knowing how or why, he instinctively reached for the moonstone around his neck. Thrusting it upwards to block the blow, he ducked behind the shield of the glowing orb.

He felt his arms would break as the tremendous thrust of the runesword sliced into the crystal. And then he was swimming through space, wreathed in blinding white light, as if caught up in a storm of swirling comets. A terrible energy burnt around him, sucking his thoughts into a maelstrom of enchantments of boundless power.

Then he heard Brid's voice and felt her hand on his. 'Great Mother, guide us. Keridwen, Morrigwen, help us,' she pleaded.

Caspar gritted his teeth, bowed his head and thrust the moonstone upwards against the force of the sword. He felt the shock as the blade sliced through the skin of the orb but, instead of hacking downwards towards his bowed head, it stuck fast. An energy stormed up through the earth, through his body, and channelled through his hands. The power surged into the moonstone, then concentrated within it before being driven outwards in a burst of supernatural violence.

He was on his knees. The force of the runesword had hammered him to the ground, but the blade had stuck fast, embedded in the heart of the moonstone.

Snags of white lightning licked along the blade towards the hilt and Gwion's hands. The wildfire blistered up the priest's forearms and flashed over his wiry body. He screeched in torment. His bulging eyes became blazing spheres of white energy. The force of the magic, concentrated through the two great talismans, bit into his brain, filling him with terrible demons that raked and shredded his diseased mind. Scorching heat stormed round his body, gathering momentum before erupting out of him in a sunburst of energy. The combined powers of sword and moonstone discharged their fiery energy into the world.

'The runespells! No!' Brid cried out in despair. 'The runes of sorcery! It's releasing the runes of sorcery!'

Caspar sensed the electrifying energy of the spell bursting out from the sword as the runes were cast into the universe, releasing their power.

'The creatures of shadow will seize the spells and take life from them!' Brid yelled in dismay.

Gwion clawed at his eyes and a sparkling red object slipped from his grip. Maddened with pain, Gwion fled and was swallowed into the storm. Through it, they heard his scream once more, a scream of terror. It howled on and on until it was no more than the point of a whisper and then silence.

'The cliff,' Brid murmured. She didn't need to say more.

They were alone in the snowstorm. Caspar stared speechlessly at the blanketed earth and stooped to pick up the ruby that was sinking down through the fine layers of snow. He felt a warm glow as he clutched it. Solemnly he handed it to Brid. A smile flickered across her exhausted face. Caspar then turned back to the moonstone impaled on the runesword. He tried to free it but failed and there was nothing he could do except strap the weighty weapon to his back. His mind was numb but he had to think. Gwion! His Uncle Gwion. His mother's brother. All along he had schemed against them, driven by the demented belief that Keridwen had existed only to subjugate him. Gwion had sought to be master of the world just to have revenge on his sister.

Brid's mind evidently struggled with the same thought. 'He was just jealous of his younger sister. He couldn't accept her success while he failed.'

Caspar leant into the wind and forced his exhausted legs to carry him higher. The ground ahead narrowed and they were once more on an ibex track. It curved around the edge of the peak that lanced upwards like a horn. With Brid's nails digging into his flesh as she clutched his hand, he strode onwards, praying that as they skirted round to the far side of the peak, the weather would ease.

Too cold and exhausted to move further, they cowered down behind an overhanging boulder and drew their cloaks over their heads to form a tent, breathing in the warmth of each other's heat. Caspar looked into Brid's red raw eyes and saw the echo of his own emotions.

'Hal,' she choked, unable to say anything more, and fell against Caspar's shoulder, sobbing. He hugged her tightly, sharing her grief and glad of the bodily warmth. If Gwion had confronted them with Hal's sword, how then could Hal be alive? Without the runesword, Hal and Ceowulf stood little chance against a troop of barbaric Vaalakan warriors. Two Belbidians alone against possibly half a dozen muscle-bound Northmen ... The odds were impossible. Caspar refused to give up hope for his raven-haired kinsman and, judging by the way Brid brushed away her tears and stiffened her pose, he guessed she was doing the same.

They waited more than an hour in the shelter of the rock before the winds subsided. Caspar felt he could do nothing more than sleep but he knew they must move on. The air was too thin and when night drew in, the cold would kill them. They couldn't rest any longer. As the storm receded, a sheer horn of rock climbed high into the bright blue air above them.

Burdened with sorrow, they battled upwards and Brid began to sing as if trying to encourage their spirits. Though sad, her voice was as sweet and welcome as the warming sun, so filled with life and energy that it seemed to woo the very rocks around them and urge the world to protect them.

> 'Up, up to the mountain peak,
> Where the eagles soar and the hawks shriek.
> Up, up to the mountain heights,
> Where the snow stings and the wind bites.'

She stopped and Caspar whispered the rest.

> '*Up, up to the cruel, ice air,*
> *Fear the dagger of cold, fear the dragon's lair.*'

They looked at each other with foreboding.

'It's just a song,' Brid said, trying to sound light. 'Just a silly song.'

Nevertheless Caspar felt nervous. He wished he could wield the runesword but he knew it was now useless as a weapon. Instead he hurriedly unslung his bow from his back.

'Shh!' Brid ordered.

Caspar looked round. 'What?'

Urgently she waved him to be silent and cupped her ear to indicate that she was trying to listen to something. He could hear it too; a strange snuffling sound.

Caspar felt the hairs on the back of his neck tingle in fearful anticipation. It was definitely the sound of a predator sniffing out prey. Suddenly he relaxed and laughed as Trog came snuffling round the corner.

At first he thought the dog had been running, nose to the ground, to seek out their trail. But, after greeting them with enthusiasm, Trog remained uncharacteristically distracted, his nose still twitching urgently at the air.

Caspar looked at Brid disconnectedly. 'What do you suppose he can smell?'

'Well, I've only ever seen him look like that when he can smell snakes,' Brid remarked with a dismissive glance.

At the mention of the word *snakes*, Trog spun round and round, excitedly snuffling over the ground, and then went stiff again, his nose pointing upwards towards the peak.

Caspar laughed nervously. 'Well, one thing's for certain, he can't possible smell you-know-what up here.' Trog slouched low and began to creep forward like a wolf stalking its prey. 'It might be something like them, maybe lizards . . . or wyvern,' the youth suggested with horror.

They followed the path as it wound upwards, now manoeuvring with difficulty from one rocky ledge to the next until they found themselves climbing up above the clouds and below a near vertical seam in the rock. Trog whined and sniffed around the sheet of tilted rock until he found a fern-lined gully that cut like a staircase through it. Following the dog's lead, they scrambled and clawed their way up the slippery couloir. Caspar felt the sweat pour off his brow with the effort of hauling himself ever upwards for the next handhold and he stopped for a second to draw breath. Standing above the sheer face, the mountains seem to fall away forever.

He looked down at the foaming bank of snow cloud that cloaked the Lake of Tears. Apart from the mist still trapped in the bowl-shaped valley beneath them, the atmosphere around the crags was clear. He could see far beyond the snow-capped peaks. Like an eagle, he could see it all: the churning roof of the clouds, the deep, rich colours of the lower mountains, the red, gold and black of the heathers, the scrubby trees and exposed rocks, and the silver garlands of river that tumbled in white sashes towards the plain far, far below. Camaalia stretched out like a golden carpet, the dry parched land fed only by the melting snows off the Frosted Peaks. Squinting into the distance, he could just make out the grey plain of the sea. Beyond that he knew lay Torra Alta, thousands of leagues away.

Trog dislodged a loose flint from a crack in the rock and Caspar whisked his head aside to let the pebble skim past him as it tossed downwards. Up here in the heights he felt most at home and most alive, breathing the air that no one else could breathe. As he turned his head he caught a movement some way to his left.

'Brid,' he whispered, 'there's something following us.' He looked down at her wind-scrubbed face, her hair, tattered and drenched from the storm, clinging to her cheeks. Her wide, dazzling green eyes urgently searched around them.

'I can't see anything,' she whispered uncertainly, 'but . . .'

'There's something there,' Caspar concluded for her. 'The shadows have eyes. I can feel them staring.'

He shuddered and drew the heavy weight of his damp cloak

tightly around him. He could sense something breathing, something big and powerful. Trog looked around for a moment, his small black eyes fixed on the same point of empty space as Caspar's. He whimpered softly but quickly turned back towards the sharp peak ahead, intent on his prey.

Fifty yards above them, the slope steepened sharply to form a horn and, at its base, Caspar saw something white, a beautiful silvery white, moving with the energetic grace of a high stepping horse. For a second he caught sight of the shadow of its head and a long thin horn. 'The unicorn,' he murmured. It moved fully into view and pawed at the ground with one cloven hoof. An animal so beautiful yet so infused with evil.

'They're taking form,' Brid whispered. 'When the sword struck the moonstone the runes of sorcery were released into the ether. We must hurry.'

A shadow swooped overhead, plunging them into darkness as a thirty-foot wingspan blacked out the sky. A terrible scream, like the caw of a monstrous raven, filled the sky and for a moment Caspar felt burning heat. He saw nothing but he knew what it was.

Brid's mouth formed around the word *dragon* but she seemed reluctant to actually voice the word. 'Just hurry,' she begged. 'We must get there before they are fully formed.'

Caspar clambered upwards.

At the base of the horn was a narrow ledge and the black mouth of a cave. Trog was cowering before the cave with his hackles up and his lips pared back. He slunk forward, whimpering, and then fled back to Brid and stood trembling between her legs.

'Mother, have mercy,' she murmured.

Chapter 24

The tip of Hal's sabre snapped under the force of Kullak's axe. The next series of blows beat the Torra Altan down onto one knee and the big Vaalakan warrior showed no signs of tiring.

Ceowulf grunted with the effort of every blow. Hal heard the sudden thrust and cut of the knight's blade as he made better ground but then the Caldean was beaten back as another Vaalakan came shrieking to the attack. There was a stifled gasp as the big knight suffered a blow to his left side. He fought on, though his grip was slipping as blood oozed out over his hilt.

Hal knew they were no longer fighting for their own lives: their lives were already lost. They could no longer hope to defeat the seven men around them, who hacked at them with increasing ferocity. They were only fighting for time, fighting for Caspar to reach the Egg. Hal was ready to make the sacrifice. His only regret was that he had never told his nephew that he no longer resented him for being the heir to Torra Alta. He realized now that there were other things that were more important – like Brid.

He had been so jealous when Brid had given him her favour at the tournament. He had been furious with Caspar for it, even though he knew it wasn't his fault. He understood that the scarf had been given not as a token of her love but to bestow Caspar with strength and the ability to win. He was sorry, now, for being so unbearably churlish.

He wished that he had kissed Brid at least once and told her that he loved her. Unfulfilled, his only solace was that he would at least die a hero and would take with him as many of these fiendish barbarians as he possibly could. As long as Spar and Brid could reach the Egg they still had time. If he could hold out only a little longer, they would save the castle and all Belbidia.

Kullak towered over him, hacking and slicing with his double-bladed cleaver, clearly aiming at the peak of Hal's head. He would only need one clean blow and the smooth plates of Hal's skull would be split asunder as cleanly as a log on a chopping block.

It was then that he heard it. Above the maddened screams of battle came the song of warlords riding to the fray. The heartening sound was accompanied by the furious blasts of a clarion and the snorts of charging horses. Hal fought with renewed vigour as he recognized the colours of the approaching knights. Kay, Grinwal and Tylot were at the head of a party of eight horsemen. Amongst the noble battle standards and garish colours, he caught a flash of bright pink satin, which he knew could never have been worn by any knight.

Grinwal, who was in the lead, dropped his lance in favour of his black-metalled sword, obviously fearing that the fighting was too close for the longer weapon. He charged straight for the nearest Vaalakan, who wheeled to meet him, and split open the Northman's face with one clean stroke.

Tylot swung his mace into Scragg's back. Though the brutish warrior was not mortally wounded, he staggered and fell on top of Hal, pinning him to the blood-soaked turf, his axe blade wavering over the Belbidian's exposed neck. Hal wrestled one arm free from the crushing weight of Scragg's body, desperately struggling to hold the man off, but he was too weak. As he fought back against the Vaalakan's strength, the axe blade jerked closer in juddery bursts towards his jugular.

He squirmed his other arm beneath the crushing weight, found his dagger and then thrust upwards until the blade embedded so deeply in the barbarian's gut that he felt its tip jar against the man's spine. As Hal felt the warm tissues ooze out over his hand, the Northman's eyes bulged in sudden realization, his lips called for his God's embrace and, in his last breath, he whispered, 'Vaal-Peor.'

The prayers of the dying warrior charged the air as his departing spirit reached out to the Ice-God. The atmosphere was suddenly choked by a miasma of evil.

As the Belbidian youth struggled to his feet, the last Vaalakan was felled by a well-executed cut and thrust of Kay's blade. His father thumped him proudly on the back and then the eyes of the Camaalian knights were on the two Belbidians. Hal's left arm was cut and he clutched it protectively to his body. Ceowulf was still on his knees, bleeding from gashes to his thigh and face. He tried to stand but stumbled and sank down again, defeated.

Looking completely out of place in her swirl of pink satin, Cybillia unexpectedly came dashing through from somewhere behind the knights and flung herself down beside the big Caldean, shredding bandages from her petticoats and fussing over Ceowulf's wounds.

'You're injured. Oh, Ceowulf, you're injured,' she sobbed fitfully.

He laughed, a deep-throated laugh. 'It's not so bad, lass. Dry your eyes; I'm just exhausted.'

He slumped forwards into her arms and Hal lay back on the rough heather, wondering if his muscles would ever work again. He didn't know how long they had been fighting but it had seemed like hours and, at high altitude, he no longer had the strength to move. He envied Ceowulf the restorative kisses that Cybillia heaped upon him but he grinned at their happiness. They deserved each other.

Hal looked up into Kay's face.

The young Lonisian looked concerned. 'Are you still living?'

'My mind is, though I'm not sure about my body.' He accepted Kay's hand and hoisted himself to his feet, though once there he nearly buckled under his own weight. 'How on earth did you get here?' he asked as Grinwal expertly strapped his left arm with a field-dressing.

Kay nodded towards Cybillia. 'She came hammering on our doors and fair demanded our help. At first we thought she was trying to set us up, you know, as some sort of prank. She said she was worried for you all riding up alone into the mountains and felt helpless at being left behind. We couldn't see what harm you could come to but she was insistent. She couldn't say that anything was exactly the matter, just that she had this feeling. Anyway, to be honest a ride into the mountains seemed like a great idea. It wasn't until we were high in the Frosted Peaks, where by rights a young lady should be afeard for her own safety, that we realized she was in deepest earnest. She rode fearlessly through the difficult terrain, whipping on her horse as if possessed by a demon. Real spirit.'

Hal laughed. 'Did you hear that, Cybillia? Kay says you're a true Belbidian.' He admired the girl for her courage and determination, yet they were the two qualities that he had previously despised in women. Now he realized there was another maiden who had those qualities – and many more a hundred times over. He turned to look up towards the great horn of the crag that overshadowed the tarn. 'Brid,' he whispered.

All along it had been Gwion who had betrayed them. Somehow he wasn't surprised – he had never liked the man's eyes. He looked at the hacked bodies around them. Gwion's was not amongst them. The treacherous priest was after Caspar and his Brid.

He turned to the others and pointed wildly to the sharpened peak that stabbed at the sky. 'Spar and Brid! They are still in danger!'

Around the mouth of the cave lay the remains of recent kills and from its dark mouth came a familiar hissing like the sound of the sea rushing over rocks, loud, insistent and compelling. The sound came from snakes and he hated snakes.

The place stank of death and Caspar's skin felt clammy with fear. He had harboured a mortal fear of snakes ever since Cailleach had captured him in the Boarchase Forest and wrapped him up in her sinuous arms, breathing sibilant words of lust across his face.

The cave was writhing with coiling shapes, hundreds of them. But why was Trog afraid? The animal normally liked nothing more than to seek and destroy these legless reptiles but now the fearless terrier was cowering behind Brid.

Caspar pulled his eyes away from the gloom of the cave and looked at the young Maiden. She swallowed hard and smiled bravely. 'Well, who's going to look first, you or me?'

Caspar gulped; his legs felt weak. He couldn't go into the cave. He was petrified by the merest thought of snakes but he couldn't possibly let Brid go first. He must protect her. As Brid moved forward, answering her question for herself, he snatched at her arm and pulled her back. 'No, I'll go.'

'We'll go together,' she suggested, looking fearfully at the threshold of death before them. But they took only one more step forward before leaping back as a long snake lashed out like a bullwhip, its mouth gaping open ready to strike. It would have caught Brid's leg if it hadn't been for Trog.

Like the precursor to lightning, the dog burst out from behind her ankles and latched onto the neck of the vast fifteen-foot black and yellow viper, before it was halfway across its strike. The hound was lifted up and lashed back and forth, beaten against the cave wall, but he held on tenaciously, a crimson cowl covering his neck and shoulders. Caspar couldn't tell if it was Trog's blood or the snake's. Despite Brid's screams of dismay, as she watched her dog being beaten against the rocks, Caspar could do nothing to help. There was a shrill cry as the dog's teeth finally sliced through the scales of the snake and punctured its spinal column. The serpent slumped lifelessly. Trog staggered up and limped towards Brid, wagging his tail.

Caspar could no longer hear the all-enveloping sound of hissing snakes and wondered if the immense noise had not just been the echo of this one vast serpent reverberating throughout the cave. But, as he stepped forward and his eyes adjusted to the dark, he realized he was wrong.

The hissing returned. Immediately in front of him what looked like a hundred snakes awaited his next step. Their wide mesmerizing eyes fixed his and their forked tongues quivered with anticipation, their necks arched back, ready to strike. Behind the first rank of poised snakes, countless others, their necks reaching up into the air, swayed back and forth like tall grasses. Their combined breath caressed an oval object, which floated at the centre of the chamber in mid-air, buoyed on the breathy cushion of their united hisses. Cream in colour and veined with blue marbling, it was no bigger than a fist. Despite the snakes, Caspar found his gaze compelled to the oval sphere, transfixed by its unworldly sorcery. He had no doubt that he beheld the Druid's Egg.

The nearest snake spat and Caspar stepped slowly back in horror. He tried to run but tripped. As he fell, the viper lashed out towards him, but Trog was there, flinging himself past Caspar's panic-stricken body.

The dog was too slow to catch the serpent in his jaws and the snake's curving fangs punctured his hide just beneath the throat. Trog let out an agonized squeal, limped precariously away from the mouth of the cave and collapsed.

His noble sacrifice had given Caspar enough time to retreat. 'There must be a thousand of them,' he gasped, reaching forlornly for the snake-catcher.

Brid caught the dog in her arms and tried to comfort him. 'Oh Trog,' she despaired. 'I have nothing for snakebites.' She hugged the dog to her while she raised her eyes to examine the cave and the Druid's Egg.

Caspar followed her gaze. 'Look,' he pointed at the arch of stone above the cave mouth. 'There's an inscription.' His eyes scanned across the weather-worn runes carved into the rock.

Brid moved a little closer and read aloud.

'This is the threshold. Wise is he to have got thus far but wiser still he who turns back now. What lies within was begat from the combined labours of a thousand serpents. It is the seed of an unnatural power, and such power is an ill womb where foes from friends are bred.'

'But we have to use that power,' Caspar said heavily, his mind grappling with the enormity of the Egg's fantastical properties. He was suddenly aware of powerful wing beats above them. A big black shape was taking form.

'When the sword entered the moonstone, it released the runespell, drawing the beasts of legend to us and giving them form. We've summoned their spirits from the Otherworld. If they grasp the Egg before us, they will be free to control the earth again.' Brid stood up, trembling. 'Help me raise the sword.'

Caspar stumbled to her and put his hand on the hilt. The moment he touched the weapon, he sensed the throbbing energy of the moonstone rippling through it.

'Great Mother, help us,' Brid pleaded.

Impaled halfway down the length of the sword, the moonstone flashed and swirled with blue-white energy. As the Maiden summoned the Goddess, Caspar sensed her strength grow. Though he could not see them, Caspar was certain that he sensed the presence of the other two priestesses of the Trinity as Brid's small, slender arms lifted the weighty sword higher without his help.

'Spar, let go and get the Egg,' she ordered, fearfully gritting her teeth, her eyes focused on the black shimmering apparition that hovered above her. Wispy claws sharpened into hard definition and a long warty snout pushed down out of the murky cloud towards them.

Caspar stepped back and stared at the shimmering air around Brid. Like the dragon's, the shadowy auras of Morrigwen and Keridwen condensed out of the charged atmosphere. They lent their strength to Brid as she held the sword aloft to defend them from the beast who hovered like a giant vulture above them.

Brid turned to speak and Caspar heard a trinity of voices as her words mingled with the other priestesses'. 'Complete your quest. This is your time. Take the Egg. You are the Seeker. Do it now!'

Rich reds and golds began to colour the dragon's outline.

The hazy contours crystallized into detail: scales, a barbed tail, long rows of curving fangs and a vast maw that inhaled deeply to fill the furnace of its belly. A spurt of fire gushed from the dragon's shimmering mouth. Though it was still not fully formed, the flames had life and energy. Caspar could feel their scorching heat. But as the blast of churning flames struck the runesword the fire parted. Torrents of red, orange and blue flame were channelled aside, like the tumbling waters of a spating river dividing round a boulder.

He stood in the protective lee of the sword while the fire circled away and gushed into the cave mouth, burning alive the first ranks of snakes. The courage in Caspar's heart chilled as he watched the vipers shrivel in the crackling flames. Then his mind was galvanized, alarmed that the fire might destroy the Egg. Or if it cracked . . .

All was lost if the Egg cracked. He had to stop the dragon. Taking his bow, he aimed and loosed an arrow. He didn't know what else he could do. It needed only one well-placed shot, but it had to be accurate since the dragon's armour plating of scales was impenetrable except at the throat, which it kept protectively coiled. Brid held up the runesword like a shield and he fired again and again, but his arrows were ineffectual, glancing off the dragon's scales.

He could see the beast more vividly now. Its wingspan was thirty or forty feet across, its body a pale leathery green with a long coiling tail. But it was still not quite real; its translucent shape shimmered and wavered between the two worlds. Only the fire was real as it scorched the atmosphere and consumed the air.

Caspar's quiver was emptying rapidly. The dragon's shadowy falcate claws raked at the sky and Caspar could feel the disturbed air though he could not yet focus on its flesh. For one brief moment the torrent of scarlet and gold flames roaring from the dragon's maw was sucked back into its monstrous belly as the beast drew breath. Caspar seized his opportunity and burst forward until he was beneath its bloated throat. Drawing a steady breath, he pulled back the bow-string as taut as it would go, sucking in a deep scorching breath to get maximum tension on the string.

His father would be proud, he knew it. At last he let the arrow fly and the second the string slapped his left wrist and the bow sung, he knew it was enough. The quarrel split the dragon's soft palate and the air around Caspar blazed as the insubstantial beast was absorbed back into the Otherworld.

The air was suddenly cold and he could again hear the hissing sound of snakes. Caspar, however, did not turn to look at them but looked out towards the far horizon. Angry thunderheads blackened the skyline and at first he thought it was a storm brewing, but as the dark rolling mass approached, three more fire-breathing beasts began to take form out of the cloud.

'We've little time,' Brid stated with controlled calmness. The sound of Morrigwen and his mother was now barely detectable. 'We might have destroyed one dragon but three is impossible and if they crack the Egg and spill out the magic into the atmosphere, the rest of the beasts of power will become whole. You must get the Egg now.'

'But how do I get it, Brid?'

Caspar looked in despair at the snakes. The dragon's fire had burnt scores of them. Their black shrivelled corpses littered the cavern floor like charred sticks from a raked-out fire. But over three score still remained, swaying above their dead companions. Their tongues flickered upwards, their combined breath still supporting the precious talisman.

It was the most perfectly formed thing he had ever seen and, despite the sickening fear that he harboured for the abhorrent reptilian creatures, he felt himself drawn to it.

The Egg was the very symbol of life; whole, perfectly formed and yet so very delicate. Its surface was a smooth pearly white threaded with blue gossamer marbling. It was as unremarkable as any other egg, but he sensed the potential of its power, knew that he beheld a talisman that could sway the destiny of the world. Yet it was as perfect and as delicate as a newborn baby – and just as vulnerable.

'I can't get to it, Brid,' he cried helplessly. 'There's no way I can get it. The snakes . . .'

He was far more petrified of the squirming legless creatures than he was of the approaching shimmering forms of dragons, though they were a thousand times more dangerous. The snakes could not come out and attack him, that would mean abandoning the Egg, and yet he was terrified of them. His mind was filled with the image of Cailleach coiling him in her snake-like arms and sucking at his breath.

'You've got to,' Brid yelled at him before her voice was drowned in the thunder of wing beats.

One of the dragons was nearly on them but, instead of sweeping above Brid and Caspar, it dipped below the ridge and beat back on its wings to hang in mid-air like a bird of prey. It shrieked out an appalling scream, dodging and darting as a volley of javelins were hurled up from below, peppering the air around it. The unmistakable clank of armour heralded the appearance of a gauntleted hand on the lip of the ridge on which Brid and Caspar stood. Ceowulf held a spear aloft and launched it at the dragon's throat. More men clambered up, thrusting javelins at the insubstantial beasts until eight knights stood side by side before them, holding back the dragons.

And then Hal was there too. He looked faint with exhaustion and his limbs drooped but his eyes were alive with excitement. To Caspar's relief, his uncle took no more than a moment to assess the situation.

'Brid, the sword,' he commanded. 'Give me the sword.' He frowned briefly at the moonstone impaled near the hilt of the weapon before roughly pushing Brid aside. 'Stay there, out of harm's way,' he growled. Caspar instantly knew that his uncle's harsh tone was not born from a need to command but out of protective love for the girl.

The raven-haired youth held the sword out sideways and made a few practice swings though he grimaced with pain and winced as the movement stressed his left arm. Blood oozed through the white bandage above his elbow.

'The moonstone alters the feel a little but I don't think it'll matter,' Hal announced to them through gritted teeth. His black brows pressed down until his eyes were barely visible in the darkness of his face. 'I will have to do it with one cut and, Spar, you've got to get there before the Egg falls.'

Caspar tried to think above the roar of the dragons as Ceowulf, Grinwal and the other knights held them back. He nodded weakly at his uncle. He tried hard to think only of the Egg but had to draw the image of his mother into the forefront of his mind to sweep away his horror of the snakes.

'Ready,' Hal demanded impatiently as he drew his sword back sideways so the blade was parallel to the ground.

Caspar didn't think he would ever be ready but he nodded all the same. If Hal said he could do it, he could do it. For a brief moment it was as if nothing had ever changed and they were back in the Yellow Mountains of Torra Alta and Hal was leading him off on another hare-brained adventure that Branwolf would later punish them for. But the moment was fleeting and grim reality loomed. This mattered, this mattered more than anything else had ever mattered before.

Crouched on tightly sprung legs, Caspar prepared to leap forward just behind the cutting blade of the sword. His uncle began to advance, swinging the runesword in an intricately powerful weave. Caspar looked at the snakes and froze. He just couldn't do it.

'Spar,' Brid's voice pleaded. 'For Torra Alta's sake, Spar, run!'

The image of his home filled Caspar's mind and his fear was swamped by his sense of duty. Screaming out the Torra Altan war-song to allay his dread and steel his courage, he spurted forward behind the scything blade. The sword whistled as it spun out of Hal's hands, sheering sideways through the air in a series of flat, elliptical loops. The steel edge sliced through the necks of the snakes, felling them like ears of wheat before him. Then the Egg was falling. Caspar lunged forward, his arms outstretched, his eyes fixed on the delicate Egg as it fell towards the solid rock floor. He could hear the triumphant roar of the dragons as they anticipated the freedom that would come with the Egg's destruction.

His body brushed through the falling snakes, fountains of blood gushing upwards as the bodies of the decapitated beasts still swayed upright. He reached forward as the Egg came hurtling towards the ground, just managing to cup his hand beneath it as his body thumped onto rock, pinning the headless bodies of the serpents beneath him.

He had it. He held the Egg. He could feel the surging power wash through his body. He grasped it in both hands, looking deep into its wondrous patterns, marvelling at the perfect delicacy of its oval shape. Then he felt the agonizing pain stab through the back of his neck. First came the needle-like jabs as fangs punctured his flesh then the whip-like sting of poison being injected into his bloodstream. He could feel his body weakening, and he slumped to his knees amongst the carnage, concentrating all his thoughts on keeping his hands cupped under the Egg, cradling it like a baby to the very last.

Simultaneously Hal and Brid ran forward, crunching over the crisp and charred carcasses and rolling on the squelching bodies of those hewn down by the sweep of the runesword. Through a blurry daze, Caspar saw Hal deftly cut down the last snake and tentatively crouch down beside him. Someone was gently prising open his fingers, freeing him from the Egg and, although he could no longer see, he knew it was Brid.

Hal scooped him up and he lay slumped in his arms. 'Just one snake. It must have been the moonstone that stopped the sword from slicing through that last snake, but that was enough.'

Caspar's mind was working but he couldn't move, speak or respond as he slid into a stupor. He was vaguely aware of echoing speech and people's hazy features around him but he was unable to feel or react. He sensed a power near him. At first he thought it was the moonstone but gradually realized it was the Egg. He relaxed: she had the Egg, that was all that mattered. He could die now, die in peace, content that they held the power.

'Lay him by the dog and keep him warm,' Brid commanded, her voice unfaltering.

In utter exhaustion, Caspar could only raise his blurry eyes and watch as he lay on his side, staring out of the mouth of a cave. Crouched on the ledge in front of him was a vast beast with hunched shoulders and a long neck like a vulture. His green scaly snout jutted forward and splayed out to form two cave-like nostrils. White fangs, the length of walrus tusks, pushed out between serrated lips. With wings neatly folded and hunched onto angular legs, he crouched perfectly still – apart from a long barbed tail that twitched back and forth like a cat's. His skin was a shimmering green, glistening with points of silver and gold, and his emerald eyes seemed to be filled with ancient wisdom.

Strange, Caspar thought dreamily, that those dazzling eyes should be so very like Brid's. The dragon's back was ridged with barbed armoured plates and he stank. Foul gastric juices boiling inside his belly reeked like charred and rotted fish. Caspar wondered whether it wasn't the rank smell that was stopping him from slipping completely into oblivion. Even from here he could feel the double beat of the monster's heart. He vaguely wondered why it wasn't attacking but soon the effort became too much. He closed his eyes and let himself slide like a feather drifting down on still air from the top of a high tower – falling, tumbling, gliding into the abyss of the unknown world that lingered just the other side of dreaming.

'Is he dead?'

Caspar could hear his uncle's voice; it was clipped and taut with strain. He wondered whether Hal was talking about him and tried to open his eyes to reassure his kinsman but he couldn't.

'No, but he's not doing as well as the dog. Feel Trog's heartbeat. It's strong and even now.' It was Brid's voice, soft, caring and deeply concerned, the voice she always used when tending the sick. 'Trog will recover, though he might not care for killing snakes again.' Her tone was steady as she kept her emotions tightly in check. 'I'd stake my scrip that Ophidian snake-catchers have a natural immunity to snakebites. I should imagine the resistance to snakebites is bred into them. It's in their blood.'

'But not in Spar's.' The words faltered on Hal's lips.

Caspar knew Hal's words were significant but couldn't quite grasp what they meant. Did it matter that, unlike the dog, he lacked resistance to snakebites? He didn't know, didn't care terribly anymore; he just wanted to feel warm again.

'Will he . . . ?' Hal's sentence was left unfinished.

'Keep him warm,' Brid ordered laconically as Caspar heard the rustling noises that he associated with the priestess rummaging through her precious herb scrip. 'I don't think I have anything that will counteract it,' she despaired.

Caspar could hear a grating sound that he couldn't place and then he felt a tingling energy close by. It was the moonstone. Brid must be dragging the runesword across the stony ground to bring the orb closer to him. He could feel her hands grip his and his mind slipped away into the dazzling white world of the Druid's Eye.

It eased the terrible choking pain that stilled his blood. He felt lost in a mist but then Brid was guiding him, drawing him towards the light. All around him snakes writhed and hissed in a knotted coil, thousands of sinuous creatures spitting at him. One seemed to be swallowing his leg whole and another his arm. The jaws peeled back and he could see the scaly body stretch and the shape of his foot bulging inside its maw. He would be swallowed alive.

Then Brid looked into his eyes and the snake was gone. He stumbled but Brid's guiding hand held him up. She seemed to be struggling. Using both hands, she was dragging him, tears sparkling on her cheeks as she braced herself against his weight. Grunting, she heaved him after her, always towards the light.

Then *she* was there. He felt like a baby being rocked back and forth. Giant arms embraced him and he felt blissfully happy. He didn't need to open his eyes to know he was in the comfort of his mother's arms. He could hear her soft honey-silk voice caressing his ears as she cradled him, singing as sweetly as a summer breeze sighing through a leafy glade, like a skylark climbing to the heavens on the notes of its lament.

'He's dying,' Brid said simply, 'and I cannot help him.' She was sobbing. 'I have brought him to you.'

'Thank you.' Keridwen's voice was filled with pain but she didn't cry as Brid was doing. She merely continued to sing, filling him with the knowledge of her love, keeping him warm and comforted to the very end, easing his passage to the other side.

'It is part of the cycle.' Keridwen's voice was soft and soothing though the sadness was so deep it was almost beautiful. Caspar could have wept for her. 'Death is part of the cycle because without it there can be no rebirth.'

The boy lay there excluding everything from his mind except his mother's blissful touch. This was what he had missed all his life. She had been taken from him before he could remember but, somewhere deep in his subconscious, he recognized the delight of her embrace.

He was aware of a change in his mother's emotions and she looked up. He turned his head to follow her gaze. Through the threads of white gossamer that seemed to veil the dreamlike world of his trance, he could see a figure approaching very slowly, very painfully, with broken hobbling steps.

Her bedraggled hair fell in wisps around her shoulders and her clothes hung like a tattered standard from her emaciated body. He didn't recognize her face; it was little more than a skull. She was leaning on someone, someone small but filled with caring that intensified her strength. Just for a moment he thought he glimpsed a swirl of chestnut curls and big pleading hazel eyes. May, he thought, surprised by his sudden sense of hopeful expectancy, but then her hazy image faded away, unable to reach this part of his subconscious. The shrunken creature hobbled towards them alone.

When she spoke, he recognized her instantly. Morrigwen's eyes were glazed and unseeing but, behind their opaque surface, he knew they still sparkled with a brilliant azure blue, flecked with the shards of silver-white. He sensed the love of the Great

Mother burning brightly within them, giving them colour and life. At first she seemed strangely confused as if woken from a deep sleep. Blurrily, she stared at them uncomprehendingly for a moment.

'I must save Torra Alta. You must let me,' she began. 'Don't make me sleep.' But as her eyes fell on Caspar they suddenly focused and it was as if her other thoughts were swept away in a tide of urgent concern. She reached out and put a bony hand on the boy's forehead, marking him with the runes of healing.

'It is too late for that,' Keridwen sighed. 'Let him go peacefully.'

'Have I taught you nothing?' the Crone slammed her words into Keridwen's face. 'Must I be dragged from my pallet, barely able to lift my own eyelids, to remind you and Brid of your lessons? Has all my teaching been in vain? When I'm gone there's only you two left to hold up the knowledge of the old ways, and to think I have taught you so little. The boy must live. It is he and not us that must wield the Egg. The Goddess decreed that the sword was for Hal and the Egg for Spar. He is the heir to Torra Alta and must prove the castle's dedication to Her future worship.'

There was fury and scorn in the old woman's voice though Caspar sensed no resentment from the other two women. They looked at her in dismay.

'Let me help you.' Brid ran to catch the ancient Crone as she stumbled.

'You cannot help me much longer,' Morrigwen sighed. 'Mine is a wound that cannot be cured; it is age and I have fought it this long to see the tides of time change, and must hold on still a little longer. My only duty is to see all you young fools through.' She bent over coughing and wheezing, then wearily dragged her skeletal hand across her furrowed brow.

'I cannot think clearly,' she moaned, rocking her head from side to side as if to shake off the deep lethargy that drained her strength. 'I'm unnaturally tired. They made me sleep.' She frowned uncertainly at the boy for a moment while she gathered her thoughts. Suddenly she stiffened with resolve. 'Open a deep vein in the dog, a big thick deep vein,' she ordered. 'And, Brid, take a stem of reed and push it into the vein. Then cap the end of the reed with a small bladder. You must have something in your scrip.'

'The skin of a toad?' the girl questioned.

'Yes. Collect the dog's blood and then slit open a big vein on the boy and insert the reed and squeeze the dog's blood into him.'

Caspar's brain was swirling. The numbness was fading and he felt a deep and fearful pain surge through his body. He wanted to scream but he didn't have the strength. He could feel his mother being dragged from him. One second her arms were tight around him then he slipped from her grasp and she was desperately reaching out for him, a swirl of fiery red hair washing around her shoulders. Her eyes, deep vivid violet, wide and imploring, yearned with protective love.

She began to turn grey and frost over. Her muscles jerked into spasm, ridging the tendons on the back of her hand until they were like hooked talons, clawing for help. Her eyeballs were like cold hard sapphires glazed over with an icy film. Her stretched lips faded from lush deep pink to pale white, to deathly blue, and her mouth stuck open in a scream, a scream of unbearable agony.

'Mother,' Caspar spluttered, desperate to save her. 'Mother!' He wrenched and struggled to claw at her but still she slipped back into the frozen torture of the glacier. Caspar felt himself being dragged up towards the pain of the living.

His hands were still hooked around the moonstone. In his desperate efforts to drag his mother from the claws of the glacier, he had somehow wrenched the orb free from the shaft of the blade.

'I'm not convinced that's a healthy thing to do,' someone was muttering but Caspar couldn't quite place the voice. 'The dog's blood might kill him. It's not healthy to mix man and beast.'

'Don't meddle in things you don't understand.' Brid's voice was harsh.

Caspar was aware of the mutterings still continuing though they now grumbled a little further off. 'And I don't believe my eyes. I can't believe my eyes. That's a dragon sitting there behind us and I just daren't look.'

'I'm not going to look.'

Caspar recognized the last voice: it was Kay's. What was Kay doing here? He groaned and tried to raise his head.

'How are you feeling?' someone else whispered very close by. Caspar blinked and looked up into familiar olive-green eyes and his uncle's grin.

Caspar tried to speak but his voice only came out as a weak splutter. Hal gripped his hand, then squeezed it tight. He opened his eyes again and looked up into Hal's face, aware that his uncle had been crying.

Something wet and slobbery was annoying his right ear. Caspar slowly turned his head to be faced with Trog's enormous white snout butted up against his face. 'I thought he was dead.'

'Lucky for you he wasn't,' Brid remarked softly. 'We put some of his blood into your veins so that it could fight the poison within you.'

'Oh.' Caspar shrugged, caring little for the details. He felt wretched and the fear for his mother swamped all other thought. He could still hear her agonized scream ringing on and on in his head, haunting him, pleading with him to save her. He tried to sit up but Brid pushed him back down, ordering him to rest.

'You'll feel well again soon,' she told him. 'Trog is already much stronger and it's only been a few hours.'

'A few hours!' Caspar had thought only a matter of minutes had passed.

'We're going to stay here tonight; tomorrow you'll feel a great deal fitter and –'

'We can't possibly stay here. The temperature will drop at dusk. We'll freeze,' the man whom Caspar had heard muttering objected and this time he recognized Grinwal's voice. 'Ceowulf, aren't you going to take command here rather than let us all be ordered about by this young girl? We should move the boy now while there's still some light left.'

Ceowulf laughed dismissively. 'Brid has been in charge right from the very beginning. She is the Maiden.'

There was something in his words that Caspar didn't understand though he knew what the knight meant. Brid represented the Great Mother and, yes, in a way she had always been in charge all along. She was so very much more than just a young girl.

Brid showed no sign of reacting to the knights' conversation as she continued to tend Caspar. There was a wistful look in her eyes as if she were troubled by something else altogether. 'We won't freeze,' she nodded towards the dragon whose snout was level with their heads. Holding the Egg in one hand, she stepped over and patted his nose. The monster batted an eyelid in obeisance to her touch. 'Light a fire for us, dragon,' she ordered imperiously.

Hal snorted. 'Doesn't she ever learn? No self-respecting chap likes to be spoken to like that.'

'Why ever not?' Brid replied. 'Trog doesn't mind.'

Caspar was quite taken aback when Hal laughed. He sounded almost as though he were agreeing with her.

The youth's raven-black hair flopped forward over his face as he stooped over his nephew. 'She's beautiful, isn't she?' he confided as Caspar began to feel rapidly better. The younger Torra Altan looked up at Brid. Her hair was matted, her breeches torn and stained and her face was a bruise of colours. Hal had never before thought her beautiful when she looked like that.

The dragon dipped his head and flew off to snuffle together some dry wood from the lower slopes. He carried the load in his jaws like a bird preparing to make a nest and carefully placed the bundle of wood by the humans. He breathed gently over it and the fire darted into life.

Just as Caspar began to look more comfortable, Brid's attention was caught by the scarlet fire-drake, which had finally found them. It struggled up over the ledge and advanced, with its ruff raised, hissing and spitting towards the moonstone. Brid gave a stifled gasp of dismay. Caspar sat up with a start. 'What's the matter?'

'The Druid's Eye! Look!' Brid held the orb out towards him. It appeared to be impregnated with smoke. There was a thin open wound where the sword had gashed through its skin and cut deep into the crystalline heart. Smoke from the dragon must have seeped in through the gash. The smooth creamy patterns that had swirled and danced over the iridescent orb were gone, replaced by clouds of thick black smoke and flashes of fiery red that sizzled deep within its form. Brid pressed her palms to the orb.

'Morrigwen!' Urgently she tried to summon the old Crone but the Druid's Eye remained closed, a haze of dun smoke choking the once-lucid orb. 'I can't summon her,' Brid sighed. 'For the first time I can safely use the Druid's Eye, because we are no longer afraid of the creatures of power following us, and now it is closed to me. The breath of the dragon has ruined it. I saw her while you were unconscious. I'm sure something was wrong with her.'

'Did she say how they fared? Did she mention Torra Alta or the Vaalakans?' asked a worried Caspar.

Brid shook her head and tugged at her plait. 'No, though she seemed confused and strangely distracted. Perhaps she was sleeping when we summoned her or perhaps the forgetfulness of old age has finally crept up on her.' The Maiden shrugged, tossing her thick plait dismissively over her shoulder. 'It's no use worrying; the runes of war will hold until the end of Fallow so we still have time – a few days yet. As soon as we have Keridwen safely with us, we will see them all again.'

'But Gwion said he had destroyed the runes,' Caspar despaired.

'Gwion was mad; we should not heed his testimony,' Brid stated calmly. 'We still have time.'

She scooped up the salamander in her hand and let it wriggle beneath the folds of her shirt. 'I suppose at least the heat of the dragon's breath will keep Keridwen warm.' Resignedly she reknotted the leather thongs that formed a net around the orb and slid it round her neck next to the fire-drake.

Ceowulf sat on a small boulder, his thigh and head bandaged, but still he kept his sword drawn and looked alertly around him for danger while Cybillia sat at his side. Caspar couldn't imagine how the Jotunn noblewoman had made it all the way up here.

Grinwal was still grumbling. 'I'm trying very hard to believe that creature is there, but I'm failing. I mean, kiss my lance and shield, I'm looking at a live dragon and it hasn't eaten me. Is it the young lady's eyes that command it?'

'No, Father, it's that egg,' Kay told him. 'Haven't you noticed how everybody and everything watches it? Even the very mountain seems to be looking at it.'

'Everyone except Hal,' Grinwal pointed out.

Hal's attention was fixed on Brid as he continually sighed, 'She's beautiful, isn't she?'

Brid was gently soothing the dog who had crawled lovingly into the cradle of her lap. The girl's clothes were in rags. Half of her hair had worked free from her braid and her elfin face was covered in smudges of soot and blood. She looked as if her mind were elsewhere.

'I thought you only liked complacent girls in beautiful dresses.' Caspar stumbled over the words, struggling to pull his mind away from the fascination of the Druid's Egg. 'She's always telling people what to do, her hair's a mess and she's as grubby as a blacksmith's apron. You've never liked anyone like that before.'

'Who are you to tell me what I like or don't like?' Hal had evidently forgotten his worry over Caspar's fate and had returned to his normal self. 'When I was fighting in the valley and thought I was going to die, I realized that all I wanted was Brid. There was suddenly nothing else that mattered.'

Caspar sighed and suddenly felt deeply alone. He had lost. He had wanted Brid right from the very start but had known that his only hope in winning her lay in Hal's fickle attitude and rejection of the Maiden. But now Hal wanted her and not for her lithe, curvaceous body nor her bewitching eyes. He wanted Brid for herself and herself alone.

The auburn-haired youth could see Ceowulf hold Cybillia close and wrap her in his cloak. The girl's head rested against his shoulder. Hal looked towards them and then towards Brid. He stood up as if suddenly decided.

'You'll be all right for a moment, won't you?' he whispered to his nephew. 'There's something I need to say to her.'

As he got up and left him, Caspar knew he had lost Hal too. Hal had always been his constant companion and now he had abandoned him in favour of Brid. It was natural and understandable but he felt terribly alone, alone with his fears for Torra Alta and his dreadful grief as he remembered his mother's pain.

The raven-haired youth sat down next to Brid and gently took her hand in his while lifting her chin to face him. He brushed back a drift of hair from her face. Caspar thought his heart would break. He had expected his uncle to say something eloquent and irresistible to female ears but he said nothing. He leant forward and kissed her on the forehead and then on both cheeks and finally on the lips, long and lingering.

Caspar closed his eyes against his pain. After all he loved them both.

Chapter 25

'Get the women down below. Get them down into the cellars,' the Baron thundered over his shoulder. Staggering backwards down the stairs, he was desperately hacking at a fanged creature with long clawed arms and hairless leathery skin. Reared up onto its hindlegs, the roach-backed troll towered over the Baron and bellowed like a bear as it thrashed out with raking claws.

'The trolls have scaled the keep walls,' Branwolf warned. 'Dozens of them! Get the women down to the cellars!'

Rosalind was nearest to the bottom of the staircase and stood stupefied, staring up at the fighting men while the rest of the women retreated to the far wall. Shrieking Vaalakans followed the trolls, huge men with long, almost white hair. May focused instantly on the war plaits, the hair braided into several strands then knotted with bones twined through the ends. Some had strings of ears looped around their necks; others bore the raised decorative scars of self-mutilation across their bare chests; all rippled with greased muscles.

She focused on one more than any other. His smooth breast was bare. Reindeer-hide leggings were laced to his legs and lower body. The symbol of an axe was carved on his chest and it rippled and moved as he hefted his huge weapon. She watched as it swung through the air, slicing its arc towards Rosalind's neck. Her head splattered against the far wall before her body hit the ground.

For a moment the world seemed to go silent and May stumbled back against the stone wall. Vaalakans poured down the central staircase, the remaining Torra Altan men forming a wedge to hold them back, fighting furiously in the narrow confines. One swordsman rushed through the Vaalakans, who had already made the hall, and alone held the staircase for several minutes. When he fell, his mutilated body was trampled underfoot as more Vaalakans pressed their way into the lower keep. The Belbidians fought on, determined to stand to the very last. Though they killed ten barbarians for each one of their own that fell, still the Vaalakans came on.

Branwolf had Morrigwen by the arm and was shoving her towards the trap-door that led down into the cellars. 'We can escape through the cellars. There's a tunnel to the curtain wall,' he cried to his men. 'Get the women down there.'

He stood over the door, cutting and thrusting viciously as more Vaalakans swarmed towards them. Only twenty men stood around the few remaining women. Elaine fell in the chaos as a Vaalakan axe hurtled into their midst but she was on her feet again, clutching her arm and struggling towards May.

'Ma!' May tried to fight her way towards her flame-haired mother but was swept back by the press of Torra Altan women. She was aware of Cook grabbing her hand and dragging her into the tunnel.

'Ma! Ma! Where are you?' the girl cried out in the gloom, terrified that she would lose her mother in the chaos. 'Ma!'

Pip! There at least was Pip. He found her hand and held on.

'Go with them,' the Baron yelled at the Captain. 'Take a rope and go now. I'll hold the rear and light the powder kegs. You must stay with the women.'

There was still a thin shaft of light coming down the trap-door as they slipped into the tunnel, running in maddened panic. Ma was just ahead. May could see her now, holding Morrigwen as they stumbled and twisted through the labyrinth. Elaine's right arm hung limply at her side. Then they were plunged into darkness as the trap-door slammed shut, muffling the roars from above. May could hear footsteps running behind them and her heart beat in her mouth, fearing they were

Vaalakans'. Her thoughts were swept away as a flash of bright yellow light and a thunderous explosion snatched away her air. The blast hurled them to the floor.

They were quickly on their feet again, following the Captain's lead until he drew them to a halt. May heard footsteps behind them in the dark and she held her breath.

'The explosion will delay them.' It was the Baron's voice. 'The blast has sealed the entrance to the tunnel.' His voice was steady. 'Now listen; the tunnel runs east and comes out just within the curtain wall. When we get there we're all going to climb down towards the river. If we're lucky they won't spot us in the dark until we're well away. They may well think we all died in the explosion back there.'

'Are we the last ones?' Pip asked in a small voice.

'Hush, child,' Elaine soothed. 'We'll make it, Pip. We'll make it through.'

Branwolf pushed his way forward until he was at the Captain's side. 'Have you got the rope ready?'

The tall thin man grunted grimly.

The nobleman drew a steady breath and drew back a small wooden shutter. Moonlight lit the narrow passage and he scanned the sorry party around him as if counting numbers. Then he lifted a metal bar from the passage wall and pulled the large stone inwards.

Silently he signalled for them to creep out through the low, narrow opening and into the moon-cast shadows beneath the curtain wall. May felt like a rabbit emerging from its bolt-hole as she crawled out of the tunnel. Scrambling onto the cobbles, she saw that the east quarter of the courtyard was deserted. Black shapes silhouetted in the glow of their firebrands, a few of the Vaalakans were still concentrated around the entrance to the keep. But the castle was alive with the violence of pillage as the barbarians hammered on doors and destroyed everything that could be splintered, crushed or shredded with their axes. No one had yet noticed their small party.

The Captain flung a thick rope over the wall and fastened it securely with grappling irons to the battlements.

Branwolf sent one of the men down the rope first to secure it at the bottom. 'Over you go, quickly. Quickly!' the Baron urged, as he waited for the inevitable attack, his sword in one hand, a short length of fuse rope, its end smouldering with a glowing flame, in the other. Two powder kegs were strapped to his belt.

Five of the women climbed out of the tunnel but then hesitated. The two boys from the kitchens had made it safely through the attack and they slithered quickly over the wall, followed by Frieda, who had been stricken by the ergot mould earlier in the siege.

The Baron turned to the Captain. 'You must take Morrigwen. You'll have to carry her. She's too weak to lower herself.'

'But, I can't, my lord. I can't leave you to stand alone.'

'I'll hold the rear. You take her. It's an order. Over the wall with you.'

'My lord,' he assented as he swung Morrigwen's frail body onto his back and she clung to his neck. The Captain's long fingers coiled around the rope and he swung himself over the wall.

'I'll see you at the bottom,' Branwolf replied. 'Now get moving.'

Suddenly there was a scream of outrage as two Vaalakans spotted the escape. Their outcry was swiftly followed by the fiendish roar of a troll, charging out of the dark. The creature loped awkwardly towards them. Without thought, one of the last Torra Altan soldiers flung himself at the troll, leaving the Baron and two remaining soldiers to fight off the two Vaalakans.

'Get everyone over the wall,' Branwolf screamed at Elaine.

They were the last of the women and children left on the castle battlements now. Elaine shoved her son towards the rope and he slithered over the wall, his teeth gritted against his fear of the precipitous height.

May froze. The sides of the castle fell away from her for what seemed like an eternity into the giddy blackness.

423

'Get to the rope,' her mother screamed.

May looked over the parapet and as she did she saw Frieda slip. She seemed to fall forever, cartwheeling and tumbling, her wailing screams filling the canyon, before she smashed onto the jagged rocks that jutted above the frothy waters of the Silversalmon.

'Get over the side, May,' Elaine pleaded. 'You can do it.'

The young girl turned to look helplessly at her mother.

Clutching at her wounded arm, Elaine looked helplessly towards Branwolf as he sliced through the bull-like neck of a Vaalakan warrior. One of the Torra Altan soldiers fell under the crushing blow of the troll, its claws raking across his face and tearing out his eyes. Branwolf stabbed his sword between the troll's shoulder blades but it was too late to save his countryman or the last remaining garrison soldier who was hacked down just as he spun round to help him. An enemy war axe sliced first through his leg and then through his stomach but, in his last breath, he thrust his sword deep into the Northman's naked torso. Only the Baron was left now as another Vaalakan warrior was alerted by the sound of battle. The barbarian slowly but deliberately advanced.

'Branwolf,' Elaine cried. 'Take my daughter. After this one there will be another and then another,' Elaine cried. 'Please, my lord, take my daughter. Give me the powder kegs. If I have them, they won't rush me and I'll be able to hold them just long enough for you to get over the wall. You must save my daughter. You've got time now to do it if I threaten these men with the explosives. I'm not strong enough to carry May. You must take her. Do this for me, as you would do for your own wife, Keridwen.'

'Get over the side, woman!' Branwolf bellowed as he ran forward to meet the Vaalakan. His sword split the man's skull but yet another Vaalakan with a towering antlered head-dress turned away from the keep door and confidently approached.

'I've been cut,' Elaine explained. 'My arm is useless. I won't be able to hold the rope. My life is lost already. Better I die here protecting my daughter than fall uselessly onto the rocks below. Please take my daughter. I cannot save her and you must do it for me. I can at least light the powder kegs and hold them back for a moment longer. I must do this for my child. I beg you in the name of the Mother, help me save my child!'

The Baron thrust the fuse rope and powder kegs into the woman's damaged grasp. Reverently he kissed her. 'I do this because you ask me,' he murmured. 'I promise that while I still draw breath I will look after your children.'

May shrieked as the Baron scooped her up into his arms. 'Ma, Ma! Don't!' She beat furiously at the Baron's chest as he strode towards the battlements. 'Ma! No!' Her cries were desperate but she could not resist the Baron's strength as he slid over the wall. With the threat of the drop beneath her, she was forced to grip his neck as he lowered himself over the side.

'I love you, May,' Elaine cried. 'Look for me in another life.'

The big Vaalakan approached, his towering head-dress swaying above his blond head and the skulls of ibex strung about his neck rattling as he marched towards the red-haired woman. In slow, deliberate movements, he flung his axe up into the air, letting it swing through elliptical loops in a taunting, elaborate display as he stalked the woman. That was the last May saw as they slid down the rope towards the cold waters of the Silversalmon. A yellow flash lit the sky above their heads as they slithered the last few feet towards solid ground.

In the darkness she clutched at her orphaned brother.

Chapter 26

'It's already started!' Brid shouted into the rushing air. Her hair streamed out like a pennant behind her, brushing against Caspar's face as he clung to the barbs of the dragon's back. The clap of wing beats mingled with the roar of the wind as they sped across the sky. The exhilaration was breathtaking. He tightened his grip on the dog's collar and pressed forward to look past Brid's shoulders.

Without taking her hands from their tight embrace around Hal's waist, the Maiden turned to look sideways at Caspar. 'There's a change in the air. The tides of time are already changing.'

His mind was too ablaze with the power of the Egg to think clearly about what she meant. It throbbed with the energy of life struggling to break through its shell, trapped angry souls, storming with hatred for his kind, yet eager for his control, too, as long as he focused his will through the Egg. At first it drained his energies and his mind shrank from the ferocity of the beasts he summoned but gradually he was learning to relax as he discovered the extent of his dominion over them. That was extraordinary enough in itself but this . . .

He looked down at the patterns far below, the strange geometric shapes of cultivated fields, the aimless meandering rivers, the vastness of the plains and then the sea. A few spangled sails were keeled over in the stiff breeze, the choppy white horses flickering in the deep blue depths. Around him were the clouds. It was cold, icy cold but it added to the excitement. He was flying, flying higher than the hawks, higher than the eagles.

On Brid's orders, they had delayed their departure for several days. While fashioning a protective scrip for the Egg which she hung around Caspar's neck, she had insisted that they waited until he had recovered enough to properly wield the might of the Egg. She had assured them that they still had time. Though, following Gwion's revelation, Caspar hadn't been so sure.

Precariously, he reached inside his jacket and caressed the Egg. Such power. Smooth and cool like marble, it would have felt as inanimate as stone if it were not for the restless prickling that fed back through his fingertips as he stroked its surface. It was like placing his hand on a steel dungeon door suddenly aware of the pressure of lives that lay imprisoned behind it. And he was the gaoler. In his hands lay the power to release or hold the captives. He felt numbed by the sense of responsibility. He didn't want it. He had wanted to pass the orb to Hal, but Brid had pushed the Egg back into his hands. 'The Goddess wishes it for you, not Hal,' she had told him firmly.

It wasn't like touching the runesword. The sword infused its bearer with courage and a sense of invincible power but it also brought with it a despotic ill-will that possessed the user's mind. When Caspar first touched the Egg, he felt omnipotent, god-like, but the feeling was transitory. Quite suddenly the sense of his own unimaginable power evaporated and his soul bowed before the awesome presence of the Egg. What he sensed was not his power but the energy of creation. This power of life was so much more fearful than the power of death. He had the ability to summon the creatures from the Otherworld, to give them life and let them breathe on the surface of the earth again, his to command, but only while he held the Druid's Egg. He felt very much better when the Egg was hidden away from sight and safely protected from touch.

As they swept over the swell of the Caballan Sea, his mind turned to the Caldean knight and his golden-haired lady and to the long journey they would have to make home. Midst fond farewells and wishes of good luck, Ceowulf and Cybillia had taken all their horses and left the Frosted Peaks to catch a ship for Belbidia. Grinwal confessed that he wished to leave the Camaalian guard and Kay and he had offered Ceowulf their services.

'I've tried for five years now to win that tournament and I'm getting too long in the tooth for it,' he had told them. 'A man should know when it's time to give up chasing impossible dreams. It turns the rest of life sour. I want to enjoy just being who I am again.' He had smiled at Brid. 'Besides there are better causes to serve than my own. Over these last days, you've opened my eyes to the beauty of the world around me.'

When they had turned to leave, Cybillia had grasped Brid's hand. 'After the Vaalakans scarred my cheek, you said you'd heal me so long as I gave thanks to the Great Mother every day. You have healed me and I will give thanks, but not because I promised.' She looked deep into the priestess's dragon-green eyes. 'Every morning as the sun rises I will thank the Great Mother, not for my smooth face, but for life itself. I have found a happiness and freedom of spirit that was forbidden to me by the New Faith.'

Brid's eyes had sparkled with joy as she hugged the girl farewell.

Only the three Torra Altans had remained alone in the Frosted Peaks, kept warm by the breath of the dragon. The salamander periodically poked its head out from the top of Brid's shirt to gape at the vast dragon. It blinked and seemed almost to purr, its flesh darkening with emotion.

Brid had laughed. 'Poor little fire-drake. He must think he's looking at his God.'

She had tossed her gaze towards the steaming monster that crouched over them, the sound of its rushing breath drowning out the noise of the mountain winds. As Caspar carried the Druid's Egg, the creature's vast green eyes stalked his every move.

'It knows; it thinks,' he had said to Brid as he felt its eyes crawling all over him. 'It thinks like you or me – not like Trog.'

Trog had looked up at the mention of his name and cocked

his ear in a curious but helplessly ridiculous expression. The dog then yipped and kicked his heels into the air, throwing himself into a sideways spin that he practised for use in battle. The dragon seemed to smirk in disgust at the little creature and drew back his head fractionally, drawing in a breath. For a moment Caspar feared that the vast monster might breathe out a gush of acid fire over the dog but, before any harm was done, Brid jumped fiercely to her feet and rapped the dragon's vast snout with her knuckles.

'No,' she had scolded as if talking to a small child. The dragon had blinked apologetically as Brid turned to Caspar. 'Spar, you must learn to command through the Egg. It's no good just holding it; you must command.'

Now Caspar held the Egg and the dragon was bending to his will, carrying them northward on powerful, effortless beats of its leathery wings. The boy couldn't help wondering how terrifying this would be for someone afraid of heights. There was nothing, absolutely nothing beneath them except thin air, thousands of feet of thin air.

'Lower. Make him lose height,' Brid anxiously shouted at Caspar. 'Stop willing him higher otherwise we won't be able to breathe.'

Caspar sensed the dragon's disappointment as he encouraged him to spill air from beneath his veined leathery wings. The skin was so finely stretched across the bat-like wings that it was almost transparent. He was disappointed himself. He loved the height.

He could see their shadow carving across the plain of water below. At his command, they swooped down and he could hear, very faintly, the dismayed shouts of sailors on a three-masted schooner. They looked up in disbelief at the creatures flying overhead. Two more dragons swooped down behind them, one of them diving within yards of the ship. As it skimmed the mast, the downbeat from its wings fanned the water, sending the vessel reeling and rocking as the waves sloshed around its wooden hull.

Brid twisted round furiously to face Caspar. 'You must learn to concentrate effectively. They only did that because you thought it.'

Caspar felt guilty. What she said was true. He was showing off, wanting the whole world to know that he had control of this incredible power. He sensed it now, spreading out over the world. The ancient beasts were bowing to his will, turning towards Torra Alta, answering his call to battle. But he must not let his instincts escape to become as wild as the creatures.

The dragon's great wing beats swept them effortlessly across the reach of the Caballan Sea and north-west towards Torra Alta. Hardly able to breathe for the rush of air and the exhilaration of flying, Caspar finally spied land and the distant gleaming peaks of the Yellow Mountains. Home! Soon he would be home. They would fly past Torra Alta on the way to rescue his mother. His heart pounded in his throat.

Now he could see it! The towers of Torra Alta thrust up above the canyon walls, gleaming in the rose of the morning sun, an invincible shield guarding Belbidia from northern attack and yet . . . The blush of morning was too crimson. Columns of black smoke belched into the sky from flickering yellow fires that dotted the canyon floor. Caspar's mind reeled. Clinging to the horned spines of the dragon's back, he hung out sideways, squinting down at the devastation below. White-haired men crawled around all sides of the Tor, even wading through the Silversalmon. Carcasses littered the land. Bodies were heaped in great piles and put to the torch, the crackling flames filling the air with a dreadful stench.

They swooped down low to take a closer look. Dark-haired Belbidian men still entangled with their long bows were dragged by bare-breasted warriors into piles. These heaps of human flesh were not ceremoniously burnt with honour but left to rot as the vultures circled the sky. Sickened with grief and despair, Caspar forced the dragon to circle above the castle.

Like an outer skeleton, Vaalakan war-engines were lashed to what was left of the outer walls. Bodies were still jammed in the parapets where they had fallen. Above the keep spiked a bare flagpole. The Dragon Standard was gone and the west tower was a burnt-out ruin, the once smooth continuous stone of the curtain wall now breached in three places. The keep, however, remained stolidly intact.

'Father,' Caspar yelled out into the bleak ruin. 'Father.' His piercing cry was like an eagle's pealing out of the sky but there was no answer. 'Father,' he cried again but the only reply was a crossbow bolt that rose up out of the smoke and skimmed past his ear. The dragon yawed to the right and the Torra Altans hung on tightly.

'Land,' Hal yelled at his nephew. 'Land now.' The youth was shaking with anger. 'I will kill them. I will kill every last one of them. We must find Branwolf. Branwolf!' he screamed desperately down into the canyon, his words spluttering with rage.

'No,' Brid tugged at the distraught youth. 'No, we must find the Mother. We must bring Keridwen back first. The Goddess promised she would save Torra Alta only when the Trinity was restored and stood united in the castle. We cannot save Torra Alta without her; we must get her first. It's not yet the end of Fallow. The keep still stands. We must release Keridwen.'

Through a haze of choking tears, Caspar stared back at the smouldering towers, that had once been so beautiful; the pale gleaming whinstone was now blackened to slag. He could hardly think. Where was his father? He couldn't face the possibility that Morrigwen, and worse his father, were somewhere amongst the bloody carnage. No, Branwolf must still be holding fast. There was nothing they could do now except find Keridwen. Great Mother, protect us, he prayed, protect Torra Alta and its garrison. Protect Father.

He wrenched his mind away from the chaos and forced himself to look northward towards the barren tundra as he willed the dragon away from his homeland. Parched and bleak, the northern landscape was veined with dried-out riverbeds that had once watered all of Vaalaka with the summer melts from the northern ice-cap. For years now the ice-cap had remained permanently frozen through the summer months and the Dragon Scorch had become totally devoid of surface water – but something was altering. He could sense that feeling, like waking in Ostara or early Merrymoon to find the birds already singing and a different scent in the air. Summer was coming at last. Now he knew what Brid meant when she had said that the tides of time were changing. Vaal-Peor's wintry grip was failing.

They threaded beneath the peaks of the three Black Devils and skimmed across the thin belt of grass that was decayed down to its grey roots by the long winter. A collection of circular tents covered with stretched reindeer hides marked where the Vaalakan women had sheltered through the bitter cold. Caspar shielded his eyes from the glistening whiteness on the horizon.

'The tundra,' Hal pointed ahead of them, releasing his hand from the barbed spike that sprouted from the dragon's back. There was a splintering crash like a sudden clap of thunder and a creaking and groaning as if they had entered the abode of warring giants.

'It's the ice-cap melting. I said it had already started,' Brid cried delightedly. 'The Great Mother be praised, the seasons are restored. Without our realizing it, our travels have taken us to four confluences of energy lines in the Mother's mantle. The lines of power radiating from those four points form the rune of the Mother and, in tracing out this pattern across the earth, we have proclaimed our love to Her. Now the tide has changed. The cycle is restored.'

'Nearly restored,' Caspar corrected her. 'We must still rescue Keridwen.'

Brid nodded. 'But it has already started. In a way, I don't think the Great Mother really wanted the Egg at all. All She wanted was for us to prove our love for Her.' Holding Hal tightly, the priestess stretched out over the dragon's neck to scan the distant ground. 'Down, down here. Look; there's the cairn that marks the confluence,' she shouted ecstatically.

As Caspar complied with the urgency of the girl's wishes,

the dragon swooped suddenly and the youth felt the blood rush to his freckled face. Trog's ears were pressed to his skull and his lips were pulled back from his teeth by the force of the wind. Caspar tightened his grip on the dog. Hal gets to be held by Brid, he thought resentfully, and I get to hold Trog. All this power, all this immense power and it's Hal who gets the prize.

Caspar was amazed by the powerful thrust from the downbeat of the dragon's wings as they neared the parched ground and stirred a cloud of dust into the air. They alighted right alongside the cairn as gently and as gracefully as a lark might have touched down on a twig.

Hal slid down the dragon's leg, clutching hold of the triangular scales to ease himself down the last half-dozen feet. He waited to catch Brid. The Maiden relished his attention, and no longer reproached him for looking after her, so long as the raven-haired youth never attempted to tell her what she could or could not do.

Caspar thumped down onto the hard ground and turned to catch Trog. He pointed to the spot where he knew Keridwen was buried in the grey glacier. The rippled ice-river, wallowing in the valley of the craggy mountains, was very different from when he had last seen it. No longer were there long black shadows clawing out across the filmy layer of snow that had previously frosted the glacier; no longer were the surrounding mountains bleakly stark, their parched grasses dried by the icy wind to old man's whiskers. Now there were tiny crocuses pushing up through the soil and field pansies peppered the gentler slopes. The glacier itself was brighter and a clear glaze of meltwater swam over its surface. Caspar could not only see the changes, he could hear them.

The temperature was rising. As the earth basked in the welcome sun, absorbing its rays, the ground around the glacier warmed and melted the frozen river, the effect spreading upwards through the solid blue-white crystalline layers. The surface creaked and groaned as the ice was melted from beneath. The whole plain seemed to be moving. Crevasses opened up and then snapped shut again like the mouths of gaping crocodiles. Caspar put one foot on the ice and felt it trembling with mobile energy. The flood waters were forming. He flinched back as he heard a giant crack, like the sound of an ogre's thigh-bone splintering. The entire glacier shook.

'Quick! Back on the dragon,' he yelled as they were threatened by a rumble from the slopes above. The peaks at the head of the glacier ruffled and shook out their snow-cloaks. A puff of white billowed up, churning and storming, as it thundered down in a sweeping cascade towards them.

Hal threw Brid up to snatch hold of the barbs at the back of the dragon's neck and scrambled after her. More aware of self-preservation than the rest of them, Trog had run up the dragon's tail and was already up on the creature's back, claws spread wide to balance himself. Caspar lunged for a claw as the great beast took to the air and then scrabbled up to cling on tight alongside the others.

'Fly over the glacier,' Caspar demanded, pointing out the spot where he knew his mother would be. The thundering boom of the avalanche dwindled to a rolling roar and finally a grumbling murmur. The air was choked with dusty particles of snow. The dragon glided backwards and forwards through the glittering haze as Brid and Caspar craned out to the side, scanning the surface of the glacier beneath. Blocks of ice shook and shuddered, great sections folding and subsiding to be swallowed into the meltwaters foaming beneath the glacier's white belly.

'There,' Brid shouted. 'There! I can see her.'

Caspar tried to steady his thoughts as the dark shadowy form of his mother was visible just for a moment in the translucent ice, an arm's length beneath the surface. His eyes fixed the spot as the dragon circled. They just needed to get close enough. The ice was melting and soon he would be able to lift her out.

'Brid, hold this.' He thrust the Egg into the Maiden's hand and slithered down onto the dragon's front claw. Clinging to the great curving nail, he stretched out his hand, skimming the ice-cold water, reaching down towards his mother. But just as his fingers brushed her hand, she vanished.

He cried out in horror as the glacier shifted and water burst up from the crevasses to either side. The point where she lay had fallen through to the roar of the meltwater tumbling below. Caspar gave no time to thought but let go of the dragon's claw and fell through after her.

The water's chill hit him like the flat of an axe blade. The air was shocked from his lungs and, as he plunged deeper, the current hurled him against the river bedrock before he tumbled upright in a froth of bubbles. The swirling waters continued to turn him and over and over. For a split second they spat him teasingly to the surface for a gasp of raw air before he was plunged down again into the deathly cold.

Spar, save yourself. He sensed her thoughts in the water. The water was the substance of life, the element that linked them all and he knew her mind was clawing out towards him.

Caspar kicked on furiously. It was dark beneath the blue white belly of the glacier but, through the storm of water around him, he glimpsed a point of light ahead. They were being swept rapidly towards the open mouth of the glacier. He willed the water to drive them on faster. In these temperatures they would last barely a minute. The churning roar of the meltwaters, pounding against fallen boulders, burst in his head. They seemed to be just sitting there, waiting, as if Vaal-Peor Himself had flung them there in His rage, to break their bodies as they smashed against them.

'Mother!' he shrieked, 'Mother!' He caught a flash of red just ahead and to the left of him where her long hair was spinning like a maelstrom around her inert body. Caspar dived like a cormorant, turning his body and kicking furiously through the turbulent waters. He felt something soft in his fingers and realized he was grappling with her white robe. At last he held her. He hauled her towards him and kicked for the narrow gap of air trapped between the tumbling meltwater and the underbelly of the glacier. Her eyes were unseeing and her face was bony white and hard to the touch, like marble. She looked as if she had been dead for years.

He gripped her tightly to him and used his rapidly numbing legs to fend them off the approaching rocks. They were rushed along in the churning water that tunnelled beneath the belly of the glacier, tumbling towards the light at the mouth of the glacier. The sapping cancer of cold had spread throughout his body and he didn't know how much longer he could hold his mother above the water. He felt numb and was no longer sure whether his legs were still kicking or that they were still there at all. His head lolled back in the freezing current and at last he saw blue sky above him just as Keridwen began to slip through his fingers.

'There! Down there!' It was Hal's voice, urgent and compelling. Caspar was dimly aware of a great black shape swooping towards him. Then the weight of his body was being pulled taut as he was dragged clear of the water by a vast claw that enveloped his body. In his last moments of lucidity he was thankfully aware of Keridwen dangling lifelessly beside him.

His skin itched. The skin on his back was definitely too hot and was beginning to irritate though he didn't have the strength to move his hand to rub it. Someone was trying to choke him. He tried to cough and push them away but he was too weak and the person continued to pour a sickly sweet liquid rather messily down his throat. Spluttering, he opened his eyes and looked up into Brid's concerned face. He raised a hand to stop her. His flesh was covered in runes.

'The runes of healing and the runes of fire,' the girl said simply.

For a moment, he inspected his swollen red fingers with detached curiosity. The water . . . Suddenly it all came back to him. Urgently sitting up, he looked for his mother. 'Is she . . . ?' He could say no more.

Brid turned sorrowfully away.

Hal knelt down next to him. 'No one could live through that. No one could live trapped in the ice. No doubt her image in the moonstone was an illusion all along,' he said almost resentfully.

'Oh please shut up,' Brid begged as if she didn't have the strength to argue anymore.

Hal looked at her indignantly and then his expression softened. 'I'm sorry. I know how you must feel. I was just trying to be realistic.' He pulled her down towards him and held her while she wept.

But Caspar had no one to hold. He crawled over to his mother and looked into her ashen face. Her hair was a sodden mass that twisted around her neck and clung to her skin but her eyeballs were still frozen. The dragon was very gently breathing flickering flames into the atmosphere, enclosing them beneath a ceiling of blasted red and golden fire but it did nothing to ease the cold in Caspar's heart. He wondered if Keridwen's image was still trapped within the moonstone, whether he could still see her as she once had been. Perhaps he could still reach her through the Druid's Eye, even if he was only reaching her spirit as it walked in the shadows of the Otherworld.

'Brid, please, the moonstone,' he begged. 'I must try to reach her.'

'The dragon's breath has darkened it,' she reminded him as she reached inside her shirt and pulled the salamander from the orb, handing the murky sphere to the youth.

'It's not as smoky as it was,' he said hopefully, staring into the orb.

Still, it contained a storm of thunderclouds, churning and boiling with snags of lightning skittering along the length of the gash that scarred the sphere. Tentatively he cleared his mind and cupped his hand over the orb. At first he felt nothing and fought back his disappointment, determined to keep trying. He scooped up slush from the edge of the glacier and bathed the stone in it, hoping that it would rinse away the smoke, but as it cooled, the moonstone merely dulled more. At last he thought of the Egg. Surely, with all that power, it could give the moonstone new life.

'Brid, pass me the Egg,' he asked politely without taking his eyes from the moonstone.

Holding the murky sphere in one hand and the blue-marbled Egg in the other, he willed the moonstone to clear. The Egg tingled on his palm and gradually began to feel heavier and heavier as if the entire weight of a universe pressed against his palm. He knew the force was the spirit of the beasts of power that hovered behind the invisible gateway and that he alone held the key to their liberty. But what could they do to help? They might have vast powers of strength and speed but they still couldn't clear the clouds from the moonstone. He slipped the Egg back into its cushioned scrip on his chest and looked at the moonstone in defeat.

'Blow on it,' Hal suggested.

'What good will that do?'

'You never know. Sometimes the simplest things work,' Hal shrugged. 'It might be like trying to crack an egg open with a hammer whereas all you really need is a tap with a spoon.'

Caspar took a breath and blew gently into the crack in the side of the moonstone. The clouds rippled and stirred and little by little they wafted out through the crack and dispersed into the atmosphere. The moonstone's gleaming iridescence flashed with white energy once more, though sparks of blue-white lightning still flickered around the line of the crack. He smiled gratefully at Hal and pressed his palms firmly to its translucent surface.

He welcomed the pain of the blinding flashes that arced through his mind and jerked his muscles into spasm. Once the shock had passed, he let his mind slip into the subconscious world of the moonstone, desperately seeking his mother's soul within the channels of magic. He found himself pushing through ghostly shadows into an icicle-filled cave, the entrance crusted over with hoarfrost. Some preternatural instinct told him his mother was close. Repeatedly, he shouldered against the wall of frost until finally it cracked and he forced his way through the spikes of icicles.

Towering before him stood a dazzling throne with frozen

cascades tumbling down its sides to form beautiful spirals of twisted ice. The throne itself was like blue diamond, hard and perfect, hewn from a single block of tundra ice.

There was someone there or rather something, something so big and terrible that he could not imagine it, could not look at it. It was like staring into the bare teeth of the north wind. Apart from the terrible vastness of the presence, he perceived only horns, fangs, talons and a vast axe.

'She is mine now, little boy. I will keep her here in the Otherworld where I can dip into her power whenever I choose. I will absorb her strength until her soul is one with mine, leaving her body as nothing but a crisp outer husk. I will drain the life-force from her body like wine from a cup.'

'Give her back! Give her back to me!' Although he could not as yet see them, Caspar could smell the foul stench of trolls snuffling around the hem of the God's throne. He knew who the being was but he sensed that if he voiced Vaal-Peor's name the God would swoop down and crush him beneath His thumbnail.

'She is not yours to claim, little creature,' the wind howled in Caspar's ears.

'No, she is not mine. But she belongs to all the world and not to you. She is a part of the Great Mother,' Caspar screamed, hoping his thin voice would carry to the heights of the throne.

'You have no authority over Me, mite.' Vaal-Peor's voice shuddered the cave. 'Those who worship Me, I have rewarded. They already hold your precious lands and I will leave you to live so that you can fully suffer the pain of your loss. Torra Alta has fallen,' he boomed. 'Now leave Me.'

Defeat engulfed Caspar's heart but as he staggered in his grief, he put his hand to his chest and felt the power of the Druid's Egg. He reached inside his shirt to pull it out. It seemed so small, so insignificant in his hands, hardly a potent talisman at all. Focusing on the Egg, he thought of the creatures it commanded and said quietly, 'Bring her to me.'

He didn't know exactly where the creatures were, only that

they lingered just beyond the threshold of his conscious mind and would, at his command, take solid form while he held the Egg. Gradually, shimmering shapes began to appear. The claw of a dragon, the tail of a griffin, the fang of a wolf, the spiralling horn of a unicorn. As the bodies of the beasts condensed and flexed their solid muscles, Caspar's eyes fixed on one single pure white stallion.

He was like Firecracker in every detail bar the single horn that spiralled to a tip four feet above his forehead and the two swan-like wings that sprouted from his withers. He was the most magnificent beast Caspar had ever seen. The horn was tapered like an icicle, pearly white and threaded with silver and gold that highlighted the coil. The wings spread to a span of over twenty feet.

'Fetch Keridwen to me,' the youth ordered again, deepening his voice to mimic the authority in his father's.

The unicorn charged into the stormy mist that veiled the God's body and in one graceful leap took to the wing, soaring up into the heavens. Maned wolves far bigger than those of the Yellow Mountains, with long cat-like fangs protruding from their jaws, scrambled at the walls of the cave. They leapt from frosted rock to frosted rock, struggling to scale the heights. Then came swarms of dragons and, as Caspar summoned them, each bowed its head in recognition before flying up through the swirling mists that shrouded the mountain throne. They went so high that even the dragons became blurred specks in the vast, far distance before they disappeared from view.

A minute figure in the limitless heights of the ice-cave, Caspar felt terribly alone. He couldn't sense his mother's presence anymore as the ferocious cold crept into his brain. He tried to move, but his joints were already stiffening and his fingers were turning a sickly blue. If he stayed much longer, so close to the will of the Ice-God, he knew he would die.

At last, high in the faded distance of the frosted mists that hid the form of Vaal-Peor, dragonfire flashed across the heavens. Suddenly hail was crashing down from above. He clapped his hands to his ears as a monstrous scream of rage shocked the air. The icicles snapped and shattered around him and he flung himself to the edge of the cave, cowering behind a rocky overhang as lethal daggers of ice fell from the blue white throne. Then at last a few bedraggled beasts returned.

First came a half-dozen wolves, limping and bleeding, then three dragons, scales shredded from their bodies to reveal the soft pulsing flesh beneath. Their wings were torn and they flew with awkward beats of their tattered wings. Caspar waited, his breath forming a dense cloud of vapour around him. He could hardly blink now as the penetrating cold possessed his body. Then at last he saw the graceful sweep of the unicorn's feathered wings. His heart leapt to his throat as he saw a swirl of golden red against its wings. His mother's body lay slumped across the animal's back.

The winged-unicorn trembled as Caspar approached, fearless to all but the touch of a human hand. Tentatively the boy raised his hand and grasped his mother in his arms. The wild beast shied away and the ground beneath Caspar's feet shuddered and rocked as a peal of thunder slammed through the air. Again icicles shattered to the ground around him. He flung himself on top of his mother's body and, in that instant, felt himself released from the mystical world of the moonstone. For a second, as his mind spun away from the crystal cave and he was hurled back into the reality of the Vaalakan tundra, he looked into the eyes of the unicorn.

The beast was free, released from its captivity in the Otherworld and free to roam in this. Caspar was aware of the savagery of the creature and wondered if he had done wrong in letting him go. Should he have banished it back to the parallel world of shadow?

His mind, however, was too concerned for his mother to give it more than the briefest thought. All he cared was that he was holding Keridwen in his arms, rocking her to and fro. After a while he was able to sit back and look at her and as he did he realized that he was no longer clasping the moonstone. All around him shards of sparkling crystal lay like fragmented icicles on the ground. The orb must have shattered under the impact of the God's fury, he thought sadly, and quickly turned away from the glistening crystals to look mournfully at his mother.

Her body was still stiff and inert but her eyes were closed and the extreme expression of pain was gone from her face. The last of the ice was melting from her eyelashes and Caspar pushed her hair back from her face, combing it with his fingers. She looked so young. Was this really his mother? Branwolf was grey at the temples and had a careworn expression cultivated by decades of onerous responsibility. This face, with its firm high cheekbones and immaculate skin, belonged to a woman still in her early twenties – only the skin was so very pale and cold, like frosted porcelain. Her hair was drying in the warmth of the dragon's breath to a deep rich auburn, more fiery than his own hair and more lovely for it. The white silk cloth that clung to her small and delicately proportioned body looked more like a shroud than a dress.

'Mother,' he whispered. 'I have missed you all my life. You left me with a terrible emptiness. Throughout my childhood, I thought you had abandoned me. You cannot abandon me now, not now when I have found you. Please, please don't leave me.'

He hugged her to him, breathing his hot breath onto her cold cheeks, rocking her to and fro until the pain of grief overwhelmed him. He laid her down on his cloak and wrapped her tightly in it, his mind so full of despair that he couldn't think beyond the moment. His grief was pierced by Brid's sharp intake of breath.

'Look,' she stammered, pointing at Keridwen, her voice no more than a whisper as if she feared to break a spell. It was early evening and, with her back to the rapidly darkening east, she was silhouetted by the hazy crescent moon that hung, like a ghostly sickle, in the sky.

'I didn't see anything.'

'Look. I saw it just as the moon rose,' Brid insisted.

'It's just the evening light,' Hal argued.

'No, look,' Brid begged. She pressed closer.

With great concentration, Caspar stared at his mother's long curling eyelashes until his eyes hurt. Then at last he was rewarded. 'They flickered,' he breathed in wonder. 'They definitely flickered.'

'The wind,' Hal continued before either of them could say anything more.

Trog pushed his snout in between all of them, violently wagging his tail and evidently fascinated by what drew their attention. He cocked his head quizzically at Keridwen and then darted forward, slurping at her face with his long wet sticky tongue.

Hal pulled him roughly back but Caspar no longer noticed what the dog was doing. He was intent only on his mother as her eyelids fluttered. Her chest heaved upwards, sucking in a rasp of warmed air from the dragon, and her eyes blinked open. Nothing had ever prepared Caspar for their true beauty. They were as limitless as the deepest blue skies seen from the highest peaks, a blue full of the intensity of life. They flickered and blinked and looked round at all their faces before frowning with a curiously puzzled expression.

Her mouth moved to speak but no sound came. She closed her eyes and swallowed, before opening them again. 'A dragon,' she whispered. Her voice was a harsh croak as if it had dried up and seized up with disuse. 'There's a dragon standing over me. Am I alive or . . . ?' Her words faltered as if it were all too much for her to take in.

Brid took her hand.

'Keridwen,' she whispered. 'You are alive.'

'I truly don't feel it,' the woman spoke in a broken hoarse whisper.

'Shh, don't talk for a while. I'll give you something to ease the pain and soothe your body. Wintergreen for the cold, syrup for the throat. Sleep and rest is what you need. We will talk later,' Brid told her.

Keridwen obediently slumped back and, all the while she slept, Caspar watched over her.

The western skies were robed in the smudged colours of evening. Smoky brown clouds billowed in the soft breeze, swelling into dark and hidden mists, to blanket the far horizon. As darkness fell, the sound of gushing water swelled as the vast plains of ice began to crack and spill their meltwaters out onto the arid plain of the Dragon Scorch. Life was returning to Vaalaka, and it was all too late. Life came to the northern plains just as death stormed through Torra Alta and into Belbidia. He thought of the howling words of the Ice-God, claiming that Torra Alta was lost.

The night clamped its hand over the valley. All that could be heard was the eerie creaking of the unstable glacier. They piled the fire high to stave off the fierce northern cold and, by its flickering light, Caspar and his two companions kept vigil over Keridwen.

Hal was staring at her, his mouth ajar. 'She's very beautiful,' he murmured reverently, almost as if he saw her as a vision.

Her eyes blinked as his voice disturbed her sleep. She tilted her head to look at him curiously, a smile lighting up her face and a laugh coming readily to her lips. The sound was as free and as uplifting as a lark on the wing but then, as she peered at the youth in the twilight, her laughter died away. She looked at him uncertainly.

'Branwolf? Is it you?' Eased by the herbs, her voice was now smooth and melodious.

Hal shook his head and Caspar's heartstrings snatched tight around his soul as he thought of the deep sorrow that welcomed Keridwen from her long sleep. Torra Alta had fallen. And Branwolf . . . Still he could not truly believe it.

Keridwen continued to stare at Hal. 'Branwolf, it must be you; so dark, so handsome, with that same daring look.'

'I'm Hal,' the youth replied as gently as he could.

'Hal! But you can't be. No, Hal is only six at the most and if you're . . . ?' The question died on her lips.

She turned with sudden realization to the red-haired youth sitting beside her, his eyes wide with expectation and innocence. 'I thought it was all a nightmare but it was true. I've been in the ice for ... Spar!' She said no more but hugged him to her, her tears splashing down her cheeks. It was several minutes before she could speak again but after that she wouldn't rest until they had told her the full story in bursts of tearful emotion.

'And Gwion,' Caspar nodded. 'It was Gwion all along.'

'Gwion,' she echoed heavily. 'And Vaal-Peor claimed that Torra Alta was lost and you yourselves saw all but the keep sacked.' The sparkle was dying from her eyes. 'Torra Alta, Morrigwen, Branwolf ...' Her voice shook, but then her lips pursed as if she were arming herself against her grief. Sweeping her hand through her long red hair, she coiled it into a knot as if she were furling in her sorrow. She gave Hal a long sideways look and smiled mournfully. 'He was so very, very like you.'

Chapter 27

A great sense of pride welled up inside the young boy as he watched his mother settling on the dragon's neck. She held tightly to the creature's horns, the wind ruffling and sweeping back her billowing white robe as they flew towards the distant peaks of the Yellow Mountains. He still couldn't quite believe she was real. The colour had returned to her cheeks and now, with the rushing wind in her face, she was as rosy and as mysteriously beautiful as an autumn sunset.

'Faster, Spar, ask him to go faster.' Her words were whisked away in the airstream. Caspar knew she was in her late thirties but in truth she looked little more than a girl. But when she spoke it was with a certain mature authority, defying any to disobey.

Caspar felt for the Egg secured around his neck and willed the beast to greater efforts until they could barely breathe for the speed of the air in their faces. Meeting his mother and seeing her true nature had given him a new sense of his own identity. Before, he had imagined her as flighty and docile, subdued by the strength of Branwolf's personality. Now he saw her as wildly brave, possessed of purpose and driven by love for the Great Mother that extended to all living things. He was proud to have her blood flowing in his veins. The woman's presence added support and unity to them all: not even Hal dared to question or doubt her. Caspar smiled at his mother and a new confidence was born in the Baron's son.

The moment Caspar had told her that the Vaalakans were storming the castle defences, she had ordered them to return to Torra Alta. With more impetus than even Brid, she had instantly taken control of the youngsters.

Below them now they could see two Vaalakan columns; one heading south-west towards the Jaws of the Wolf and one heading south-east towards the head of the Pass at Torra Alta. 'Spar, summon the wolves,' she ordered as they approached the green strip of the Boarchase Forest.

'I – how?' he stammered.

Her imperious note startled him and he expected her to be cross or patronizing as he failed to understand her command but instead her smile sweetened.

'It's all right. Put your hands on the Egg and look about you.'

Instantly he saw what she meant. Running wild through the woods were the hazy outlines of savage wolves, long since extinct, the forefathers of the mountain wolves. Tall, long-maned creatures with cat-like fangs, they were the size of large rangy ponies.

'Give them form,' Keridwen whispered, her hands covering her son's palm. Caspar felt his mother's confidence infuse him with a steady control over his emotions. Beneath the white silken dress that floated around the curves of her young body, she was smaller and more delicate than Brid. But despite her lack of stature, she commanded great presence born from decisive confidence. 'First the wolves, then the unicorns and lastly the old trolls of the mountains,' she whispered. 'You can do it, Spar. Draw them out of the shadows and give them form.'

'But, is it safe? So many at once?' Caspar stammered. He sensed the ferocious beasts of power everywhere around him now, the ghosts of thousands of savage beasts all with wills and minds of their own, all baying for their freedom. For a moment he faltered. What if he summoned them but then was unable to control so many? Think of the wild savagery he would unleash on the world. He wasn't sure that he was strong enough to keep them subdued.

'You can do it, Spar,' Keridwen told him firmly. 'Look at

me, child.' She lifted his chin and stared for a long moment into his eyes. 'They will obey but first you must command.'

'Give the Egg to me and I'll do it,' Hal offered eagerly.

Keridwen sniffed in disapproval. 'Spar can do it. He only needs the confidence, but he at least understands the responsibility of the power he wields. In his hands there is less danger. We must trust the judgement of the Great Mother and she decreed the Druid's Egg was for him to wield.'

Hal withdrew his outstretched hand, defeated by Keridwen's authority.

'Command, Spar,' Keridwen repeated to her son. 'You have it within you. Believe in yourself.'

Authority did not come naturally to the boy. Even where Firecracker was concerned he never commanded, only suggested. But he needed to command now. Gradually the shapes of running wolves tracked across the forest paths below, heading for the mountains.

Clinging to the bony spines of the dragon, they flew over the Yellow Mountains. The peaks were a golden ochre in the spring light with only the tallest crags around Mirror Lake and the Jaws of the Wolf still clad in snow. A Vaalakan column, like a black scar on the pale landscape, sliced unchecked towards the high mountain pass to the west. Caspar knew that, while the enemy seeped through the Jaws of the Wolf, Torra Alta was open to attack from the south as well as the north. His mind swept towards the treacherous Pass. Instantly the dragon yawed to the right, following his wishes.

'No,' Hal objected. 'Spar, no. We must go to Torra Alta first.'

Caspar's resolve wavered and the dragon's pulsing wings slowed to a hesitant glide.

'Command, Spar,' Keridwen told him. 'Once you've made a decision, stick to it otherwise we'll achieve nothing. We're in your hands and you must command.'

'First to the Jaws of the Wolf. With this army, we'll be able to stem the flood of Vaalakans. Then at least the castle won't be vulnerable from all sides.'

'You're right – and Keridwen's right,' Hal uncharacteristically conceded. 'We've no time to waste in argument. Let's go!'

Caspar's stomach was left in mid-air as the dragon swooped to the right and sliced up through the mountain air. The marching Vaalakan column was vivid now, struggling to climb the steep slopes leading to the narrow ravine that cut through the spine of mountains. Caspar felt sick with anger. The valleys all around were crawling with bare-breasted Northmen and the landscape was grey and torn where they had destroyed huge swathes of his forests.

He wanted only to kill them and his desires were channelled through the Druid's Egg. They swooped lower and he could see the dark shapes of the tall wolves emerging from the shadows. The dragon belched out fire, scorching ten Vaalakans, and then flew on, leaving the screaming barbarians to the wolves.

'Morbak's hordes are vast,' Hal said gloomily. 'There are too many.' He was sitting close to Brid. One hand held hers; the other gripped the runesword. 'Even a thousand wolves won't kill them all.'

'Whoever said we wanted to kill them?' Keridwen looked at him haughtily. 'We must drive them back to their own lands to rebuild their irrigation channels and repair their lands. The Dragon Scorch is flooded with meltwater again and, if they return, the northern plains will be workable again. The Great Mother has restored the balance.'

'If Vaal-Peor's words are true and Torra Alta has fallen then She might have restored the balance for the Vaalakans but not for us,' he retorted bitterly.

Keridwen looked as if she were about to chastise him for his blasphemy but then her look softened into one of sorrow and she shook her head. 'No, indeed, possibly not for us. Perhaps we didn't deserve it.'

'She misled and betrayed us,' the youth declared blackly.

Keridwen shook her head, unruffled by the youth's outburst. 'No, Hal. It was Gwion who betrayed us, and before that it was we who betrayed the Great Mother by allowing her faith to be persecuted.'

The air cooled as they soared above the Jaws of the Wolf. To either side the mountains rose like serrated teeth with gouged sides where snow permanently clung to the gullies. Even though it was now late spring, cowls of snow still capped the higher peaks, glistening in the sun. Deep shadow darkened the pass below and where the sun warmed the upper crags, rocks were loosened by the thaw of ice to scatter down the scree slopes, tickling and tumbling towards the valley. But nothing stopped the trudge of marching feet.

'There must be thousands of them,' Brid despaired. 'Once they are through here no army will stop them.'

'Once through, yes.' Hal agreed, suddenly brightening. 'But it wouldn't take much to stop them, not in this narrow Pass.' A cheeky grin spread across his face. 'What do you think, Spar?' He pointed to the couloirs and snow-capped peaks. 'In this weather when the black rocks are warming quickly . . . ?'

Caspar nodded. 'No, I wouldn't choose to march through here in early spring let alone late Fallow. The layers of snow will be loosening from the warming rocks. Given the right circumstances . . .'

All four Torra Altans looked at each other; the first signs of triumph shining in their faces. With his hand on the Egg, Caspar sensed the spirits of six dragons that had once, more than a thousand years ago, swarmed thick over the Yellow Mountains. He wasted no time nor fearful thoughts on summoning them. At first only their shady outlines could be seen circling around the topmost peaks but gradually their forms condensed. Two were plain green, the younger ones Caspar thought, while the others were streaked with gold and silver fringes to their barbed scaled armour. Six in all, many still carrying the scars of their death at the hands of the first men of Torra Alta.

They screamed and shrieked, the vast bladders beneath their throats filling with gallons of air, and, as they roared, the flames gushed out across the mountain tops. The blast from their shrieking throats shook the air but the roar from the ensuing avalanche was louder. It started with a rumble, drumming the ground like stampeding bison, and culminated in an ear-splitting clap as one side of the snow-clad Pass sheered off and slid down to choke its narrow base. The dragon on which they rode launched into the sky as the backwash from the imploding pass buffeted and rocked the air around them. For a moment Caspar couldn't breathe as the atmosphere became clogged with fine particles of sparkling snow blown upwards by the shock of the blast. The dragon circled lazily until the billowing clouds of snow had settled.

Below them the valley was choked in tons of dirt-laden snow, bearing all and washing everyone before it to their deaths, crushed and suffocated in the mountain's white cloaks. To the north, the vast enemy column had turned in fearful retreat of the treacherous mountains.

'No one will get through that until the autumn,' Keridwen sighed with a degree of satisfaction. 'Those great slabs of compacted snow will take months to thaw.'

Caspar willed the dragon east towards his home. 'What of the ones that are already through?' he asked.

'King Rewik will deal with them and if not they'll head to Torra Alta where we will see to them ourselves,' Keridwen confidently told him before Hal managed to say a word.

'Our job now is to defend the Pass,' he said heavily when she had finished.

Caspar thought on his words. Vaal-Peor had claimed there was nothing left to defend, that Torra Alta had fallen; all was lost. All they could do now was attempt to find his father and Morrigwen. Father, he thought in despair, and sensed the same grief in his mother though her face remained composed in determined concentration. He couldn't contemplate the thought that any harm had come to his father but he knew in his heart that the castle was lost and likely his father and friends with it. But Vaal-Peor was wrong; there was much to defend. Torra Alta might have fallen but it was only a castle and it was his job to defend the Pass from northern attack with or without a castle. An act of fate had made him heir to the Barony and as such he must command.

It was only moments before the top turrets of the frontier fortress spiked into view above the surrounding pale golden peaks. Numerous columns of dense black smoke pumped into the sky, casting a dark shadow over the plain. Vaalakans, seething like millions of ants, teamed and streamed over the ground, as they spiralled up the Tor to engulf the castle. The doors of the keep were hacked open and belching flames leapt from the narrow window-slits of the blocky tower.

'No!' Brid screamed defiantly down at the scene. 'No! No! Morrigwen! She must live. The Three must be united!'

Hal snatched her to him, evidently fearful that she might tumble from the dragon's back in her grief. Caspar looked down, too shocked to speak. No one could be left alive in that, no one, not Morrigwen and not Branwolf.

They circled several times with the other six dragons in their wake, searching for a safe place to land. The towers of the castle had crumbled, their wooden interiors burnt through and roofs fallen in. The failing turrets had tossed great chunks of masonry down the sides of the Tor to crash into the canyon. Clouds of smoke rose in columns around the pillar of rock that lanced out of the canyon floor.

'She's like an old witch that's been burnt at the stake,' Brid said, her voice choking with tears.

Caspar summoned the wolves out of the mountains. Then soon after, a herd of pearl-white beasts thundered from the southern tip of the Pass. They ran back and forth, gouging and raking with their long spiralling horns amongst the barbarians. Caspar left them to their task.

'Down,' he commanded. 'Take us down to the central courtyard.'

White-haired warriors crawled like tiny ants over the remains of the battlements, turning over the remaining Torra Altan corpses and mutilating their bodies before chucking them over the wall. They fell as cartwheeling limbs and torsos onto the jagged rocks below where flocking ravens picked

452

them clean. Caspar had his bow ready and Hal drew his sword.

'Stay on the dragon's back with Keridwen. I'll feel better if I know where you are,' the dark youth commanded Brid. 'No one can touch you there.'

She nodded, strangely obedient.

In blind terror, the barbarians on the castle battlements fell to their knees, cowering, as they looked up at the dragons swooping down from the sky. Demented with fear, they ran shrieking in all directions, some hurling themselves from the battlements to flee the tongues of fire spuming from the monsters' belching maws. But three Northmen stood their ground and as the dragon turned his snout to shrivel the life from the first of the approaching barbarians, Caspar instinctively raised his hand to command the dragon to stop. With Hal at his side, he leapt to the ground. He needed the satisfaction of personal revenge.

The steadiness of the barbarians' pale eyes declared that they were not afraid to die. Like most other Vaalakans they wore skins bandaged to their bulging thighs, a stiff crude belt buckled their breeches and only a tattered black bearskin over one shoulder covered their naked torsos. Numerous feathers and beads, knotted into their long white war plaits, declared them to be of high birth.

Caspar wasted no time. He drew back his bow and let the arrow fly. The barbarian before him instinctively tried to deflect the arrow with his arm but the movement was too slow. While his hand was still only halfway to his chest, the arrow had already bored into his pumping heart. The second Northman had taken two strides towards Hal before Caspar could release his next quarrel. The wide barb split the tight skin of the Vaalakan's cheek, the force of the blow snapping back his head, though he continued to stagger forward. Hal threw him aside.

Only one Vaalakan remained. He was broad and muscular but there was a gaunt, hungry look to his face that the boy had also noted in Gwion. The man unslung his axe, wielding it with the skill of a Camaalian knight. A troll's leathery hide adorned his shoulders and a necklace of trolls' teeth jangled around his head. He had a tall spiked helmet with ibex horns jutting from the top. Impaled on the spike at the very top of his helmet was a head. A hacked and bloodied head.

Caspar was revolted to the pit of his stomach. It was the head of a woman with long red hair, like his mother's. Elaine, he thought, if they have done this to you what of the others? He couldn't bare to think what had happened to his father, Morrigwen, nor even of little May who had looked at him with such resentment. The thought of the small girl with her large vulnerable eyes and thoughtful expression filled him with strange emotions. He had seen her through the eyes of the moonstone, and felt her mind, strong and caring. If Morbak had harmed her, like he had harmed her mother . . . His anger was roused to madness.

Hal moved forward. Gone was the rage that would previously have possessed him. Now with cool calculated control, he wielded his sword with the same skill as Ceowulf tilted a lance. He feinted in on the left, drawing the Vaalakan's guard, and then spun away, his sword swirling round in a giant arc. The blade sang out its awesome magic. The sunlight caught the honed edges and was reflected back into the air as a burst of white energy. It was over quickly. The man's frozen stare saw the raw cutting edge of the blade for only a moment. He had no time to raise his axe and the realization was plain on his horror-struck face. He tried to duck, but the whistling speed of the runesword was too fast. The blade hit at eye level, shattering the temple guards of his helmet and cleaving through his skull. The gruesome head-dress slid from his shoulders, clattering to the cobbles, and Elaine's severed head rolled free. The barbarian's body still swayed for a moment on solid legs before tottering and slumping in a heap midst his black bearskin cloak.

Caspar stared at him blankly for a long hard minute before taking in the rest of the scene around him. Screams of terror and pain echoed back and forth between the bare canyon walls. The fearsome beasts of legend wreaked havoc, with fang and fire, horn and hoof, as they drove the Vaalakans north. Many of the northern warriors chose to fling themselves into the freezing waters of the Silversalmon, rather than be crushed in the savage jaws of the wolves or impaled by the unicorns. The churning rapids of the turbulent river dashed them onto rocks and sucked them into its foaming depths. The Pass was emptying. It would take days yet but the work had already begun.

With his foot, Caspar cleared the debris from Torra Alta's heartstone and sat in the cleared space staring at the cream marbled surface of the Egg, controlling the creatures while the others began their search.

Not one woman was found alive in the keep. Isabel's and Rosalind's hacked bodies were still recognizable but many others were not. Brid and Keridwen examined each and every one carefully, hoping beyond hope that they might yet find someone alive.

'Don't go into the towers,' Caspar ordered. 'They're too dangerous and could topple at any moment.'

But in the end they all felt compelled to look. The foot of each tower was a tumbled mass of charred timbers and broken blocks of masonry. They all instantly understood that no one could survive beneath the rubble.

Keridwen's face was long and drawn. 'I have suffered for thirteen years, thirteen very long years, but that pain was nothing to this. Where is he? Will I never find peace?'

Caspar tried to comfort his mother. 'There are still more places to search. Father searched for you for years, always searching, never knowing whether you were dead or not, and in the end we found you. There is always hope.'

Keridwen looked down at the smouldering Vaalakan funeral pyres and the mounds of rotting Torra Altan dead. 'We must sort through all of them until we find him.'

At last the vast sabre-toothed wolves, the unicorns and the dragons had swept the canyon clear of all signs of living Vaalakans and they were free to descend the road. Caspar replaced the Egg in its cushioned scrip and started down the winding ledge that spiralled to the bottom of the Tor. His mother walked at his side.

'Send them home now,' Keridwen told him gently. 'Send the creatures back to the Otherworld. Left here to roam they will become a danger to all of us. Send them back. They have served their purpose: the Vaalakans will not return.'

As if he had heard her words the dragon flew down and landed on the path. Caspar looked into its vivid green eyes. The beast had carried them across the Caballan Sea and stayed by them ever since. 'I cannot send him back to a world of shadows. He has helped us beyond measure.' The dragon looked at him condescendingly as if he didn't want this gratitude but still Caspar didn't have it in his heart to send him back. 'No,' he said. 'I'll give him his freedom so long as he goes across the western ocean to whatever lies beyond.'

The dragon blinked, seemingly in comprehension. Caspar was certain the great monster understood even if he could not speak their tongue.

'It would be worse to be alone and without a mate, to wander forlornly on the earth forever,' Hal mused.

'Well then, I will send him with one of the young females.'

The dragon blinked again, more quickly and insistently. Caspar was sure he was doing the right thing. 'Go,' he said. 'Take one of the young females and fly across the ocean.'

Keridwen shook her head, 'Spar, no. It's wrong.'

Caspar pouted. 'I cannot repay them with a half-existence.' He closed his eyes and his will was done. When he opened them again the dragon and all the other creatures were gone.

Keridwen's eyes were moist and she shook her head sadly.

They began their grisly task and continued until it was nearly dark. The valley stank and, as late evening threw its sombre cloak over the Pass, Caspar felt his flesh crawl. He could almost see the souls of the unburied dead hanging over the valley. Many were his friends, men he knew well. His day's search had proved fruitless and he could bear the sorrow no longer. As they piled the bodies ready to light a funeral pyre that would at least mark their deaths with dignity, the tears began to roll. He wept like a small child.

Keridwen wrapped him up in her arms and hugged him to her, rocking him back and forth, but he quickly steadied himself. 'I cannot be weak. Without Father I must command the Barony – whatever is left of it – and live up to my responsibilities.'

'Here, quick! Help me!' Brid cried.

A man was groaning. A troll gash had opened up half his chest but his heart still pumped.

Hal ran to the Silversalmon with a water flask in his hand while Keridwen and Brid did what they could to ease the man's pain and bandage his broken body. Renewed hope kindled in the boy's heart. If one was alive there could be more. He hadn't recognized the man at first; his face was too smothered in blood. But by the time he was cleaned up and given water and herbs to cleanse the poisons in his blood, Caspar knew him for the archer Brock. But the man couldn't speak for his wounds and Brid finally gave him a draught to ease him into restful sleep.

Within two hours they had found three other Torra Altans miraculously alive amongst the hundreds of dead, but not a trace of Branwolf.

'He would never have left his men to die alone,' Hal repeated continually. 'The Vaalakans must have taken his body and . . .'

Keridwen was fighting back tears as she struggled to the point of exhaustion. Without resting, she continued to pull broken bodies away from the heap and drag them to the new pile to burn.

'Make her stop,' Brid pleaded. 'Oh, Spar, make her stop before she kills herself. She must rest.'

But there was a desperate energy in Keridwen that Caspar could not control. They all worked on until they reached the very last layers of the piles of Belbidian dead. There were no more alive and, of the three that had been spared, one had since died. And there midst the fuming funeral pyres and the rotting stench of death at last they slept, exhausted by work and grief.

Keridwen was awake first, looking like a ghost drifting through the mists that lazed over the Silversalmon. Her feet were engulfed in drifts of hazy cloud and she seemed to glide as she searched further afield for the dead and the dying, hoping beyond hope that they might find Branwolf. Caspar rose to join her, listening to the ever swelling roar of the Silversalmon as its waters were fed by the Vaalakan melt-waters.

'The river will soon flood the canyon and wash them all away,' she sighed. 'It will cleanse the land of all the carnage and the Vaalakan bodies heaped about our land and yet what for? He is gone. Branwolf, my Lord Branwolf is gone. Morrigwen is gone.' She smiled sorrowfully at her son. 'But I still have you.'

She reached out her hand and, despite the grief in the woman's heart, Caspar sensed her strength as she sadly continued, 'Morrigwen is surely dead and the Trinity lost. Whatever the powers of the Druid's Egg, we have still failed,' she sighed. 'But the waters will refresh the land.' She pointed to the rubble that scarred the canyon floor. 'We must take shelter in the hills soon because the floods from the melting ice-cap will drown the entire canyon floor. Would that it would drown that forever.' Her slender hand thrust angrily towards a vast slab-sided altar that stood in the foundations of the cathedral to the new God. 'That is what failed us. Torra Alta and my lord are fallen because of that.' Angrily she strode towards it and beat it with her fists. 'Mother, have I suffered so long only to be brought back to life to this slaughter?'

She pummelled the altar stone in fury while Caspar stood silently behind her, wishing he could absorb some of her grief, but he could not. He felt too numb, drowned by too deep a sorrow. He broke down, slumped to his knees and wept. He had no strength left and yet he knew that all who remained now relied on him. If Branwolf was lost, then he was the

Baron, but he did not feel strong enough. He had no more courage left.

A light touch on his shoulder could not bring him out of his despair, though he drew strength from his mother as she enfolded him in her slender but strong arms. 'You are still just a boy, Spar. You don't have to be strong yet. I shouldn't have broken down on you. I'm sorry.' She kissed his forehead and smiled. 'Come, we will keep looking.'

Caspar dried his eyes and drew courage from his mother's strength. The morning sun scaled over the eastern peaks and Keridwen stood up on the altar of the New Faith and raised her hands to hail the waking deity.

'It is the Sun and a new beginning is born.'

She looked down at the foot of the altar and froze. Trog was digging frantically at its base, snuffling and whining. Picking up one of the many Vaalakan war axes that lay discarded on the canyon floor, Caspar nudged the dog aside and hewed frantically at the ground. He could hear sobbing. He knew he could hear voices down there.

Brid and Hal came running at the signs of their frantic activity.

Hal took one look at the situation. 'Spar, save your energy,' he said, putting his weight against the top slab of the altar stone and grunting.

The stone gave way and grated over its plinth. As the sunlight fell through the opening, Caspar caught his breath at the sight of the wretched human beings that lay huddled together, wide eyes staring out from blackened faces in the confined space. They looked half-starved and were smeared in dried blood and dust. With their eyes blinking in the light, they raised their arms to shield themselves from savage attack. Hal leapt back as a figure burst forward from within the altar, roaring with a last determined effort to save those he guarded.

'No! Wait, stop! Friend, it's us,' Hal cried urgently.

The tall, lank figure halted. His tattered hauberk hung from the skeletal frame of his shoulders and his eyes were sunk back beneath hooded brows that met over a jutting nose. He dropped his raised arms in exhaustion. Standing speechlessly, he blinked at them without moving and then behind him rose up a thin woman, unrecognizable in the smudged dirt.

'Mercy, Mother, it's Master Hal, Master Spar and Elaine.' Her eyes gaped open in shock. 'Mercy Mother, it's not Elaine but Lady Keridwen and not looking a day older than when I last saw her,' she stammered before stirring herself into action. 'Well, just don't stand there, Captain. Let's get these others out.'

'Cook!' Caspar cried with sudden realization. 'Cook, it's you! And Captain. I would never . . .'

'You would never have known me,' he said falteringly, 'hiding here. But all else was lost.' He looked reverently towards Caspar's mother. 'My lady,' he bowed, 'I wish I could give you a better welcome home.'

Five of them emerged from beneath the altar stone; the Captain, Cook, one woman and the two young boys from the kitchens, all weak with hunger. They looked giddily around them at the rotting Vaalakan corpses and then sadly at the black smoke that still rose from the smouldering Belbidian funeral pyres. Caspar led them to the campfire where Hal cooked a half-plucked pheasant and a small gutted fawn. Once given a sip from a bladder of water, Cook insisted on getting to work.

'I had more reserves than most,' she said, slapping her slender sides.

Her voluminous clothes looked quite absurd on the scrawny woman that now lay beneath. She wiped her hand quickly across her eyes. The Captain, too, would not rest though he had ordered the others to lie peacefully. His red eyes searched the canyon, sweeping hungrily back and forth.

Keridwen clutched at his arm, 'Have you . . . did you . . . ?' Her eyes followed his gaze.

'We stood around the Dragon Standard on the upper battlements of the keep. All around us the men were dead and dying but we stood to the last. Then the trolls breached the walls and we were forced to retreat downwards. Finally only he and

I with twenty of the last men stood over what was left of the womenfolk, a few from the kitchens and the two little woodcutter's children. They closed in on us and we fought long and hard but they had trolls and there were too many. We managed to retreat into the cellars, keeping the Vaalakans back with the last of the sulphur kegs, and made it to the outer walls where we threw a grappling rope over the side. We struggled down until we reached the craggy rocks where we crawled through the dead all around us. We tried to cross the Silversalmon but a party of rogue trolls headed us off and we were forced west.'

He paused to take a long draught from the water canister. 'If a Vaalakan came close, we lay slumped like carcasses and that's when we got separated. Branwolf stayed with the children, as he had promised their mother, but they were weak and frightened. Elaine . . .' he faltered. 'She died helping us escape from the castle.'

Caspar swallowed hard, feeling his stomach rise into his throat as he remembered Elaine's decapitated head on the helmet of the Vaalakan barbarian.

The Captain continued his woeful tale. 'Morrigwen was too frail to run so she stayed with Lord Branwolf and Elaine's children. He told the rest of us to go on ahead. In the cover of darkness we made it here to the canyon floor but we were too weak to flee further and the canyon was crawling with enemy warriors. We hid here until you found us.'

Brid's face was white at the mention of the old Crone. Her clenched fist kneaded Hal's hand.

'But what of my father?' Caspar begged.

The Captain shrugged sorrowfully. His nose looked large and protruding on his spare face though there was something comforting about the way his hawkish eyebrows hooded together over his dark eyes.

'He's out there,' Caspar suddenly cried with conviction, looking west towards the steep, wooded rise of the canyon wall. 'He would head for the mountains.'

Cook looked doubtful. 'It might look like some giant has

461

marched through here and trodden down the enemy for us but when we climbed over the walls – something I might say I thought I would never do – the canyon was thick with the northern varmints. No one could make it across to the mountains.'

'He's out there,' Keridwen echoed her son's words with equal conviction. They looked despairingly at the steep-sided canyon and then at the poor wretched people who had fought so long and hard. 'We must get you out of the canyon. With all this rotting flesh there's too much danger from infection and soon the floods will come as the ice-cap melts. We'll be caught in the spate if we don't climb higher.'

It was a painful and slow climb for those who had suffered the long siege at Torra Alta but half-dragged and half-carried by the other four, they eventually made it to the top.

Encouraged by his mother's presence, Caspar turned to give orders to the Captain. 'You must stay with the others and rest. Make camp here so that we can find you.' The Captain nodded and then without a word Hal, Brid, Caspar and Keridwen turned west into the valleys.

They climbed on throughout the day until in the far distance they saw a lake cupped in the claw of the mountains, the last rays of the evening sun glimmering on its waters. To their left, a peak with a small spinney of rowan bushes clumped around its base overlooked the valley. At its summit a slab of flat bedrock jutted into the air.

Keridwen looked up at it. 'Once we rode out here and there was a vast black wolf on that rock. It was full daylight and he stared fearlessly straight back at us, sleek and as black as a raven. I told Branwolf that it was his spirit, the spirit of the old Black Wolf. We climbed right up there and . . .' she looked meaningfully at them, 'we found a deep cave.'

They ran through the rowan wood and breathlessly scrambled up the steeper slopes but as they approached they slowed. The sun had dipped behind the mountains and the light of the moon danced on the highest snow-capped peaks. A flicker of firelight and the smell of cooking came faintly to them through the trees. Hal gripped Brid's hand as they approached and carefully tiptoed towards the glowing light. Four figures sat hunched beneath their thick bearskins around a fire. A small spitted animal sizzled in the roasting flames as its flesh browned.

'The young nowadays, they have no respect. Can't you see I'm tired? I can't tell that story again.' An old shaky female voice grumbled and croaked.

'Oh please,' a young girl's voice cajoled.

The old woman sniffed in disgust and then finally sighed as if in surrender as she began her tale. 'In the beginning, the Sun smiled out alone in the great black universe and, after an eternity of meditation, its thoughts formed together, manifesting themselves in the great subconscious; and the Annwyn was created.'

Brid drew in a deep breath. Caspar felt Keridwen's grip tighten on his wrist and sensed her pulse quicken as she chanted in unison with the Maiden. 'And from the Annwyn have all things been created, from the smallest creatures in the oceans to ourselves. We are all of one and come from one and, in the end, return to the one.'

The moonlight shone on Morrigwen's face as she turned, open-mouthed. Brid and Keridwen stepped forward just as the lonely howl of a wolf filled the night. For a moment the three women stood staring in silence.

'You have the Egg?' Morrigwen asked, her tone matter-of-fact as if she daren't allow any emotion to crack into her voice in case she crumbled entirely.

Keridwen nodded.

'The Trinity is restored,' the ancient Crone raised her voice in thanksgiving.

Branwolf stood in the blessed light of the moon and held out his hands to his wife. Wordlessly they fell into each other's arms.

May looked up at Morrigwen and sniffed. 'She's so like Ma.'

'I know,' Morrigwen replied. 'But she is, you see. She's everyone's mother.'

Epilogue

In the dim torchlight that cast deep shadows in the lowest dungeons beneath the keep, Caspar reverently replaced the Druid's Egg in its moss-lined oak casket. Through the last weeks of recuperation and rebuilding of Torra Alta, none ever spoke of the talisman's terrible power and only in secret did Caspar sneak down to caress it. Every day since their return, he had come to be near it, for despite the bustle of rebuilding the castle, he felt alone. Keridwen rarely left his father's side and Hal was generally too preoccupied with Brid to pay him much attention. Only the Egg seemed to speak to him now as he sensed the pleading souls of the beasts of power beg for their release.

He slid the casket back under an altar slab carved with the pagan symbol of the pentagram, where the fearful talisman was hidden for safekeeping. He rose from his knees and, taking the firebrand from the bracket in the wall, he gazed one last time into the hollow chamber before closing and locking the solid steel door. Reluctantly he withdrew from the dungeons and ascended the cold stone steps to meet his father.

Above the blackened towers a new Dragon Standard, hastily embroidered, fluttered in the breeze. Ant-like, wagons crawled up the spiralling road towards the castle with supplies and building materials. The masonry from the half-built cathedral was already being dismantled to rebuild the fortress.

'It will take generations, generations of your descendants,' Branwolf told his son as they stood at the barbican to greet the first of the day's wagoners, sweated and breathless from the steep ascent.

Trog growled at the intruders and hastily lifted his leg on one of the vast wagon wheels just to make sure everyone knew of his presence. Then to add measure, he trotted to the barbican and marked his territory beneath the portcullis. He yipped delightedly at the sight of Brid and charged to welcome her, bowling her over in his exuberance.

Hal protectively pulled the dog off the Maiden, only to be knocked over himself. He laughed good-naturedly. Caspar watched them and pushed self-consciously at his crooked nose. He didn't begrudge Hal's good fortune in winning Brid, but had simply wanted her for himself. He jumped as a feathery touch brushed his hand.

'She's not for you. She may be as beautiful as the day and as mysterious as the night but she's also as wilful as the tides and as stubborn as rock. She needs someone like Hal who will stand up to her.'

Shamefaced, Caspar looked at his mother. 'But . . . but he doesn't understand her.'

'He doesn't need to. He need only love her. When you are older, you will need a wife who won't tell you what to do all the time. Spar, you need to be more honest with yourself.' She patted his shoulder reassuringly before rejoining Branwolf. The Baron took his lady's arm and together they returned to the keep.

He shrugged. Perhaps that was true but how could he ever look at anyone else while he was forever dazzled by Brid?

Below a young girl with chestnut hair laughed with the wagoner – only to Caspar, she didn't seem so young anymore. She must be about thirteen, he thought as he watched her petting the big wagon horses. She must have sensed that she was being watched for quite suddenly her big hazel eyes looked up to meet his gaze. He flushed a brilliant scarlet, grinned sheepishly and hurriedly turned away to look out over the canyon.

He studiously avoided looking round to see if she was still there but finally his imagination was stolen away by the breath-taking views over the mountains. Lost in reverie, Caspar hung over the parapet, gazing out at his barony. He jumped again, violently this time, as someone nudged him in the back and he lurched towards the sheer drop.

Hal laughed loudly as he yanked Caspar back into balance. 'It never fails, never. You always jump.'

'Oh, shut up,' Caspar implored, fearing that May might notice how his uncle made a fool of him.

Hal caught Caspar's quick glance in the girl's direction. His olive-green eyes glinted with humour as he raised his eyebrows and gave his nephew a knowing look. 'She watches you.'

'I know but . . .'

Hal wasn't listening anymore. He pointed down into the canyon where a company of knights galloped towards the castle on a stream of brightly coloured horses, banners fluttering in the morning breeze. Caspar instantly recognized the purple colours of Jotunn and the red and white chequered caparison of Caldea. He stood on the parapets, the wind lifting his hair, uncaring that the world dropped away hundreds of feet directly beneath him.

They could see the lead rider struggling to retain a gleaming red beast who bucked and tugged to pull ahead. 'It's Cracker,' Caspar cried. 'Ceowulf and Cybillia are bringing Cracker home.'

Pulling at his uncle to follow, he jumped excitedly from the crenellations and into the courtyard. Just as he crossed Torra Alta's heartstone, his eye again caught the chestnut-haired girl who still chatted amiably to the wagoner.

Caspar turned to his uncle. 'I'll teach her to ride. I'll teach her to ride Cracker.'

'May on Firecracker? You're mad.'

'Well, Brid can ride Cracker so why not May?'

'Ah but Brid is Brid,' Hal said proudly as they strode, side by side, under the portcullis to greet their guests.